I0629019

ZERO
TRUST

A FENDER HACKER THRILLER
BOOK 2

HELEN HANSON

Published by Domino INK, P.O. Box 1614, Little Elm, TX 75068

DOMINO INK

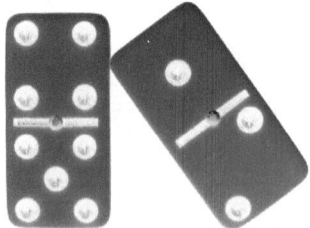

For Tom, Ted, Paula, Chuck, Mary Kay & Hannah.

I love you always.

Even that time you put me in the dryer.

1

Byron Suliani was sorry he'd worn his new leather boots. As he walked along the sidewalk, he heard a distinctive squeak with each uncomfortable step. They felt great on the carpet in the shoe store. But after handing over four hundred and ninety-five dollars for the pair, he realized, they still needed to be broken in for real comfort.

The day held expectations for serious comfort, even if his feet ached. The meet he had planned in the park would bring him years of comfort. Finally— a life of ease. Once the money transferred to Byron's offshore account, he could do what he wanted. Buy what he wanted. Last week he withdrew ten grand from his bank and carried it everywhere, just to get used to the idea. After his recent purchases, he was down to eighty-five hundred dollars, tipping with twenties and leaving the change in his wake.

Maybe he'd move to a different coast. A coast much warmer than the foggy, soggy, groggy city of San Francisco. Last year, Byron spent a week in the Bahamas and reveled in the sultry clime. After today, he could afford a house somewhere in the Caribbean. Despite the sore feet, it was his turn to strut.

Byron's instructions were to arrive at noon for the rendezvous with his contact. Given the stakes, Byron didn't fully trust the situation, so he arrived early to reconnoiter the park and make sure it wasn't a setup. Just being prudent. A man needed solid footing when his future rode that single giant wave. But if things didn't go down as planned, they all had something to lose.

He left his car a few blocks away and only brought the satchel containing the remaining cash and the package for his contact. He resisted the urge to bring his cigarettes. After smoking three on the drive from his place and downing a third cup of coffee, his nerves jangled. He pushed his belt below his protruding belly, where it didn't cut into his skin. Maybe if he'd parked closer, his feet wouldn't hurt, but he wanted to approach the meet site, not land in the middle of it. He'd fire up another smoke as soon as he completed the trade.

From across the street, he located the bench amid the bushes where he was supposed to sit and wait. Byron patted the tan leather case strapped across his chest. The case was smaller than most,

just big enough for a tablet and constructed from the softest leather he could find. He wished he could say the same about the boots.

A crisp Saturday morning, activity in the neighborhood park was lively. Older kids played basketball on the court, while the younger ones clung to the playground where the adults aimed their attention. At the edge of the grass, a white man in tattered jeans urinated into a stand of juniper. Other than that dude, Byron didn't see anyone who concerned him. He kept to the park perimeter and made his way to the bench.

While he sat, Byron kept a steady watch for his contact but was having trouble focusing with both eyes. One of them seemed clouded. As he went to rub it, a searing pang jabbed his forehead. Too much caffeine. Two packs a day wasn't doing him any favors either. He needed to start that diet today. Clean up his act. Get his body in shape for the beach.

As the pain in his forehead settled into a thumping ache, pins and needles tingled his left leg. He stood to relieve the uncomfortable sensation. Walking behind the bench, a trail in the grass led to a neighborhood. The movement helped, but now his leg felt weak. Byron leaned against a tree, and the pain dulled.

When he put his weight on the leg, it gave way beneath him. He stumbled into the bushes.

A thick branch scratched his face as he fell, catching the satchel strap, snapping it against his Adam's apple. He coughed and slipped the strap off his shoulder.

The fall left him dizzy. He pulled himself to a stand and backed out of the bush to get his bearings. He tried to rub his eyes, but only his right hand responded.

Byron wanted to cry out, but the words in his head didn't seem to form any sounds. He concentrated on his surroundings.

Trees. Bushes. Houses. Nothing looked familiar.

The images lost shape and melded into colors and then reformed.

He came here for a reason. What was it?

The houses loomed over the foliage. He focused on the houses.

People there. Get help.

Byron staggered toward the neighborhood.

He spied a blue house. He'd go to the blue house.

His grandmother lived in a blue house.

2

Solomon Price saw that his mama's bedroom door was open, so he knew Tyrone wasn't in there with her. Sol peeked around the door to see if she was sleeping. Waking her was always a risk.

He stepped over the dirty clothes and nudged her shoulder, his heart slapping like a loose pinball. "Mama, get up. It's today!"

Toya Price glared with a single open eye, making him wish he'd waited for the alarm to ring like she'd told him. He ran from the room before her wild swing caught his backside.

He peeked in from behind the doorjamb. "Sorry, Mama."

She rolled over and buried her face into a pillow. "Double shift, Sol."

He hated those words. Being a nurse, mama had to stay and help all the sick people at the hospital. Sol understood that. But like last night, double shift meant he spent the evening alone, while Mama came home late, her hair smelling of smoke.

"It's today, Mama." Sol bounced on his toes. "We can pick up the money today."

She turned toward him, her eyes snapping open. "That's right. It is today." The covers came off her in a single sweep, and she was out of bed. "I'll be in the shower. You make me some coffee, hear?"

Solomon ran to the kitchen and pulled the coffee pot to the edge of the sticky counter. The glass pot needed washing, along with the other dishes in the sink, but he was too excited to wash them the night before.

He swished water around in the pot and thought about how much coffee to make. If he made a full pot, she might want to drink it all. Instead, he filled it only half full with water. That was enough.

When his mother came out of the shower, she didn't spend her usual time doing her makeup. Sol wasn't sure anyone would know who she was with a bare face. Instead, she downed a cup of coffee, dressed quickly, and they left the apartment.

On the street, they walked to the corner where some of the bigger kids liked to hang out before school.

"Hey, Sol," one boy called.

Solomon turned to wave, but Mama tugged his backpack, pulling him closer to her. "Mind your business, son."

He heard laughing behind him, but they kept walking.

Normally, he'd be on the way to school right now, but she let him skip because today was too big. He liked school because he could see the San Francisco Bay. Mama didn't like the water much, so he'd sneak down there by himself. She said most third graders didn't get to see the big boats from the schoolyard, that they only had four sad walls to look at, and he should consider himself lucky. But Solomon never really felt lucky until the day he found that leather case.

They reached the bus stop, where several other people waited. With all the new buildings going up nearby, he didn't recognize any of them.

"Let's wait over here." Mama led him away from the rest of them and got on her phone.

When the bus came along, the group climbed aboard. Sol liked to check the bus number when they went into the city, but today, he forgot to look. Nineteen. It was usually nineteen. Mama sat near the front and spent the time texting on her phone. He took off his backpack and sat next to her. He could tell by the sparkle in her eye, she was excited, too.

"After we get the satchel, can we go to the water?"

Her eyes did that thing he hated, where the brown part rolled behind her lids. All he could see was stark white.

It meant no. It always meant no.

"You act like we won the lottery." She went back to her phone. "You still have to go to school, and I still have to go to work."

"What about the park? Can we at least go to the park?"

He could tell she was about to say no, but then her shoulders fell. "Alright. Just this one time."

"Thanks, Mama."

The park wasn't as good as the ocean, but today, nothing could make him sad, not even a city surrounded by water without the chance to see it. The big buildings were always in the way. They even kept out the sun. He'd ask her again later, after the park. Maybe she'd change her mind because today was special.

Solomon name-checked every street they passed to watch their progress. It was mostly a countdown from 26th Street to 15th, with a big jump to 7th.

But the streets seemed to go in circles, with some odd names like Mariposa, just to confuse people. Sounded like a girl's name. Mama didn't know any girls with that name, so he looked it up. It was Spanish for butterfly, but he doubted there were many butterflies that lived in the city. When they finally reached 7th street, he knew they were close.

"Mama, we're here."

"I know, son." She pocketed her phone. "We would've had that money a long time ago, if you'd listened to me."

The bus finally slowed to a stop in front of the police station, and he jumped off the top stair to the curb.

Mama held onto the rail, taking careful steps in her red high heels. How could she move so slow? This was the best day ever.

But Sol couldn't wait for her, and he ran around the corner, looking for the entrance to the Hall of Justice. When Mama appeared, she scooted down the sidewalk in that bent-knee run she did when wearing her big shoes. Special day or not, she was mad.

"Don't you run off like that again. You hear me?"

She tugged his ear hard before they went up the stairs and inside the building.

A metal detector made a beeping sound until the man in front of them took off his belt. A policeman looked inside Sol's empty backpack before he and Mama passed through the metal detector. They took the elevator to the Lost and Found department.

When they approached the desk, a male cop with pink-white skin said, "You must be Carl Martin."

The day Sol found the money in the leather case, he was so excited that he screamed. The cop walking by thought Sol was hurt. While his mother couldn't stop the cop from taking the satchel, she gave him one of the fake names, and Sol's had to match. He used so many names, it got confusing.

Sol said, "You must be Officer Peyton." He called the Lost and Found every Friday and talked to Officer Peyton.

The officer lifted an eyebrow. "I've been expecting you."

Ninety days was a long time to wait. "It's still here, right?"

The pink lips spread into a smile. He put a clipboard on the counter. "I just need your mother to fill out the paperwork, check her identification, and you can take possession of the case and the money."

Sol jumped into a spin, his fist shooting into the air. "Yes!"

Mama took the clipboard. "He's a little excited."

"That's a fine young man you have there, ma'am. Smart, diligent, and polite." Officer Peyton pointed at Sol. "He's one to watch."

His mother's eyes brightened. "Yeah, he's a house-a-fire, my boy." She ran her hand over Sol's hair.

As she filled out the form, the thumping in his chest went even faster. She gave the clipboard back to Officer Peyton, and he asked for her driver's license. Mama held her license for him while he took down the information.

She used LaShawna Martin that day in the park.

The cop said, "I'll be right back."

Solomon danced to some song in his head. He didn't know if it was one he'd heard on the street or if he made it up, but it sounded just like—

Her hand landed on his neck. "Stop that, son. You can go crazy later. But not here."

The officer returned with the leather case and opened it.

"Please inspect the contents, and if you're satisfied—" He pointed to another form. "—sign here, and you can be on your way."

She took a deep breath and reached inside the case.

Maybe they didn't win the lottery, but $8,500 was a lot of money.

While she counted, Sol dreamed of all the things he would buy, including some new dresses for Mama. Most of hers were too small.

She breathed as if the weather were cold. "Eighty-five hundred dollars. It's all here."

"I can't believe I finally get to take it home." He spun around until he was dizzy.

Mama signed the paperwork with her free hand.

Sol found the tan case under a bush at a park in the city. It was made of soft leather and had a couple of pouches inside, a flap cover, and a long strap. Finding the pack of money inside, though, he figured someone would need it for food or shoes or rent. Mama was so mad when the policeman took it to Lost and Found. She made sure they got a receipt.

Anyway, it was theirs now, and she promised Solomon that he could carry it home, but only in a backpack. She didn't want them flashing an expensive case out on the streets. He looked up the name on the satchel, and that brand sold for hundreds of dollars. Mama said there were too many people who wanted to steal it.

He opened his backpack wide. Mama whacked the stack of hundred-dollar bills against her palm. He could tell she didn't want to let it go. Eventually, she sighed, put the money and the leather case in Sol's backpack, and helped thread his arms through the straps.

Wearing this much money on his back, Sol wondered if this was how Superman felt with his cape, knowing he could fly.

But he wouldn't run, not in the building or out on the street. This was serious. Like Mama told him, he was the man of the house, and he needed to act like one. So he trudged down to the elevator and out of the building with all the self-control he could muster.

In the fresh air, his head spun a little as if he were sick, but without the feeling-bad part. Good dizzy.

Mama was texting again, but she'd promised they could go to the park for a while before going home. The park was several blocks away from the Hall of Justice, and Sol skipped ahead of her. He checked a few times to make sure she was still behind him, but Mama stared at her phone the whole time.

About ten minutes later, they neared the park, and her voice hit his back. "Solomon James."

The sound of her voice told him she was angry, so he waited on the sidewalk until she clacked over in those tall, red shoes. Silly, old things. If she couldn't run, why wear them?

She wagged a finger at him and dropped her phone. Sol picked it up.

Just then, a car with dark windows pulled over to the curb beside them. A man got out from the back seat. Even with the mask, Solomon saw white skin bunched up around the angry blue eyes.

"Give me the backpack, kid."

When Sol noticed the shiny gun, his muscles went soft, and warm pee rolled down his leg.

Mama scowled. "Solomon, you give him what he wants. Hear me, son?"

But Sol couldn't move. His muscles wouldn't do anything he wanted.

From nearby, someone screamed, "He's got a gun!"

The gunman turned toward the voice, the blue-eyed stare broken. Sol didn't think, didn't decide. He just ran across the street.

"Sol!" His mother's voice hit his back.

Then he heard the gunshots.

A corner of the building next to him turned into dust. When he looked back, his mother lay on the ground.

Tears spilled from Sol's face. Mama.

Another shot sounded.

He turned and ran as fast as he could.

This was his fault.

Now, they'd take him away for sure.

3

The doorbell sounded throughout the Fender's house as Maggie called out to her half-brother Travis. "Where are the dogs?"

She scooted down the hall to the front door, slowing to a more leisurely, professional gait. Flipping her ponytail behind a shoulder, she checked the front of her blue suit for any coffee spills. In the past few months, Maggie and Travis worked a couple of cases together, and the prospect of a new adventure sent her heart rate into a patter.

Travis strode into the hallway. "I took them on a beach run earlier, so they both crashed on their pillows."

Maggie peered through the security viewer. Two men stood on her porch. One was round and sturdy, impeccably dressed in a suit. The other wore nearly the same thing as Travis, a white Oxford shirt and jeans. "Oh, my. He's even more handsome than his picture." She lifted an eyebrow at Travis, who waited down the hall.

"Client. Remember?" Wearing his own version of business casual, Travis added a wool vest and looked much older than his sixteen years.

She sneered. "Part of our job is to observe. So I'm observing."

The time was straight-up ten in the morning when she opened the door and let the attorney and his blond client in the door. The blond roboticist was slightly older than Maggie's twenty-three years and a local legend. He had the steely-eyed gaze of a man on a mission.

When they made eye contact, his expression softened. "Maggie Fender?"

"Yes." She steadied her hand to shake his. "Please, come in."

They stepped into the foyer.

"This is my corporate attorney, Jerry Katana."

The attorney carried a briefcase and said, "It's a pleasure to meet you, Ms. Fender."

"Please, call me, Maggie."

She led them into the living room, where Travis had retreated. "Baxter Cruise, Jerry Katana, Baxter, I know you've worked with my brother and partner, Travis Fender."

Travis was an old soul. With raven black hair and sage green eyes, he was as tall as Baxter and had the poise of a diplomat. "It's good to meet you in person, gentlemen."

Maggie gestured toward the seating area around the table where a tray of hot coffee awaited. After prepping all morning for this meeting, she was jonesing for more caffeine. Plus, she wanted to know how this big fish landed on her tiny boat.

Travis sat on one end of the couch while she sat on the other and served coffee. "So, what brings you to our door today?"

"Sorry," Jerry said, "but I have to ask you to sign non-disclosure agreements before we can have this discussion." The two men sat in the chairs across from the couch.

Katana handed her the document.

"Of course, we expected the NDA." She scanned the agreement to make sure she wasn't signing away rights to any internal organs and put her scrawl on the appropriate lines. She passed the document to Travis. Since they'd skipped the preliminaries, she had a few questions of her own.

"I'm honored, but with so many companies like ours in the area, why did you call us?"

"Travis was helpful when I needed decryption work." Baxter's icy blues trained on her brother. "I also spoke with Kurt Meyers, who assured me you could handle this job. I trust his judgment."

Maggie and Travis started their penetration testing business months earlier after their financial windfall from the Paddy O'Mara dark pool scandal, where they met Kurt Meyers. Meyers was tracking the money O'Mara stole. The settlement would work its way through the courts, but after repaying the jilted investors, the attorneys, and a multitude of brokers, Maggie and her brother expected to keep four or five hundred million dollars in assets across the globe. While they could never bring the entire fortune into the country, they planned to fund charities where it was. In the meantime, they were finally flush.

As for their business, they had a couple of solid wins, earning them esteemed referrals. But they were new to the security game. In Silicon Valley, data and computer systems security were vital to innovation and survival. Hiring companies like theirs was a way to find the vulnerable areas before the hackers found them first and stole their data. Like pouring water into a vessel to look for leaks, if there was a crack in the security, a savvy hacker would find it.

Kurt Meyers brought the Fenders their first client.

Travis' expression turned solemn. "Kurt has been good to us."

"Kurt spoke highly of you," Baxter said, "and I wanted people who aren't well known in the industry and offered more than a routine scan of my systems."

Travis wrote software and scripts to probe computer security systems. It was a programming project he continually refined. It also earned him homeschooling credits for computer science.

"Like any company, technology is our lifeblood. It's what sets us apart from the competition." Baxter glanced at Katana, who took notes. "We're at the point where we need to hire beyond the core team, but I can't yet because I suspect we have a spy."

"Do you have any evidence?" Maggie drained the last of her cup and poured another.

"We developed some unique algorithms for curious robots. They're autonomous underwater robots that roam the ocean floor, exploring, recording data, and sending images to operators, who can intervene and redirect them if needed." Baxter propped his foot on the other knee. "We also plan to adapt them for industry. Anyway, at a recent show, I ran into a guy I went to school with. He works for a robotics company but isn't a direct competitor. He told me that someone approached him online, offering to sell him our algorithms."

Maggie watched for any reaction from Travis and said, "That doesn't sound very sophisticated."

"Actually, it was." Baxter rubbed his chin. "My friend was on the dark web, doing a routine check to see if any of his company's secrets were out in the wild. He got an anonymous tap on the shoulder, but the tapper knew my friend was trolling for robotics information."

"I have a crawler program that can search the dark web." Travis stretched an arm along the top of the couch. "I can find out what's out there with your name on it. The dark web isn't as big as many people think."

Maggie bit her lip. It was his engagement on the dark web, specifically the hacker forums, that had caused their family so much grief. But the kid was smart and in his element. Computers, the internet, even his hacking skills, these were the colors of his rainbow.

"That's a great place to start," Baxter said, "but I also want someone on the inside. Can you work for me undercover?"

"Undercover." Maggie's heart pumped faster. Travis was too young for that job, but she wasn't. "Tell me about the situation. Is your team working remote?"

"No. Since everyone is new, I wanted them on-site, so we could develop a strong working relationship and resolve issues immediately. Tougher to do that on a conference call."

"What do you have in mind?"

"I need someone to work with the engineering team." Baxter leaned forward in his chair. "What's your background?"

Meager. Her ambitious plans were stymied by money troubles, legal hassles, and wasting disease. Now that she had the freedom to do most anything, she wanted to keep a low profile and build a business with her brother.

"I took some engineering courses—"

"Do you have any document management experience?"

Her mood brightened. "I do. I worked part time for my father starting in junior high. It was mostly data entry, but I processed all the engineering documents. Change orders, bills of material, procurement specifications, schematics, diagrams."

She'd considered pursuing this kind of work when she first sought a full-time job. But none of them were close to the house. With Travis being a kid and Dad's dementia, she needed to stay near home.

"Perfect. That role gives you higher level access and maneuverability within the company. It also puts you in direct contact with the engineering staff. As much as I hate to say it, they're the prime suspects."

"Who would I report to?"

"You'd report to me. We have an actual candidate for the position once we plug the security breach." He sighed. "Until then, I'm not making any other moves."

"Troubleshooting 101." Katana didn't look up from his notes. "Change a single variable at a time."

Baxter pointed at his attorney. "Exactly."

"Who's managing the system now?" Maggie wondered if she would step on delicate toes.

"Lynn Moyega. She runs IT and security." As if he read her mind, Baxter added. "She'll be happy to give it up. She's buried."

"What about hiring? That's usually a long process." She may have experience, but she didn't have an actual résumé that matched the hype. But she could fake one if needed.

"We're so new, the process is relatively informal."

"That may be part of your problem." Travis cleared his throat. "Especially if the controls aren't in place to keep your secrets safe."

Baxter leaned forward. "That's why I want to hire you. Lynn runs security scans on our systems routinely, and she says the environment is secure. But I didn't tell her that our intellectual property is already out on the web."

Maggie laid her hands on her lap. "Because she's a suspect."

"At this stage in our growth, everyone's a suspect. Only Clint Masters, our CEO, and Katana here know about the breach. It's one thing to lose head knowledge from a defecting employee, but with documents, others can recreate our work. Only an insider would have that access."

"If you're losing documents, it could be the new system."

"We thought that, but we monitor file access by the employee."

Her role would be similar to the spy's, if one existed. "How soon do you want me to start?"

Baxter's upper lip stiffened. "Can you start tomorrow?"

4

Augie Barrett stood, shoving his chair so hard it slammed into the credenza. "How could you lose him?"

The man in his sights was Gilbert Adams, someone Augie thought he could trust.

"We planned to snatch the case before they got on the bus. I had a guy on the street ready for the play, but they took a different route." His bulky shoulders rose in a shrug, which only pissed Augie off. "We had to improvise."

"Making the six o'clock news is how you improvise?" Gilbert earned a certain latitude because he'd never failed so miserably. Still, it couldn't have happened at a worse time.

"No one can identify us or the car." The big man wasn't stupid, but he didn't appreciate all the ramifications of his blunder. "We jacked the car before the hit, wiped it clean, and ditched it in The Tenderloin with the keys. Whoever took it from there is probably still sweating with the cops."

The room grew warm, and Augie shed his jacket. "But you lost a kid, Gil. A freaking kid." He looked heavenward and covered his eyes, the absurdity of the loss fully sinking in. This wasn't even a disaster. It was suicide.

"I've got people at his house and the club where his mother works, but I don't think the kid's part of that scene. After we realized what happened to the satchel, we watched them for a few weeks." Gilbert wiped his forehead with the back of his hand. "The boy stays in Hunter's Point, while mom does her thing in the city. Even in the city, she doesn't stray far from the club."

"Any friends in Hunter's Point? Anyplace he might go to hide?"

"None that we know. Besides, with all the names that chick was using, she's hiding from something. Doesn't look like she made many friends."

"How old is he?" Augie figured he was still in elementary school.

"Eight."

"Make sure he doesn't make it to nine." He pressed the heel of his hand into an eye. "And find the damn satchel."

"I'll comb the streets once the cops move out of the area. Can't risk getting on their radar. But we'll find him. I mean, where's he going to go? His mother's in the morgue. "

"You're kidding, right?" Augie said, "This is San Francisco. If you don't find him, sure as hell, someone else will. You know, nothing on the street is safe. By now, he could be the star of a kiddie porn shoot."

Gil shrank under the assault, but had enough sense to back out of the room. "I'm on it. We'll find him. I promise."

"You better." Augie barely got out the words before the door closed.

But the problem didn't end with merely finding the kid. Russian mobster Vladimir Penniski was neither understanding nor patient. He expected Augie to eliminate any witnesses. Once again, his ass was on the line.

After securing the package from their contact, Gil was supposed to pop the mother and her son. Now, the kid was a liability. While his men scoured the streets for a scared black kid, Augie had to make an uncomfortable phone call to a man without a conscience.

5

Solomon didn't know how long he'd been hiding behind the dumpster, but his ears finally started to work again. He'd heard gunshots in his neighborhood before, but none that close. He swiped a wet cheek with his fist and ran down the sidewalk, not daring to look back until he was far away from the dumpster.

The man who shot Mama had mean blue eyes with dark rings around them and bread-white skin. Who was he?

He wasn't the man Mama told Sol to worry about. She told Sol to stay away from a big black man with a torn earlobe because someone told Mama that he was after her. Mama said that if the raggedy-eared man ever caught up to them, Sol would end up alone.

Mama also told him not to trust strangers, cops, or white people. But who did that leave? She said none of them could mind their own business, and none of them would help him.

Sol's feet pounded along the pavement, taking in as much street as he could gather. The weight of his backpack bounced against his bones.

He turned at the next corner and leaned against a window to catch his breath. His throbbing hand drew his attention. He still clutched Mama's phone in his fist. Sol could call Tyrone. He'd know what to do. Stiff fingers uncurled, revealing the shattered screen. He pushed the power button, but the screen stayed dark.

If only he'd listened to Mama and given his backpack to the man in the mask. If Sol had, Mama wouldn't be hurt. He wasn't trying to sass her, but after seeing the gun, he couldn't move. How did the man even know about the money?

Sol had to find another place to hide and quick.

He ran down the street and saw a delivery truck with an open back door and a ramp leading to the pavement. The man wheeled some boxes down the ramp and onto the sidewalk. Sol went over to look inside the truck.

It was half the size of the huge trucks on the freeway. At the back of the open part was a stack of plastic crates. It smelled like the fruit section of the grocery store, but he saw nothing he could eat.

Sol ran up the ramp and crawled into the corner, pulling a plastic crate over him like a turtle's shell. His body trembled, and he tried to slow his breathing so it didn't make so much noise.

Sol wished now that he'd never found the stupid satchel.

He stayed there for a long time, without peeking, hoping his hiding place was a good one.

For an instant, Sol felt airborne, and it startled him awake. He pushed off the covers in a panic. But it wasn't his blanket—only the plastic crate. The truck he hid in was now bouncing along a road to somewhere. He remembered what happened to Mama, but this time, he vowed not to cry.

Tears won't fill your belly, she always said.

Sol took off the backpack and rested his head on it while listening to truck sounds as it moved on the road. Creaks and squeaks, with the wind whistling even louder. The worst of his ear aching was over, but he didn't know how long he'd been asleep or where they were going.

Wherever they ended up, Sol would have to figure out what to do when he arrived. He had Mama's phone. Maybe it just needed a charge, and he could get Tyrone to take him home. He pressed a knuckle against his eye. Mama was right—being the man of the house was hard.

Hunger clawed his belly like a tiger trying to escape. His last meal was marshmallow cereal for dinner the night before. Sol wished he'd eaten some breakfast. At least he had money. Plenty of it. He hoped the truck stopped soon, so he could get some food.

After a long time, the truck finally slowed down. But going at the slower speeds made it bouncier, and it stopped and started every other minute and made a few turns. The ride made him queasy. He rubbed his tummy the way Mama did when he was sick.

Maybe Sol didn't feel good, but what about Mama? Was she okay? He wasn't even sure how to find her. He could pretend to be a grownup and call the police. They might tell him what happened. But she said they couldn't be trusted.

Still, after they took the leather case and the money, they returned both like they promised.

Sol could decide later. He couldn't think with an upset stomach. After his long wait for the satchel, it brought him nothing but trouble.

The truck rumbled along so slow, Sol figured he could open the rear door and jump out. Then the truck made another turn and stopped, but this time, the backup beeper came on, and the truck moved a bit more before the driver turned off the engine. Sol pulled the crate over his head.

He heard the driver get out. When the back door rolled up, Sol clamped his eyes shut. When the clanking noises stopped, he let one eye crack to a slit. The truck was backed against an open building.

Sol crawled out from under the crate and crept to the end of the truck. Inside the building, he didn't see any people around, just boxes. He checked the parking lot for the truck driver before jumping to the pavement.

He saw several other trucks backed against the building. A painting on the side of them showed pumpkins, grapes, apples, and other stuff spilling out of a pointy basket and onto a plate. It said: Vaughan Foods. So that was why the truck smelled like a grocery store.

Thick bushes lined the back side of the parking lot. After looking both ways, Sol ran to the bushes and stopped to look around. Wherever this was, there weren't any tall buildings. Didn't look like any place he'd been.

Sol pushed his way through the bushes into another parking lot. There were only cars and pickup trucks in this one. The sign said: Surfside Motel. Was the water nearby?

The sounds here were different, and the air, too. Smelled all salty and fishy like the ocean. Across the road from the motel was a big patch of grass—not like a park—this had rows of something growing and a big red tractor parked in the middle.

Wherever this was, it didn't look like San Francisco.

6

Maggie tried to peer inside Ginger's house, past the screen door, but the mesh was too dark. She called out, "Ginger?"

"Hang on. I'm in the kitchen with Denesha."

Maggie's small, Samoan neighbor padded to the door and unlocked it. Maggie stepped inside.

"You want some soup?"

"No, but it smells delicious." Some of Ginger's soups were fruit-based, like the sweet banana soup called *suafa'i* now scenting the house. While it tasted delicious, it looked like a brain smoothie. Others, like *sua i'a*, she made from fish. The whole fish. Eyeballs and all. Travis would eat absolutely anything Ginger Baker put in front of him—another reason she adored him. Maggie, however, politely spooned around anything in her bowl that might wink.

She followed Ginger into the kitchen and found her best friend, Denesha Roberts, at the table. Denesha's pretty, brown face lit up with its usual brilliance. That smile and her encouragement brightened Maggie's sorry days when her family's health, finances, and reputation raced to win the downhill.

Maggie hustled to Denesha's side and put an arm around her. They had waitressed together in a variety of restaurants. Both women leaned in for the hug.

"Are you all settled?" Maggie said, "Excited?"

"I am. Started school today." Denesha always wanted to be a nurse, so she signed up for nursing school at the College of San Mateo and found a rental in the neighborhood with a roommate. "Thanks for all the help moving my stuff. Came by your place, but Travis said you were out."

"Doing some prep work for tomorrow. Trav and I took a new job today."

Maggie and Travis considered both these women family. About the same height, Denesha was Tinker Bell tiny, while Ginger lived up to her Samoan stereotype.

"What this time? I hope it's not with another junk food company." Ginger took her bowl of soup to the kitchen table, resting her feet on the step stool beneath it. "I finally got those clowns to pay you."

When they opened their company, Ginger joined them as their accountant, since she ran a bookkeeping business out of her home.

"No food this time." While the snack food job was a success—Travis found a security hole in the company's online ordering app that allowed price changes and ordered an entire truckload of lemon Ring-a-Dings for thirty bucks—the district manager was so embarrassed by the incident, he delayed their final payment. Ginger was their five-foot enforcer.

"You're going to like this one. Completely high-tech." Maggie settled into a seat beside Denesha.

"Right." Ginger dipped a spoon into the gray matter. "What's the gig?"

"They think someone on the inside is selling their secrets. I'm going undercover as a document management specialist to find him." Maggie's head bobbed. "Or her."

"Undercover." Denesha squeezed Maggie's shoulder. "You going to be safe, girlfriend?"

Safe.

With all the tragedy in Maggie's life, she knew there was no such thing as safe.

"I'll be fine. I have some experience in this area from working with Dad, but I've been on a crash course of their document system since we took the job." Maggie tapped her cup with a fingernail. "I need to seem like a new employee, not a clueless one."

Maggie's original goal was to become a patent attorney, which meant she needed a science or technical degree. She didn't love the idea, but a job and excellent money were practically guaranteed. Now that Maggie didn't fret about money, she put her energy into Travis, her clients, and fixing up the house.

"The job will give me access to their engineering team and the files they want to protect."

"Engineering team?" Ginger said, "You mean suspects."

"That would be anyone with access to the files."

Denesha said, "What's Travis going to do? His usual?"

"Yep." Maggie scooted her chair closer. "He has all the tools to probe the company electronically, and if I need any tricks while I'm inside, he's the man to provide them."

"He's got plenty of tricks, that one." Denesha rose from the table. "So who hired you?"

"The local talent. He hired Travis for some decryption work a while back. I can't disclose his name, but boy does he have talent."

Ginger flashed a smile to Denesha. "Is that so?"

"Besides being incredo-smart, he's blond, blue-eyed, and dripping gorgeous. Looks like that South African model, Devin Paisley."

Denesha brewed a cup of tea at the Keurig. "Since when are you an expert on male models?"

"Since the day I reached for a candy bar and found his face on the magazine rack." Maggie sighed. "Famous models aside, the local hottie has an equally gorgeous girlfriend who works in the FBI." She blew air from her lips. "Yes, I googled him."

"The desperate act of a lonely woman." Ginger said, "What's up with you and Fyodor?"

Her handsome Russian neighbor, Fyodor Umanov, ran a personal security firm and encouraged her to open the penetration testing company. They'd worked together on a case of his and dated. A bit. Nothing serious, but only because they were both too busy with work. At least, that was what she told herself.

"No doubt protecting somebody somewhere." Hopefully, someone male.

Ginger finished her soup and pushed away the bowl. "When do you go undercover?"

"Tomorrow," Maggie said.

"I'm not sure I like you going undercover." Ginger carried the dishes to the sink.

"Me either." Even Denesha's disapproving face glowed.

"It's part of the job." The part Maggie enjoyed most. She helped Travis when he needed it but preferred the field work: gaining sensitive information over the phone, wheedling her way into a secure location, listening in while others revealed secrets they were supposed to protect. In the hacker vernacular, she was a social engineer. The title held a certain cachet. Maybe she would've been an excellent spy.

"I'll be careful." Maggie stood. "If I do my job right, no one will see anything but a hard-working employee."

Ginger hugged her. "Then do your job right."

Denesha tilted her head toward Ginger. "What she said."

Maggie dismissed their concerns with a wave. "C'mon. It's a group of nerdy engineers. How much trouble can they make?"

7

Marcus Fisher walked the ten blocks from his hotel instead of taking a cab. With a fresh breeze blowing in from the lake, the exercise would do him some good. He'd eaten scrambled eggs and some bacon that morning, recording his blood sugar before setting out for the day. He kept a pack of raw almonds in his pocket in case he got hungry.

The address was in a dilapidated part of Detroit, which was saying something. The military worried about fixing up Fallujah, but someone ought to have a look around Motown. Corruption, war, and waste burned the innocents in both places. Some said Motor City was moving again, but this part of town hadn't made it out of first gear.

When Marcus reached the apartment complex, it looked like another abandoned building. Weeds crowded wherever they could grow, plywood covered several of the windows, and graffiti expressed the sentiments of an artist with talent. Marcus marveled at what people could do with spray paint. It could either be another depressing evidence of decay or a tiny glimmer of life amid the blight.

The street address, 17314, reminded him of his service to the country with the 173rd Airborne in 2014. Some things never slip from a man's memory. The apartment building's decrepit condition only reinforced the association.

The woman in Baltimore who gave him the address wasn't what Marcus would call a reliable witness. Meth and a parade of men with no soul had seen to that. But hers was the only lead he'd gotten in the past six months, making her dubious information worth the trip to Detroit.

A cyclone fence around the apartment building leaned badly in places. In others, only the metal poles remained. He spied an overgrown path to the building and wished he'd worn his old shoes. Probably full of ticks. Did they have Lyme disease in Michigan? That'd be just his luck.

As Marcus made his way through the weeds, a dog yapped from the right side of the building. Maybe someone lived here. Could be one of the feral dogs roaming the city, but it sounded small. Too small to make it on the streets without a pack. He saw a curtain move from a unit on the lower right side of the building.

He climbed the stairs to the second floor and found unit 216, where particle board covered the windows. There was no chance of peering in, so he listened. After a full minute of silence, Marcus rapped on the door. It sounded hollow.

The next units he tried also seemed empty, or no one wanted to deal with a man nearly in a suit. Slacks and a jacket didn't exactly peg him as "the man," but the people in this neighborhood were more a jeans and work shirt crowd, for those who had a job. Those who didn't either wore hip-hop t-shirts or Versace. The crack houses he'd been through seemed to have equal numbers of both.

Marcus took the stairs down to the first floor in search of the unit with the dog. The mutt started yapping before Marcus reached the ground floor, and he followed the sound to unit 105. He knocked, and the curtain moved again. The door had a security viewer, so he expected the occupant was giving him the once-over. That was fine. He turned his head so his jagged earlobe wasn't obvious. Have a good long look. But either way, that door was going to open.

"What do you want?" The voice was female. Probably older.

Polite always greased the wheels of old women.

"I'm sorry to bother you, ma'am. My name is Marcus Fisher. I just want to ask you a few questions." He knew what her next question would be. It was always the same.

"About what?"

His lips were ready with the standard lie.

"My sister, ma'am. I'm looking for my sister, Toya. She's been missing for a lot of years, and I was told that she lived here. Apparently, she's not using her real name, and I don't know what she calls herself now. I hoped to show you a picture of her, so you could tell me if she's around."

He played the role of grieving brother for the peephole in the door, taking the picture from his wallet. He did his best to appear pained. "I promise not to take too much of your time."

The woman was probably considering it. If she lived alone, she might even want the company. Plus, with his Southern manners, Marcus didn't resemble the local thugs. A slide lock screeched open.

When their eyes met, he gave her his softest smile. "Thank you. It's very kind of you, ma'am." He dipped his head toward her as the door opened wider.

She was somewhere north of seventy, slightly hunched, wearing a sack dress and a big sweater over her skinny frame. Her sagging skin wore the burdens of her years and the strains of the neighborhood. Dark spots, common in people of color, dotted her cheeks. Marcus had one such spot near his left ear. While they hadn't hurt Morgan Freeman, he hoped he didn't get more.

He showed her the picture.

She squinted one eye at him and then at the photo. "Your sister, huh?"

"Yes, ma'am."

The yappy dog growled, baring its yellow teeth in a snarl. It had pointy ears like a Chihuahua, but with long hair. If that ugly pooch came near him, he'd kick it through the nearest goal posts.

"That's a mighty fine watchdog you have there. Loyal. A quality missing in most people nowadays."

"Ain't it, though?"

He kept his distance, though he'd normally try to pet it for the owner's sake. The dog hid behind the woman's scrawny legs and growled.

"Well, come on in, so I can take a better look at the photo." The old woman even smiled and opened the door wider. "Cedric won't bother you none."

As he walked into the apartment, he tucked the photo in his pocket and kept watch of the dog. "Cedric, huh? He must keep you entertained."

"You got that right." Her laugh revealed a full set of teeth. "What's your name again?"

"Marcus Fisher."

The small apartment had furniture against every wall——a decent leather sectional, two chairs, and end tables with lamps.

"Well, Marcus Fisher, I'm Cordelia Jackson. You have a seat. I was just fixing some coffee." She ambled into the kitchen. "Black okay?"

Marcus preferred his with a little cream, but he doubted it was on the menu. "Yes, ma'am."

He surveyed the seats and noticed a chair. Obviously, her preferred spot, she'd placed all her daily tools within her arm's reach. Magnifying glass. TV remote. Cough drops. Bible. Box of tissues. Lotion. Crossword puzzles. He sat on the leather sectional and glared at the ugly dog.

When she returned, he stood and took the cups from her. "Thank you, ma'am." She settled into her chair as expected. The dog found a spot beside her.

Holding out her hands for a cup, Cordelia took it, sipped, and set it down. "Now show me that sister of yours."

Marcus removed the ten-year-old photo from his shirt pocket and gave it to her. "This is my Toya." He forced himself to breathe.

Cordelia slipped the glasses over her nose and took the photo. "I know her." She tapped the image with a bony finger. "Regina Sampson. Lived upstairs with her boy, Erik."

Lived.

Not lives.

He'd missed her again.

Regina Sampson this time. Marcus cleared his throat. "How are they? My momma would surely like to see them."

Her head dropped toward Marcus. "I don't think you're going to enjoy hearing how she earned a living."

His lips folded inward. "No, but it wouldn't surprise me either. Was she dealing or hooking?"

She handed back the picture and cradled her coffee cup. "This place used to be decent. But the entire city done been through it. I met my husband Earl at the GM factory in Poletown back in '72. That's what we called it then, because of all the Poles living in the area. My Earl worked for Chrysler at the Jefferson North plant the day he died of a heart attack. He put everything we owned into this building. Now, it ain't worth much."

Marcus figured the sixteen-unit building was worth around a hundred grand. If they could find a buyer.

"But that's my troubles, not yours." A loud shot of air heaved from her chest. "They might've been dealing, but I'm guessing she used the place to entertain. There were a few of them upstairs who worked together then. They moved the kids around at least while they were working. Sometimes they sent them to visit with me. But even that money seemed to dry up."

"When did she leave?"

"About a year now, several of them left without really saying goodbye. Or paying rent." She gestured around the room. "Instead, I got a few pieces of furniture that was too big for them to move."

Gray-brown eyes fixed on him. "You know she warned me you might come looking for her?"

His jaw muscle flexed with tension. "Did she now? Our parting wasn't easy, but it's been a long time. Our mama's been ailing, and she wants to see Toya." He tried to sound earnest. "So do I, ma'am."

"She said you were out to kill her. Man with a torn ear like you got." She pointed at him. "That girl could twist a lie right fast. Heard too many from her to count."

"Isn't that just like Toya." Marcus released his breath. "Where did she go?"

Her thin shoulders lifted in a shrug. "I heard them talking about San Francisco. One of them had a friend that lived out that way, worked at some kind of club."

"Do you know the name of it?"

24

"Oh, my." Her brown eyes looked up. "High rise. High hat. It was high something."

High something. Fitting for Toya. It was the same story he'd heard every time he found her cold trail. The dumb bitch. But he was supposed to be a caring brother. Time to act like it. "My mama worries about her all the time. Was she in good health?"

"Good as can be expected. I tried talking to them girls, but they didn't have no interest in my opinion. Told them that kind of life always ends early." Her mouth puckered in a frown. "You can't tell nothing to those girls. They think they're going to live forever."

8

After leaving the place where the truck parked, Sol slipped into a convenience store and bought some donuts and potato chips for his dinner. When he paid for them with a hundred-dollar bill, the girl at the register asked him where his parents were. He lied and said his Mama was waiting outside for him. After marking the bill with a special pen to make sure it was real money, she shrugged and rang up his purchase. Sol stuffed all the change in his pocket.

Inside the store, he'd seen a map of a place called Half Moon Bay and figured out that's where he was. Sol found the ocean easy enough, since it was right next to him the whole time. He smelled it before actually seeing the water. It didn't have all the boats nearby like the ocean by his house, and there weren't any bridges.

He kept checking Mama's phone, in case it started working, but the screen was dark and cracked. Probably needed a charge. He just wanted to know where she was. How she was.

The sounds of those gunshots kept ringing in his ears. Those were so much louder than he'd expected. He'd seen her on the ground, but was she still alive?

Sol was on the bluff by the beach when the sun sank and the sky turned pink and orange. The weather was turning cool, and it was going to get cold during the night.

The satchel held all the money in his world, and he needed to keep it safe. Bigger kids sometimes messed with his backpack, so he didn't want to carry the case with him. But the trees and bushes all looked the same. He had to find a place he could remember.

He searched and found a small group of trees that was different. One tree had a branch like an arm, bent up all straight at the elbow like it was trying to stop traffic. That tree would be easy to find again.

Sol found some hard sticks and spent a good while digging a hole at the bottom of the elbow tree. The hole had to be deep enough to cover the satchel. When the hole was ready, he dropped the leather bag in it and refilled the hole with dirt. Then he took all the dead tree stuff lying around and spread it on the packed dirt to make the ground look the same as the rest.

Digging the hole wasn't as hard as he thought it would be, and another bigger hole would be a good place for him to hide at night. Just because he hadn't seen any scary people yet, didn't mean they weren't out there.

He dug the second hole faster and deeper until he could fit all of him into it. Not stretched out, of course, but curled up, the way he liked to sleep. Some nearby plants had soft, fishbone-like leaves that were big like fans. He tore off a bunch of these to cover his sleeping hole.

As he sat by the hole, he checked the phone one more time. No lights. No messages from Mama.

By now, the air was damp, and Sol shivered. Mama always made him get up and walk around if he was cold, so he slipped on the empty backpack and climbed down the embankment to the beach. He didn't see anyone, which was fine by him. The sun was almost past the edge, and he knew it would be dark really soon.

A house down the beach had a light on, and he followed the edge of the bluff until it came into better view. It had a nice back porch with a couple of chairs. Sol spied a jacket hanging off the back of one chair. It looked warm.

Mama always said we need to help ourselves sometimes. Was this one of those times? What if he got caught taking the jacket?

He heard barking from inside the house, and then a couple of dog noses appeared at the back door. He always wanted a dog, but Mama never did. She said he was enough trouble. Didn't need no dog either.

Sol waited to see if anyone came to the door. He noticed an outlet for electricity. If he had a cable, maybe he could charge the phone here.

The dogs continued to bark, but no one ever came to the back door. Just the dog noses. Whoever lived here with the outlet on the back porch probably had lots of warm jackets. Sol just needed one.

He ran to the chair, grabbed the jacket, and sped off down the beach.

When he was far enough away that he couldn't see the house, he stopped and slipped the jacket over his arms. It was huge on him, but man, he was right. It was warm. And he wouldn't keep it. No. Just borrow it a few days until his Mama came to find him.

9

The morning sky was twilight dark when Travis rose from bed and entered the kitchen to make breakfast for Maggie's first day undercover at R-Bot Systems. While the coffee pot sputtered on the counter, strips of bacon sizzled in the skillet, and he cracked four eggs into a bowl.

By the time the meal was ready, Maggie entered the room fully dressed in a red skirt and a white blouse. She'd even woven her long blonde hair into a rare French braid. Her eyes briefly closed as she seemed to take in the scents of the kitchen.

"Mmm. Smells great, Trav." She leaned against the counter and tugged at her tights around her ankle.

He divvied the eggs and bacon between the two plates. "Can you grab the coffee?"

Maggie filled the cups while he set the plates in their usual places.

She sprinkled some pepper on her food. "Thanks."

"Even spies need a decent meal." He tried to keep the worry from his voice. "Let me know if you need anything."

"I'll call you at lunchtime," she said. "But Baxter told me to expect all the orientation stuff today. Payroll forms, photo ID, and several training sessions. After that, they'll set up my work space and introduce me around the place." She wrinkled her nose and rubbed it with the back of her hand. "Nothing like my first day waiting tables at Osakane when I pulled a double shift. They're going to pay me to sit around and listen to lectures on company culture and sexual harassment."

"Ha! As a waitress, you could write that last one."

"No kidding." She hoisted her cup. "Other than finding the industrial spy, my personal goals are to locate the coffee pot and the ladies' room. In that order."

"You are full of ambition." Travis knew she was kidding, but it was her way of trying to reassure him.

Maggie was his half-sister through their late father, Martin. Ever since Travis' mom Trisha died, Maggie assumed the maternal role. She just wasn't very good at it.

"While I'm slaving away at the office, what are you going to do?"

He swallowed before answering. "System probe. Baxter thinks it's an inside job, but I want to see for myself."

She stabbed her eggs. "The customer isn't always right."

"I need to rule it out before I assume anything." Travis felt the cold, wet nose of a beagle probing his hand. It was Belli. He cupped her chin. "Go to your bowl, girl. I already fed you."

Belli's brother, Bailey, made crunching noises from his bowl. Her ears perked, and she tottered over to her litter mate. Named for famous attorneys, they were also known as the legal beagles or simply The Firm.

Maggie finished eating and took her plate to the sink. "I've got to run. It's about an hour's drive from here."

Travis got up from the table and went to the counter, where she was digging through her purse. He got a travel mug out of the cupboard and filled it with coffee. "You sure you're up for this? Your other gigs were just episodes. This thing is full time."

Maggie stopped rummaging, and her body went slack. Her features softened into what Travis called her motherly face. His late mother, Trisha had a similar expression, but Maggie's came with inadvertent condescension, like a little girl talking to a plastic pig. Maggie meant well. That's what he told himself, anyway.

"Trav, honey, I'll be fine." She squeezed his shoulder. "Besides, if I need to cut out early or leave, Baxter gave me plenty of cover."

"What kind?"

"They have a host of seminars and training sessions I can attend." She made air quote marks when saying the word attend. "Or I can have a dental emergency." Her shoulders bounced up. "Whatever. He made sure I've got room to maneuver." Her hand came out of her purse dangling keys, and Travis regained eye contact. "For once, I don't run the usual risk of getting fired."

She'd been the sole wage-earner for several years. Losing her job had been a constant worry.

"Hmm." Travis hadn't really considered it from her perspective. "So, this is really fun for you?"

"Absolutely." Her voice quickened. "Not only do I get to play spy, but I get to experience the interesting parts of working in a company without the responsibilities. Kind of like taking a corporate test drive."

"Plus, there's a building full of smart guys."

"Well, now." She lifted an eyebrow. "I hadn't thought of that." Maggie's lips spread into a grin, easing his apprehension.

"Yeah. Whatever you say." Travis looked at the clock. "Unless you want to make a poor showing on your first day, you'd better hit the road."

She hugged him with one arm. "Will you give the dogs their heartworm meds? I forgot to last night."

"Done." He handed her the travel mug. "I'm here if you need anything."

"I'll be fine." Maggie took the mug and left.

Travis watched until she drove away and made sure the front door was locked. He gave the dogs their medicine and let them outside, before heading to his office to work.

Technically, his felony conviction had been reversed, but the mental strain of the ordeal followed him like a rain cloud. Eventually, the local newspapers picked up the reversal story, briefly putting his name again in the headlines. At least this time, the news was positive.

While some people assumed an accusation is as good as guilt, others conferred on him the full benefit of his respectable legal standing. Travis didn't care what the community at large thought. The people who really knew him stood by him in their own ways. It was because of them that the conviction reversal held meaning. Their faith in him hadn't been wasted.

He was court-ordered off the computer long enough that it still felt as if the brown-shirts might break down his door whenever he logged on. An overreaction, but he wasn't fully acclimated to his new respectability.

Travis set up his office in Dad's old bedroom at Maggie's insistence. She wanted him to have a dedicated work space for school and their new business. A section of the room was ostensibly hers, but she never used it. Travis liked the closeness he felt to his father while he worked.

Before logging on, Travis heard one of The Firm barking at the back door. Probably Belli. She was quick to sound the alarm if something curious appeared on their stretch of beach. Last year, she barked when a wounded pelican took up residence on one of their Adirondack porch chairs. She left it alone but didn't quiet down until she'd alerted one of the creatures with thumbs. Travis and Maggie took it to the seabird rehab center later that day.

He opened the back door and saw Belli wagging from nose to tail, but she wouldn't come in. Bailey wasn't with her. Overhead, white mist kept the rising sun from spreading any warmth, so he took a jacket from the peg before following her outside.

The dog ran off, gathering speed down the beach. With tides rolling out, the wet sand kicked up behind her as her paws clawed the shore. Both dogs had coloring typical of beagles: white legs and undercarriage, black saddle, brown patches on their shoulders and head, plus white again on the muzzle and the strip between their soulful, brown eyes.

Travis whistled for Bailey. He probably had his nose in a rotting crab or a dead fish, but so far, Travis didn't see him. Too many coves and shrubs to be certain where he might be, but this was one of the few dog-friendly beaches left, and everyone knew The Firm.

Bailey eventually appeared above Travis, standing on a bluff.

"C'mon, boy."

The dog looked back at the sage scrub that dominated the coastline. Whatever was in there, Bailey had staked a claim. Travis thought he might have to go after him, but the dog dropped his head and sought a sure-footed path along a gradual slope down to the beach. Belli waited at the bottom until he descended, before scampering toward the water and racing into the surf. Ramping to a jog, Travis led the pair back toward the house.

All around, seabirds squawked for their morning meals and jostled for position on the rocks. While still hidden by the fog, the sun was up in earnest, and it promised to be a glorious day.

Travis' mind drifted to Maggie's first day as a spy. She was smart and could take care of herself, but they both knew the job might be dangerous. Unless it was a military secret, industrial spies were usually in it for the money. As they learned at great personal expense, greed brought out the worst in people.

When Travis neared the house, something seemed off. He stared at the back porch, taking in the details, sifting the visual inputs for a tangible source of his dissonance. Dad's Adirondack chair. He always kept his jean jacket on the back of that chair.

Even after his funeral, they left the jacket in place. Travis enjoyed watching the ocean from that vantage point, taking in the remaining scents of their father.

As if reading his thoughts, both beagles raced to the chair, bombarding it with sniffs.

Dad's jacket was on the chair yesterday. Now it was gone.

10

By the time Maggie reached Santa Cruz, any apprehension for the job ahead had burned off with the fog. The hour-long drive on Highway 1 gave her time to plan and absorb the negative ions of the coast. Listening to Ledisi's mighty pipes belt I Blame You at full volume lifted her mood to the hilltops. So far, being a working stiff was totally chill.

Yesterday, she tracked the flow of documents from beginning to end in dozens of scenarios to make sure she understood the process. These scenarios formed the basis of her duties at R-Bot Systems and were part of the normal learning curve for a new hire. Her crash course in their document management system—DocuLocker—was enough to give her the confidence she needed to do the actual job. The current version of DocuLocker was new enough that no one was really an expert.

Having a comfortable car for the long drive also boosted her confidence. Since their financial windfall, she bought a modest vehicle that didn't go through oil like a fast food joint. A late model Mazda MX-5 in white pearl, it was a sporty car without getting stupid. Even if she could afford stupid, she wasn't comfortable spending money on something she didn't need. Too many years with her fingers pressed against each penny to let that happen.

After Travis got his driving permit, they picked up a gunmetal gray Jeep Wrangler Rubicon for him, which cost far more than hers. While they could easily afford it, the purchase felt like a splurge. She wanted it to be. The kid was unjustly accused and jailed, missing many final days with his father. A vehicle wouldn't give him back that time, but it lessened the tension on Maggie's guilt.

As she descended the hill to her temporary home, the building complex for R-Bot Systems sprawled before her. It was a terraced glass and concrete structure with outdoor green spaces on each level. Nestled amid redwoods and Douglas fir, the complex was built ten years earlier by an internet company that eventually went out of business. So far, Maggie didn't hate the place.

She tucked her car into the parking space and sighed with satisfaction. Their family had been in a tailspin for so long, she'd forgotten how to feel hopeful. Now, Maggie needed to scan a brighter horizon for herself as well as for Travis.

She got out of the car, slung her purse over a shoulder, and walked to the building. With windows running the full height of the first floor, the lobby let in all the sun the surrounding trees would allow. It was a cheery space. She hoped they had decent coffee.

Inside, Maggie stopped at the reception station attended by a young man with too much hair gel. The receptionist said, "Welcome to R-Bot Systems. How can I help you?"

"Hi, my name is Maggie Fender. I'm a new employee, and I'm here to see Gail Everly." Maggie wouldn't have any unusual contact with Baxter while she was here. She had to act like a regular new hire, starting with a visit to HR.

"Oh. Cool. I'm Aiden Costa. Welcome aboard." The receptionist pulled out a tablet. "May I verify your identification, please?"

"Of course." Maggie pulled out her driver's license. Aiden compared it to something on his tablet and then made a phone call.

"Ms. Everly will be down in a minute." He handed her a lanyard with a card dangling from the end. "Please wear this at all times until you get your permanent badge. It will let you move through the low security areas only."

Maggie looked around for the restroom. "I hope the ladies' room is low security."

He laughed and pointed to the wood paneled section near the lobby windows. "You should be very secure, but you won't need a badge for entry."

"Thanks." She walked casually, but the long drive and large travel mug took its toll on her patience. Her two first-day objectives came to mind. Find the ladies' room. Check. The morning was already a success.

Before leaving the bathroom, she did a mirror scan. Her wardrobe got a makeover a few months back when she and Travis spent a full day shopping over in the valley. It wasn't the carefree trip she'd expected it to be. After years of living on the edge, it was hard to spend the money needed to portray an image other than struggling. In the end, she knew it was important to set an example for Travis.

When she reentered the lobby, a pale woman with short, dark hair approached the reception area. No doubt it was Gail Everly because she was as Baxter described her. Tall and curvy, she wore a black dress with an uneven hemline that swished past her knees. The chunky, polished rock necklace around her neck looked like an accessory for Wilma Flintstone. But the woman wore it well.

"Maggie Fender." Her voice was bright and expectant.

Maggie held out her hand. "It's a pleasure to meet you."

While they walked upstairs, Gail briefed her on the day's plan. They went into an area where new employees were processed, including a booth for taking badge photos.

The HR department. Scratch that. What'd they call it? Talent Acquisition. Yeah, that sounded a lot better.

Actually, Gail ran accounting. She was a high-profile consultant before joining R-Bot Systems, but everyone wore multiple hats, except the engineers. Thankfully, she was friendly and never questioned Maggie's fake background, setting Maggie more at ease.

They spent the next hour going over the basics. Employee portal. Payroll forms. New badge. And where to find coffee. Check. After completing all the forms on the website, Gail led Maggie to a room full of freestanding L-shaped cubicles. The area was roomier and cheerier than Maggie had expected. The word 'cubicle' conjured images of clones manacled to their desks.

"We use cubes in this area." Gail gestured like someone on the ground crew at the airport. "But there's some separation for noise control and privacy. The rest of the team will be along later. They're in a design review with Baxter."

"I look forward to meeting everyone." Maggie had the names and roles memorized, but soon she'd be investigating actual flesh and blood.

Gail patted the top edge of the cube wall. "Lynn can give you a deeper dive on DocuLocker when she's got some time. Meanwhile, login and check it out." Gail stepped toward the door. "I'll be around, so let me know if you need anything."

"I will. Thanks."

Maggie dropped her purse on the desk. It made a louder noise than expected now that she was alone. After waitressing for so many years, working by herself felt slightly awkward. But, it was a startup company, so they weren't long on formality or hand-holding. Like everyone else, they expected her to jump in and contribute.

She found her way into the system and had examined the filing structure for a while, when she heard a group enter the area.

Baxter appeared by her cube and said, "Welcome, Maggie. All settled in?"

"I am, thanks."

"C'mon. Let's meet the team."

He didn't make any overtures beyond the routine. They agreed to only discuss matters directly related to her fake role at R-Bot Systems.

When Baxter stopped by the first cube, the occupant rose. "This is Yang Tunan, head of mechanical engineering."

"Nice to meet you, Maggie." His face was smiling and expectant.

Word was out about her already. "You too."

He was tall, with a swimmer's build, his broad face widening into a smile as he shook her hand. Wearing classic casuals, he was catalog handsome. When Travis bought work clothes, she encouraged him toward this style. Of course, he was back to t-shirts and old jeans the minute they didn't have clients around.

Yang's warm hand held hers briefly. "I'll stop by later."

"Sounds good."

Baxter gently touched her elbow, and they moved to the next cube.

A bespectacled engineer with long black hair and a flawless complexion, he stayed seated and barely looked up from his work until he noticed Maggie.

"Meet Jason Gupta." Baxter seemed to stifle a smile. "He leads our electrical engineering."

"Oh." Jason glanced over at Baxter. "So you're Maggie."

She knew she'd cleaned up particularly well that day. Made a point of it. Instead of a big clip holding a wad of hair at the top of her head, she got up early to coax her locks into a loose French braid. After that, she slid into a lacy, white blouse, a Ferrari-red skirt, and a pair of ankle-strap heels. The outfit cost more than the automatic garage door opener she'd recently installed, and it was far more useful.

For a first half-day, it rocked.

Baxter led her to a room with another set of cubicles, where a man and a woman conferred over a monitor.

"Meet Lynn Moyega and Pavel Rokotov. Lynn runs IT and security, and Pavel runs software engineering."

"Oh, hey. Nice to meet you, Maggie." Lynn was a small, solid blonde with blue eyes, wearing a short-sleeved shirt and jeans. She looked as if she spent her free time in the sun.

Pavel stood. "Yes, we heard about you yesterday. Welcome, Maggie." He dressed like someone who noticed the trends and conjured his own colorful combo from the mix. He had a high forehead, deep-set brown eyes, and perfect eyebrows, the kind women tortured themselves to achieve.

Baxter leaned against the cube wall. "We run a lean operation. Once we build our production prototypes, we plan to expand the team. For now, we have a solid group of talent."

She and Baxter had spent some time discussing who did what, but he couldn't believe that any of them would betray his trust. Clint Masters' reputation was also at stake, as much as Baxter's.

Lynn said, "If you check your calendar, I set up some time for us to dig deeper into the system."

"I planned to hit you up for a tour, so thanks." Maggie added, "Are all the servers and IT operations on-premises? Or are you running some workloads in the cloud?"

Travis rehearsed that line with her. Running in the cloud just meant the computer server hardware was physically somewhere else, and they accessed it with their local computers. It made her sound as if she knew more than she did.

Lynn shook her head. "Nothing in the cloud yet. Maybe down the road."

One of Pavel's perfect eyebrows rose. "You are working with the DocuLocker system. How do you like it so far?"

"It's similar to one I used elsewhere, but much newer. I hope to tame it soon enough with Lynn's help."

"She knows the system better than anyone here."

"I have a lot to learn from you all." Maggie glanced at Baxter. "I appreciate the introductions. Did we miss anyone?"

"That's it for now," he said. "You know your way back?"

"I do. It was nice meeting you."

As she made her way back to her desk, she wondered. Which one of them was it? Maybe it was like the Murder on the Orient Express, where they were all guilty.

While she kept her mind on the job of finding the spy—if there was one—she couldn't help thinking about how much she'd missed. She was rarely around this many people, outside of the restaurants where she waitressed. Even during her college classes, she never slowed down long enough to get to know anyone. Including any men.

It seemed trivial, given the events of her life, but she hadn't really dated. Her school years were consumed with her stepmother's painful descent into death, her father's loss of lucidity, and the false, devastating accusations against Travis. Between running their home, juggling school, and becoming the sole breadwinner, she didn't have time for frivolous relationships.

Eventually, all the men in her orbit found someone more accommodating.

Until she met Fyodor.

But lately, he'd been gone, and she and Travis focused their time with work, regrouping their lives. She thought Fyodor was different, but maybe that's only what she'd hoped. Maybe he considered their relationship frivolous.

Maggie settled in at her workstation and spent the time exercising her new powers on the computer. As promised, Baxter gave her full rein to everything that related to their intellectual property, along with a list of what was stolen.

Eventually, Lynn came by and spent ninety minutes showing Maggie the workings of DocuLocker. Throughout that day, the other employees stopped by to check on her. People were friendly, seemingly unguarded. Considering them all suspects was harder than she'd imagined.

When Maggie was alone, she checked the access logs. If someone downloaded the relevant files, those records might give her some clues. But the logs didn't reveal any smoking guns. Engineers are supposed to have access, so seeing their names wasn't enough to raise suspicion. She could compare the timing of access to whatever Travis came up with from his search of the dark web. But even if the timing was close, it wasn't enough to accuse someone of industrial espionage.

As Maggie finished her day, Yang stopped by her desk again. He was taut and fit, as if he ran or rode a bike or did that swimmer thing. Yang also seemed friendly and kind. A few times that day, he stopped by to see if she needed anything. Maggie had to admit she savored the attention. Her killer new outfit felt like a superhero suit. Red skirts for the win! The last white blouse she wore to work had stains from a tenacious Shiraz.

"How was your first day?" He sat on the edge of the cabinet outside her personal space.

"It was great." She smiled. "I already feel at home."

They chatted for a while about the projects, Santa Cruz, all the usual small talk.

His head tilted to the side. "How about a drink after work tomorrow? Or dinner?"

She wondered what she'd say if someone asked her out, but she didn't think it would happen this fast. There were good reasons to say yes from a surveillance standpoint, since these people were her suspects. But in the end, it sounded like fun. "That would be nice."

Yang bit his lip and nodded. "Cool. I'll see you later."

He wandered out of her area, and Maggie gathered her things to leave. She promised to call Travis before her commute, but she wasn't going straight home. Maggie had to do something on her own, and she couldn't share these plans with her brother.

She hit speed dial, and Travis answered. "Hey. How was your first day?"

"It was great. I'll tell you all about it when I get home, but I'm going to be a little late." Maggie felt a twinge in her gut.

"Everything all right?" Travis sounded worried.

"Yeah. It's all good." It wasn't, but the lie was necessary. "There are a couple of shops I want to check out before heading home. Only an extra hour."

"Oh. Okay." His words were tinged with disappointment. "Stopped at the fish market today. I'll grill some salmon when you get home."

"Sounds great. Thanks, Trav."

Maggie hated deceiving her brother, but she wasn't sure what he'd think about her latest project. She'd tell him, eventually.

For now, it was something she had to do alone.

11

Gilbert Adams walked down the sidewalk, avoiding the area of the shooting from the day before. If the police were still gathering evidence, there was no good reason for him to end up on the witness list. Only arsonists or psychos put themselves in the middle of an investigation. Gilbert was neither, but he had to fix this problem for his boss, Augie Barrett. The only way to fix this was to find the kid.

In reporting the murder, the media ran his mother's picture from her ID as LaShawna Martin, which was the name she'd given the police when the kid handed over the satchel. Even people who knew her might not recognize her from the photo. Given the circles she traveled, her friends wouldn't talk to the police. They were even less likely to read the news.

The shooting was blocks away from the police station, and witnesses couldn't agree on details. When someone brandished a gun, that's all people saw. Those who noticed Gilbert saw only a mask, and even those details quickly faded. For now, there was no mention of the missing kid.

His mother called him Solomon. Was that his real name? Whatever his name, Gil had to find him.

After his mother got hit, the kid bolted from the scene, and Gilbert only knew the initial direction.

Gil planned to ask around today. If he thought someone wasn't forthcoming, he'd happily dangle a carrot, but if needed, he'd just as happily wield the stick. Before either, he had to find someone who actually knew something.

Gilbert stood at the intersection, looking past the homeless bodies slumped against the stucco and steel, imagining the way the kid might have run. What choices did that kid make in the aftermath? Gunfire ringing in his ears, his mother bleeding out on the sidewalk—the kid would hide. But where?

Maybe with another relative, if he could. But Gilbert had watched that kid and his mother for the last two weeks since finding out they turned in the leather case to the police. As far as Gil knew, they didn't have any relatives in the area. Or any friends.

The mother worked at a strip club, but the only person she associated with outside of the club was its owner, Tyrone Craig. Gilbert went by Tyrone's house the night before, but there was no sign of the kid.

Gilbert asked a few of the shop owners and derelicts around the scene of the shooting, but no one saw the kid. He left the busy street and strolled another block.

He kept up his canvass to the next intersection, where human traffic subsided and storefronts secured with bars gave way to buildings boarded with plywood. It was a better place to hide.

He entered the first open business on that block: King's Castle Hotel. The king had obviously ceded his palace to transients after losing his empire. Minus two stars on any decent travel scale.

Gilbert pushed open the door with his foot and entered the lobby. The man at the counter eyed him as if coming in alone was unusual. Gilbert offered the fable he'd perfected after repeating it all day. "I'm looking for a kid who stole my wallet yesterday. Small, black kid about eight or nine. Had a backpack. Did he run past here?" He waited for some flicker of recognition, but the clerk showed no signs of life.

"Nobody sees nothing around here. Including me."

If there was some possibility the guy was lying, Gilbert would offer him ten bucks to pique his interest. A starting bid of sorts. If they couldn't reach a deal or someone gave him too much mouth, Gilbert had a set of brass knuckles for added persuasion. But this guy wasn't a curious type. Gilbert kept his ten and hit the street.

He tried a few more places. A kebab joint. A wig store. A place that traded vinyl. When he got to the nail salon, he finally caught a break. The shop owner remembered a kid with a backpack.

"Yeah, black boy lean against window. Scare my customer. He look like he up to no good."

"Which way did he leave?"

The woman folded the two tens he'd given her and tucked them in a pocket. She pointed to an opening between buildings. "Ran that way."

"Thanks."

Gilbert headed toward the opening, checking his map app to see what businesses were located there. A shared parking lot serviced a dance club, a tattoo parlor catering to bikers, and a shoe store for the fetish crowd. None were ideal for a kid seeking refuge.

Where would the kid go from here?

The back door of the dance club opened while Gilbert was trying to decide his next move. A guy walked out wearing worn jeans and a plaid work shirt. Not exactly club chic.

"Got a minute?" Gilbert called out,

They were alone. It was San Francisco. It was a crappy part of town. Of course, the guy looked apprehensive.

"For what?"

"Sorry, man. Just looking for some help." He held up both hands and kept his distance. "Kid stole my wallet yesterday morning around nine. Someone said he ran back here. Any chance you saw him? Or find my wallet."

"No. Got a delivery yesterday. I was inside, restocking the cooler."

"What kind of delivery?"

"Produce. People come here to get loaded, but they still expect organic arugula salads on the menu." The guy shrugged. "Go figure."

Gilbert looked around the lot. "Any chance you've got cameras out here? It might tell me which way the kid went next."

The guy pointed to the tattoo parlor. "Got them all over." Then he jacked a thumb behind him. "We take care of each other around here." He checked his phone. "Even got an app for it." He ran through some screens, swiping away. Then he turned the phone towards Gilbert. "Is this your pickpocket?"

There he was. Carl Martin. Or Solomon. Whatever. The snot-nosed brat that caused him all this grief.

Gotcha, you little bastard.

"Took my wallet and a hundred and twenty bucks. Had to cancel all my credit cards. Such a bloody hassle."

"Your pickpocket is also a hitchhiker. Check it out."

The guy tapped the screen, and the still image of the kid entering the parking lot turned into full-motion. After surveying his surroundings, the kid crawled into the produce truck parked at the back of the dance club. Eventually, the driver closed the roll-up door. The kid never got out.

The side of the truck listed Vaughan Foods, Half Moon Bay, California. Gilbert now had something to tell his boss, Augie.

After a few more taps, the guy from the club said, "You want a copy of the video?"

It was a risk providing any information, even if the only person around who might care about the kid was dead. Plus, Gilbert now knew his own visit to the parking lot was recorded.

"Thanks, but it's not worth it. I just hoped to find my ID. I'm sure the money is long gone. The kid would've jumped out at the next red light."

"We're usually Dave's last delivery on his morning run before he returns to the warehouse."

"Had to check." Gilbert shoved his hands in his pocket. "But at least now I know it's a lost cause. Thanks."

As he wandered toward the main street, he started the audio app on his phone and recorded the information he learned, "Plate number 14226M3. Driver named Dave. Vaughn Foods of Half Moon Bay."

Gilbert planned to take an early drive there in the morning.

12

The sun was full-bright when Solomon woke. Warm rays streamed through the leaves that covered his head. He crawled out of his sleeping hole and found the last of the donuts and chips he bought the night before and ate them. He still wore the jacket he'd taken from the house, but he couldn't wear it anywhere else. If they found him wearing it, he might go to jail.

He took it off and placed it in the hole, then covered it all with the big leaves. Even the spot was hard to find unless you knew it was there by the elbow tree.

Sol decided to find the town that day, so he walked toward the main road. There had to be more stores around somewhere. The cars on the road went both directions, but there was a lot of nothing in between buildings. Trees. Fields. Some even had pumpkins growing in them. He checked Mama's phone again, but it was still dark.

Mama told him he might have to run someday, but she never told Sol what to do if that happened. Mama only told him to stay away. Now he was away from everything, including home.

He eventually found a busy road with lots of businesses, but with none of the tall buildings that towered overhead, blocking the light. As he walked, Sol counted the blocks, noting the road names as he went. He couldn't get over how quiet it was here. There were noises, but nothing like the ones in the city. Plus, it was clean and shinier than the places he usually went, with none of the trash on the ground. It was foggy and cold at night like San Francisco, but people here didn't seem to be in such a hurry. The only thing in San Francisco's favor was there he had a bed. And Mama. He hoped he still had Mama.

Sol avoided talking to other people, but he didn't know how long he was going to be here. When Mama got better, she'd come looking for him. He had to believe she'd come looking for him. Then, maybe they could stay here.

This Half Moon Bay wasn't an awful place. Most of the people were white, but they seemed to mind their own business. He didn't see any of the scary-looking people around, the ones who made sure everyone knew they were tough. He also didn't see any of the ones who smelled funny and peed on the sidewalks. Leastwise, he hadn't yet.

Plus, the ocean was everywhere, and all the buildings had lots more room around them. Sol saw a building with a giant wave painted on the side that was as big as the building. Someone stood on a surfboard in the middle of the wave as it curled. He wondered if waves ever really got that big.

His hand slipped into a pocket to check his money. Sol had the change from the one hundred dollar bill, and he planned to buy a charger for the phone. That house had an electric outlet on their porch, but they also had dogs.

After two meals of donuts and chips, his stomach hurt. Living outside, he needed food that didn't go bad. At one place he and Mama stayed, they didn't have a refrigerator. Or a stove. He remembered which foods they ate then. Canned goods with flip tops. As long as he ate it all in one meal, he should be safe. But he remembered those cans were heavy, so he couldn't buy too many at once. He was so thirsty, too, but he'd get just one bottle and then fill it up again later. If he could carry everything in the basket in the store, he could carry it in his backpack.

Earlier, he passed a drugstore at the other end of the road. If they were like the ones in San Francisco, they carried electronics, plus lots of food that didn't need a refrigerator. That was the best place for him to start.

Sol crossed the street and worked his way to the drugstore. He was worried about Mama, but there was a side of the adventure that was kind of fun—exploring this little town, counting the streets. Since he knew where he was going, it wouldn't take him as long to get back. The sun hadn't gone down yet, but he didn't want to stay out after dark.

At the drugstore, he got one of their carry baskets and found the food aisle. He picked out two boxes of granola bars and six cans of meat that didn't need an opener. Ham, corned beef hash, and Spam, plus some chicken in a pouch. He had some plastic forks left over from his visit to the convenience store the day before, so he didn't need to buy those. Sol scanned the shelves and found a bottle of water. Once it was all in his basket, he tested it for weight and then traded in the bottle of water for a smaller one.

Next stop, the electronics counter for the charger. That couldn't weigh much. Electronics were near the cash register. Sol stood on his toes to look at the packages on the wall.

A white woman popped up from behind the counter.

Sol gasped.

"Sorry, honey, I didn't mean to frighten you."

"I didn't see you back there."

"Can I help you find something?"

He didn't want her help, but he didn't see the charger Mama used.

She leaned on the counter. "Are you by yourself?"

Mama was right, old white women never can stay out of your business. But in this case, he needed her help.

"My mama sent me in here to get a few things, and I need a phone charger. The kind that plugs in the wall."

The woman raised an eyebrow and then rifled through the display, pulling out the right charger. "Is this it?"

Sol nodded. "Yes, ma'am." He put it in his basket.

"I can ring you up if you're ready to check out."

He nodded and handed her the basket. He dug out the money from his pocket and laid two twenties on the counter.

As she scanned each item, she handed it to him, and he put it in his backpack, which sat on the floor.

The total came to thirty-nine dollars and eighteen cents.

"Wait." Sol grabbed a chocolate bar and slapped it on the counter. He slipped his backpack over his shoulders and dug in his pocket for his other money.

"You owe me one dollar and seven cents, son."

Just then, a big man walked in the front door next to Sol. Not just any man, a cop.

Maybe he knew about the stolen jacket.

Sol's beating heart threatened to break through his chest. Down deep, the shaking started, like an earthquake rumbling his insides. Sol couldn't stop.

He grabbed the chocolate bar off the counter and ran out the door.

13

As a flock of seagulls circled overhead, Travis' best friend, Javier Modesto, dropped into the Adirondack chair beside him on the back porch. "How goes the hacking business?"

"Sweet so far. First day blues, though."

"New gig?" Javie picked up the smooth stone from the table. It was the stone Travis' dad always kept in his pocket.

"Hired us yesterday. Maggie's gone inside and undercover."

"What's your role?"

Travis put his hands behind his head. "Barbarian at the gate."

"Right in your wheelhouse. Nice to know you can't get busted for it this time."

"We get everything in writing. My job is to breach the fortress if I can. Give Maggie air cover and teach her what to look for." Travis checked the time on his phone. She'd be home soon.

"Anything you can discuss?"

"Working with a company that thinks they might have a spy. High-tech. High-value IP."

"What's IP?" Javie's interests ran more toward science rather than technology.

"Intellectual property. Company secrets."

Travis gave him a rundown on the project without mentioning the specific company or technology involved.

"Found a way in yet?"

"Thought I did earlier, but no. Besides, I'm convinced it's just a honeypot. The server doesn't go anywhere or seem to do anything."

"I thought honeypots were supposed to let you in. Aren't they just servers with sloppy security?" He laid the stone back on the table. "You know, without the patches."

"The good ones aren't. The good honeypots are set up like a regular server but are isolated on the system. If you find a way in, you can't access anything of value. Meanwhile, the internal crew is tracking your every move. Gives them a better understanding of the genuine threats coming their way."

Travis opened the door to let out the pair of beagles. They went straight to Javie for a welcoming sniff. He gave them a quick rubbing before they trotted out to the beach.

"Some companies put honeypots on the same backbone as their live servers, but they're just begging to get hacked. Guys we're working with aren't that stupid."

"So Maggie's pretending to be an employee." Javie put both feet up on the chair. "I'd ask how she drew the short straw, but I guess you're not old enough for inside jobs."

"I still can't drive my new Jeep by myself." Travis was counting the days until his birthday. "This place wouldn't touch me until I was at least eighteen. Or had a Ph.D." He got up to clean the grill. "Maggie loves her role as a social engineer. Worries me a little."

"She's due for a little adventure. That girl wore it all for years."

She was due. With him in prison and Dad sliding into dementia, Maggie had to carry the whole family. She deserved some fun. Instead, she wanted to work, get their business going as quickly as possible.

"Too hard for her to slow down after the wind up she had, I guess."

"Where's her bodyguard boyfriend these days? The Russian hulk."

Hulk was an appropriate description for him. He was 6' 5" and as sturdy as a tank.

"Haven't seen Fyodor the Great in a while. Think he's got a few jobs out of town." Travis checked the propane level in the tank and turned on the gas burners.

"Seen some people at Frodo's place this week." Javie sat upright and looked at the back of his chair. "Hey. Where's your dad's jacket?" He resettled into the seat. "Finally retired his jersey?"

As far back as Travis could remember, the jacket was either on Dad or on the back of that chair. "No. Some dirtbag stole it."

"Stole it? Bro, that's cold." Javie was one of the few people who understood.

"Hella cold."

"Can't trust anybody these days."

"Got that right."

Travis called for the dogs. He wanted to feed them before dinner. They eventually heeded him and returned with Bailey in the lead.

He nudged Javie. "Grilling some salmon. You in?"

"You grilling or Maggie?"

"Me. Plus, scalloped spuds and apple pie."

"In that case, I wish. But I promised to help my sister with chemistry." The Modestos owned the apartment building on their street. After Travis got out of prison, Javie's mom helped with the paperwork so Travis could homeschool like Javie and his siblings.

"Yeah. Maggie's making me take chemistry next year. I may need that service, too."

"Cool." He stood. "We can make stink bombs."

"As long as I get an 'A'."

Javie walked off the porch toward his place. "You want an 'A'? That'll cost extra."

Travis took the dogs inside and let them eat while he prepped the meal for the humans. The potatoes and salad were ready, and the salmon had marinaded long enough. Time to grill. He'd talked Maggie into buying the gas grill once their financial situation changed. Besides being a manly art he wanted to master, it took the load off of her. But mainly, Maggie was a terrible cook.

Over the years, Travis watched his mother, Ginger, and Javie's mom work in the kitchen, and he whipped out some decent dishes just from doing what they did. But after waitressing all those years in the finest local restaurants, with direct access to professional chefs, even the dogs considered Maggie's food marginally edible.

He heard the front door open and went to the foyer to greet his sister. But she dashed upstairs, and all he saw was her back.

Jeans. Now she wore jeans and a long shirt instead of the red skirt and white blouse she had on when she left that morning. She said she was stopping at some shops in Santa Cruz. Maybe she bought the clothes there and wore them home.

The Firm sauntered past him and charged up the stairs to visit Maggie, with Belli leading the way. Travis returned to the kitchen. Now that they could afford more than macaroni, cooking a nice dinner was actually fun. He put the salads and potatoes outside on the table. Warmer than usual, it was way too nice a night to eat indoors.

Maggie opened the sliding door. "Looks great, Trav. What can I do?"

He noticed her clothes. It was the same stuff she had on when she came home. Not new either. She obviously took them with her. Why would she change before coming home?

"I've got everything but the dishes. Can you grab those?"

"Sure," she said and retreated into the house.

Travis brushed the grill with oil and put the steaks on the fire.

Maggie returned with their dishes and a glass of wine. "This smells as good as any place I ever worked."

"Thanks." He checked the time. Three minutes before he needed to flip the salmon. "Tell me what happened at R-Bot."

She gave him all the details about her first day on the job. The people she met, the meager beginnings of her undercover work. By the time she told him about the engineer who asked her out, they finished dinner.

"You said 'yes'?" Travis thought she and Fyodor were almost an item. "What about Frodo? He might not like other hobbits in his shire."

Maggie kicked him.

"Hey!" He rubbed his shin. "That hurt."

"Didn't mean to kick you so hard. But I'm not in his shire."

"Just an expression."

"Find a new one." She gave him that look that told him she knew she'd overreacted. "Sorry."

"Sensitive. Much?"

"Thought I'd hear from him by now. Even if he's working." She picked up the dirty plates and stood. "Besides, meeting offsite with a suspect might be helpful."

Travis opened the door for her, and they went inside.

"My day wasn't a total bust, but I learned nothing new either." He told her about the probes he ran on the R-Bot systems and the suspected honeypot. Process-of-elimination work. Dull but necessary.

"How was the shopping?" He pointed at her clothes. "Did you get those today?" He knew she hadn't, but it was a probe of her systems. No excuses. It was what he did.

"Oh, no. Old stuff. Ran upstairs to change as soon as I got home." Her face dropped behind a curtain of blonde hair. "I didn't find anything I wanted." Maggie loaded the dishwasher.

Why would she lie about something as simple as changing clothes? Did she even go shopping? If not, where was she? Travis was going to call her on it, but decided not to. Maggie had her reasons. But it hurt that she didn't trust him with the truth.

A bark from Bailey interrupted Belli's snoring from the other room. He scrambled to his feet and ran to the back door. Belli lifted her head and reluctantly joined her brother at the door.

The salmon.

Travis couldn't let the beagles outside with the leftovers on the table. They were well-behaved dogs, but they were still dogs. Only the salad was safe.

He pushed past them to open the door to the porch. On the table, the plate that held the leftover salmon steaks was empty. The dish with the scalloped potatoes was gone. Raccoons definitely would eat the food, but they couldn't take the casserole dish.

Maybe it was the same dirtbag that took Dad's jacket.

Whatever else they had going on, now, Travis had to catch a thief.

14

The morning sky was a near blackout when Gilbert rolled into town after the winding drive over Highway 92. Most cars would head the other direction for an eight-to-late somewhere in the valley, but few alarm clocks chimed this early, still ten minutes before five a.m. Gilbert wanted to hit Vaughn Foods when they opened. To supply restaurants with their daily deliveries, Vaughn Foods started the day with the roosters. Finishing the last of his C-store coffee, Gilbert dropped the cup in the holder and followed the route given by his GPS.

The reports of the murdered woman had now faded. Local headlines moved on to a minor earthquake centered in Vallejo that rumbled an old school to the ground.

Augie Barrett was a man Gilbert couldn't afford to disappoint. They were old friends, but Augie was still the head of the organization, and he didn't suffer the sin of sentiment. Gilbert didn't know why, but somehow, this job was different. He knew he'd screwed up when he lost the kid, but the pressure from Augie amplified. Gilbert didn't know what was in the leather case. Didn't care either. But once he found it, then all was well. Popping a kid wasn't something he'd normally do, but it was for Augie and an extra $100K when they found the satchel and the kid stopped breathing.

He'd been to Half Moon Bay only once before today. There wasn't much to do there unless you liked the ocean and outdoors. Gilbert preferred indoor games like blackjack or roulette or a sweaty round with Misty when his wife didn't expect him home. Misty got him breathing hard enough. Who needed exercise?

Following GPS, he passed Vaughn Foods, parked his black Chrysler 300 two blocks down the street, and walked to the back parking lot.

It was before sunrise, and a bank of lights lit the work area. Several men were visible. Each attended to a truck that was backed up to a loading bay. From inside, the loading bay doors opened.

Gilbert strode past the first driver he saw, a man wearing a Western shirt, jeans, and cowboy boots. The only driver that interested Gil was the big-headed fellow with a mop of curly brown hair he'd seen in the video from the alley. Dave. He'd know him by sight, plus, he knew the license plate number of the truck the kid hitched a ride in from the city.

Gilbert wouldn't mention the kid. No reason to give the driver and the bar owner reason to discuss Gilbert. If the kid's body was ever found, he didn't want the video from the alley to be presented as evidence.

To make sure that didn't happen, Gilbert bought a bottle of temporary hair dye the night before. His own hair was in the blond range, but the box he bought promised him silky highlights along with dark brown hair, at least until he washed it. He covered most of his head in a ball cap—which he never wore—tugged low over his eyes and a plaid flannel shirt from a thrift shop.

Further down the line, he found the truck with the right license plate number. The bay door to the building was open, and the driver was approaching the cab from the opposite side.

Gilbert walked around the front of the truck, inspecting the grill and front bumpers.

The guy gave Gilbert a once-over and said, "Can I help you?"

"Hey. I'm John." He stood upright and held out his hand to shake the driver's. "I was in the city two days ago, and my car got hit. Someone told me they saw your truck nearby." The story Gilbert rehearsed spilled easily.

"My truck? I didn't hit anything." The guy strapped his arms across his chest.

"Oh, I know." Gilbert gestured toward the truck. "It's in great condition." He put his hands in his pocket. "No way it's this truck. The witness was half sober, and the truck's the wrong color."

With those words, the driver seemed to relax. "Weird."

"Yeah, I got a license plate number and the name of the company for my twenty bucks. But he said the truck was green."

He laughed. "Reliable, eh?"

"My fault for paying the guy."

"When was this?"

"Monday. Around noon."

"Nah. I'm long gone by then. Finished my morning delivery before ten and came straight back. My second route is over in the valley."

"Where'd you get hit?"

"Over on Arguello Blvd." Gilbert picked a street much farther west than where the truck was located.

"My last drop was a nightclub off of Eddy."

The same place the kid crawled into the truck.

"I was on my second delivery by the time your car got hit."

"Sorry to hold up you, man. But I had to check it out, you know?"

"Sure."

"See you around." Gilbert spun on a heel and left the parking lot.

He walked the wrong way from his car, going around the block. Augie was probably still asleep, but he expected a progress report.

Gilbert's call went to voice mail. "Just talked to the driver. It's possible the kid jumped out before leaving the city, so I've got people watching his neighborhood, in case he finds his way home or back to school. But I think he hitched a ride out of town. The club is close to the Central Freeway." Gil turned away from the sun. "That truck would've been out of the city and on the 101 within minutes. The kid couldn't jump out of a moving truck. Anyway, I think he's here in Half Moon Bay. I'm going to camp here for a few days and find the little brat."

But Gilbert couldn't just wait to get lucky. So far, the kid defied all his expectations of how a kid should behave. He knew the kid wasn't some Eagle Scout, but he seemed to have an instinct for survival. He'd probably seen a few tricks living with that mother of his. Another waste of a good bullet.

Gilbert had to treat this kid with more respect. Like a more cunning target. Like an adult. A smart one. Underestimating him had only brought Gilbert to this low point—stuck in a crap town and diminished in the eyes of his employer. He had a solid rep with Augie before this gig. For that alone, the kid needed to pay.

His moves wouldn't be predictable, and he wouldn't walk up to Gilbert with open arms. He didn't run to the police or even to his neighbors. Would've been what most kids would do. This kid didn't trust anyone. He was a city rat with a built-in antenna that kept him alive.

For now.

Gilbert needed a backup plan to deal with him once he found him. Snatching a screaming kid off the sidewalk brought unwanted attention. And if he wasn't carrying the satchel, then what?

Gilbert wasn't just screwed. He was dead.

He considered his options. The coastal mountain range looming over this damp town offered privacy. The hills were sparsely populated with private estates, farms, and houses, but there were also trails, fire roads, and byways that dead-ended in thick forest. In the hills, he could find some abandoned building left to rot.

It was a good plan.

For now, he'd hole up in a local hotel under an assumed name. Gilbert could scout the area for a secluded place to go in case the kid needed persuading. After an hour with Rocco, the kid would scream for his mama.

Gilbert laughed at the thought.

If a kid screamed in the forest, did he really make a sound? Plus, the forest was the perfect place to dispose of his body.

15

On Maggie's second day on the job at R-Bot Systems, she greeted all her coworkers and then spent the morning trying to determine which one of them was a spy.

She focused on the access logs of their engineering files to see who was viewing what. In the old days, if someone made a copy of a file and passed it on to another person over a drink, that activity would be impossible to trace. Edward Snowden was a constant reminder of the human factor in data security.

But R-Bot's data-loss prevention software system was outright paranoid. If Maggie tried to copy a file to a thumb drive, the software would check her access rights against the data she was trying to save.

A memo about the espresso machine in the cafeteria? Prove employee status. The salary list for the entire company? Um, no. Access denied.

Baxter told her the process was called Zero Trust network access.

Never trust. Always verify.

All the layers of extra security slightly slowed the engineer's work. For R-Bot Systems, it was a delicate balance between protecting their data and keeping their employees from smashing their computers.

Most network security groups operated like a fiefdom from the Middle Ages. Once the wall and moat were built around the castle, security teams only guarded the perimeter. Anyone who made it through the inner gate was given free access. With Zero Trust protocols, palace guards challenged anyone who wanted to step inside the royal keep.

As for networks, no matter who asked for the information, every single request was assumed to be a breach until the requester was verified.

Requesters wanting access had to prove who they were, and that they had a right to see that specific information.

Verify every user login. Verify every data request. Every single time.

At R-Bot, even when the right person could access critical data, they recorded every step taken by that user in the access logs that Maggie studied. Every keystroke made in that building was recorded and monitored.

Spend lunch sniping that vintage Van Halen vinyl on eBay?

Recorded.

And now, Maggie's inspection of the access logs was going into the same files. As the security manager, Lynn Moyega would come justifiably unglued if she knew Maggie was the one making these entries. Since she was using Baxter's login credentials and one of his computers, Lynn would never suspect.

Baxter said that each type of data was categorized by sensitivity. Basically, what kind of firestorm would occur if the data were stolen? Lose health information—face public backlash and major fines. Lose customer data—face public backlash and lawsuits. Lose trade secrets—face lower market share and bankruptcy.

All résumé updating events.

But no system was entirely safe. Humans were always the wild card. In the Snowden case, he was allowed unrestricted access to files the NSA didn't want him to see.

People. Always a risky draw from the deck.

At the sound of sharp conversation, Maggie instinctively closed the windows on her screen.

She rose to stretch and saw Pavel and Jason near the entry. Jason's complexion appeared less perfect now that he was angry. But Pavel didn't seem to be the focus of his tirade. Maggie lowered to her chair.

She couldn't make out much of their conversation, but she heard Jason mention the name Yang. Was Jason mad at Yang Tunan?

While Yang designed the moving parts of the robot, Jason developed the electronics to actuate the parts, and Pavel wrote the software that controlled the movement of the parts. The three men had to work in concert for the company to succeed.

Startups often demanded long hours and intense make-or-break-a-company decisions. Conflict was inevitable.

The conversation escalated until Pavel said, "Lower your voice."

She heard a loud exhale, and then Jason said, "This isn't over."

The exchange left Maggie intrigued and a little rattled. Baxter didn't mention any disputes within the group.

Just then, her phone sounded with Travis' ringtone, One Foot by Walk The Moon. Maggie flinched and clapped a hand to her chest. She took a sharp breath before checking the text from her brother.

Call me.

They wouldn't talk about the job while she was inside the building.

After logging out of the program, she slipped the laptop into a lower drawer and locked it. Ready to loosen her muscles, she walked down the hall to the veranda on her floor before calling her brother.

"Hey, Trav."

"Magpie. How's the job going?"

"The work is fascinating, but I already hate the commute."

"You and everyone else."

"And I just heard part of an argument." She replayed the scene for him with all the detail she had. "Could be something. Could be nothing."

Travis said, "You sure it's a good idea to go to dinner with Yang?"

"It'll be fine. We're meeting in a public place. Separate cars." She inhaled deeply from a cool breeze scented with the smoky, sweet scent of cypress. "None of these people seem dangerous."

"But one of them might be."

They stayed quiet a moment.

Maggie said, "Anything else go missing off our back porch?"

"This time the thief returned some things."

"Not the salmon, I hope."

He laughed as expected. "No, just the casserole dish. It was clean and contained several sea shells. Weird, huh?"

"Seashells? Is that some sort of beach-theft currency?"

"Wondered the same thing myself. Whoever did it was only after the food. If it was the same person who took dad's jacket, my guess is the person's living on the beach."

"Then there's a chance we'll get it back." She hoped so. To anyone else, it was just a jacket. To Travis, it was a part of his history, his psyche. When he was little, he ran up to strangers who had similar jackets, thinking it was their father.

"I didn't think of that." Excitement tinged his voice. "That would be cool."

"Might not hurt to set up some cameras. See who we're dealing with." She thought about the many transients that came along the beach. "Could be harmless, but if not, we should know."

"Good idea. I'll see if Ginger will ride with me to the hardware store." He said, "Once I get it set up, I may leave some bait."

Maggie said, "I'll keep digging, but I see nothing obvious." She thought about her evening plans. "Remember, I'm gonna be late tonight."

"You were late last night too. Something I should know about?"

What had she told him? "No, just went shopping yesterday." She hated lying to him. But was he ready for the truth?

"You might know someone at the restaurant."

Maggie knew a lot of the restaurant staff from her years of waitressing. There were several of those people she never wanted to see again. "Probably not this time. It's a Mexican restaurant in Santa Cruz."

"What time do you think you'll be home?"

"Can't stay out too late. Still a work night for me, but maybe I can learn something from this guy. At least impressions of the staff, if nothing else. It's really the only reason I agreed to go with him."

"Is he good-looking?"

His question made her cheeks hot, but she wasn't sure why. "Well, yeah. But I really want to talk to him about the staff. Jason sure seemed unhappy. Unhappy people will go to great lengths to make others miserable." Her own mother came to mind. Maggie hadn't seen her in years, and that arrangement worked just fine.

"Just checking." His snark annoyed her.

"Enough about me. What progress have you made?" For the client's sake, she hoped it was significant.

"I've started a new line of investigation on the dark web. Baxter's friend was approached anonymously about Baxter's tech. By searching for anyone offering R-Bot systems information, I can filter through the monikers. It won't give me a real life name, but it's a start."

It was a smart angle. "What have you got so far?"

"Nothing, but I've dropped feelers at a few sites. If someone on the dark web is actively looking for a buyer, I should get approached."

Maggie knew he had friends on the web with access to questionable forums. "Are you using any of your contacts?"

"Any objections if I do?"

It was a fair question. The kid had suffered from his undeserved conviction. From the beginning of that saga, she'd assumed he was guilty, and it undermined their relationship. She wasn't making that mistake again.

"If you have questions about legal issues, then let's address those. Otherwise, Trav, I trust you to do the right thing."

"Thanks." She heard the good cheer in his voice, could almost see his spine straighten. She'd been such a bitch to him over the years. It was an ongoing wonder that her opinion still mattered.

"To answer your question, yes, I asked one of my online buddies for help. If I can get some extra mileage this way, all the better. Besides, it's better to have it look as if there are multiple parties interested in the robotics info. Competition never hurts."

Travis told her that someone had assisted him on the dark web when their father was missing. For that she was thankful. The more she understood her little brother, the better she viewed his judgment. Then again, he had to grow up faster than most.

Maggie said, "I plan to check in with Baxter at some point. Is there anything I can tell him?" Baxter wasn't certain they'd get any results, but she wanted him apprised of their plans.

"I don't see any obvious holes with any machines on their network. No unpatched devices, out-of-date software, or wonky routers. Which makes sense since they're so new. They wouldn't start out with antiquated equipment or software. But, someone could have brought equipment from home. If a machine is turned off, I won't see it until it's online. For what it's worth, I'm running my scans continuously, in case some vulnerable machine is currently offline."

"That makes sense. At least we have to eliminate it as a possibility."

"Exactly."

She checked the time on her phone. "I still have to do some non-spy work before I leave today, so I have to roll."

"I'm going to Ginger's now, see if she'll drive with me to the hardware store, so I can pick up the cameras. Probably buy her lunch, if she's hungry."

"It's about time you fed her." Maggie added, "Take her someplace expensive."

"Have a nice time on your date, but I'll be waiting up for you."

"Funny man. I'm going out with an engineer. I hope I can stay awake."

16

Marcus got off the plane and grabbed a taxi outside the terminal. He could've hired a less expensive driver, but he wanted the experience of someone who really knew the city. Someone used to questions from tourists.

"Not sure where I'm going yet. Just here for the day."

"Sightseeing." The driver was Middle Eastern, with an accent to match. "I'll drive around until you decide on a destination."

"Sounds good." In all of his travels, including his search for Toya, Marcus had never been to San Francisco.

The driver left the airport and gave Marcus a quick tour of the bay side attractions: Pier 39, Alcatraz Island, fog rolling through the Golden Gate Bridge.

While the sights resembled the postcards he'd seen, the world always looked dingier in real life. Postcards stripped out the layers of living grime the city didn't want to promote.

Marcus didn't want to hang around any longer than necessary. "What clubs are open now?"

"In San Francisco?" The guy raised an eyebrow toward the rearview mirror. "You need to be a little more specific than that."

Between all the gay clubs and those who catered to swingers or the bondage crowd, the type Toya worked in might be in the minority.

"Girls. Dancers." He straightened his tie. "Just girls."

The driver smiled. "Plenty of those in town, despite what you might have heard."

"Someone recommended a club called high something. Know any place like that?"

"Hightop Honeys?" The driver made eye contact. "That might be the one you're talking about."

"Sounds like the place. What's it like?"

"Not the most expensive club in town. But plenty to look at. Or whatever."

Marcus frequented these places only in his search for Toya. "Take me there."

"Awfully early. Place won't even open till noon."

"It's fine. Plan to get out and do some walking."

They small-talked about things to do and see while Marcus was in town, but it was only for the driver's benefit. He was here with a single aim.

They passed the expected images. Victorian houses. Glimpses of the Bay. Homeless on street corners. The high-tech companies owned certain areas from what Marcus knew. But this street had seen none of the new money circulating in town.

When they arrived at the club, Marcus had the driver pass by the front. No one would confuse the place with Carnegie Hall. Brass doors, darkened windows, neon lights flashing images that belonged on mud flaps. The joint opened at noon.

Typical of the places he'd trailed after Toya. Nothing upscale, but not the worst place in town either. He attributed that to her looks. Despite being on his hit list, she was a beauty.

On the corner, Marcus got out of the car and paid the driver. He walked toward the club, but not to the front door. First, he wanted to get a look around the place, find the employee entrance.

Behind the club was a private parking lot. On the sidewalk, a man and his belongings leaned against a fence. His feet stuck out from a small tent draped over his head. Marcus walked around him and found the rear door of the building.

Bars covered all parts of the structure that weren't solid cinder block. Marcus pressed the doorbell. If anyone was inside, he didn't pass the test for entry. So he waited.

It had been a while since he'd eaten. He snacked on some beef jerky to keep his blood sugar in check. On the streets, human traffic kept a steady flow. The man on the sidewalk eventually moved on, tucking his tent into a box and dragging it to another location. Cyclists moved faster than most of the cars. He watched an endless stream of people shopping, mumbling, searching for a bright moment in the city.

Eventually, a silver car pulled into the lot. A beat-up old Toyota with a peace sign on the rear bumper. A white girl stepped out who looked as expected. Blonde extensions, outlandish makeup, and a body designed for anime. Only her clothes weren't ready for showtime. She wore sweats that still tripped the imagination, carrying something on a hanger that would eventually turn into nothing on the stage.

He'd met many of them over the years. From Ratlanta to Shitcago—they all wore the same impassive look, the armor of fake hair, the glittering war paint for another long night of battle. Out here, they didn't want to meet you. They needed the field advantage of the stage, where they stood above you, riding the brass pole. Only then could they imagine they were in control.

Marcus walked toward her as she neared the door. "Excuse me, ma'am. I'd like a word with you, if I may."

"Come back at noon and bring your money." She wouldn't make eye contact.

"Not interested in the show. I'm looking for a lady who works here."

Maybe it was the use of the word lady, but the blonde glanced at him while she rang the rear bell. "Can't help you."

He pulled out the picture of Toya to show her as the door opened. Marcus was six-foot two and a solid 200 pounds, but he had to look up to the tatted white dude standing in the doorway.

The tatted dude put his hand on the woman's arm. "This guy bothering you, Lacey?" Lacey. Undoubtedly a stage name.

Marcus took a step back. "Not here to bother anyone. Just looking for the lady."

The guy checked the photo while pulling the woman through the door. "Don't know her. Now either come back through the front door when we're open, or don't come back at all. You read me?"

"Just looking for the lady." Marcus repeated this mainly to himself because the door slammed shut.

He understood a serious warning when he heard one. The dude could probably bench press Marcus and the blonde. But he hadn't flown all this way to get blown off by Vanilla Ice. He wouldn't confront the man unless he had to. For now, he had time to kill.

The parking lot offered a great place to watch pigeons for the next ten minutes. A slice of bread kept half a dozen of them fighting for crumbs, while Marcus cooled his nerves.

Suddenly, the back door opened and out came Lacey. Still wearing her sweats, she had a new swagger to her walk. He figured she left something in her car, but she veered toward Marcus with wide, glassy eyes. Coke maybe. A snort of indifference before taking the stage.

"Why are you looking for her?" Her voice was louder, harder.

Marcus wasn't sure which lie he should tell her. In the past, he'd tried the truth, but that didn't get him any further than a good lie. Once, the truth got him into a knife fight. Since then, the lies seemed easier to manage.

"She's my sister."

"Sister my ass." Lacey's lips hitched into a sneer. "She warned us about you. Coming to look for her one day."

Marcus instinctively reached for his ear. He'd thought about plastic surgery. Even some big ass earring that might cover it. But his shredded lobe was a daily reminder of his tour in Iraq. He'd earned his scars, but it made him a marked man.

"If you won't help me, why are you here?"

The sneer dropped from her face, false eyelashes lowering to touch her cheek. "I don't like her. Used to be Tyrone was my boyfriend until LaShawna showed up."

LaShawna. How many names did the woman have? "LaShawna. How is she?"

"She's a bitch." Lacey crossed her arms. "Don't think you like her much either. One thing you learn in this job is how to read men."

He'd been looking for Toya for too many years to invest in emotion. Ahab could have his white whale. For Marcus, this was just a job he had to finish. Another mission.

"She's caused the family a bit of grief. I just need to find her. Will she be working today?"

"Don't know. She was supposed to be here last night but didn't come in. Tyrone was pissed." Lacey tossed her hair over a shoulder. "Maybe I'll get him back."

Did Toya know he was in town? Had she skipped out again? He nodded as if the news was no big deal. "LaShawna miss work often?"

"Not since I've been here. Tyrone frowns on it. Even for his pets."

"Can you tell me where she's living?"

"I don't like her, but I don't want to see her hurt."

"No." Marcus wasn't sure what this woman wanted. "Real men never hurt ladies."

The woman rocked back on her hip. "LaShawna said you wanted to hurt her, but she wasn't easy with the truth."

"You know her better than most then." Marcus laughed under his breath. "She's been gone from home a few years. Mama's been sick, and she just wants to know that her daughter is okay."

"I lost my mom a year ago." Lacey's lips tightened. "Yeah. I'll give you her address."

17

On the cab ride over to Toya's, Marcus talked to the driver about the neighborhood. What he learned didn't surprise him. Originally a segregated neighborhood on the outskirts of the city, Hunters Point was former home to the Naval shipyard and Candlestick Park, where the San Francisco Giants and 49ers played ball.

It was one of the worst neighborhoods in the San Francisco area, arguably the most polluted. When they tested the early atomic bombs at sea, the attending ships caught the fallout, returned to the shipyard, and contaminated the surrounding area. Cleanup was still going on. Meanwhile, the gangs and drug pushers claimed part of the turf, while the tech gen-Xers built upscale apartments, put up fences, and hired guards. With Toya as a neighbor, Marcus didn't blame them.

The ride to Hunters Point took about 30 minutes. They drove past her place once, just to verify the address. The two-story apartment building was on the side of a hill, with the parking on the street. He'd have to hoof it down a set of stairs to get to her place. If Toya was home, he didn't want her to see him arrive. Over the years, he'd been on her heels before. Once, he missed her by three days, but he'd never felt this close to catching her mangy ass.

Marcus' promise of a fat tip convinced the driver to stay in the area while he checked out Toya's place. Marcus donned a hoodie and grabbed his rucksack before getting out of the cab to scout the area.

A guy parked in a car down the street looked out of place. Marcus had been doing this too long not to know a watchdog when he saw one. Maybe a cop. They probably tailed someone once a week in this neighborhood.

Few people around this time of day. Still school time for the kids. There were a few young guys hanging around the front stoops across the street.

Marcus made his way down the stairs and walked to another building so no one would know his destination. Some buildings were further down the hillside and accessible by a series of stairs. The lower units required a healthy walk from the parking lot. With a million-dollar view of the bay, many of the occupants had to look through bars to see it. Some would have to remove the plywood.

Considering some of the other places he'd trailed her, this wasn't the worst place she'd haunted. The signs listed the owner as San Francisco Public Housing. She probably scammed someone to get in here. The waiting lists for Section 8 housing in this real estate market had to be years.

But Toya could figure an angle faster than Euclid. Must be a man involved somewhere. Maybe that Tyrone mentioned by the woman at the club. As a stripper, she was probably an independent contractor, had to pay for her spot at the club. Then she had to split her take with the house. Toya might not even be on the guy's register. At one club, she worked entirely off the books. Men went stupid for her. One guy even sold his car to give her travel money out of town.

From somewhere amid the stucco forest, he heard a baby wail. Once he was out of view, he doubled back to confirm the address Lacey gave him. The buildings were two stories and terraced along the hillside. Toya's unit was on the first floor.

He checked the back of her place first. Curtains covered the window. He listened for sounds of life, but heard nothing coming from inside. The only way to make certain Toya lived here was to enter the unit.

He pulled a small kit from his pocket—a few slim tools to coax open an unwilling lock. He steadied his hands, but the lock needed little convincing.

Whether it was the breaking and entry, finally finding Toya, or low-blood sugar, he didn't know, but Marcus felt perspiration moisten his shirt. He stepped inside and ate some raw almonds from the pack in his pocket, just in case.

Blood thumped his temples as he peered into the living room. Would this chase finally end here? He hoped so. For everyone involved, he hoped so.

It was a small apartment with a stained coffee table, a bookcase with no books, and a yellow tufted couch with sagging cushions. The walls were bare except for a plastic clock and a framed print of a red rose floating over a valley. He didn't know the name of the piece, but the artist was Salvador Dali.

Surreal.

An apt description of Marcus' day. Like Dali's painting of the drooping clocks, Marcus felt his own pending meltdown.

Another city. Another state. Another dirty hovel.

Finding this woman was the longest mission of his life.

He passed through the living room into the spartan kitchen, where the smell of burnt coffee lingered. The coffee maker rested on the edge of the counter with a single cup next to it. Dirty dishes in the sink. On the floor, a step stool sat against the baseboard—the first sign that a child might live here. He still hadn't seen any toys.

Marcus opened the fridge, a few cabinets, but the contents would've disappointed Mother Hubbard. Or was it her dog? The boy was about nine now. Wasn't much for him either.

On the other side of the hall, Marcus checked the bedroom. A single bed and an air mattress on the floor comprised the bedroom furniture. But finally, he saw some toys.

At least two people then. A woman and a boy. The clothes in the closet and those strewn around the room confirmed it. He took a quick peek in the bathroom. Makeup in every variety. The sharpened tools of Toya's trade. A bottle of Shalini perfume sat atop the dirty, laminate counter, the scent clinging to the stale air. That bottle cost more than the entire contents of the kitchen.

It was the closet that most interested Marcus. There, he found a trove of Toya's sordid history. Her life on paper: fake identification, social security numbers, past addresses, a few old letters from her mother. He got his phone and snapped photos of all that he found. A few of the addresses were familiar, but not all of them. He'd probably chased her in places she'd never been.

But he had her nailed.

He took his time and set up the small cellular cameras and microphones. Nothing CIA level, but they were discreet and would record any activity inside the apartment.

Marcus returned all her things to where he found them. He had some business to conduct with the boys across the road before taking the cab to his hotel.

He expected to go back to Florida, report what he found, but with her this close, he decided to stay and prepare for a final, decisive move.

18

Yang Tunan met Maggie in the lobby of El Corazón, a trendy Mexican restaurant close to the office. "Hey, Maggie." He swept his bangs to one side. "I hope you like this place."

After her days waitressing, she appreciated being table-side any time. "It certainly smells fabulous."

"Also, I hope this doesn't offend you," his voice lowered, "but you look great."

"It's all good. Thanks."

She'd worn another killer outfit, a pale pink dress with long sleeves that contoured in all the right places. In the past, she never focused on clothing, but lately, the new things made her feel more alive. Maggie felt a little shallow admitting that to herself, but facts were facts.

Yang pointed at the wine rack above the *maître d's* counter. "How about we start here?"

"Sounds good to me."

The *maître d'* checked their reservation and led them to a table overlooking the San Lorenzo River. They passed through a rock archway surrounded by walls painted in jewel tones. Colorful mosaic parrots brightened the floor.

At the table, Yang helped Maggie with her chair.

Smart and well-mannered.

He picked up the wine list. "Glad you could get away. First few days of a new job are always a blur."

"I'm getting a grip on the software and the specific procedures. Everyone's been great."

"It's a talented group. Amazing company. I was flattered that they hired me."

Every time Yang spoke, she liked him a little more. He wasn't the egotistical egghead she thought he might be. She wondered what Jason had against him.

"I'm sure you're more than qualified. A startup like this one can certainly be selective."

He lowered his head and studied the wine list. "Is there something in particular you'd like? Unless you're going to have seafood, I recommend the Ladera Malbec. We could split a bottle."

"The Malbec sounds lovely, but I think a glass might be a better idea." He might live nearby, but she lived an hour away. "I need time to regroup my gray cells before hitting the road."

"Yeah. It's still a work night."

He signaled for the waiter, who came and took their drink order. Soon, she luxuriated in a goblet of Napa Malbec.

"Ooh, this is nice." She swirled the red liquid in the glass, mostly because she liked the way it glittered in the lights. She'd been known to enjoy a glass from a box.

"Found that vintner on my last trip north." He laid back in his chair. "So, what do you think of the document software?"

As a fake employee, the software was her mainstay function. A real employee would have an opinion. "It's adequate. There are certainly systems with more elaborate functionality." It was a safe general comment and likely true.

"I've warmed up to it," Yang said. "I recommended they get a different one." He hoisted his glass in a toast. "I hope that doesn't make us enemies."

"I'm not the only who one has to use it." She felt bad offering an opinion that was meaningless, but deceit was part of the job. From what she saw of him so far, Yang seemed decent.

Maggie lifted her glass and looked across the room. Staring back at her from another table was Fyodor the Magnificent.

Her gaze fixed on him for several embarrassing seconds. She put down the glass and resolved not to melt. Maggie forgot the effect he had on her. But who would remember? He hadn't been around in ages.

Fyodor was with another man, possibly a client. Whereas Maggie was also with a man, possibly a client. Still, something about the look on his face seemed hurt. Maybe she just hoped that was the case.

She offered a slight wave. He waved back. And they returned to their respective table companions.

Yang didn't miss the exchange. "A friend of yours?"

"An acquaintance." Maggie turned the subject to the personalities of R-Bot Systems. "So tell me about the other engineers." She focused on him to get her mind off the brooding Russian at the other table. "Jason seemed upset earlier today. With all the pressures, everyone needs a relief valve."

"We're still in the forming and storming stages of an organization." He rearranged his napkin before laying it on his lap. "At least I hope so."

"Where did you work before this?" Yang changed the topic.

Maggie developed an imaginary résumé for herself, so she was prepared for the question. Plus, Baxter made sure her listed jobs didn't overlap with any of his real employees. "I worked for Cat-Sat Laboratories."

It was a good choice for her because the company was huge. Plus, their founder was the CEO.

"I met Clint Masters on one of his trips out here. Great guy." Yang leaned forward. "Well, a legend."

"What about you? What did you do before?"

"I wrote software starting in grade school, but the mechanical side of products has always been my first love. I competed in robot battle competitions during college."

"My brother is a big fan of those." The words slipped out before she realized. Maggie chided herself for adding personal information. A real spy would be more discreet.

Fortunately, the waiter returned to take their order and brought another round of wine and the subject changed.

Maggie tried to get him to talk about his coworkers, but invariably, Yang returned the topic to her. Either he was infatuated, or maybe, he just wasn't a gossip.

As they conversed, the food eventually arrived, and Maggie tried to keep her eyes away from Fyodor.

She didn't want to stick around for dessert, but Fyodor was gone before she finished her second glass of wine. He didn't bother stopping by the table, perhaps because he was working. Perhaps because he didn't think her worth his time. The possibilities were endless, and not productive for Maggie to consider.

With dinner concluded, Yang offered to pay, but Maggie insisted they split the check. When they left their table, he put his arm on her elbow, an old-school gesture which some women didn't appreciate. For Maggie, it reminded her of her father. Whatever the conclusion with this job or Fyodor, she had to admit that Yang held her interest. If he weren't a suspect—

She shook the thought from her head.

Outside, the evening air coming off the ocean was balmy and with the seductive scent of salt and eucalyptus.

A canopy of trees graced the parking lot, with accent lighting throughout to illuminate the property. When Yang walked her toward her car, she wondered if the moment would get awkward. He was a coworker, ostensibly, and she wanted to keep things casual.

Fortunately, he just extended a hand and said, "I had a nice evening, Maggie. Can we do this again sometime?"

She took his hand in return. For all she knew, Yang could have dismembered pig parts in his fridge, but he certainly was a gentleman. "I'd like that." She meant it.

He squeezed her hand and let it drop.

Whether the case went forward with his help, or whether he was the thief of the company secrets, time would tell. Outside of Fyodor, he was the closest thing to a promising relationship she'd met in years.

Figured.

She unlocked her car. "Thanks for inviting me, Yang. I had fun."

"Me too." He opened the car door for her and said, "I'll see you in the morning."

A girl could get used to this.

Yang stood aside to let her enter the car. Before she took her seat, his lips lifted at the corners, widening into a bright smile, until a sharp sound cracked the air, and his head exploded in a furious cloud of red.

19

That night, Sol lay in his sleeping hole near the elbow tree wondering if the police were going to take him to jail. They eventually did that to all the black brothers, according to Mama. And he did steal the chocolate bar.

By the time he'd stopped running after leaving the store, the chocolate bar was all squished in his hand. He ate it anyway because Mama didn't like him to waste food. But it didn't taste as sweet as he expected.

He also stole that pink fish and the potatoes. Maybe he should go to jail. But it was still warm and smelled so good when he walked by that house, and the dogs weren't around. It was nothing like he'd ever eaten. Whoever lived in that house was lucky. Nothing Mama ever made was that tasty.

Sol pushed away the soft branches that covered his hole. There wasn't much light out, just the stars and a moon sliver. Sol tried the power button on the phone again, but the screen was still dark, cracked. He covered his head again and burrowed into his hole.

Once he got the phone charged, maybe there'd be a message from Mama. Or even Tyrone. Tyrone didn't always talk nice to Sol, using bad words sometimes. But right now, Sol wouldn't mind the bad words if Tyrone would take him to Mama.

Sol had the charger. He'd paid for that, at least. But he didn't have a way to plug it in except at the house where he stole the jacket and fish. Charging the phone would take a while, so he'd have to leave the phone there and come back later.

And those two dogs lived there. The dogs seemed friendly, but dogs remembered smells. If he left something at that house, they could track him and figure out where he was hiding. The dogs couldn't track him from the dishes because he washed those, but he couldn't wash the phone.

Maybe there were other houses nearby with outdoor plugs. He'd look for one of those. No, he wasn't leaving anything at that house. He didn't want any trouble with a pair of sniffy dogs.

Just then, Sol heard something rustling the brush nearby. It was close. Too close. His chest tapped in fear. He hunkered beneath the soft denim jacket and quieted his breath.

He really didn't want to see whatever was in the bushes near him. What if it was the cop? If Sol could go back and pay for the chocolate bar without getting arrested, he would. He never stole anything before, and he had plenty of money.

Now the noises were right next to him, sounding more like a grunt. Animal grunts. He and Mama had mice or rats once in a while, but whatever this was, it sounded bigger.

Oh, where was she? Sol knew she was hurt. Hurt bad. But was she still alive? Part of him didn't think so. The gunshots were so loud, and she was on the ground.

Sol couldn't stop being scared any more than he could make the dark go away. When it was daylight, he could be brave. But not alone at night. Not with animals grunting close to his ear.

He pressed his palms tight against his eyes, but tears slid down his cheeks. Mama left him alone lots of times before, and she always came back. If he really was on his own, then he'd live here on the beach.

As long as that cop didn't find him.

Sol would return the jacket eventually, and he scrubbed those dishes with sand until they sparkled. It was easier than using the sponge he had at home. When he dug up the satchel again, he'd get out some money to leave on the porch, but for now, the seashells would have to do.

The grunts started again. Louder, grunting too close for him to sleep. Whatever it was, he had to get rid of it. Scare it away.

He eased away the leaves above his head and spied the eyes of a white-faced rat. When it saw Sol, it bared fangs and hissed.

"Git!" Sol ducked under the leaves, his stomach thumping with every heartbeat.

He'd seen plenty of rats, but that was huge. Rats carried babies in their mouths, but that one had some on its back.

Maybe it was an opossum. He'd never seen a live one, but he knew they came out at night.

Thinking that through made him bolder. He stuck his head out again and looked at the creature more carefully. A bunch of babies rode piggyback, but it was leaving.

That thing was an opossum. He was sure of it. And he'd scared it away.

A deep breath left Sol feeling stronger. He'd faced the enemy and won. With $8,500, he could stay here by the elbow tree forever. He could do this, even alone, if he had to.

But he wanted his Mama back. She'd come find him if she could. How bad was she hurt?

Sol had to know. Was he on his own for good? She told him that day might come. And if he was alone, well then, he'd live at the beach and play in the water by day and scare off animals by night. But if she was okay, he had to find her.

With his mind made up, he settled in for another night of sleep. Then he heard it.

Tap. Tap. Splat.

The rain came fast and hard, seeping into his dug-out bed. When the warm jacket got too wet, the cold water reached his skin.

No lights. No power. No Mama.

Sol swiped his face.

No crying neither.

Now he had to figure out how to survive.

20

Maggie didn't trust her eyes. Her mind rewound and replayed the horrific scene in ever slower motion. Yang's head ruptured like a pin-pricked balloon, his body crumpling like a marionette with a snapped string. The sharp crack she heard before was now replaced by dull screams and the steady thud of blood against her ears.

From the road, the squeal of tires caught her attention, but the vehicle was already gone. Like Yang.

Was this a drive-by?

She pushed away from the car, her new pink dress snagging on the lower corner of the door.

Before touching Yang, she knew he was dead. Blood seeped out of him, glistening on the pavement like an oil slick. Still, she squatted to check his pulse at the neck.

That was the first step in first aid. Check the pulse. Even if a man is missing half his skull.

Oddly, she still expected to find a pulse, but his warm body was still. Her hand came back to her covered in blood and smelling of iron.

No pulse. Yang's fading heartbeats only hastened his exsanguination. Bled him of any tenacious remnants of life. Maggie wiped her hand on her pink dress.

Others were around her now, a din of voices competing with the pounding in her head. They pointed toward the roadway.

Yang was dead. Who would want to kill him?

Her stomach convulsed. She covered her mouth and ran to the other side of her car before throwing up in the bushes. With each expulsion, her breaths came shallow and short.

A woman came near Maggie and said something. The woman's posture was consoling, but Maggie couldn't focus on the words.

Her tongue felt thick, and her head shook out a 'no.' The woman patted Maggie's hand and rejoined the crowd.

While others tried to tame the chaos, Maggie leaned against her car, sweat trickling from her forehead. She wanted to run, find the ocean and dive under a wave to etch the acrid stench from her nostrils. But the police would be here soon, and she was a primary witness.

From several directions, Maggie heard sirens caterwauling in lament. One was close. Soon, the first police car rolled slowly into the parking lot, and the crowd divided. The hypnotic bounce of lights colored everything and everyone with eerie hues.

She thought about calling Travis, but she'd have to wait. The officers took control of the scene, blocking the entrance. Men and women in blue approached the onlookers. Someone pointed at her and many eyes followed her direction.

If only they'd left earlier. Maybe Yang would still be alive. She scanned the faces of the crowd for Fyodor. But he was gone. Yang was gone. Maggie was the only one left.

A police officer approached and said, "I'm Lt. John Truett from the Santa Cruz Police Department. Can you tell me your name, please?"

His words were muted, but she could understand him. "Maggie. Margaret Fender."

"Are you all right? Do you need medical attention?"

Even as he asked the question, he seemed to assess her, making sure her answer matched his observations.

"I'm fine." She wasn't, but there was nothing anyone could do to make her feel better.

The officer led her to the back of a squad car and got in next to her. The seat was hard and uncomfortable.

He said, "I need to ask you some questions."

Maggie stared at the steel mesh between the front and rear seat.

"Can you tell me the victim's name?"

"Yang Tunan." Mere minutes ago, Yang was breathing, laughing, and making her want to know him better. "We had dinner together."

Officer Truett took notes. "What was your relationship with Mr. Tunan?"

Was. Past tense. She'd spent an evening with the man, and now he was past tense.

"We work—worked together. Just out for a meal." But really, she'd been spying on him. Did it have a bearing on his death?

"Tell me what happened when you left the restaurant."

Maggie stepped her way through every detail that she could remember. Then the officer had her recount the events inside during their meal.

She gave them new information as it came to her. Fajitas. They ate fajitas. Hers now lay in a disgusting pile behind the hydrangea. No, she didn't know Yang well. Enemies? Not that she could name. Too early to know if Jason counted as an enemy. What else? She waved to a friend at another table.

"You knew someone in the restaurant?"

One detail too many. She paused. "He was long gone before the shooting."

"We'd like a name, please?"

"Fyodor Umanov. He's my neighbor." Great. Way to drag him down, too. Bound to remind him of why he'd stayed away from her.

The officer asking questions was relentless.

No, she didn't see the car, but she saw one speed away. Gun? No, she didn't see the gun. Only the grisly result.

Around them, police officials snapped photos and gathered evidence, while Yang's body grew colder on the pavement.

While the puzzle pieces had scattered in her brain, they were there, and eventually, she completed the picture in her mind.

An ambulance arrived and medical staff poured from the truck, but it was too late. Whatever the EMT's best effort was today, it wouldn't be enough to save the young engineer.

Eventually, someone came to the squad car. She got out so they could take photos and collect samples from her dress. Tiny bits of her dinner companion swabbed and stuffed into a vial as evidence. They swabbed her hands. She assumed they were testing for gunshot residue, but they didn't treat her as a suspect.

As the night air cooled, the questions continued until even the officer seemed weary.

"May I go home now?" She didn't know what time it was, only that it was late.

"We might need to ask you more questions. Where can we reach you?"

Maggie supplied him with her contact information.

"Do you think you're able to drive?" His countenance softened. "You've been through a traumatic experience, and Half Moon Bay might feel like a long drive under the circumstances."

"Thank you, but I'll be fine." She looked forward to the long drive, couldn't wait to let the night air cleanse her lungs of death.

He offered his card. "If you think of anything else, please call me."

"I will," she said and wrapped the card in her fist.

Maggie got in her car and idled out of the lot. When she made it around the corner and down the road, she pulled over and started to shake.

Yang's death was heinous, wanton.

She opened the car door and threw up again. Leaning further, she wretched until the bile burned her throat and the emptiness of her stomach drove the gruesome video replay from her head. When she could focus, she put the top down on her car and got on Highway 1 to go home.

A head-banger radio station accompanied her on the drive, and a salted wind blasted through the open car. It was foggy. The mist made her damp and cold, but it kept her senses sharp.

Her thoughts focused on Yang when he was alive. Did he have a family? More to the point. Did he have enemies?

There was a reason the police asked that question first, but she never really knew him. Their conversation at work over the two days she'd been there might total a couple of hours. That included meetings. Sharing a meal seemed a safe outing with someone who was virtually a stranger, and at the outset, dinner provided more comfort for her than she expected.

Now the man was dead, and she had to find out why.

By the time she reached her house in Half Moon Bay, Maggie was exhausted. She parked her car in the garage and went in search of Travis. Her face streamed with tears as she opened the door.

21

It was 12:58 a.m. when Travis heard the garage door rattle open. If Maggie didn't come home by one, he was going to call the police. Maybe he was overreacting, but she'd trained him to keep in contact with her, and she never intentionally left him hanging for a return call or text. He worked on his main laptop in the kitchen that evening and figured she'd be home around ten. Eleven if the night went really late.

She'd already lied to him once this week about where she'd been. He didn't like it. After Dad died, they each promised to stay close and tell each other the truth.

Bailey and Belli roused from their beds and toddled to his side. They often slept upstairs, but they never went up before everyone was home. It took them several weeks after Dad's death to realize he wasn't coming back.

Travis moved near the counter, caught himself tapping a foot until he saw her.

When she entered the kitchen, he noticed her clothing first. Her new pink dress was torn and smeared with blood.

"My God, Maggie! Are you all right?"

Glassy eyes looking through him, not at him. Shiny trails lined her cheeks. And she smelled bad. Bus station bathroom bad.

"What happened?"

His stomach tightened as he braced for the worst. But she didn't answer. "Talk to me!"

She walked silently toward him and then hugged him around the waist. Her face burrowed into his shoulder, and Travis held her while choking sobs made his skin wet beneath his sweatshirt. His knees threatened to give way, and he leaned against the counter for support.

Maggie didn't do hysterical. She was the mortar between the bricks. He mentally tripped through a dozen horrible scenarios that could cause her to lose it.

Travis gripped her upper arms, prying her far enough away to look her in the eye. "Magpie, talk to me."

She took a deep halting breath, dragged a sleeve across her face, and said, "Yang. He was murdered."

"Murdered?" Travis slumped. That scenario wasn't on the list. If anything, Travis thought he might want a piece of Yang's hide for messing with his sister.

"What? How? Are you hurt?"

"No." She held out the skirt of her ruined dress and let it drop. "Looks bad, but I'm not injured."

The beagles flanked her, nosing her hands, sniffing her as if she were a stranger.

Travis helped her into one of the kitchen chairs, but really, he needed one himself. He sat beside her. "Okay, tell me everything."

When he finally got Maggie talking, she was like a wind-up toy let loose on the floor. He didn't want to interrupt her, so he just let her tell the story as she remembered it. While she talked, he poured some red wine for her. She drained the glass as if it contained an antidote.

Her story finally made it to the part where she came home, and Travis found himself relieved. Her saga ended with a noisy, stuttering breath. He resisted the urge to hug her again.

"Do they have any suspects? Any witnesses?"

"Not that I'm aware of." Maggie poured herself a second glass of wine. "I can't believe he's gone."

Questions pinged inside his head. "Do you think this is related to our case?"

Her lips pursed. "I wish I knew. I just met Yang. Had one quasi date with him to get some information." She dropped her head. "We talked. We ate. It was just a nice dinner, you know?"

A thought occurred to him, but he didn't want to give it room. But Maggie lied to him, and it still pissed him off. If they were partners in this, then everything had to be on the table. "Was Fyodor jealous? You said he left first."

She blinked to a stare. "You think Fyodor killed Yang?"

"Just raising the flag." Maybe Travis' timing was bad, but he wanted her to get this because he had more to unload. "If we're trying to find hackers or a company mole, we need to think like investigators. No matter how crazy. Even if it has nothing to do with our case, if we think it's possible, we raise the flag."

"Fair enough." She put her elbows on her knees and pressed her fingers into her eyes. "No. He wasn't jealous enough to shoot a guy just because we shared a meal. If anything, he avoided us. Maybe he suspected I was there with a client. It's not like I was trying to hide."

"Maybe not from Fyodor, just from me." Travis squared off with his sister.

Her face dropped behind a curtain of hair. "What do you mean?"

"You lied to me about going shopping the other day. I don't like it." Travis crossed his arms across his chest. "Where were you?"

Maggie hesitated, as if she were running through a list of options, but then her body slumped deeper into the chair. "I'm sorry I lied to you." She bit a lip. "I've been going to the gun range to learn how to shoot."

"The gun range?" His arms fell to his side. "For real?" He didn't have a solid guess about where she'd been, but the gun range never made it to his fantasy list. She was full of surprises tonight. "When did you buy a gun?"

"Dad had a couple. When he first showed signs of dementia, I hid them from him."

"Why would you lie about that?"

"I wasn't sure how you'd feel about your sister packing heat. I want to get my concealed carry permit." She wiped her face. "Not that I could've saved Yang."

"Look, if you want to learn how to handle a gun, I'm all for it."

"But—"

He couldn't stop his chin from quivering. "Don't ever lie to me again. Either we're a team, or we're not."

"You're right. And we are a team." She lightly punched his arm. "Want to come shoot with me?"

"I can't. Remember? Convicted felon." Travis kicked a chair leg.

"Record expunged. Remember?" Maggie gave him a full-on bear hug. "Legally, you don't have a record anymore."

22

When the news about Yang Tunan's death rippled through R-Bot Systems, everyone was in shock. No one more so than Maggie. She arrived at the office that morning, and the people who worked closest with Yang already gathered in the lobby. Gail Everly, Jason Gupta. Lynn Moyega. Pavel Rokotov, and Aiden Costa, the receptionist, were among the mourners.

They huddled on the long leather couches near the windows. Maggie had their full attention when she told them her version of the tragic events.

"We met for dinner. Talked shop." She held her breath. "When we left—it happened so fast."

"My God, Maggie." Gail touched her arm. "I heard about the shooting on the news, but I didn't know it was Yang." She covered her mouth. "Or you."

Jason looked as if he'd been punched, while Lynn and Pavel seemed to grip each other for support. Once each found an emotional footing, anguish for Yang and Maggie came in a torrent.

Their compassion toward Maggie was touching. Three days ago, she was a stranger.

"I'm fine. But I can only imagine how Yang's family is doing. If they even know. He told me they lived in Southern California."

"Santa Monica." Jason's voice was weak. "His parent's live in Santa Monica." He pressed his knuckles against his lips. But whatever he felt, he kept it to himself and wandered away from the group.

Pavel said to Maggie, "You should be home. Doing something other than coming to work."

Lynn reached over and gave her arm a squeeze. "I'd be at the beach. Or a bar."

"I didn't really want to be alone."

She'd considered staying home, but she had to figure out if his death was related to her case. If someone at the company was involved, she had to see the reactions first hand. But the reactions were universal: horrified.

Oddly, as she answered their specific questions, the retelling of events ratcheted down her tension. Maybe it was a random act of violence. Not that the thought should make her feel better.

The conversation broke when Pavel's attention was diverted to the front door. Baxter entered the lobby with a woman, who Maggie recognized as the FBI agent dating Baxter, Claudia Seagal.

She was tall with dark brown hair, olive skin, and a perfect complement to Baxter's Nordic good looks. He said something to Claudia and walked up to the group by himself.

"You must be devastated by the news." His voice caught when he spoke. "I know I am. Yang was a kind soul." He touched his chest. "I spoke with his parents this morning. They plan to hold the funeral down south. When they get around to the arrangements, they'll let me know. At some point, we can do something here in his honor. As for today, everyone is free to go home or stay." Baxter looked as distraught as Maggie felt. "There's no formula for grief, so do what you need." He turned toward her. "Maggie, would you come with me, please?"

The words made her clench in all the uncomfortable places. But that was just her reflexes. She wouldn't lose this job.

"Of course." Maggie cast a sympathetic eye toward the other employees before leaving their fold. Their pain and grief at the tragic death of a close colleague was honest. Maggie just met the guy and was shattered.

Maybe it was also a sense of guilt. She'd only agreed to have dinner with Yang so she could slide him under her microscope. Unless he was their industrial spy—which she had to admit was still a possibility—he was just a nice man she would've liked to know better.

She followed Baxter to where Claudia stood, and he made quick introductions. They didn't hang out in the lobby, but hiked the stairs up to Baxter's corner office.

After they entered, Baxter said, "Claudia is here in an official capacity, Maggie. The FBI is involved at my request. They also have jurisdiction in industrial espionage cases that might benefit another country, which could be the situation here. The shooting wasn't random."

Any solace she'd found commiserating with the others fled like a bandit. She turned toward the agent. "Are you sure?" Maggie melted into a chair. "How do you know?"

Claudia glanced at Baxter and then sat next to Maggie. "First off, I know what you experienced was traumatic. This kind of situation sometimes confuses people. It's common, and I've been there." Claudia touched

Maggie's arm. "I read your statement to the police. You thought it was a drive-by."

"Yes. I distinctly heard tires squealing on the street after—after Yang was shot."

"I know you heard tires, but it wasn't from the shooter. The streets around the restaurant are only 30-40 yards from the where Yang stood. His shooter was much farther away."

Maggie was confused. "How far?"

"At least 100 yards."

Trees, other businesses surrounded the parking lot. There wasn't any line-of-sight that distance on the ground. The shot came from another building. The full impact of the situation sharpened into focus. "It was a sniper?"

Claudia gave a deep nod. "The trajectory of the bullet confirms it was fired from above street level. Investigators didn't find the bullet casing, but a site on the edge of another building tested positive for gunshot residue. We know where the shooter was when Mr. Tunan was killed."

From her time at the gun range, Maggie knew that any decent hunter could make a 100-yard shot. "What was the weapon?"

"We don't know, but we sent the bullet to ballistics for analysis."

A sniper had to set up, wait, know who was coming out the door. "I didn't tell anyone that we were going out."

"You need to think like an investigator on this one." Claudia clasped her hands together. "You told Baxter. Who else did you tell?"

Dammit. None of Maggie's memories were reliable. "Yeah. I told Baxter. Give me a minute." After Yang asked her out, she decided not to tell anyone at the office. On that point, she was certain. "I told my brother Travis and Baxter. That's it."

"Whoever killed him knew you were going to that restaurant. Do you know if Mr. Tunan mentioned it to anyone?"

She thought about the reactions from people that morning. No one seemed surprised that Yang and she had dinner. The only shock was the shooting. Maybe she shouldn't have been so quick to come to work and tell them. Maggie had a lot to learn.

"I don't. I think maybe they heard it from me this morning." She hated admitting it.

Baxter said, "I saw your picture on a news website. It's possible some of them found out that way."

That lessened her burden a bit. But she had another thought that weighed her down. One she didn't tell the police, but now she felt obligated.

"A guy I date sometimes, my neighbor. We occasionally work together." She tried to think of all her affiliations with Fyodor. "He was at the restaurant, but left early. I trust him with, well, my life. I don't have any reason to believe he's involved, but I'm also not confident of my ability to determine what's relevant at the moment."

Claudia's head bounced in agreement. "Good. That's a good sign. And you're right, he's probably not involved, but sometimes you just need to think the best and let the facts speak for themselves." She shot a sad look at Baxter and said, "We'd check out everyone eating in the restaurant that night as part of the investigation anyway, so you haven't done him any harm."

"Thanks." It was still early in the morning, and Maggie was running on only four hours of sleep. "Do you think Yang's murder has something to do with company secrets on the dark web?"

"It's possible. That's why I'm investigating. But Occam's razor cuts most victims, so the police need to follow the usual lines of inquiry first. Did the man have any enemies? Any expensive habits? Any dangerous friends?"

"Baxter," Maggie said, "you knew Yang best, but I've heard nothing that would make him a target."

"I agree, but I've only known him a couple of months longer than you." He rubbed his face. "If his murder is associated with the company, I don't think you should be this involved, Maggie. It's too dangerous."

So this was about losing her job. She'd watched a man get his head blown off. For what?

"No. I'm not leaving. If Yang was the spy, then let's prove it. If not, I want to find the sonovabitch who killed him."

"I understand the sentiment, Maggie," Claudia said. "I really do. But there's also a chance that Yang wasn't the target."

"What do you mean?"

Her eyes cut to Baxter and back to Maggie. "It's possible that you were the target."

23

After spending the prior day scanning every street for the kid, Gilbert was sick of Half Moon Bay. His night was a dull sequence of takeout, warm beer, and cable TV. He couldn't even find a decent card room. The local thing was big-wave surfing when the weather was crappy enough to generate them. What a joke. Nothing in this soggy city passed for entertainment.

While going home was the fantasy, he couldn't seriously return without news of the kid. Since the little brat hadn't been seen near Hunter's Point, this was still the likeliest place to find him. Gilbert would have to suffer the sand and surf another day.

At least he could get reliable coffee. That morning, he found a java joint that rivaled any in the city. Breakfast was decent when he stuck to the basics. None of those turkey, avocado, and alfalfa sprout omelets for him. Just bacon, eggs, and a short stack, thanks.

Gilbert reviewed his options over breakfast. Originally, he'd figured the streets were his best bet because the kid was from the city. Plus, it was easy for Gilbert to cruise around in his car, covering more territory that way, but he saw nothing. But maybe the kid was near the water. To the east, it was uphill and wooded. If the kid was sleeping rough, he'd probably stay away from the dark forest. He would if he knew what lived there. Gilbert decided to check the waterfront.

The shoreline wasn't a great place to hide because some beaches got wet during high tide, according to the locals. And it got cold at night. He was sure the kid didn't know anyone here, but it was possible that someone took him in. A real Samaritan would turn the kid over to the authorities. Anyone else who had him probably wasn't doing him any favors. If anyone found the kid,

Gilbert expected to hear about it through his contacts. As much as he hated the idea, he had to search the coast.

Gilbert was a full-on loafer man, right down to his tassels. The idea of wearing gym shoes of any kind was anathema. Walking on the beach just meant getting sand in his favorite suede shoes.

After breakfast, he drove to the nearest beach parking lot and looked around with his binoculars. In some parts of San Francisco, that act alone could start a minor war. In a tourist town like this one, it was nothing, least of all suspicious. But there was nothing to see. Birds squawking and crapping overhead. The droning sound of the water. A loathsome place, Gilbert would say screw it and head back to the city, if Augie weren't both a friend and dangerous.

There were only so many places the kid could go without wheels. With his upbringing, maybe he already knew how to boost a car. That mother of his used at least one alias and worked in places Gilbert wouldn't waste his singles. But realistically, the kid could only be a couple of miles from the place he crawled out of the truck. This location was at one end of that range, also near food.

But it made little sense to hike down there when Gil couldn't see the kid. It was a school day, and all he saw were a few scattered people, none of them kids. Gilbert watched for a while and then moved his Chrysler 300 down the beach.

The next parking lot was by a hiking trail that ran parallel to the water and a stretch of brown sand. Lots of hiding places for a kid. But kids weren't good at staying put. They liked to play, had to eat and piss, and maybe the kid was looking for a ride home. The last time they met, Gilbert wore the balaclava, so the kid didn't know what he looked like. All Gilbert had to do was offer him a ride, get the satchel, and then go dump the body.

Gilbert slipped on a pair of blackout sunglasses that covered his eyes and brows. He got out of the car and followed the trail along the bluff.

His cell phone sounded. It was Dwayne, one of his men watching the kid's neighborhood. Gilbert answered and said, "Talk to me."

"She had a visitor."

"What kind of visitor?" Gilbert squinted at the sun.

"Big black dude. Over six feet. Wore a green hoodie."

Gilbert knew it wasn't Tyrone. "Anything else?"

"The guy went inside her place."

"When?"

Dwayne hesitated. "Yesterday."

Heat rose in Gilbert's chest. "Yesterday! And you're just telling me now? What the hell have you been doing?"

"Gil, we're still covering Tyrone's and the club. Can't be everywhere at once. Got some locals watching her place, and it paid off."

"Yeah, we'll discuss that later. What did the guy want with LaShawna?"

"Not sure. We're in her place now. Looks quiet. Still no sign of the kid."

Gilbert thought watching the house was probably a waste, but he had to cover all the bases. "I think the kid would've gone home already if he could."

"Maybe you're right about Half Moon Bay, Gil. Any luck tracking him there?"

"Not yet. But I'm not giving up until we find him. Call me if you hear anything else. Or if that guy comes back."

"Will do."

While it wasn't good news, it didn't surprise him. The dude could be an angry lover, a drug dealer, or someone interested in the leather case. If needed, Gilbert would deal with him later. In the meantime, Gil continued his hunt for the kid along the bluff trail.

He wished he were somewhere else. Anywhere else. The wind blew steadily from the ocean, bringing damp, salted air to his lungs. The undeveloped land was mostly barren. What grew was low, scrubby trees and hardscrabble brush that looked down on its luck. The wind beat down everything that dared stand up to it.

Fresh air? That crap liked to kill him.

He passed walkers, joggers, cyclists, even a geezer cruising in an electric wheelchair. Gilbert had five miles to cover along the coast until he ran out of town, but not all of it had trails, and a lot of it was too open to make a good hiding place. Some of it dropped off a cliff into the ocean. If the kid found an unlocked shed or garage, the job would be tougher. Gilbert stopped to shake the gravel out of his shoes.

Solomon was still out there, somewhere. Hopefully within Gilbert's reach. Hopefully, the little bastard was close enough to choke.

A pair of hot young mamas in jogging suits ran past him with strollers. Overhead, a flock of brown pelicans soared, briefly blocking the sun. One of them relieved itself, and the droppings landed on his right shoe. Gilbert grimaced and yanked a handkerchief from his pocket and wiped it off. Miserable place for a vacation.

Augie didn't share all the details of this job with Gilbert. He often would, but when he didn't, Gilbert knew better than to ask. Some of Augie's connections were big time, not their usual customers, and keeping his end of the deal was a condition of future breathing. Augie was in it to make money, but some of their clients were only interested in power. Smart money always followed.

The bluff trail wended to a spot further from the water, making it harder to see the beach. As much as he hated the idea, he knew he'd eventually have to walk on the sand. The only time he intentionally ventured near sand was when he got a bad bounce on the fairway. He didn't enjoy it then either.

At the next bend, a gentle slope led to the water. At least he didn't have to mimic a mountain goat to reach it.

He took the beaten path down to the beach. With each passing minute, the water seemed to come closer to his suede loafers. He jogged around a wave that cut too close and glimpsed movement that held promise. A flash of dark skin briefly appeared around a bend in the cliff. The body seemed small.

From this distance, he wasn't sure if it was a kid or an adult. Male or female. He'd have to see the person again.

He cut toward the water this time, even if his suede paid the price. It gave him a better view around the cliff.

It was a kid. Male. Tossing a something to a seagull. No other people in sight.

But was it him? Gil had to be certain. Just needed to get a little closer.

The kid darted toward the water. When he noticed Gilbert, he froze.

Oh yeah. That was the kid.

Gil felt for the knife in his pocket. The kid couldn't possibly recognize Gilbert, but he had to be on edge. After all the grief that kid caused, Gilbert would gut him like a flounder. Gil already found a few isolated properties in the hills where he could bury the body.

But first, he had to get a hold of the satchel. Now that he found the kid, should be easy. Kids weren't that smart.

His mother called him Solomon.

Not so wise after all.

24

Sol didn't like the way the big man was looking at him. Too much attention, as Mama would say. Be careful when a stranger pays you too much attention. Especially if he's white.

He thought maybe it was about the jacket, but Sol didn't have it on, only with him. The man was still far enough away that he couldn't catch Sol, but why take chances? Sol grabbed the big jacket from the ground and headed down the beach in the opposite direction. He'd hide the jacket again once he was safe.

When he came to a trail that led from the bluff, he saw a black woman running toward him on the beach. His heart hip-hopped. For a moment he thought it might be Mama. But she never ran anywhere. The woman slowed when she saw Sol.

"Hey, little man." She jogged in place near him, her eyes scanning the shoreline. "What are you doing out here by yourself?"

He glanced at the scary white man. "Just looking for seashells. My mama's down the beach."

Her eyes narrowed at Sol as if she didn't believe him.

She was a pretty lady, but small and kinda skinny. His mama was taller than her. Of course, Mama never wore shoes that were flat on the bottom.

"How about we go find her?" The pretty lady put a hand on his shoulder. "My name's Denesha, little man. What's yours?"

Sol's head spun with the choices. He'd gone by so many names over the years. Kobe. Isaiah. Freddie. "Sol. My name is Sol." Telling the truth didn't feel much different from a lie.

He didn't want to go with her, but the white man still seemed like a threat. Just then, an old couple appeared on the same path from the bluff. For once,

Sol was happy for all the extra company. When he turned toward the white man, he was throwing something into the water. Maybe he wasn't scary after all. Maybe he was just white.

Sol coughed. "Yeah, let's go find her." More than anything, Sol wished that could be true.

Denesha kept a hand on him while they walked. The old couple followed along in the same direction, and so did the white man.

Eventually, they neared the house. The house. The one where he stole the jacket and the good fish. He even had the jacket with him. He forgot to leave it behind, and he couldn't go past that house with the jacket.

"Shouldn't you be in school?"

Even the black ladies were nosy. "We're here for a funeral." It was a line Mama taught him. It fell easily.

The skin between her eyebrows rumpled. "I'm so sorry, honey. I'm so sorry for your loss."

Maybe he wasn't lying about the funeral this time. Maybe Mama was gone. Sol turned around and couldn't see the white man. "Yeah. I gotta go."

At this spot on the shore, the bluff came down to meet the beach. Sol ran as fast as he could up to the tree line.

"Hey!" Denesha called after him.

When he found some cover from the thicket, Sol hid and watched the woman. For a moment, she stared in his direction with that same scowling face Mama made but didn't follow him. When Sol looked over at the beach, the white man came into view. He stopped to shake sand from his shoe. He didn't pay any attention to Sol.

Denesha walked over to the same house where he stole all the things. She knocked on the back door and waited. Maybe they knew each other, the lucky people who live in that house and this Denesha. Either that, or she knew Sol was a thief and wanted to turn him in for a reward. He had the jacket out this morning because it needed to dry. He couldn't do that again. Denesha seemed nice, but Sol couldn't get too close.

When she spun around and left the house, Sol followed to see where she lived. The lady was the first he'd met around here like himself. Not that he'd met many of any kind.

Sol stayed in the trees as long as he could and still keep up with her. He thought she looked his way a few times, but she never came over. Eventually she turned down a road, and he had to break cover to keep her in sight. He dropped from the trees and followed her.

He and Mama didn't have a TV, at least not in San Francisco. But he remembered seeing a show where the kids acted like detectives. When following somebody, they stayed far enough behind to keep from being seen, ducking down behind cars and trash cans whenever that person looked around. It was easier than Sol thought.

Denesha kept to the road, until she reached a little, yellow house and cut down the side of it toward the back. Sol sneaked through the bushes along the next-door neighbor's driveway and found a spot behind a red pickup truck where he could see her standing on a small porch.

She went inside and came out with a cup of something and wore a small towel wrapped around her neck. Denesha sat in one of the plastic chairs and put her feet up on a low table. Within a few seconds, another black woman came out and sat in the chair next to her. They were saying stuff to one another, making each other laugh, but Sol couldn't hear the words, just sounds that reminded him of Mama.

The two women talking and giggling made his insides feel like jelly. Sol slapped his hands over his eyes to keep tears from slipping out. He slid to the ground with his back against the red truck and leaned against a tire.

Usually, he could push his eyes hard enough to make them stop, but all he did was make his eyes hurt. Sol couldn't see the women anymore, but he didn't want them finding him, coming over to see what was going on.

They seemed friendly, and maybe they were even nice. But Mama told him to never trust strangers.

He rested against that tire for a while before getting to his feet. By now, the ladies were gone. Sol looked around their back porch. It had a tall potted plant in the corner that wasn't dead. Someone kept it good and alive. One of them left a cup on the table. He didn't know why, but he wanted to touch it. It was still warm.

He glanced around the porch in case there was anything he could use. Doing that, even thinking that way, made him feel bad, but he reminded himself he was just borrowing things like Mama said. Either way, there was nothing here he wanted.

As he left, he noticed an outlet behind the plant. He'd have to come back when he was sure no one was around, but this would be a good place to charge Mama's phone. Now he was stealing electricity.

Stealing stuff was getting too easy. That's how it worked, he guessed. Stealing good fish and electricity one day and robbing banks the next. But he had money. He wasn't stealing money, just stuff.

Still, a thief was a thief.

Then, a siren sounded in the distance, making him jump.

If they were going to take him to jail, they'd have to find him first. He got up and ran out a different way than the way he came. When he got to the end of the street, he glanced back.

That big white man was standing on the sidewalk.

What did he want? Was he following Sol?

Probably another do-gooder who wondered why Sol was alone.

But he couldn't think about that now. He had to hide from the police right now. He'd return and charge Mama's phone later.

25

A notice from his phone sounded as Marcus took his first spoonful of clam chowder. He dropped the utensil onto the plate, where it clattered. His waitress at the bay side restaurant turned toward him with an air of concern, as if he didn't like his soup. He waved her off with his hand.

The icon at the top of his phone showed he got a hit at Toya's place. The cameras recorded something in her apartment. Could it finally be her this time? He inserted an earbud and opened the recording.

There were a couple of files, one from outside the building and another from the inside. When he saw the featured stills for the videos, he wasn't shocked—just disappointed. Couple of dudes. Not Toya. There was always someone else looking for her.

Marcus played the file recorded inside Toya's house. He saw two guys—a stocky black dude and a white dude with neck tats—both in their mid-thirties. They made a call. Marcus listened as they described Marcus entering Toya's place. He only heard their side of the conversation.

Someone had seen Marcus enter Toya's the day before and reported that event to these two. Marcus was paying some locals to watch the cars near her house. Maybe the men on the video were also paying the locals for services. Money rarely bought loyalty, but it was great for buying information.

The guys in Toya's neighborhood were quick to take Marcus' hundred bucks. If they also took money from others, he couldn't blame them. Marcus left them with some equipment, that bit of cash, and no way to verify what they did with it. Not his preferred method for even the smallest of contract jobs, but they didn't give him a choice.

When the waitress came by offering him coffee, he covered the screen. He waited until she was gone and replayed the video. This time, he listened more carefully. They seemed more concerned about the kid than Toya. They were surveilling her house, Tyrone's place, and the club where she worked, but they wanted to find the kid.

What could they want from him? Whatever it was, Toya had to be involved. She always left a wake for others, never smoothing the world for anybody but herself. At least three people searching, and she wasn't their focus.

Leave it to her to make her own kid a target.

Stupid bitch.

Marcus tried to imagine why they wanted the kid. Was he even old enough to start serious trouble? While trouble didn't have an age requirement, he seemed young. Living with Toya aged him faster than most. He likely saw stuff no kid should have to see. Lord knows Marcus saw plenty of misery just tracking her. One place she'd lived was as dangerous as a war zone. Toya's lifestyle was just a slower route to death.

His shoulders dropped, and he laid the phone on the table. For now, Marcus had a new location to search. Half Moon Bay. Wherever the hell that was. Some guy named Gil was there looking for the kid. If the kid was there, Toya had to be nearby. Whatever the effort, Marcus planned to find her first.

He finished his soup and paid his bill. He'd have to check his blood sugar later, but for now, he went outside and found a bench along the wharf. A sea lion slid along the waterline, breaking the surface. Marcus searched for Half Moon Bay on his phone. Down the coast from the city about 30 miles, it wasn't as big as Toya's usual haunts. She preferred the bright lights, a nightlife. She was a nocturnal creature.

Along with the hundred bucks, Marcus left a few cellular GPS devices with some brothers near Toya's. They agreed to install the device in the OBD port of any strange cars near her house. It was a quick install under the dash. Just plug and play. Unless someone was looking at the port, it didn't stand out.

The move wasn't legal, but he didn't care. Neither did the guys who took his money. If they bothered to install the GPS devices as arranged, Marcus could monitor a car's movements from his phone app. He figured the odds were fifty-fifty that they resold the devices.

Marcus opened an app on his phone and navigated to the car registry menu. Inside, he found a new entry. He clicked on it, and the map showed a car's movements in real time.

Seems he owed the brothers an apology.

Currently, the car was cruising north on Dolores. He changed the settings, so the app would notify him whenever the car was in motion.

Marcus couldn't confirm it was the same one driven by the guys he saw in the video, but it was another lead to chase. Eventually, that car would make a decisive move. Until then, he needed to rent a car. The drive to Half Moon Bay was about forty minutes. Toya could be there now. Marcus felt close.

He hoped it wasn't another dead end.

26

After checking the clock on his office wall, Augie Barrett stood and paced to ease some tension. Gilbert was supposed to give him an update every hour on the hour, and Augie wasn't in the mood for excuses about trying to find the kid. Three days had passed since Gil lost the satchel. Today, Augie needed to make critical decisions.

After Gil shot that broad in public, the incident barely registered a blip in the local news. But press of any kind was unwelcome. Unless you were digging for it, the story was buried. Fortunately, the people LaShawna hung out with weren't news junkies. Mostly just junkies.

Losing that case set Augie's payday back by three months, and the lost revenue was compounding. He considered claiming it from the police, but he only knew that it was tan-colored, with no idea what it contained.

The past few months were more painful than when Augie was circumcised at age twenty-six because of infection. The doctor started cutting before the anesthesia kicked in.

No one knew what happened to the satchel until recently. Now that they did, Augie promised delivery to Vladimir Penniski within the week. Otherwise, Augie's carcass might chum the waters off Bird Island.

He rubbed his eyes and looked out the window, checking the time again. Two minutes before Gil's update was due.

The deal with Byron Suliani was supposed to elevate Augie's position with Vlad, get him out of this ratty, fourth floor office, hovering above the city's grime. Augie needed to be at least twenty floors up to cleanse his view of the homeless.

Vlad was big time, notorious, impatient. Living large in the penthouse suite with a dominating view of the city and the bay, he could overlook the peasants below. Vlad dwelt among the clouds.

The setup was perfect.

Once Augie understood Byron Suliani's assets, Augie brokered the arrangement with Vlad and waited to reap the harvest. With this deal, money would grow on trees. But all of Augie's plans withered when Byron missed the meet in the park. At that moment, Augie's life span measured in hours.

Everyone figured Byron sold to another buyer until they located him in the morgue. What a time for the dude to stroke out. Augie had the worst luck.

It took some effort, but Augie figured out what happened and tracked the leather case to the police Lost and Found, where it sat until the kid claimed it on Monday. Gil was supposed to make a simple street snatch. Now, he was on a freaking wanted poster.

Augie rolled his shoulders. He needed to get to the gym, or at least to a legit masseuse.

Gilbert was loyal to Augie, but he wasn't part of this deal, didn't understand the stakes. If he couldn't deliver, Augie had to get him off the payroll. Permanently.

Exactly on the hour, Augie's phone rang with a call from Gil. The guy had some survival skills.

Augie answered. "Tell me you found the satchel."

Gilbert breathed heavily into the phone. It didn't inspire confidence. "Not yet. But I found the kid."

Augie felt a throb in the back of his neck. "How could you find the kid but not the case?"

"He's here. In Half Moon Bay."

The news was better than nothing. "What's he doing there?"

"I found him on the beach, playing like he was on vacation. Doesn't he know his mother is dead?"

What Augie knew about the kid's mother, Augie figured the kid was better off.

"The kid isn't walking around with the case. Looks like he's staying with someone here. I saw him walking around with some black woman."

Augie leaned against a window. "I need that satchel, Gil. He could've stashed it before moving down coast."

"Maybe. But I don't think he had time. I'll find it. Don't worry."

Don't worry. Augie was past worry and on to anguish. "What do you plan to do about him?"

There was a long pause before Gilbert said, "How many details you want over the phone?"

Gil had a point. "How soon?" It was all that really mattered.

"Very."

"I'm counting on it." Augie ended the call.

He slid the phone in his pocket and heard a siren howl beyond the window.

While he normally kept Gil in his confidence, this deal was too big. Vlad was too volatile. Since his stint in San Quentin for biting off a man's nose, he rebranded his public image as a philanthropist, a man of letters, a patron of the local arts.

Exposing Vlad's involvement in this fiasco was a quick ticket to the bottom of the bay. Augie couldn't leave anything to chance.

When Byron Suliani went and had a stroke during the meet, the sheer absurdity of it was the only reason Augie was still alive. No matter the outcome, Vlad expected delivery.

Augie felt his heart beat in his stomach. A woman on the street walked at the same pace. Dressed in goth gear, she bumped her way through a group of tourists exiting the trolley car. Probably a pickpocket.

Welcome to San Francisco.

Augie's phone buzzed, and he noted the caller ID on his way to his desk: Unknown.

Could be several people on his payroll who preferred to stay off the books. Calling Augie might put some of them at risk.

He answered, "Yeah."

"Hey. I've got some news on the vic."

The voice was hushed, but Augie recognized his informant inside the police station. He was supposed to report any developments on the broad's murder case. With over a hundred homicides in the city each year, Augie didn't expect this one to be a police priority.

"What do you know?" Augie leaned back in his chair.

"Her name is Toya Price."

"Toya Price?" His informant was worth every penny Augie paid him. They knew her by LaShawna Martin, but found documents in her apartment confirming she'd used other names. "Is Price another alias?"

"Nah, this name's legit."

"What's she running from?" The more aliases, the longer the rap sheet.

"Probably her own shadow." The informant laughed. "No loss on this one."

"Where?"

"Everywhere. Florida for assault and attempted murder. New Mexico for robbery and drug trafficking. Michigan for fraud and prostitution. Toya is a genuine class act."

"So no surprises. A hooker and an addict." Augie remembered the surveillance photos of her. Gorgeous woman. "She wasn't going to last long, anyway."

"One other thing." The informant hesitated. "It's not good news."

Augie sat upright.

"It's about the kid. His teacher was worried about him since he missed school all week. Then she realized that his mother was the woman murdered in the city."

No. Not good news. Horrible news.

"Yeah. He's considered a critical missing."

"Damn it."

"They're going to plaster his picture everywhere. They've called in the FBI to assist."

The FBI never stepped in without taking over. When Vlad heard about this, Augie's extra few days would disappear. If Gil didn't find that satchel soon, Augie might not survive the week.

27

Travis took a share ride over to the gun range and went inside, where he found Maggie bent over the display cabinet of weapons for rent.

The man behind the counter said, "Are you here with someone, son?"

He pointed at his sister. "She's my legal guardian." At his age, Travis wasn't allowed in the place on his own. Though he was often mistaken for being much older. Mostly by women.

"Yo, Magpie. You going to claim me?"

"Hey, Trav." She looked up long enough to see him and say to the clerk, "I have a letter of guardianship for him."

Travis tapped her shoulder with a fist bump. "What's on the menu?"

"We need to work our way through the common calibers. You can start with Dad's old Ruger Mark III. It's a .22 caliber. You can try the KelTec .380, but the grip might be too small for you. I'm going to rent a 9mm."

Being at the gun range with his sister discussing weapons was surreal. His father promised to take him shooting, but by then, Dad was scary enough without a gun. Travis never saw either of the guns his father owned at their house.

Maggie rose and pointed at a small pistol. "I'd like to try the Beretta 9M, please." She pulled out her driver's license and the guardianship documents for Travis. "We'll need two boxes each of .22, .380, and 9mm ammo, please. Plus eye and ear protection for my brother."

After Maggie and Travis read and acknowledged the range rules, the man behind the counter showed them how to operate the Beretta and handed them the weaponry and paper targets. They donned their safety gear before passing through the security doors and entering the live range.

Muffled pops of varying intensity ruptured in the cool air that smelled like sulfur. The range master who watched the place stood near the back wall, reminding Travis of a hawk, waiting for something on the ground to twitch.

Maggie chose a stall close to the door. The stalls were simple structures with deep side walls between them, a carpeted shelf for the weapons and ammo, plus a clip to hold the paper target. A switch on the side wall sent the target down range for shooting and brought it back so they could see what they hit.

She unpacked a shoulder bag he'd never seen before.

"Is that new?"

"I've been hiding it in the trunk." Her embarrassment was brief. "Don't touch anything until I get it ready."

Normally, when Maggie went into Mom mode, Travis would offer some snark just to mess with her. But this was deadly serious. And if she thought he didn't think so, she wouldn't bring him again. He resisted the urge.

In handling the weapons, Maggie wasn't at all smooth, but she was careful. She had him watch her the first time, loading the magazine with 10 rounds of ammo. She fired a few rounds and then handed the pistol to Travis.

The .22 had little kick, but he also didn't hit the target. After some adjustments based on what Maggie learned from YouTube, Travis was punching holes in the paper. He emptied half a box of .22 ammo, and then Maggie took her turn in the stall.

She kept a serious tone about her, even when they were doing something fun. Maybe it was her role as caretaker that squeezed out the levity. She made handy work of the remaining .22 ammo, and they loaded the magazine of the Beretta.

Maggie went first this time. After the initial shot, her arms jumped upward from the recoil. She laid the weapon on the carpet and wiped her hands down the front of her pants.

"This is nothing like the .22." She curbed her hair behind an ear. "It kicks harder." She stepped aside. "You try it."

He expected her to get used to the weapon before handing it to him. His face must've given him away.

"You're stronger than I am. I think you'll hold on to it better." Her finger slipped under the safety glasses and wiped an eye. "All right, this one scares me."

Maggie's moments of concession were rare. But only yesterday, a man standing right next to her was shot in the head. Travis shuddered when he remembered seeing his sister covered in Yang's blood.

Travis shoved down his own emotions and got in the shooting stance, gently squeezing the trigger. He didn't think the Beretta would ever fire until it flashed.

The tension in his arms released, jerking his arms upward just like Maggie's.

He took a step back. "You're right. Nothing like the .22."

He pointed the weapon downrange and stretched out his arms, using the sights to line up his next shot. Tension built in his muscles till they throbbed. When the next round fired, hot brass ejected under his right cuff, searing his skin. Travis nearly dropped the gun on the shelf. He backed away, swiping at his sleeve, the spent cartridge falling to the floor.

Maggie's head dropped to one side as she closed her eyes. "We're done." Her chin trembled.

Travis was used to dealing with Maggie when she was bossy, bitchy, or pissed. But melt-down Maggie was a total foreigner.

Travis could only nod.

He dropped the magazine from the Beretta and pulled back the slide to remove the bullet in the chamber. The rule was to keep a red flag down the barrel of any gun to prove it was empty. He inserted the flag made of red duct tape and weed whacker string and put it back in the case.

They locked up their gear, moving through the security doors and into the quiet of the storefront. Travis yanked the earmuffs off his head, his arm still burning from the hot brass.

Maggie strode to the counter and returned the Beretta. "It's not what I'd call tame. Would the .357 be easier?"

Wherever she'd drifted, the Maggie he knew was back.

"No, ma'am. You may find you prefer different weapons or loads, but the M9 has less kick than the .357. If you're interested, we offer training."

She slumped against the counter, as if she needed the support. "Yes. Training would be good."

They discussed a couple of options, and in the end, she hired a private trainer for them both.

Whatever she was experiencing after Yang's death, Maggie wasn't giving up.

It was dark when they left the building and loaded Maggie's car with their gear. When another car pulled into the parking lot near them, Travis immediately recognized the driver. It seemed to take Maggie another half-beat until the car door opened.

Fyodor Umanov was one of those rare, muscled men with all the right proportions and who didn't have a swagger. Maggie said she saw him at the restaurant when she was with Yang.

"Maggie." Fyodor approached her.

They hadn't dated in a while and not because Maggie didn't want to.

Awkward.

Travis waved and got into the car. Whatever they might discuss, they didn't need him as a third wheel.

28

"Fyodor." It was the only word Maggie could muster when she saw him. Though after turning his name in to the police, he probably had a few for her. "What are you doing here?"

She knew he frequented this range, but didn't expect to run into him tonight.

"I need the practice." Fyodor broke his gaze long enough to acknowledge Travis with a friendly smile and a head nod. Even in the yellowish light cast by the parking lot lamps, she saw Fyodor's countenance turn serious when he refocused on her.

Was he angry?

She braced herself against the car.

"Maggie, I heard about the shooting at the restaurant." He stopped short, standing just outside her personal space. "Were you there when it happened? Are you all right?"

Not angry.

Kind.

She'd forgotten that Fyodor was kind.

Maggie drew deeply from the moist night air, and her body slackened. "I was there. I saw it." She shrugged. "I'm fine."

A half-moon glowed over his right shoulder as he shook his head. "No. No one is fine after watching someone die. Especially like that." He gestured toward the gun range. "Is this why you are here?"

Seeing Yang again at the moment he lost his life, she suppressed the full replay.

Fyodor hadn't been around in a couple of months. Maggie didn't owe him an explanation. "I need the practice too."

His weight shifted as he stood. She could tell he wanted to ask more, but he seemed resigned to let her answer stand. "Let me know if I can help."

Among his many talents, Fyodor was an expert marksman. He was the one who taught her that women have a physical advantage when shooting from a standing position. Their hips lock into place and men's don't. Maggie was stunned when she found out Fyodor couldn't rest on a back hip the way she could, and she delighted in watching him try. He looked like a Russian Elvis—the young, handsome version, before he went all Las Vegas creepy.

That sensuous image of Fyodor lingered too long for Maggie's comfort. "Thanks. We're just heading home." She opened her car door to make her exit smoother. "We'll see you later."

He placed a hand on her door, blocking her path. The movement caused her to start.

Fyodor immediately raised his hands and backed away. "My apologies."

Like a lithe tiger, his physical presence was enough to make men wary. He couldn't help the effect he had on others, but he never gave Maggie a reason to fear him or treat him this rudely.

She placed a hand on his forearm, which felt better than she remembered. "You're fine."

His posture eased under her touch.

"It's been a long couple of days." She withdrew from him and leaned against the car door. "Trav and I started a new job this week, and as you know, yesterday was a righteous cluster."

"I spoke to the police." Fyodor said. "They gave few details, but I'm so sorry." He placed an elbow on the roof of her car. "If there's anything I can do." His voice trailed off.

Maggie didn't know what anyone could do for her, and any help for Yang was too late.

"Thanks. I'm as good as I can be for now." She pushed herself from the car. "I better get going. Still need to work in the morning."

"I understand." He pursed his lips and put his hands in his back pockets. "I don't want to burden you with my concerns, especially now. But I haven't been around much, and I wanted you to know why."

As many times as she envisioned this conversation with him, she didn't want to have it here or now. Her own resolution returned. "You don't owe me an explanation, Fyodor."

"I was engaged once." He bit his lower lip. "We broke up before I met you."

Maggie's stomach fluttered. She knew Fyodor hadn't waited his life to meet her, but she didn't know he'd been close to marriage.

"My mother was recently diagnosed with the same dreadful disease that claimed your father."

She closed her eyes, wrapping an arm around her middle, which now started to ache. Alzheimer's. Memories of her father's descent invaded like marauders. She choked back her own lingering grief.

"I'm so sorry." Even if he had moved on with other woman, he faced trying years and earned all her sympathies. "It's a rough road."

Crossing his arms across his broad chest, he nodded rapidly. "Yes." His voice was low, almost a whisper. "Katya was close to my mother and lives near to her." He ran a hand through his hair. "Since the symptoms have appeared, she's spent much time with my mother, and we have been in one another's company again."

Katya. Images of a beautiful Russian princess draped in glittering gold and royal blue came to Maggie's mind. If Katya offered Fyodor's mother companionship during this time, she had to be nice. Maggie couldn't muster any ill will to hate her.

"I'm glad your mother has someone close by to watch her. The early days are tough. Sometimes, she'll be coherent and, well, normal. The next—" Maggie shrugged. "The next time, she'll think you're the guy from UPS."

Fyodor blew air into the night, a fog forming with his breath. "I just need to sort through all this, and while I'm very fond of you, Maggie, I need to focus on my mother. And with Katya around—I just don't want to mislead either of you."

She'd expected this discussion, but his reasons weren't on her list of possibilities. While it might've been nice to know sooner, she understood what he was dealing with at home. Maybe not the parts about rekindling his relationship with Katya, but at least he was honest. Even if it was bad news, Maggie preferred honest.

Now it was her turn. She leaned against the car.

"I really like you, too, Fyodor. And you know, I've had little time for relationships." The words came easily. "Katya sounds like a fine woman, and you have history. I get it." Those words were much harder. "We both have a lot going on right now, and whatever happens down the road, I'd like us to remain friends."

The furrows in his brow relaxed. "Same here."

She remembered Travis was waiting for her in the car and glanced at him. He was looking at his phone.

Maggie quickly squeezed Fyodor's hand and let it go. "Both Travis and I are grateful for all you've done for us. That won't ever change."

Fyodor stepped away from her door, and she got in the car with her brother.

Travis' green eyes held that familiar sorry-your-life-sucks look. She didn't bother to confirm his suspicions.

She'd been wondering where Fyodor was these past months. Now she knew. Katya the Great and Beautiful was the one that got away and was now nursing his ailing mother.

That was a lot of boxes ticked on her side of the tally.

It was just as well. It wasn't a competition.

Maggie started the car and cranked up the music.

She and her brother had a case to solve.

29

On the drive home, Maggie rolled down the windows, and Travis pumped his Greta Van Fleet playlist into the night air. The Zeppelinesque music launched a raucous sing-a-long, mercifully muting her thoughts of Fyodor and Katya the Great. By the time they neared their street, the high had left her, and now she was simply exhausted. She turned down the music, and they putted toward their house.

When the car's headlights hit their driveway, something reflective flickered before Maggie realized it was Denesha in her running gear. She moved to the grassy area while they parked.

"Hey." Maggie's energy rebounded as she got out of the car. Denesha always elevated her mood. "It's good to see you."

Denesha gave her a hug. "I heard about the shooting from Ginger. How're you holding up?"

"I'm sorry, Neesh. I've been meaning to call—"

"No." She pulled Maggie in closer. "You do not get to worry about me on this one, hon. Geez, Mag. You saw a man get killed."

Maggie repeatedly blocked the image of Yang just to get through the day. But here, with Denesha, Maggie didn't have to pretend. She draped her arms over Denesha's shoulders, letting her full weight rest, and convulsed in sobs.

They stayed like this on the front lawn until Maggie was empty of emotion. She found the strength to regain her footing and straightened to a stand.

"Can you come in for a bit?" Maggie gestured to the front door where Travis stood by. It was late, but she wanted the company.

Denesha kept a steady hand against Maggie's back. "Wouldn't miss it."

Travis opened the door, letting them enter first. He followed the women into the kitchen.

"Quite a week, Neesh." Maggie briefly touched her forehead on Denesha's shoulder. "Want some wine?"

"You know it."

Denesha leaned against the counter while Maggie poured two glasses of Merlot. Then they joined Travis at the kitchen table.

"Is your dad's jacket missing from his chair on the back porch?" Denesha tapped her goblet with a fingernail.

"Stolen." Travis' voice snapped with anger. "Some dirt bag took it." He cocked his head. "How did you know?"

"I may know who has it." She stretched her arms on the table. "Though he's not the culprit you expected."

"Who?" Travis said, "Who has it?"

"It's a kid. Saw him on the beach today."

She had Maggie's attention now. "Are you sure it was Dad's jacket?"

"Sure as I can be without inspecting it. It was far too big for the boy, and it looked like your dad's."

"Where does the kid live?" There were always people moving in and out of the neighborhood, plus the tourists and vagrants. Maggie thought it might be someone new to the area.

"I'm not sure. I was jogging on the beach, and he was by himself. Which seemed strange. He was only about eight or nine. But I noticed the jacket." Denesha gripped her wineglass and took a sip. "Anyway, I wanted to check on him, and he said his mother was down the beach, so we walked together until I got near your house. Then he ran away into the trees."

Travis leaned back in his chair and pointed a finger at Maggie. "That's our porch pirate."

"Could be," she said. Her thoughts floated back to Fyodor and Katya the Great. Her mind conjuring images of them on matching white steeds, riding through a snowy Russian forest, Katya clad in flowing sable. Maggie downed her glass and poured another while Travis told Denesha about the other items that went missing from their back porch.

"Interesting," Denesha said, "Because I don't think he wanted to go near your house. When I didn't see the jacket on your dad's chair, I figured that was the reason."

"Do you know where he went?"

"He followed me and then watched me and my roommate Sharla drinking coffee on the porch for a while. He hid behind a truck the whole time. You know how kids are. Think they're all stealthy, but they aren't."

"He must live close by."

"He told me he was here for a funeral." Denesha's braids bounced as she shook her head. "But I didn't believe him."

"What did he look like?"

"Little brown man with short dreads. Wore a pair of jeans, a long-sleeve rugby shirt. Mostly blue and white." She glanced at the ceiling. "Maybe some yellow. White tennis shoes." She set her glass on the table. "All of his clothes were dirty. He's been on the beach a while or something."

Travis put his hands behind his head. "So our thief is a little dude. That changes things."

"What does that change?" Travis had a soft spot for kids. Maggie knew she was pushing his button, but if the boy was stealing food, maybe he needed the jacket more than Travis.

"For one, I'm less worried about our safety. He's probably not a serial killer stalking the beach."

Denesha appeared to choke down her sip to keep it from spewing while she laughed. "Yeah." She grabbed a napkin and dabbed her chin. "You can check that one off your list, Trav."

Maggie laughed along with Denesha, but given their week, she understood his concerns.

"So maybe that scenario is a bit extreme." Travis stood and yawned. "But we need to be careful." He jumped and touched the ceiling. "Anyway, there's got to be an adult around the kid somewhere. Maybe that Mom doesn't know the boy is stealing things. That won't be good news."

"While you solve the mystery, I need to get home." Denesha stood. "Oh, he told me his name is Sol."

"Sol," Travis repeated the name. "I bought some cameras for the porch, but with all that's been going on, I haven't installed them yet. Maybe tomorrow."

Maggie rose and tapped Denesha's hand. "Why don't you come over Friday night? Bring your roommate, Sharla, and we'll wine and dine the both of you."

"Oh, she'd like that. Sharla doesn't know many people around here, yet. Thanks." Denesha's smile turned grim. "Wait. Who's cooking?"

Maggie fist-bumped her friend's shoulder. "Not funny."

"Don't worry, Neesh, I'm cooking," Travis said.

Denesha gripped his wrist. "Oh, thank goodness."

"Yeah. Yeah." Maggie moved her wineglass to the counter.

"Seriously though, thanks, guys. See you Friday." Denesha's smile rebounded. "And Trav, it's good to know you're keeping us safe from serial killers."

The noises were coming from the side yard, so Sol followed them. He found a fence, but no dog, and the house next door was completely dark. Now, the whimpering sounds got louder, but they were coming from inside Denesha's house.

Heat thumped inside him. How could she do that to a dog? And she seemed so nice, too.

The sounds were loudest by the window with the light shining out of it, and Sol wanted to see the dog.

By that window there was a gray pipe and a gray box that had something to do with the gas or electricity. Sol reached up to the windowsill, climbing from the pipe to the box to peer inside the window.

Between the break in the curtains he could see, it wasn't a dog.

All the breath rushed from his lungs. It was Denesha's friend, wearing a bright red shirt, the one who was sipping drinks with Denesha on the back porch yesterday. Sol didn't know her name, but she was scared. He recognized the big white man even though he wore a mask. He stood over the woman with a big knife, flashing the same angry blue eyes like he did when he shot Mama.

31

After Maggie left for her fake job at R-Bot Systems, Travis took Bailey and Belli for a quick run on the beach and then returned to his desk for a morning of research. Earlier in the week, he'd placed some feelers on the dark web for company secrets similar to those stolen from R-Bot.

Understanding the competition's new products gave any company an edge in the marketplace. They could then position a comparable product or at least lessen the impact to their own sales.

But if a company created ground-breaking technology, something so innovative that their products would disrupt the current marketplace, demand for those products could leap-frog them beyond the competition, giving them an advantage for years.

Then again, some companies chose not to create. They chose to steal. While others were always willing to broker trade secrets for a price. Industrial espionage was a booming global business.

Travis logged into the dark web using The Onion Router browser, aka Tor, which allowed him anonymity when he searched. While he wouldn't do anything illegal, his activities had been misunderstood by the legal system once before, earning him six months in prison. Even with the expunged record, he now lived by the axiom: fool me once.

He navigated to a hacker forum where the locals only knew him by his handle, |3ack2m3, or Back To Me. A message waited for him from his trusted associate, AreEff. Travis knew it would be terse but on point.

007s at work. list on alt.

The brief message told Travis what he needed. AreEff had a list of other companies that had been recently hit by industrial spies.

111

Whether they linked to R-Bot in any way was still in question, but it was a good start. Travis knew where to meet AreEff and get the list.

He logged into the private chat forum that was more secure than Area 51. A flashing icon told him that AreEff was online. Travis typed:

early birds and worms

The system indicated when another was typing. AreEff wrote:

2 many tourists after sunup

The tourists, as he called them, were there for drugs, sex, or some version of rock and roll. AreEff had no patience for them.

Travis didn't know who AreEff was, where he lived, whether he was male or female, or even if he was a single person. And whatever AreEff did for a living, his interests were always professional, corporate, and occasionally crossed legal lines.

On the dark web, AreEff's tentacles were numerous and lengthy. He monitored high-stakes transactions in a variety of ways, including, frequenting forums, scraping websites, and undoubtedly, through associates like Travis who were part of his vast network.

AreEff typed again:

Plenum Systems

AtWork Technologies

Quark Science

Branch Intelligence

Neverest Systems

CMD Line Inc

NlightN Dynamics

Travis wasn't familiar with any of the companies on the list, but he would be by noon. Now it was his turn to provide some value.

ur needs?

He'd recently helped AreEff with background work on some candidates for a job at a nuclear facility. They wanted to ensure they didn't actually hire a Homer Simpson. Or an OJ. One on the list was accused of embezzlement. While the jury didn't convict, the company dropped him from consideration because he didn't disclose the felony arrest on his application.

AreEff wrote:

0

They'd taken to using binary for simple yes and no answers. The number 1 meant 'yes' or 'acknowledged,' while the 0 meant 'no.' At this, Travis knew their conversation was over. It was time for a deeper dive.

Travis wrote scripts to scan the corners of the dark web, but most people used a search engine. Like using Google to find a barber's website, the dark web had search engines that navigated the depths.

Tools were necessary. Dark website URLs were intentionally impossible to remember, and some websites had the life expectancy of a mushroom. But these search engines didn't track their users' every interest. Travis never saw targeted ads for guitar strings after searching for a Gibson Les Paul.

Otherwise, dark web sites selling drugs looked a lot like online shopping at The Gap. They had star ratings and reviews from clients, offered buyer loyalty programs, and even ran the occasional sale. Especially around April 20th.

Travis navigated to the site that had offered R-Bot's corporate secrets to Baxter's colleague. While Travis didn't find any new data for sale, these postings came and went with the speed of a mouse click.

The companies on AreEff's list were unfamiliar to Travis. But R-Bot's security system challenged any user who requested information. Even so, their information was vulnerable. Clearly, there was a breach in their defenses, but where?

Intellectual property theft was a sophisticated game. The regular script kiddies couldn't penetrate a Zero Trust security system. An intruder might hack a server still running Windows 2003, but this was a different league.

R-Bot kept their systems on the latest software and security patches. With well-designed Zero Trust protocols challenging every request for information as if it were a hack, the intruder shouldn't make it past the front door. Yet, someone did.

While he considered the possibilities Travis opened the window curtain to let in more sunlight. Was the R-Bot breach simply an inside job, or were they targeted by an organized force? Hacktivists often tried to gain attention for their causes, but no group claimed this hack. Government-sanctioned hacker groups often targeted innovative companies to gain national advantage in strategic areas. Robotics certainly qualified.

Travis continued his search in the forums. He had other contacts, like AreEff, who monitored the transactions on specific sites. Travis dug in and worked through every name on AreEff's list, tapping his usual haunts, where information was traded for legal and illegal ventures. Services existed to alert companies when others offered their proprietary data for sale on the dark web. Unfortunately, it was a burgeoning market.

By mid-morning, Travis confirmed that all of those companies had their information trafficked on the dark web. He also understood what was stolen, some of which he confirmed in regular news reports. From AtWork Technologies, it was the company's employee data. While serious, it was a different kind of theft. Travis focused on those selling intellectual property that shaped the world's future.

Of the seven company names on AreEff's list, Travis confirmed that the secrets of five companies were trafficked on the dark web. Two were currently up for sale, while the other three sold within the last month. Proceeds from one sale was estimated at seven figures.

Based on AreEff's information, the only discernible common element among these companies was the seller on the dark web. While the seller may not have been the original hacker, Travis needed to explore that connection. He left a single word message on the contact page for the seller:

Robotics?

A wet nose pushed into Travis' knee. Then a second. Bailey turned quickly, knowing Travis would follow him. Belli stayed on her brother's heels all the way to the rear door.

Travis let them outside and returned to his computer. Another flashing icon awaited him. He clicked.

Mechanical schematic for surgical articulation

From discussions with Baxter, Travis knew R-Bot had a unique design for surgical equipment, capable of ultra-fine scale robotic movements controlled by a surgeon. The programming defined the refinement available to the surgeon. There were other players in this market, but this was one of R-Bot's closely guarded secrets.

Travis had to consult with Baxter about this discovery. Losing control of this information could be a startup killer. Before his death, Yang Tunan was head of R-Bot's mechanical engineering team. This schematic may have been the very reason he was murdered.

32

Gilbert didn't expect anyone to find him after breaking in to the pretty jogger's house. He saw her leave before sunup, but the kid wasn't with her.

To blend in with the minimal morning light, Gilbert had worn a mask and dark clothing as he listened at her back door. He heard the shower running, so he knew the roommate was still inside. He planned to hide in the house and look for signs of the kid once he was alone.

The tools he brought made simple work of the patio door lock. He entered the premises and found a comfortable spot to bide his time.

A few minutes after the shower stopped, he heard footsteps and thought the roommate was leaving.

Damned if she didn't open the closet at the end of the hallway where he was hiding.

She was an attractive brown girl wearing blue sweats. Late twenties. Too young for him, but there was a day. Petite, but that didn't mean she'd be a pushover. Sometimes the little ones put up the fiercest fight.

When she saw him, her eyes and mouth widened. He slapped a hand over her lips before her scream went viral. A shrieking woman only brought unwanted attention, and usually, a fight. But her full weight fell in his arms as she fainted. Gilbert dragged her into a bedroom. The photos around the mirror suggested it was hers. He sat the woman in the chair from her vanity, then bound and gagged her with a few fashionable scarves from her collection.

A quick scan of the house showed no sign of any other people. Two rooms. Two sets of girly stuff. Nothing for the kid. But the lady had to know something about him. He was with the roommate the day before, and if Gilbert knew anything, women talked.

This one now had to talk to him.

When he got back to the bedroom, she was sluggish but conscious. Her head lolled, but he got her attention with a sharp slap on the face.

"Where's the kid?"

She whimpered, shaking her head at the question.

They all did that in the first round. Nobody ever admitted anything until it got serious. Maybe she thought he'd just go away. But Gilbert never did. No one paid him to go away.

Persuasion came in many forms. A favorite was a twist with a trusty switchblade. His knife had a double-edge blade that shot out the front at the push of a button. He drew the unopened knife from his pocket and let her take it in.

A bead of sweat rolled down the side of her cheek, her breath coming in quick snorts from behind a purple scarf. Her neck craned upward as she sat in the chair.

Now he had her attention.

He held the knife close to her face and pressed the button. The blade snapped out within an inch of her right eye. Her body convulsed.

While it might damage her eye, the ejection force alone wouldn't penetrate skin. But she didn't know that. To her, the blade's action appeared fearsome.

Her face turned as he slid the blade along the edge of her jaw for full effect.

"You ready to talk to me?" By now, they usually were. "I'm going to take the gag off your mouth. If you so much as speak above a whisper, I'll carve my initials in that pretty face of yours. Got it?"

The nods came in a flurry.

Gilbert wouldn't really carve his initials. Torture wasn't a pastime for him. This was just business. But she had to understand who was the boss.

He loosened the purple scarf around her mouth.

"Who else lives here?"

She squirmed in the chair. "Just me and my roommate. What do you want?"

So the women weren't family.

He tapped her leg with the knife. "Where's the kid?"

"There aren't any kids here." Her voice cracked. "What kid?"

Morning light broke through the curtains. The entire neighborhood would soon be awake. Gilbert should've been gone by now.

"Your roommate was talking to him on the beach yesterday. Black kid about nine."

Her demeanor shifted. Gilbert could tell she knew who he meant.

"I don't know him. He was just some kid on the beach."

"Why did he come to your house?"

"He didn't." She blinked several times. "He was just on the street. I've never seen him before."

"What's your name?"

Her mouth fell open. "Why-why do you want to know?"

He was already in her house. The question was merely a formality. All he had to do was check around for a bill or something. Gilbert got in her face and tapped the knife against her cheek, emphasizing each word. "What is your name?"

The way her body drooped, he figured she was resigned to her fate.

He figured wrong.

She rocked back on the chair legs and head-butted him with a force that knocked him flat on his back.

His breath expelled with a rush, leaving a hollow pain in his chest. He scrabbled to get his feet under him as she stood to a crouch. Still tied to the chair, she rushed him.

It probably seemed like a power play in her mind, but Gilbert was far more maneuverable. He fell to his side, avoiding the brunt of her next charge.

She toppled, her chair landing beside him with a loud crack. They were head-to-head.

She lunged forward, her teeth ripping his left ear.

Gilbert screamed.

When he pulled away, his mask was still in her teeth, ripping out his hair and exposing his face. He reached for his ear and felt the warm liquid.

Dammit!

If she'd simply screamed, he would've just left. The morning was already a train wreck, and he didn't need more aggravation.

Gilbert wiped the blood on his shirt. His ear throbbed, hurting worse than if she'd kicked him in the nuts.

Stupid girl. Her smug expression faded as he pressed a hand on the chair to get back on his feet.

He grabbed a pillow from the bed. The knife would be quicker, but he only used it when required. No need to leave more evidence.

A pink, ruffled pillow served his purposes, muffling her screams while he pressed out her final breaths. She thrashed as best she could, but they both knew it was futile. When her body stopped moving, he surveyed the damage.

He went to the bathroom and cleaned up the wound on his ear., sterilizing it with some hydrogen peroxide. Human bites were notoriously germ laden.

Back in the woman's bedroom, he untied her from the chair and stuffed her body under the bed, where no one could immediately see her. He slid the chair under the vanity and draped the scarves back on the mirror, tidying as needed to leave the room as he remembered.

Augie would think this messy, but Gil had no choice. He looked around and found her purse. No woman willingly left without her purse. He'd have to take it with him. He checked her ID. Goodbye, Sharla Morris.

She should've just answered when he asked. It didn't have to end this way. This incident was on her.

With any luck, no one would find her body until the stench made it obvious. By then, he hoped to blow this hellhole of a town.

Gilbert carefully searched the entire house for the satchel. Between the two young women, they didn't own much, so the job went quickly. Unfortunately, there was no leather case, and no sign of the kid.

But he found the name of the roommate, who he saw with the kid. Denesha Roberts had to know something, and Gilbert knew how to make her talk.

He was running out of time. If he didn't find the kid today, she was next on his list.

33

From his seaside balcony in Half Moon Bay, Marcus listened to the crashing waves and wondered what Toya was going to do in this town. If she were even here.

After arriving the day before, Marcus drove every street, hoping to catch a glimpse of her. Driving past the businesses didn't take long. Other than a few hotel bars, there wasn't much nightlife, and he saw none of the places Toya frequented for employment. The town was too small for such blatant vices.

Still in his pajamas, Marcus went inside his hotel room and checked his blood sugar. His levels were right in line with doctor's orders. Cutting out the sugar and carbs in his diet helped him shed sixty extra pounds and brought him back from Type II diabetes. Eating well on the road wasn't simple, but it was possible. Like finally finding Toya, it took planning.

To see this thing through, he had to stay healthy, but he also needed caffeine. Marcus prepped the single-cup coffee maker and pressed the brew button.

From his car tracker app, he knew the car tagged in Toya's neighborhood was still in San Francisco. Could be one of the guys put the device on his grandma's Olds Cutlass. But Marcus didn't think so. The car still made passes by the club where Toya worked and her place out at Hunter's Point.

The tagged car parked along Silver Avenue each night, so it wasn't a neighbor of Toya's. Marcus thought about visiting the location, but he wasn't ready to cross that line. Whoever drove that car, they were probably still searching for Toya. Or the kid.

The coffee pot gurgled to a finish when his cell phone sounded. It was an attorney he worked with in Florida.

119

Marcus checked the time before answering the call. "Mel. Good to hear from you."

"This three-hour time difference is a killer." Fifteen years in sunny Florida couldn't alter Mel's Bronx accent. "I waited as long as I could to call."

Which wasn't particularly long, as it was only six-thirty, and Marcus was pouring his first cup of coffee. "Yeah. It's an adjustment. What do you know?"

"I'm working with the district attorney to prepare an extradition request with the Governor's office. You just tell me when you find her, and I'll get the locals to arrest her."

Marcus drove this road a few times. He knew not to get too excited. "Thanks, Mel. As soon as—you'll be the first to know."

"We gotta get her before New Mexico does."

Toya had an outstanding felony warrant in New Mexico for drug trafficking under a different name. She was dealing small amounts in Taos, but they'd arrested her with enough heroin to send her to prison. After a rich boyfriend made her bail, she fled the state after stealing his car.

While New Mexico had a legal claim on her, none of them wanted her back. Even the boyfriend wanted her to stay gone.

"Florida has her for attempted murder," said Marcus. "And they have a much bigger budget."

"A bigger budget and no sense of humor. Though she can't get the needle for attempted murder."

"I will find her." Marcus didn't want to encourage his own budding hope. Chasing Toya had been a long, disappointing game. Still, he hadn't felt this close to finding her since she skipped Atlanta. "We'll claim her for Florida."

"Let's make sure we do. After all this time, we need her here." Mel huffed into the receiver. "Gotta go, Marcus. I'll keep things primed on this end."

"Thanks, Mel." Marcus ended the call.

After a quick shower, he took the stairs down to the lobby for the buffet breakfast. While the waffles sure looked good, they wreaked havoc on his blood sugar. Scrambled eggs, bacon, and hot coffee were better choices for him. Buffets always reminded him of his days in the military, except the civilian food was usually better. He filled his plate and took a seat at a table.

He ate slowly, contemplating his next moves. Toya had to be staying somewhere. He'd canvassed the hotels the day before, especially the ones with a bar. Even if Toya wasn't a guest, she'd eventually come looking for a hot time in this sleepy burg. If there were any sparks to be found, she knew how to fan them into flames.

Marcus finished eating, taking a cup of coffee back to his room. Once he stepped inside, he received a notice from the GPS tracking app. The tagged car was on the move.

He went out to the balcony and opened the app. The vehicle traveled east on Silver Avenue, which was now a routine. Silver Avenue led to the northern section of the Hunters Point peninsula. The driver's neighborhood was only twelve minutes away from Toya's, but they had little in common. That vehicle cruised by her house at least four times each day since Marcus had been tracking it. Nothing to see here.

Just as he was ready to close the app, the car took an unexpected turn. Instead of continuing eastward on Silver, it turned right on San Bruno and then took a left onto Highway 101 South.

Marcus' heart double-tapped.

Nothing decisive about the move, but that vehicle had been on a constant sweep of the city for two days. Now it was on a major artery traveling south. The route led many places, but it was also the first leg on a trip to Half Moon Bay.

34

Maggie sat at her desk that morning and reviewed the latest entries in the log files. With all that had transpired, the office should've been empty, but the pace at R-Bot Systems hadn't really changed since Yang was murdered. Baxter encouraged everyone to stay home, but the team turned their attention to work.

Maggie understood the dynamic. If she stayed busy, her world might continue to spin. Stop, and it would crack and crumble.

Watching Yang die dumped too many disparate feelings on Maggie. While it was horrific, she didn't know him well and needed to consider that maybe he was a criminal. But she'd also had a surprisingly pleasant dinner with a handsome man whose company she enjoyed. Was he a duplicitous perpetrator or the tragic hero?

As she weighed these warring thoughts, she realized both of her hands clenched so tightly that her fists turned a ghastly white. She spread out her fingers, wiggling them until the circulation returned their color to a healthier shade of pink.

Maggie didn't like emotions. They interrupted the flow of her continuum. She never had the luxury of contemplation, and now, when it was a necessary skill, it didn't offer any certainty.

The phone rang with Travis' ringtone, and her waning concentration evaporated. She stood and took the call as she walked toward the lobby. "Hey, Trav. How's it going?"

"Good. I'm coming down there. Ginger's giving me a lift, and I'm leaving now."

Maggie stopped mid-stride. If he was coming to Santa Cruz, that meant he set up a meeting with Baxter. Travis must know something. "Sure. Where?"

"I'll meet you by your car at 11:30."

"Sounds good." Actually, it sounded ominous, but that was purely a reflection of her mood. Maybe he had good news. "See you then."

She ended the call and couldn't stand the idea of returning to her cubicle. Maggie wandered by the other offices to see who was around. She found Jason Gupta leaning back in his chair.

"Hey, Jason."

He straightened up as if he'd been caught him at something. "Hi, Maggie."

"Am I interrupting?" She didn't really care if she was, but it was the polite thing to say.

"No. Just walking through my schematics." He rubbed the bridge of his nose. "The latest prototype didn't perform as expected in our design review. Lots of plausible causes. I need to make sure it's not my electronics."

"Reexamining it all, no doubt."

"I think one of the mechanical parts was built wrong, but I'm not sure." He shrugged. "Blaming the deceased isn't winning me any friends right now."

"Is that what you and Pavel were arguing about?" Maggie tested the waters.

"Heard that, did you?" He crossed his arms over his chest. "Tensions are a little high right now. Yang's death put everyone on edge."

Her sigh faltered. "That it has."

Jason leaned toward her. "I'm sorry, Maggie. You of all people—" He didn't finish the thought.

She shrugged a shoulder. "You all knew him better than I did." She returned the conversation to their project. "What was wrong with the prototype?"

"Not sure. But I built my wiring diagram based on the specifications that were in Yang's schematic. Either I got something wrong, or he did. So far, I've triple-checked my work. But Yang's not here to defend himself, so I'm the bad guy."

"You're in a tough position." Maggie said, "And the timing makes it worse."

"That it does."

Hi-tech startups were a hotbed of ambition, competition, and ego. With such high stakes, the individual contributors were bound to clash. It was the leadership's job to keep them working toward that common goal.

Maggie would ask Baxter about this when they met later that day. For now, Jason's comments made her uneasy.

"I'll leave you to it, Jason. I think I'll get some fresh air." She left his company before he added more weight to her mood.

Down the hall, she opened the door leading to the outside terrace and stepped into the sunshine. The crisp air brought scents of juniper and the faint hint of baking bread, making her stomach growl.

Gail Everly was already there, leaning on the railing. She turned when the door closed. "Hi, Maggie."

"Gail." Maggie was hoping for a little solitude, but Gail probably was too.

"Lovely first week for you." The tall woman put her back to the rail. "How're you holding up?"

"Not sure at the moment." It was an honest answer. "How about you? Everyone here knew Yang better than I did. I just picked the wrong time to join him for a friendly dinner."

Her expression held sympathy. "I can only imagine how his family is taking the news. Yang was their eldest."

Maggie had her own grief to bear, but losing a son in this way would be devastating. "I thought about contacting them, but nothing I could tell them would make them feel any better." That moment of impact replayed in slow motion.

"I'm a CPA by trade. The HR role is mine because I understand all the laws." Gail pushed up the sleeves of her shirt. "I told Baxter we should bring in a grief counselor, even if no one wants to talk."

Maggie couldn't see herself seeking counsel, but mainly because she was a fake employee. Maybe a few sessions would do her some good. "Everyone manages in their own way." She thought about mentioning Jason, but decided not to. "It helps to keep busy."

"That seems to be the mantra around here." Gail pushed off from the railing. "By the way, Lynn said there's an update for the document software this weekend." She tilted her head. "Not that you should be working then, but you'll get an email notice." Gail walked toward the door. "That thing gets updated almost as much as our accounting package."

"Thanks for the warning."

At 11:30, Maggie was in her car when Ginger rolled up long enough to drop off Travis. He jumped in the front seat with Maggie and said, "Ginger will pick me up later. Head to the coast."

"Where are we meeting Baxter?"

"Parking lot for Wilder Ranch State Park near the beach. No one from work would go there midday."

They drove north on the Cabrillo Highway until they reached the entrance. They paid the day-use fee and parked next to Baxter's graphite gray 370z. He waited for them near the trailhead, wearing an R-Bot dress shirt.

As Maggie and Travis neared, Baxter fell into stride. "What have you learned?"

Travis dug his hands into his front pockets. "I have a list of companies with recent security breaches, and I found R-Bot's IP for sale on the dark web. Same seller in all cases, but different websites."

Maggie hadn't heard this update. "How do you know it's the same seller?"

"Cryptocurrency traces from the websites lead to the same wallet. Same wallet, same owner. Can't access it, but I can see it from the public side."

Baxter said nothing. He seemed to focus somewhere down the trail. "Thanks Travis. We'll get back to that. What about you, Maggie? What have you learned about the staff?"

"Jason and Yang apparently argued over the results of the recent prototype. I assume you are aware."

He nodded. "I was, but I didn't want to taint your investigation. Everyone on my team is a Type-A, so they're bound to have conflicts. But I want your opinion based on what you learn."

Maggie brushed the leaves of a tree as she walked. "Jason thinks Yang was at fault."

Baxter stopped on the trail. "He may have been, but do you think Jason had anything to do with his death?"

"I don't," she said, "But I also don't know if he's the one selling your company's secrets."

A pair of couples entered the trail behind them. Based on their ages, probably college students.

Travis picked up a rock and let the group pass. The scent of patchouli lingered in the air. "What about the FBI?" He bounced the rock in his hand like a baseball.

"The FBI isn't directly involved in the murder investigation. But obviously Claudia's working closely with the police on this case. Might be related to our theft."

The shooter wasn't after Maggie, or the police would've found two spent cartridges. "Clearly Yang was a threat to someone. Do you know if the police have eliminated any suspects?"

"The FBI doesn't tell me everything." Baxter's smile was tentative. "Not when the investigation is ongoing."

She didn't inquire further. "When you learn something definitive, tell us, so we focus on the right areas. On the right people."

Baxter's steely blues fixed on Travis. "What technology of ours did you find for sale?"

"It was a mechanical schematic for robotic articulation. Surgical." His weight shifted to his heels. "I know this one hurts."

"It does." Baxter said, "But I can't let this bloodletting continue."

Travis tossed the rock at the base of a tree. "What do you want me to do?"

Baxter squinted, his hand moving to his brow for shade. "I want you to contact the seller on the dark web and buy my schematic."

35

Travis wasn't sure what kind of reaction Baxter expected, but buying their secrets back from the dark web was a smart move, if they could afford it. The transaction gave them a chance to unmask the seller. And if that failed, at least their secrets were safe. The seller could only provide it to a single buyer, or the information lost value, and the seller lost reputation on the dark web. Even those who operated in the shadows, protected their reputations as closely as any Fortune 500 company.

"Find out how much they're asking," Baxter wiped his brow. "And I want a sample of the document to validate before we release any funds. Once you get it, send it to me immediately, day or night."

"I assume the FBI will be involved." Maggie leaned back on her hip.

Baxter nodded. "We'll try to catch our spy and keep our secrets from falling into the wrong hands. I already have authorization from Clint Masters. We discussed this option in the event there were additional leaks." He let out a long breath. "Do we know if the schematic was available before Yang's death?"

Travis watched his sister as he said, "We can't rule it out."

Maggie seemed saddened by the comment. After watching a man die, he earned some points as a victim.

"We need to find out for certain," Baxter said.

Pelicans flew overhead, briefly blocking the sun's glare. As a group of walkers approached their position, Maggie left the trail for the old railroad tracks. Travis and Baxter followed. Up ahead, Travis spotted a tree canopy that offered both shade and privacy.

Buying trade secrets on the dark web was illegal, but maybe not if you were the rightful owner. Travis remembered the last time he took questionable actions on a company's behalf. For his family, the consequences were devastating.

While Travis had a far better opinion of Baxter Cruise, the man would understand his need for legal protection. After all, this was just business.

Travis strapped his arms across his chest. "I'll set up whatever you need." He had a laptop dedicated to surfing the dark web. "I presume the FBI will want to monitor my dark web laptop during the transaction."

"Yes, but they'll need to keep it after the transaction, plus your equipment."

"Evidence. Of course." He rubbed the back of his head.

"We'll replace it all with whatever you want. Just let me know." It was the first time Baxter smiled. "If we can get our schematics back and take down the bastard, we're all in. Maybe we can find out who our spy is from the seller."

Maggie said, "If he even knows."

He pushed up a sleeve. "I've notified the FBI, well, Claudia, that we want them involved when this goes down. She's working with their cyber forensic team to get operational approvals, so we can go live."

This was Travis' segue. "Obviously, our company will need an addendum to our services agreement indemnifying us from this transaction." He'd rehearsed that line a few times before saying it. "We'll also need guarantees from the FBI."

"Of course. I'll contact our attorney immediately. Jerry Katana—" Baxter gestured toward them. "You met him at your house. He'll give you any written guarantees you need for your protection."

A glance at Maggie, and Travis knew she was pleased with his request. Her lips pressed together, suppressing a grin. Acquiring a similar document could've averted his fifteen rounds with the courts and his six-month stint at Cumberton for crimes he didn't commit.

"I appreciate that." He straightened his posture. "I have a list of companies with similar breaches. On a whim, I checked the website of the document control software company this morning—DocuLocker. Of the seven other companies that had a breach, four had their logo on DocuLocker's client page." Travis swept his bangs out of his way. "That seems like a high percentage."

Baxter leaned in. "Yes, it does."

"I noticed R-Bot Systems wasn't listed."

He shook his head quickly. "No. I don't see the point in advertising what we use for document security. It's like giving a burglar the make and model of your safe. Makes no sense."

"Who was involved in the software selection? I know Yang wasn't initially a fan." Maggie said.

"He joined the company after the system was deployed." Baxter breathed a heavy sigh. "I liked Yang, but he complained more than most. When you're ass-deep trying to build a company, complaints are common, and I didn't always give them a full airing. Now I wish I had." He rubbed his chin.

Travis watched his sister's expression turn heavy, as if remembering that horrible moment Yang was killed. She didn't even try to clean the clothes she wore that night. The next day, he saw them in the trash.

"But the software selection was a team effort." Baxter said, "Everyone offered an opinion on the major decisions. At least those not governed by the corporate board. Gail had certain accounting packages she favored. Lynn and Pavel had to maintain them, so they checked the references on everything seriously under consideration."

"What about Jason?" Maggie said, "Was he here then?"

"Jason only cared about the CAD system. Sorry, computer assisted design. It's a critical module of the document software. It's where he creates his schematics for the design work. Yang used it too."

Travis thought back to DocuLocker's client web page. "So, the other three companies might be using DocuLocker without being listed on their site. If it's not all just a coincidence. Is the FBI aware of your concern about the software?"

"Yes, but there's no proof it was used to commit a crime, so they won't investigate the software." Baxter's eyes narrowed. "My schematics on the web, now that's a crime. But it could've happened in other ways."

"Might be helpful to inquire about the other three companies," Maggie voiced Travis' thoughts, "plus some of the other companies listed as clients." She turned toward Baxter. "I think this is something you or Clint Masters would be in a better position to accomplish."

Baxter lifted an eyebrow. "More at Clint's level than mine, but it's a good idea. He might know some of the other CEOs, but there's not a CEO in the country that won't take a call from Clint Masters. I'll contact him as soon as we're done here. Text me the names."

"Will do."

An onshore breeze brought a welcome blast of cooler air. Travis lifted his face to take in the ocean scents it carried. The week had been so busy that he hadn't slowed long enough to breathe. Or install the cameras.

He remembered the kid who took Dad's jacket. What else was he stealing in the neighborhood? It wouldn't take long to put up the cameras once Travis got home. Someone needed to trap the little rat and inform his parents.

36

After the meeting with Baxter and Maggie, Ginger dropped off Travis at his home. The legal guarantees from the attorney were waiting in Travis' email. With that secured, He got on his dark web laptop and contacted the seller to arrange the buy of R-Bot's secrets. He posted a message expressing interest. When there was no immediate reply, Travis turned his attention to installing the cameras on the back porch.

They were USB cameras with infrared LEDs for night vision, essentially plug and play. He mounted the cameras on opposite sides of the overhang so the field of vision covered the entire porch. He found an old laptop to capture the video recordings and loaded the app.

The camera installation was hasty, but it would do the trick. He'd clean it up later when he had more time. For now, he figured their little thief was too young to notice the wires.

Travis checked on the message he'd left for the seller. Still no response. The guy could be asleep on the other side of the globe or sitting courtside at a Knicks game. Either way, he wasn't playing on Travis' schedule.

With dinner to make for Denesha and Sharla, Travis jumped on his bike and rode the three miles to the fish market. He found everything on the list to make his mom's cioppino recipe. When they made it together about a month before she died, she had him record all the ingredients and measurements. At the time, the effort just made him sad, but now he appreciated having these bits of their past.

He took his turn at the counter, paid for the ingredients, and biked back to the house. After packing the seafood in the fridge, his cell phone sounded.

It was Baxter.

Travis roused the dogs from their beds and went outside to take the call. "Hey Baxter, what's the latest?"

"Clint's been on the phone since we last spoke. Of the three other companies that had a breach, two admitted to using DocuLocker's software."

"Two out of three. Tough to call that a coincidence. Did he talk to anyone at the third company?"

"Yeah, Branch Intelligence. But Clint said their CEO is a jerk. He just wanted to posture. So nothing conclusive on them. Hang on a sec. I've got another call coming in."

Travis watched Bailey dive into the surf, while Belli rolled in the dry sand. Both of them needed a serious scrubbing.

"Sorry," Baxter said. "That was Clint. He talked to the CEO of four other companies listed on DocuLocker's client page. None of them had a known breach."

"Which companies?"

"I'll text the names to you. They're probably familiar."

"Hmm. Thanks." Travis sat in the sand. "I contacted the seller. As soon as he confirms the deal is on, I'll let you know."

"Then the FBI will take over the operation."

Maggie and he discussed the situation at length. While the scenario made them both a little nervous, this was the job they'd agreed to do. Calling in the feds was a logical next step. "Understood. We'll cooperate in any way we can."

"Clint and I both appreciate it. Let's see how far we get." Baxter huffed into the phone. "Ping me when you know more."

"Will do."

They ended the call, and the text from Baxter quickly followed with the names of the companies. He was right. Travis had heard of all the companies on this list. Seen a few of their commercials. Big companies, and none of them had a known breach.

Travis went inside with the dogs and straight to his main laptop. He checked the list of companies that reported a theft. None were familiar. The distinction made him curious.

The products offered by these companies ranged the spectrum of industries. There wasn't a pattern between those that experienced a breach and those that didn't, except their size and reputation.

Travis did a systematic search of all the companies. The ones without a problem were all publicly traded, listed on either the New York Stock Exchange or NASDAQ. None of the companies were younger than ten years.

His research on the companies with a security breach told a completely different story. Of those breached, including R-Bot, all began operations within the last year. Up-and-comers in their industries from a technology viewpoint, but few reported any revenue yet. Private investment money came from angel investors like Clint Masters, and that money went straight to research and development of new products.

The companies were all startups. So what? If there was a spy at R-Bot, the spy didn't also work at the other companies. If the problem was with the document software, wouldn't the bigger companies get hit too? They had far more secrets than the newbies.

Travis checked the time. Despite the impending FBI operation, he had food to prep. He switched to his dark web laptop and logged in to check for messages from the seller.

Nothing.

Maybe the seller was in Europe, where the clubs would already be in full swing. Travis pictured a skinny goth dude head-banging to techno beats at an all-night rave. He laughed to himself and wandered into the kitchen to start dinner for their guests, Denesha and Sharla.

Denesha was like a second sister. Ever encouraging, she even visited him at Cumberton prison a few times with Maggie, forcing Maggie to be on better behavior. For that alone, he owed Denesha. Those were rough days for all of them.

But things were simpler now, and he and Maggie both wanted to get to know Sharla.

37

After the meeting with Baxter and Travis, Maggie was back to the office by twelve forty-five, and she completed the minimum tasks required as a pretend employee. Later that day, she went to find Pavel.

There were only so many people with access to the company secrets at R-Bot Systems. Pavel was the man who designed the software to make all the other elements come alive. Maggie wanted to know what he thought about the recent prototype issues. She found him in a lab staring at three monitors.

He leaned back in his chair when she entered. "Hey, Maggie."

His cologne filled her senses before reaching his desk. It was pleasant, not overpowering. She'd spent the least amount of time with him since her arrival. Maggie played the curiosity card. "Still finding my way around here. Strange first week"

Pain flashed across his face. "Strange for any week. Yang was a good guy."

She rested against the cubicle wall. "Obviously I didn't know him well, but we spent a bit of time talking before—" Emotions choked off her words.

"I can't imagine what it was like for you."

"He seemed like a genuinely nice man." She shut her eyes to extinguish images of Yang's last moments. "But even if he were a creep, no one deserved that."

"Gail said they're bringing in a grief counselor. Probably a good idea." Pavel arched an eyebrow. "Especially for you."

Maggie didn't argue the point. "Yang seemed to get along with everyone." She hesitated. "Though I guess he and Jason had some conflicts."

His head lifted. "You heard." He swiveled his chair toward Maggie. "Jason can be intense. That test was important for all of us. Besides the financial implications, our professional reputations are on the line."

"What happened with the prototype?"

"It's not that it didn't work." Pavel pushed away the keyboard on his desk. "But it didn't work as expected. Which is equally undesirable. Controlling the robot, understanding what it will do and how it will perform is mission critical."

Maggie said, "With the different disciplines involved to make the thing work, when it doesn't work, how do you troubleshoot?" She had a general idea, but wanted to hear his description.

"Before we commit anything to a physical prototype, we create computer models, so we have a planned outcome. But if the results from the prototype don't match the results expected from the simulation, we go back and inspect the original documents."

The topic change seemed to enliven him. "Were the specifications wrong? Maybe the specifications were accurate, but they built the components wrong." He tapped himself on the chest. "Was there a software issue?"

"Trial and error." Maggie put a hand on her hip. "It's a wonder anything works."

"I agree with Jason on one thing. The type of error exhibited on this test made little sense. This wasn't our first prototype." Pavel tucked his feet under the chair. "Our initial proof-of-concept tests were successful. The design worked. This time, we tested our beta prototype. If these tests succeeded, we were going to refine the design for our production model."

She now understood Jason's anger. "So, it was a disastrous setback."

"It was. Given the results, and the behavior the robot exhibited—" His head rocked as if trying to weigh his words. "—It looks like Yang made a rookie mistake. And he's not a rookie." His shoulders raised in a shrug. "Jason may not have the smoothest delivery, but we're all thinking the same thing."

Maggie left the conversation with Pavel and returned to her cubicle. While he didn't say it, the team suspected Yang of sabotage.

Was that a motive for murder?

Everyone in the company had a huge financial stake. Each of them undoubtedly had enough stock to retire after the company went public. But none of them knew that the technology they worked so hard to develop was now for sale on the dark web. Only the spy who sold them out to their competitors.

If Yang was the spy, and someone else discovered the truth, that could also be a motive for murder.

His death took some planning and knowledge of his dinner with Maggie. She wished she'd never gone out with Yang. She also wished she hadn't run into Fyodor. He was back with his former fiancée, Katya the Great, who was now nursing his ailing mother. Maggie didn't have a chance against that stacked deck.

She heard the door open, interrupting her pity party, for which Maggie was grateful. Lynn was ending a call when she arrived at Maggie's cubicle.

"My mother." Lynn rolled her eyes. "Ever since Yang's death, she hasn't given me a moment's peace. She figures I'm next." She tucked the phone in her back pocket and said, "I get it. It was a horrible thing. But there's no reason to think it was related to work." Lynn shoved her hands in the front pockets of her jeans. "I bet your mother's totally freaked out since you were there when he died."

Maggie wasn't about to discuss her mother with Lynn or anyone else. Even if she were around, Maggie's mother filtered all experiences by how it affected her. For this event, she'd be unconcerned.

"It's been a long week for everyone. I find it easier just to focus on work."

"I wish I could. She calls me every hour." Lynn huffed. "Enough about that. We have another upgrade for the document software. Won't happen until this Saturday at 5 p.m., but I wanted you to be aware."

"Gail mentioned it. I guess that happens a lot." Maggie made a mental note to inform Travis.

Lynn nodded. "Especially on the accounting software. We have to keep up with the patches to keep our security solid. Unpatched software is the fastest way to get hacked."

"Is that what all the ransomware is about?" Maggie already knew the answer, but she wanted to get Lynn's perspective.

"Exactly. Unpatched software is like leaving the front door unlocked. Hackers come in, encrypt your data, and essentially, change the locks. Suddenly, you can't access your own data. Then they hold it hostage until you pay the ransom fee. Once you pay, they give you the key to unlock it."

"What a way to make a living." Maggie said, "I don't think I could sleep nights."

"There's big money in it. And the bad actors can be from anywhere." Lynn said, "If you have backup copies of your data isolated from the encrypted systems, you can get up and running. But it's a hassle. You never want to lose control over your systems."

"I get it. Keep the front doors locked." Maggie changed the subject. "Were you in the recent design review? I heard it didn't go well."

Lynn took a wide stance. "No. They confer with me to provision their system needs, but the robotics projects are typically self-contained. Though they upload data to other applications for analysis and diagnostics."

"I heard there were some concerns about the tests."

She breathed noisily. "Yang and Jason. The closest thing we have to a rivalry around here." Lynn swiped at her blonde bangs. "I mean had."

"Why those two?"

"I don't fully understand the intricacies of their work, but they often disagreed. From my experience, though, with two engineers, you get four opinions. No shortage of those around here."

Maggie checked the time again. Working a fake job was harder than working a real one. And slower. Still an hour to go.

"I guess I better get back to it." Lynn turned to leave. "You'll get an email before the upgrade, but I doubt you'll be working on a Saturday night. See you."

"Thanks, Lynn."

Maggie stared at her desk for a moment and then shut down her computer. Given the events of her first week, no one would care if she cut out early on a Friday night. Denesha and Sharla were coming to dinner that night, and Maggie wanted to help Travis, since he volunteered to cook. For Denesha's sake, they both wanted to give Sharla a proper welcome to the neighborhood.

38

Augie Barrett took a private elevator to the 42nd floor of the luxury condo building on Rincon Hill overlooking the San Francisco Bay. His finger slipped beneath his shirt collar, tugging it looser. During the long ride up, the air felt warm, stifling. He expected the conversation with Vladimir Penniski to make him more uncomfortable.

As a local fixer, Augie customarily met clients in prisons, bars, and occasionally, at the most exclusive addresses in town.

Vladimir Penniski, normally a man who operated his business in the shadows, made his name public when he bit off the nose of a rival in Golden Gate Park. A passing Boy Scout troop filmed the carnage that fed the 24/7 news monster's gaping maw for nearly a month. In the end, even Vlad's political friends couldn't keep him from spending quality time in San Quentin.

His unwanted media attention eventually tapered. After his release, he doubled down on his privacy and the number of intermediaries between himself and his criminal enterprise, employing a media consultant to reform his image.

As the elevator to Vlad's penthouse climbed higher, so did Augie's apprehension. He still didn't have the satchel from the kid.

From the time Vlad arrived in America, Augie worked for him, and his generous retainer meant Augie was always on call. The last time Vlad summoned Augie, he left his wife before the main course of their 10th anniversary dinner.

When he arrived on the 42nd floor, Anton and Yuri Suslov, Vlad's long-term associates, opened the front door. As his personal attachés, no one got near Vladimir without dealing with Anton and Yuri first. The Russian brothers usually wore turtlenecks and jackets, accentuating their beefy musculature. One look at them, and a smart guy assumed they carried brass knuckles.

Or worse.

As usual, Anton did the talking.

"Mr. Penniski is waiting for you by the windows."

Anton and Yuri led him into the magnificent penthouse suite. Augie had been here many times, but the Russian brothers never left Vladimir's side.

The eastern wall was all glass, offering spectacular views of the city. Most of the other tenants worked in high-tech, not crime. Though the enterprises had much in common.

Vlad gripped a cigarette with his thumb and forefinger. Dressed in all black, Augie knew Vlad planned to watch the Warriors that evening.

"I hope you brought me some good news." Vladimir gestured toward the decanters on the bar. Apparently, he was still feeling hospitable. That was good news for Augie.

He helped himself to a shot of scotch, downing it in a single gulp. "The matter is still open."

"The matter is a kid." Vlad glared at Augie. "How incompetent do you have to be to let an eight-year-old escape?"

Augie's own son was the same age and would get lost on the way to the john. "He's more resourceful than the average third-grader."

Vladimir sneered. "Is that so?"

"We'll get this closed." Augie knew he couldn't push it. While he relied on Gilbert, the man screwed up.

"You said that days ago. I expect people to meet their commitments." Vladimir sat on the suede couch and adjusted the creases in his pant legs. "That includes you."

"And I will." Augie felt a sweat bead trickle down his back. "Gilbert saw the kid. We know he's down in Half Moon Bay."

Vladimir motioned to Yuri, who hustled over to the decanters. "Maybe you rely on Gilbert too much."

Until this contract, Gilbert ran jobs with speed, accuracy, and a closed mouth. But this one—this one was a total cluster. All because the delivery man had a stroke, and an eight-year-old kid found the satchel in the park. That little snot was now the enemy.

"You know I'll make this right." Augie had always come through before. He wasn't about to risk his life double-crossing a Russian mobster.

Yuri brought a fresh drink to his boss. Vlad stared at the glass and took a slow sip.

"I'll give you twenty-four hours to get that case here." His gaze rose to meet Augie's. It held the warmth of a shark's. "Just so we're clear. I don't care about your guy stroking out. I don't care about your dead hooker. I especially don't care about an eight-year-old who gave your best man the slip."

Twenty-four hours. The kid eluded Gilbert for the last five days.

"If you want to stay on my good side." Vlad pointed at Augie's face. "Find that damn satchel."

Augie shivered. Vlad had no good side. This was a direct threat, and Augie wasn't going down for Gilbert's failure.

39

From his hotel in Half Moon Bay, Marcus monitored the tagged vehicle on the GPS tracker as it continued down Highway 101. It drove through South San Francisco, San Mateo, and then it made a decisive turn westward on Highway 92. A favorite route for weekend motorcycle riders, Highway 92 led directly to Half Moon Bay.

Eventually, the tagged vehicle neared town, and Marcus wanted to find the car while it was in motion, to see who was driving. So he grabbed his binoculars, got in the white Hyundai Sonata he rented, and drove off to meet the other car.

A 7-Eleven facing the highway was a convenient place for him to park, while the vehicle on Highway 92 drove ever closer. When the blip was nearly upon him, he started his engine and eyed the traffic as it passed—silver Honda Civic, white Subaru Legacy, red Ford Mustang. He pulled in behind the pack of three.

The driver of the Subaru was a woman with a couple of kids and unlikely to be his target. The Mustang gunned its engine, and the faux V8 sounds were even louder. Too much of an attention hog to take him seriously. But Marcus sped up to be sure. A kid. Maybe eighteen. Probably his parent's car. He raced away. The Honda driver was still too far ahead to get a good view. Marcus sped up, and they both caught the next red light.

The driver was a white guy, about thirty-five, with a tatted neck. Riding shotgun was the stocky brother. The same guys in the video from Toya's were driving the silver Honda Civic.

After the light changed to green, Marcus dropped in behind the Civic, following the car as it turned left onto Highway 1, his route tracking with

Marcus' GPS. He tailed the Civic through town at a safe distance, so the driver wouldn't notice. Then, the driver took a street that led toward the hills.

The next light turned yellow, and the driver sped through it to make his right turn. Marcus bided his time for a green light, but with the GPS, he knew where to find the Civic. The car had turned into the parking lot of a local motel down the road. Marcus proceeded slowly from the intersection, and as he passed the motel, he saw the men get out of the Civic.

Whoever these guys were, they were looking for Toya. Or maybe just the kid. Either way, Marcus planned to have a discussion with them.

For now, Marcus took a diversionary drive through a neighborhood, doubled back, and entered the motel parking lot. He found a discreet spot to record the car's license plate number. In his search for Toya, he never knew what scrap of data would be his big break.

Marcus returned to his hotel to wait for the Civic's next move. A couple hours later, the white dude with the tats was finally on the road. This time he crossed over Highway 1 to an older neighborhood nearer the beach. Marcus got in his car and followed.

The old roads were tight, and Marcus didn't want to be seen, so he let the distance grow between his car and the Civic. He pulled over and watched the car move on his app.

Suddenly, the Civic stopped in the middle of Custer Street, Marcus wanted to know what caught the driver's interest. He got out of the car and walked to the end of Custer until he could see the driver of the Civic with his binoculars. The driver's attention was on a small, yellow house on the left side, fifth from the end.

This car now in Half Moon Bay, was the same one cruising Toya's house and club in San Francisco. The house must have significance. Marcus felt the familiar triple-tap in his chest. Toya might be in the house right now. Marcus imagined her sitting in a chair, painting her long claws in scarlet. He closed his eyes and could almost hear her breathe.

Marcus walked back to his car, while the Civic made its way back to the motel. Odd. The driver came all the way from San Francisco. Why stop at this house just to stare at it from the road?

While it seemed strange, Marcus was less interested in the Civic than he was Toya. If she was in that house, now was the time to find out.

He parked at the end of Custer and walked toward the yellow house, looking at his phone as if he were on a casual stroll. With each step closer, his heartbeat spiked to the contrary. Across the road, an older man came out to check the mailbox and waved. Marcus returned the greeting. But now that the man clocked him, Marcus had to be careful.

Before reaching the yellow house, he put his camera on record. Upon arrival, he aimed his phone at the driveway, hoping the camera captured the details of the two cars parked. License plate number, makes, and models. When he reached the front door, he rang the doorbell as if he were expected.

The door had a peep hole, which gave Toya the advantage, but he listened carefully for any movement inside the house. All was deathly silent. Two cars in the driveway, but no one answered the door. This job required his constant patience, and he hated it.

He wanted to go around the back, but the man who waved had line-of-sight to Marcus' position and might be still watching.

As he walked away, he watched the video of the driveway long enough to confirm that he'd captured the information from the two cars. Marcus needed to think this through. But one thing was certain, he planned to keep close watch on this house.

He made it a few doors down, when a woman ran onto Custer Street from the other direction. A pretty girl in track gear, she gunned it. When she blew around the side of the yellow house, Marcus decided to find out who she was. Unlike Toya, this girl was petite. Maybe friends. Maybe related, but Marcus didn't think Toya had family out this way.

Invigorated, he got out of the car and jogged back to the house.

When he rang the doorbell this time, a female voice called out from the side yard, "Hey." The woman walked to the front wearing cobalt blue spandex. She was even smaller up close. "Can I help you?"

The woman breathed a bit heavily because of the run, but he detected no concern in her voice. Her skin radiated good health and cheer. Marcus tried to reconcile the two of them being friends. Toya's idea of a potluck was when one person brought meth and another brought coke. Getting high was always the main course. The only time Toya ever ran was when she was being chased.

Marcus smiled and met the woman in the middle of the front lawn. "Hi. I'm Marcus Fisher, and I'm looking for my sister, Toya. I was told she might be at this address." He held Toya's picture at arm's length. "Can you tell me if you know her?"

"Your sister, huh? Let me see." The young woman came nearer and took the photo from Marcus, but quickly shook her head. "No, I'm sorry. I've never seen her."

The woman's evaluation seemed genuine. But Marcus knew some phenomenal liars. He also wasn't big on trust. "Do you think your housemate might know her?"

She took a step backward.

Marcus sensed her suspicion. "Two cars. I just assumed someone else lives here."

She pointed a finger at him and smiled. "You'd make a good detective." She glanced at the cars. "But she's not home at the moment."

He noticed a phone tucked in her waistband. He withdrew a hotel card from his pocket and wrote his number. "Please take a picture of my sister's photo and check with your roommate. I live in Sausalito, but I'm staying in town for a few days to look for her."

When he needed to be, Marcus was also a phenomenal liar. "My sister's gone off her meds, and we haven't seen her in weeks. My mother is worried sick." He had this routine down like a rap. "We heard she came to this area."

The woman looked genuinely worried now. "I'm so sorry." She took a quick snapshot of the photo and returned it to Marcus. She also took his card. "I can ask."

Nodding, he pursed his lips. "Thank you." He put the photo in his pocket.

He turned away from her, but he wasn't done. When he got back to his car, he waited. Eventually, the woman left home on foot. This time, she wore a loose pink sweater and jeans. He followed her by car at a distance, matching her every turn, until she reached a house at the edge of the beach. A blonde woman greeted her on the front porch with a friendly hug.

Neither of these women seemed like Toya's usual crowd. But the Civic that drove by Toya's house also showed keen interest in the yellow house. And the girl from the yellow house led him to the blonde. Whoever she was, she and the petite sister were now solidly on Marcus' radar.

40

That evening, Maggie looked out her front window and saw Denesha approaching for dinner, but Sharla wasn't with her. Maggie stepped outside onto the porch.

Down the street, a white car drove slowly and parked beneath a large Madrone tree. It wasn't a car that normally visited that house.

"Hey, girl. Sorry I'm late," Denesha said, as she met Maggie on the porch.

"No worries. Trav's getting started. Where's Sharla?" Maggie ushered her friend into the house.

"I don't know. Her phone keeps going to voice mail."

Both beagles ran down the hall to greet Denesha. She stooped to rub their faces.

"Bummer." Maggie didn't know Sharla well, but she wanted to. "We were looking forward to hanging out with both of you." Maggie wrinkled her brow. "You told her Travis was cooking, right?"

Denesha's cheek hitched with a smile. "Absolutely I did." She followed Maggie and the dogs down the hall and into the kitchen, where Travis was stirring something in a pot.

He stopped long enough to say, "Hey, Neesh. Dinner will be a few. You and Magpie can have some wine and chill."

"Sounds good, Trav. Thanks." Denesha leaned against the counter while the beagles sniffed her shoes.

Travis pulled a flowered tureen from the upper cabinet. "Where's Sharla?"

Denesha patted Belli's head. "Not sure."

Maggie said, "It's Friday night. Maybe Sharla will stop by later." She got a bottle of Sauvignon Blanc from the refrigerator and poured them both a glass. "In the meantime, we can start without her."

Denesha picked up her glass and followed Maggie outside, where the women talked while an orange sun lower into a pink sky.

Eventually they heard a knock on the back door, and Travis summoned them to return to the kitchen.

"Smells awesome in here," Denesha said. "What did the master chef make this time?"

"Something seafoody," Maggie said it with a straight face.

"Really?" Travis poured the contents of his pot into a serving dish and scowled at his sister. "I slave in the kitchen, and all you can come up with is 'seafoody'. Is that what you told your diners when they asked what was on the menu?"

He reached for some green bits in a ramekin and sprinkled them over the serving dish. "I made cioppino with creamy polenta, but I bought the apple pie for dessert."

Maggie laughed into her wineglass. "Like I said."

Denesha elbowed Maggie in the ribs. "Sounds a lot better when you say it, Trav." Denesha lifted her glass and took a sip. "Maggie said Solomon hasn't been back to your place."

"Haven't seen anything missing." Travis brought the tureen to the table. "But as of today, I have cameras watching the back porch." He gestured to Maggie.

She picked up on his cue and carried the polenta to the table.

When Travis' meals hit the plate, conversation always slowed. His recipes rivaled anything Maggie tasted in the kitchens along the coast. But he readily admitted, making one meal was far simpler than making a hundred. They all agreed that Maggie couldn't even manage the one.

They lingered over dinner, catching up on Denesha's news of nursing school and wayward roommates.

"No. Thank you." Denesha raised her hand in protest when offered the apple pie. "I can't eat another bite."

"Yeah. It doesn't sound as good as it did earlier." Maggie said, "Let's go sit in the living room."

She brought the bottle with them and poured more wine into their glasses before settling in on the couch. The dogs tagged behind Travis and curled up next to him on the floor. His video laptop was open on the coffee table.

Denesha sat opposite Maggie on the couch. Kicking off her shoes, she tucked her legs beneath her. "How's your latest adventure?"

Travis dropped into a big chair and put his feet on the table. "We're working with client and the FBI on this one. The client had some secrets stolen."

"Company secrets. Like new products?" Denesha stifled a yawn with the back of her hand.

"Pretty much. Maybe not a finished product, but important pieces of the technology to make the end product."

"You two certainly get around." Her head snapped toward the back door. "You hear that?"

Belli barked and scurried that direction.

Maggie sat down her wineglass. "I didn't. But Belli sure did. Let's find out if our little porch pirate returned."

She got up from her comfy spot and arrived long after Bailey. Maggie pushed the curtain aside. "I don't see anything. Or anyone."

Travis called out, "I'll check the video from the cameras."

She padded to his side. "Do you see anything?"

"Hang on."

He drilled into the events link of the video feed. An entry appeared. It was time-stamped just moments before.

And there was the kid on the video scouting their back porch. Despite his light fingers, he was a cute little dude. Handsome brown face with short dreads, wearing a rugby shirt and jeans.

"Gotcha!" Travis pumped the air with his fist.

Maggie flinched. "Not so loud. It's late." She picked up her wineglass. "Why isn't he home and in bed?"

Travis dropped his video laptop onto the couch and ran toward the back porch.

Maggie choked down her sip. "Where are you going?"

"Where else?" He skidded up to the door. "To catch the little perp!"

41

Travis scrambled out the door, struggling to keep the dogs inside as he left the house. Having the beagles track the kid might find him faster, but Travis didn't want to scare him to death. Running to the road, Travis stopped to survey the area. Illumination from street lamps and houses didn't reveal any movement.

His breath came in short huffs. Where did the kid go? Travis counted forty seconds between the video time stamp and when he left the house. Did the kid live so close that he was already home? Travis didn't know every neighbor that well, but he couldn't think of any likely candidates.

But the kid had to be staying somewhere around here. There were plenty of rentals that routinely changed hands. He ran down the main road, scanning each street for small bodies until he reached the Cabrillo Highway, before doubling back.

Movement to his left caught his attention, but it was only a cat scurrying for cover under a car. There were too many places to hide. With hundreds of houses in his area, the kid was probably tucked in bed by now.

Unless he left by the beach trail.

While it was a longer walk, it led to another neighborhood. Far too long for a young kid to take by himself at night. But everything this kid did screamed high risk.

On that thought, Travis pivoted and kicked his run into fourth gear.

As he neared the beach trail, surf sounds rose, making it harder to hear the subtler noises. He charged up the incline to the bluff. From there, he'd have a better vantage point, and if the kid left by the trail, he'd nail the little punk.

Dropping into cooler temperatures than the previous night, the wind died with the sun, and by morning, he expected a blanket of fog. Even now, the atmosphere was moist, heavy, ominous. Travis remembered that time he found the corpse near here. A shudder crept up his spine. Even if the kid was a thief, Travis didn't want to find another dead body.

He left the trail at intervals to check the beach. Overhead, a waxing gibbous moon reflected light off the water. Travis couldn't see a long way down the beach, but there was no one in his vicinity. No one obvious.

Already he was a quarter mile from the trailhead. He slowed his pace to a jog and then to a halt. He blew the spent air from his lungs and raked his fingers through his hair.

What was he doing? Looking for the kid out here was just stupid.

As with many decisions in Travis' past, it wasn't really a decision. He ran out of the house without thinking. Was it all about the stolen jacket? Seeing video of that kid scavenge his porch lit Travis like a mortar shell.

But the jacket was just a thing. Maybe a thing Travis wanted, but having it didn't replace his father.

And what was he going to do if he actually found the kid? Kick his ass?

Yeah, that would make Travis' father proud.

Travis scrubbed his face with his hands and thanked God he hadn't found the kid. Not with his head in this space. What was wrong with him?

It was just a jacket.

Travis drew a deep breath and then another. Whatever that kid's problems, Travis wouldn't add to them. He wiped his nose with the back of his sleeve and headed home.

The trail wended through the dense brush and battered coastal trees. Travis kept a brisk pace, his thoughts about the kid now reined. In his haste, he left without his phone or a flashlight. Moonlight kept the darkness from consuming the trail, but at this time of night, the shadows prevailed.

Near the base of a tree, the iridescent glow of eyes watched him before the creature skittered away. There were bigger hunters out here at night. Travis picked up his speed to a jog.

In the brush to the right of the trail, he caught movement. Travis stopped mid-stride and dropped to a crouch. He squinted toward the source of the motion. No eyes glowed back at him, the low light revealing no clues. It wasn't a breeze pushing the flora. Something was out there.

After a few deep breaths, he steadied himself. If it were a mountain lion, he wouldn't have heard it. Black bear were rare and usually foraged in the daytime. Anything smaller, he'd take his chances.

As Travis stood, he heard a cough. Not an animal sound. It was distinctly human.

With the moon illuminating from the south, Travis saw the outline of the young boy. He wasn't standing proud or even erect. He seemed stooped, like a man of many years. His small shoulders rounded as if heavily laden.

He didn't move like a child, the way they randomly spin or hop or trudge instead of step. Even the tired ones usually burned that last burst of fuel before relenting to fatigue.

Travis hadn't really considered the boy when he watched the video, didn't notice him. Travis focused only on his personal loss. He gave no genuine regard to the kid's condition.

For God's sake, he was stealing food and clothing.

He looked so young, and it was nearly eleven at night. What was he doing out here by himself?

Travis pressed a fist against his lips and shut his eyes. This was a scene straight of Les Misérables. He was pursuing a nine-year-old boy who just wanted to eat and stay warm. It's not as if they didn't have food to spare. Or jackets.

Did the kid even have a place to sleep? Travis exhaled guilt into the night air. He had to find out.

He crossed the trail on the high side of the bluff, keeping his steps light, quiet.

When he neared close enough that the kid could hear him, Travis said, "Hey. I'm Travis. You've been on my porch. Want to come home with me? We've got lots of food and a warm place to hang—"

The kid didn't wait for the full pitch. He bolted as if sprinting the 100 meters.

Travis lit out after him. But the kid was fast and seemed to know the terrain. He jumped over a thicket that Travis didn't even see.

Once again, Travis didn't think, didn't decide, didn't reason out his next steps. He just chased a scared kid deeper into the cold, lonely night.

The kid was wise to run away with a maniac stalking him. Good street smarts. Travis' invitation to follow him home didn't sound benevolent. Only malevolent.

Travis slowed his gait and headed for the house.

When he returned, Denesha and Maggie were sitting in chairs on the back porch. As usual, Maggie was first out of the gate. "What happened? Did you find him?"

Travis recounted the events, including his remorse at driving the kid away.

Maggie pulled her legs up, her knees tucked under her chin. "So, he's out there all alone?"

"Maybe. I didn't see anyone else. But we've had homeless living out there before."

Denesha was quieter than usual, but her face was intent. "I'm running tomorrow morning before I do my homework. I'll look for him then."

Travis lowered his face into his hands. "Arrgh! I sure didn't help matters."

"No, you didn't. He's just a kid." Maggie was quick to dogpile on his guilt but seemed to realize it. She added, "But you meant well."

"The kid didn't think so. He hauled out of there so fast, I didn't even see his face."

"We'll find him." Denesha stood and stretched. "But even then, we need to call child services."

Maggie said, "We do. There's no evidence of an adult in his life." Her head leaned to the side as if it felt heavy. "Though they can be a mixed bag."

"Thanks for the awesome dinner, Trav." Denesha hugged him and then Maggie. "Since you don't have a fake job to commute to, let's touch base in the morning."

"The commute is real and grueling." Maggie got up. "My next fake job needs to be closer to home."

As Maggie walked Denesha to the door, Travis found his dark web laptop and logged in.

A message waited for him from the seller on the dark web. He named his price of $250,000. A lot of money, to be sure, but not so much that R-Bot systems wouldn't pay it.

The seller didn't know who was buying, but there were only so many companies interested in this kind of technology. Even fewer willing to buy it on the black market.

Travis typed:

Need sample to verify

The seller replied:

Agreed

Within moments a .pdf document was available in the chat window. Travis downloaded the file to a quarantine area on his computer and scanned the document to make sure it was free of viruses. When he confirmed it was safe, he texted the file to Baxter to validate the document's authenticity.

A few minutes later, Baxter texted Travis his evaluation.

Legit, proceed

Travis notified the seller:

Consider it sold. Will arrange for purchase tomorrow.

The seller didn't hesitate in his reply:

24 hours. Crypto only.

It was a strange sensation to arrange this kind of purchase on behalf of a company, after previously landing in prison when he thought a company had his back. This time, he had his get-out-of-jail card notarized upfront, and he had the authorization of the FBI.

Now Baxter needed to arrange the $250,000 in cryptocurrency for the transaction. Travis sent Baxter a quick message:

It's on.

42

When it was finally morning, the fog wouldn't let the light through to warm up Sol. He sat up against a tree and shivered, rubbing his shoulders to get them feeling again. After that black-haired man from the nice house chased him last night, he didn't want to risk going back to his camp. Sol knew he'd taken too many things from that house. When Mama borrowed from people, they usually got mad at her, too.

He'd found a place under the brush and tried to stay awake. But as Sol sat in the darkness, his head bobbed on his neck until it wouldn't stay up anymore, and he fell asleep.

He woke up wet from the fog and feeling queasy. Even thinking about food, his stomach usually roared like it had a motor. Today, food didn't sound so good. And he was tired. Now the white man with the angry blue eyes and the black-haired man were both after him. Sol hugged his knees into his achy chest.

Maybe the men knew he had a lot of money. But why did Angry Blue-Eyes go to Denesha's house and mess with her roommate? Sol wondered if she was okay. When he went back for Mama's phone, he'd check on the roommate, too.

Black-Hair probably just wanted Sol to quit stealing his stuff. No matter what Mama called it, Sol knew she never returned anything.

Since Mama got shot, there'd been no end of trouble. This Half Moon Bay was a terrible place, even if the ocean was everywhere. He wanted to go back to the city and look for Mama. He knew a couple of kids in the neighborhood. Maybe he could stay with one of them. Plus, he knew Tyrone.

He needed Mama's phone. It had to be charged by now. Sol stood. A strange feeling zapped his head like lightning, making him lose his balance.

He fell against the tree, catching his breath, resting until his thinking seemed normal.

The cold seeped into his bones overnight, and all his shoulder rubbing only helped a little. It didn't stop his teeth from chattering. The big jacket was in the sleeping hole. He'd go back to camp when he could, get the jacket and the money, but he had to make sure he wasn't being followed.

If he got the phone and called Tyrone, maybe he'd pick up Sol and they could find Mama together. With all that money, Sol could pay someone to drive him if Tyrone wouldn't do it.

His legs wobbled as he pushed away from the tree. He grabbed onto the branch of a bush to steady himself. A wavy feeling entered his head, and he hesitated a moment longer, waiting for it to pass.

Sol didn't want food, but he was extra thirsty. Usually, he got up and went pee first thing, but he didn't have any to get rid of today. He'd find some water first, get the phone from Denesha's, and then check on the roommate. Sol hoped Angry Blue-Eyes was gone, and that she was all right.

As he moved through the brush, he kept a hand on a bush or a tree in case he got wobbly again. The trail was nearby, and it was a smoother walk, but he didn't want to see any people that morning, in case they knew he was a thief.

He stole the jacket and food from the nice house. He stole candy from the store. Maybe Angry Blue-Eyes thought he stole the leather case with the $8,500. Sol wished he'd never found that stupid satchel. It went from being the best thing that ever happened to him to the worst.

But he didn't steal that money. He found it and turned it in. If it belonged to Angry Blue-Eyes, he could've claimed it during the 90 days Sol waited. He'd give it up now, if it would bring Mama back. But he was clutching on it too hard that day he saw the gun. Made his thinking go woozy. If only he'd given up the case when Mama said to.

Sol coughed, and he covered his mouth with the crook of his elbow. Something seemed stuck in his throat. He coughed again and again until his stomach was jumping. When it finally stopped, he stiff-armed the nearest tree and panted.

The fog was thinning, and he could finally see farther ahead, but it wasn't making him any warmer yet. His throat hurt from all the coughing, and now it felt dry, scratchy. Sol knew a house that left a hose in the yard. He'd stop there first. Pushing away from the tree, he pressed on.

Mama's borrowing also got her in trouble. When Sol was little, some man hit her in the face because she took some of his rocks. He said she had to pay for his rocks one way or another. It was a hazy memory, like when waking up from a dream. There were lots of rocks outside, and he couldn't understand why she didn't give him some of those. Instead, they moved to New Mexico.

That's why people were always after Mama. She called it borrowing, but like him, she was just a thief.

The sun worked hard to break through that fog, and Sol wished it would hurry. His clothes were damp, and he needed to heat his bones. Up ahead, he saw a clear patch of sunrays beaming down that looked like a sun shower. He hustled to it and let the warmness soak into his skin. With even that bit of heat, Sol suddenly felt too warm. He tugged at his shirt collar, his armpits slipping in sweat.

Hearing people sounds from the trail, he quieted his raspy breathing to keep anyone from knowing he was there.

Then he heard words, a woman calling his name.

"Sol. Are you out here?"

He positioned himself on the other side of the tree so he could see the trail through the branches.

"Hey, buddy. It's me. Denesha."

She wasn't much bigger than Sol and seemed even smaller wearing all black running clothes.

"Sol. Come on out."

She looked directly his way, but he stayed statue-still as she passed. Her run wasn't fast. Not like the day he first met her. Her voice got harder to hear, and he stayed by the tree until it was all gone.

Now Sol had three people looking for him.

With Denesha running so slow, she wouldn't be back to her house for a long time. He could check on her roommate and get Mama's phone. It would have a full battery by now. He wiped the sweat from his forehead with the back of his hand. Despite not feeling so good, he left the tree and walked toward Denesha's house.

He'd call Tyrone first, but he'd have to wait a few hours. Tyrone was like Mama and worked the night shift. When he stayed over, they never got up before the middle of the day. Sol had to keep extra quiet those mornings and get himself off to school. Sol didn't want to make him mad.

One time he was over, Sol turned on the TV too loud, and Tyrone came running out of Mama's room wearing a towel. He smacked Sol upside the head kinda hard. Mama came running out in her pink robe and screeched at the both of them. Tyrone smacked her too. After that, Sol kept real quiet whenever Tyrone was around.

Sol trudged through the thicket. He was running through this area days before, but today his legs were extra heavy and sore. That house with the hose in the yard was still a long walk from him, and he imagined how cool that water would taste running down his throat. A quick stop there, and he'd be feeling just fine.

Then he'd get his phone, wait a while, and call Tyrone. He'd pick up Sol. He just had to.

Mama's phone was the only way out of this place.

43

At 6:01 am, the Fender's usual languorous Saturday morning routine was interrupted by the arrival of the FBI. With a purchase price for R-Bot Systems' IP now established with the dark web seller, the FBI's cyber forensic team took control of the operation and the Fender's home.

While an FBI agent manned their front door, Travis stood down the hallway by the living room with Bailey & Belli at his side. Two agents entered his house carrying a pair of long, folding tables and some chairs. Baxter Cruise and Agent Claudia Seagal followed and approached Travis.

"Good morning." She reached her hand out to Travis. "It's good to meet you." Claudia was instrumental when Baxter hired Travis the first time.

She wore navy slacks with an Oxford shirt, flat shoes, and her dark hair in a ponytail. The weapon holstered at her hip completed the picture of operational efficiency. The rest of her crew wore similar business casual clothes. It was going to be a tense morning. For Baxter, probably the most tense of all.

Claudia lifted her chin toward the activity. "We appreciate your cooperation and the use of your home for this operation. Our team wants all the conditions from your side of the transaction to remain the same when you contact the seller."

Travis watched his sister frantically collect dog toys from the floor and throw them into their toy basket. "Maggie and I want you to nail this guy."

"Me too," Baxter said.

"If it's who we think he is, he's been on our radar for a while." Claudia's dark eyes set on Travis. "Your work accelerated our timeline, but we have a real opportunity to bring him down."

He swallowed hard. Being under the scrutiny of law enforcement, in any scenario, made him uneasy. Travis tightened his gut. "I'm still trying to figure out how he got the documents to begin with." He broke eye contact with Claudia and focused on Baxter. "The only system that carries the information is the document control system. But R-Bot's monitoring access on everything. No one can even write to a flash drive without that activity being recorded."

She said, "Agreed. Our team reviewed the logs, and we haven't found an anomaly that would account for the data loss."

The feds agreed with him. That was a fresh development. Travis stood a little straighter. "Are you continuing to monitor the systems?"

Claudia shook her head. "We didn't find evidence of a federal crime. We don't know how the document came to be on the dark web."

"The next update to the document control system is later today, Travis," Baxter said. "You ready?"

"Yeah. Maggie told me when the notice came out yesterday." Travis tapped his phone. "I've got an alarm set, so I'll be on and scanning the packets as soon as the data moves."

"Lynn and Pavel run the same tests intermittently since the system was setup a few months ago, but maybe they missed something."

"Where are the results of those packet scans? I'd like to compare them to what I find today."

"I'll send the folder location to you." Baxter scanned the room. "You already have access."

"Cool."

Baxter's eyes fixated somewhere else, and he released a noisy exhale. "No matter what happens, it's going to be an interesting day." He touched Claudia's elbow. "If you both will excuse me, I'm going to talk to Maggie."

Claudia flashed him a quick smile and turned to Travis, wearing a full-on game face. "Let's review our plans for today."

He moved a little closer. "Sure. I'll do whatever you guys need."

"We're going to link our equipment with your system. Our team will monitor your movements to the dark website. Once you begin communications, they hope to unmask the seller with their forensic tools. We need to find out who he is before we complete the transaction."

Her gaze went toward Baxter, now on the other side of the room. Then she pointed his way. "Baxter was on a call with Clint Masters early this morning, and they transferred cryptocurrency for today's buy to your wallet. I need you to confirm that it's there."

"Absolutely."

"We'd rather not lose control of a quarter mil, but it's the plan laid out for this op."

A quarter million dollars. Travis wiped his hands down the front of his pants. "Understood."

"As discussed, we got a warrant and looped in resources from your internet provider." Claudia said. "They have access to parts of the connection that will assist our team."

He wondered how many people would watch his keystrokes. No checking the tide charts today.

"Just so we're clear." Claudia curbed some stray dark hair behind an ear. "I'm not privy to the process our forensic team will follow. Even within the Bureau, the specifics of these operations are confidential."

"No worries." He said, "I'll get my gear and verify the crypto coins are available." Travis headed to his office and called over his shoulder to everyone in the room. "Coffee and cups in the kitchen. Help yourselves."

He knew the FBI never shared all their secrets. When they found a vulnerability to exploit, they often kept that news to themselves, so they could use it to expose criminals. On the flip side, they hacked US companies to remove malicious code they'd found in unpatched Windows systems. While a white-hat hack, the move met with much controversy.

But Travis understood the drill. The usual process was that they had a vulnerability within a specific browser, like Firefox, Chrome, or even Tor— the Onion Router.

Tor was named for its layers of security—the volunteer network of relays designed to keep the user's internet address anonymous. By routing a dark web request to duplicate relays, some of which are false signals, it was difficult to determine the exit relay, where the original request reaches its destination.

Unlike regular internet browsers, Tor changed the routing path every time a user requested a site—like driving a different route to work every single time. With relays located across the globe and encryption at every hop, identifying a specific user was almost impossible.

But the FBI had their own cyber team who constantly probed systems for a way to read a user's request, unencrypted, as it hit a relay, so they could track down the person at the keyboard.

Travis got his dark web laptop, monitors, and internet equipment from his office and brought them to the FBI tables. He reconnected his gear to make sure it was working properly before letting the FBI experts tap his system. He logged into his cryptocurrency wallet, which now showed a balance of over $250,000.

Across the room, Maggie had her hands on her hips as she talked to Baxter. Bailey and Belli sniffed around Baxter's shoes, and he reached down to scratch Bailey's head, the dog stretching toward his touch.

As the FBI team prepared to monitor the transaction, Maggie and Travis kept the coffee pot in constant production. Travis stopped by the FBI tables to answer the occasional question. Otherwise, he stayed out of their way as the forensic computer scientists verified configurations, connections, monitoring, and prepared to launch their payload to track the seller.

Travis wandered outside. The FBI van buzzed with activity, a satellite dish extended above the van, and cables ran from there to his living room.

He approached the burly redhead at the door. "How's it going?"

"I'm sorry." The agent replied, "I'm not allowed to comment on live operations. The team inside will keep you briefed."

But no one inside briefed Travis, either. Only Claudia spoke with him and only about the activities he needed to perform. For now, it was a waiting game.

Travis saw movement across the street at Carl Pinkerton's house, who reveled in all the Fender misery. But he wouldn't be the only one. As the neighborhood awoke, more people would wonder what now was going on at the Fender's. Even with the family's newfound respectability, they were once the local pariahs. With that memory, Travis still felt the sting.

As if a tonic to his souring mood, Denesha appeared at the street corner, jogging toward their house. He waved.

But when she neared, she wasn't smiling, wasn't happy to see him. His sinking feeling lowered. Denesha was an easy read, and right now, he read only fear.

44

Maggie put the dogs on the back porch to keep them out of the agents' way. While they didn't seem to mind the nosy beagles sniffing about their equipment and persons, they were probably just being polite. She left the dogs with fresh water and pillows and stepped back in the house.

At the far end of the living room, Denesha stood talking with Travis. She was in her usual running gear with an added jacket. When they saw Maggie, neither seemed in good cheer. She rushed over to find out why.

"Is everything okay?" Their dour expressions told Maggie it wasn't, and she didn't like the options her mind considered.

Denesha bounced on her toes. "It's Sharla. She's still not home."

That wasn't on Maggie's top ten list of horrible happenings, but if it concerned Denesha, it concerned her. "C'mon. Let's go To Travis' office." Maggie put an arm over her friend's shoulder and led the way. "How long has Sharla been gone?"

"I don't know. I saw her the night before last." Denesha said, "We've only recently become friends, but blowing off our plans like that seems out of character. She said she looked forward to it."

"She might've forgotten," Maggie offered her a less dramatic alternative as they entered the office.

The three stood in the middle of the room.

Travis said, "You tried calling her?"

"Yeah. It goes to voice mail. She often keeps the ringer off from what I've seen." Denesha wrapped her finger around a braid. "I peeked in her room. Everything looked normal. I'm not sure what else to do."

He jabbed a finger toward the door. "We've got an entire squad of FBI agents out there, if you need one."

She twisted the watch on her wrist. "No. I don't think it's come to that yet. She might be out enjoying herself—" Her head bobbed. "I mean, she doesn't answer to me."

"What about a boyfriend?" Maggie knew some women who completely flaked out on their friends when men were involved. "Maybe a wild weekend?"

Denesha's shoulders raised, her palms turning up. "She doesn't have a steady, and we talked about having guys over before we became roommates. I didn't want to wake up with strays in the house, and she agreed."

"It's still early." Maggie said, "If she stayed somewhere last night, she probably remembered your plans and is now just embarrassed."

"Or still sleeping," Travis added. "I would be if the feds hadn't arrived."

Denesha's brow furrowed. "Is this about the case you're working?"

"Yes, but I'm sorry. We can't talk about it."

"The agent at the door almost didn't let me in until Travis insisted." Denesha rubbed her hands together. "I'm sorry to bother you with my nonsense."

"Hey. If you're worried, it's not nonsense." Travis was quick to jump in. His black hair dropped to a curtain as he hovered over Denesha. "If there's anything we can do, name it."

She laid her head on his shoulder. "Travis, you're the best." She grabbed Maggie's arm and shook it. "Your sister's all right too." Denesha's smile returned. "I'm sure everything is fine." She tugged down her shirt. "My roomie may not be as reliable as I'd hoped, but we'll see. Benefit of the doubt, baby. Benefit of the doubt."

It was the same thing she'd told Maggie during the months of Travis' ordeal, and she was right.

Denesha hit Travis' shoulder. "Hey, I went looking for the little man this morning out on the bluff. I called to him, but he didn't answer. It was so foggy, though. I couldn't see much ahead of me."

"Yeah, visibility was short." Travis pushed the chair under his desk. "I lost the dogs in the fog as soon as they left the porch." He glanced at both women. "After last night, I'm done chasing the boy. I don't want to be that guy. I'm also done leaving anything I care about on the porch."

"Maybe he lives in a house nearby." Denesha zipped her jacket. "I'd hate to think he was sleeping outside in that area. It's not safe."

"He must have someone around here." Maggie said, "A kid that young couldn't take care of himself, especially outdoors."

"Not likely." Denesha said, "I better get back and start on my homework. Lots to do this weekend." She led the way out of the office and into their living room, abuzz with pent energy. "How long is your house going to be occupied?"

"Not sure." Maggie raised her eyebrows at Travis. "We're along for the ride."

He checked his phone. "We have an appointment this morning. After that, not sure."

They set up the buy for 4 pm UTC, which converted to 9 am in Half Moon Bay. The feds seemed to be done testing their equipment, and now everyone anxiously waited.

Denesha said, "Well, I'm going to get out of the way. Thanks for listening." She hugged Maggie. "I'll let you know how the drama ends."

"I'm sure it will all be fine." Maggie added the platitude without conviction. After witnessing the demise of Yang earlier that week, nothing was a certainty.

They made their way to the front door, and an agent entered with bags of food for the team. Maggie had offered to cook for them, but Travis' cracks about her cooking convinced them to get takeout.

As Denesha put her hands in her jacket pockets and walked toward home, Maggie watched. Across the street, that twit Carl Pinkerton set up camp to watch the Fender's latest disturbance. She smiled, which she hoped would piss him off.

Over at Fyodor's, the place seemed empty, but his car was out front.

Maggie went back in her house, hoping there was a good reason Sharla stood up Denesha. Even Denesha didn't know her well enough to have an opinion. But it was probably a simple explanation.

Other than having Maggie in her life, Denesha didn't attract drama, didn't have that aura of ruin that enveloped the Fenders. Maggie was the misery magnet. In contrast, Denesha was a rock solid half-full optimist. Her world was calm and content.

No reason that should change now.

45

As Sol walked to Denesha's house to get the phone, he felt sick. It was like that time at school when he was shivering, his stomach all flip-floppy. After his teacher took him to see the nurse, they called Mama. He could tell by what the nurse said that Mama didn't want to come get him. It wasn't until the nurse mentioned the police that Mama agreed to pick him up.

Staying on the flat trail was easier, but Sol didn't want anyone finding him. Instead, he climbed down the side of the hill.

He got on the ground and lowered his legs over the edge. His left foot found a toehold, and he tested it before letting down his full weight. His arms stretched as his right foot bounced against loose dirt for a place to rest. Sol kicked his toe in deep until it bit. Winded from the effort, Sol leaned into the hillside to catch his breath.

Working the hill like that got him halfway down until his left foot broke through. Sol clawed at the dirt. His face sliding along in the grit, only the drag of his body slowed his fall to the bottom.

When he landed on his back, Sol heard a crunch. Pain flooded his chest. Something warm trickled down his neck.

He struggled to catch a breath.

The way Sol felt, he had to be dying. He wondered if this was how it was for Mama when she got shot.

As he waited in the dirt for death or darkness to take him, a sharp gasp brought air to his belly, burning his lungs. He tried to sit up but didn't have the strength. He lay there panting until he decided he wasn't going to die.

His head ached like a firecracker exploded inside. He rolled over in the dirt, his empty stomach lurching.

Sol opened his eyes. Sweat rolling off his face, he swiped at his cheeks.

No time for the house with the water hose now. He just wanted Mama's phone.

Only a couple of blocks to Denesha's. He could make it that far.

He took a painful breath in and got his feet beneath him, throwing his arms out for balance as he stood. Sol put one foot in front of the other. His steps were slow and stiff, but he was moving.

Once he was back on the pavement, it was a little easier to walk, but the thumping in his head was just as fierce. He didn't know where Angry Blue Eyes might be, so Sol kept to the edges, moving behind whatever he could find to stay hidden.

When he got to Denesha's street, he checked both ways to make sure no one else was around. Some old, white lady was in the yard digging around some yellow flowers. He tried to run past her house, but Sol couldn't go faster than a skip, which made his chest ache. With each inhale, his chest stung worse than when that scorpion crawled in his shirt.

Sol slowed to ease the pain. Just one more house, and he'd be at Denesha's. Mama's phone was charged by now. Tyrone had to come get him.

When he stepped onto the grass at Denesha's house, he heard the sound of running. He turned to see Denesha bearing down on him, wearing her running clothes and a jacket.

"Yo, little man." She caught him by the arm and twirled to a halt. "I've been looking for—Oh my, God!" The blood on her hand was bright red. "What happened to you?"

"Is that mine?" Sol didn't remember getting cut, but she couldn't stop him now. "I just want my phone. I didn't come for nothing else."

Like her eyes, her mouth was wide open, but she wasn't making any sounds. She touched his back where it hurt, but he kept quiet as best he could so she wouldn't know. He didn't want her up in his business. He needed to get the phone and be on his way.

"Your phone." She didn't look as if she understood him, but she wiped her hand on the grass and said, "We need to clean you up first. Then you can have your phone." Her hand slipped into his. "Can I get you anything? You hungry?"

Sol's throat and stomach still burned from all the puking, but he was powerful thirsty. "Water. I'll take some water."

He didn't resist when her hand gently tugged him toward the front door. She kept looking down at him and then back up, as if she thought he might disappear before they got inside. Her grip was firm but didn't hurt his hand the way Mama's did when she was in a hurry. Or mad.

There weren't any steps up to her door, which made him glad. It was hard enough walking on flat ground. Sol's head thumped like he had a drummer inside, making it feel all swirly. He needed to sit. Drink some water and just sit. Once he did that, he'd be ready to get his phone and leave.

She went in first and closed the door behind him.

Inside, the house was shiny clean. No dirty dishes or clothes lying around. Angry Blue Eyes didn't mess up the place. Sol looked down the hall and figured out where Angry Blue Eyes had been with the knife. He hoped the woman was all right. "You have a roommate."

"I do. Her name is Sharla." She smiled.

Denesha didn't seem worried. That was good.

She led him to a brown sofa with bright green leaves. "Go on. Have a seat, and I'll get you some water."

He looked himself over and stepped back. Mama wouldn't let him sit on a sofa that nice being all dirty like he was. Sol remembered getting mud on a white-striped chair in one of their houses. Mama slapped him so hard, she knocked out his loose tooth.

He checked his hand to make sure it was clean and held onto the couch arm. Sol lowered himself to the floor, his insides feeling crushed. When his bottom finally touched the carpet, his body went slack.

Denesha returned with a pink washcloth and a glass of water. Her forehead scrunched up at him. "Here you go." She leaned down and handed him the glass.

Sol took it in both hands. He wasn't trusting just one hand to hold it steady while he drank. The first sip seemed to sizzle on his tongue. He checked to see if Denesha was still watching him. She was.

But the water was so good, he drank it down in gulps, stopping to catch his breath. The pain in his ribs made him grunt like that opossum poking around his camp. He tried to be quiet, but the aching talked for him.

When he finished the glass, he was still thirsty, but the cold of it made his stomach hurt. He shivered.

"Little man." Denesha sat on the floor next to him. "Sol." She put her hand on his forehead. "You're burning up." She wiped his face with the cool, wet cloth. "Where's your Mama?"

He wished he knew. "Mama's in the city."

She tilted an ear toward him. "What city?"

The water was soaking into him now, and he was feeling a bit revived. Sol didn't want to sit and answer a bunch of nosy questions, even if Denesha was nice. "I just need my phone off the back porch. I can get a ride home."

"Your phone is on my back porch." She leaned against the sofa and spoke softly. "How did it get there?"

Stealing electricity. She might call the police on him, but he needed that phone. "I had to charge the phone, and you have an outlet on the porch."

"I can drive you home. Where do you live?"

He'd rather have Tyrone pick him up. Mama didn't like people knowing where she lived. "I can get a ride."

Denesha pulled her own phone out of a pocket. "Let's just call your Mama right now. What's the number?"

Sol didn't know Mama's number. With every new city, she got a new number. Even if he knew it, it would only ring on the back porch. "I just need my phone, and I'll be on my way."

Her lips pressed together. "You've got cuts and scratches all over you. What happened?"

More questions. Didn't anybody mind their business? "I'm fine."

Her hand felt his forehead. "You're running a fever, Sol. You're not fine."

He didn't feel all that good, but he couldn't stay here. Angry Blues Eyes might come back. "You ain't scared?"

"Scared of what?"

Didn't she know? "That big white man was in here yesterday. I don't want to see him."

"What big white man?"

"He was in there with your roommate." Sol pointed at the door. "He wore a mask and had a knife." Sol had to find out. "Is she okay?"

46

The burly, redheaded agent Travis met earlier at the van took command of the operation inside the Fender home. At his direction, the FBI team completed testing the telecoms, internet bandwidth, and satellite connections via the van in the Fender's driveway, including a connection with someone in Annapolis. Whoever or whatever was on that call, the team in Travis' house now took their instructions from that source.

As Travis paced the living room, he saw a phone number flash across one of the FBI monitors: 410-XXX-XXXX. The prefix and line number were obscured, but the 410 area code tied the caller to Annapolis, MD, home of the US Naval Academy and a quick ride to the nation's capital.

Travis suspected that the Annapolis caller, whether a person or a team, owned the code payload for the transaction. No one at the Fender's would be entrusted with that critical information. Whatever vulnerability the FBI planned to exploit, they would inject their control code at a critical moment, when a firewall was down or credentials were being passed.

Presumably, once the tracking code was released, the FBI could read all the packet information in clear text, without the usual encryption, and gain instant access to the dark web seller's location and internet address. Then they could arrest the person working the keyboard. The trick was to do it before the seller found out and moved his operation.

As they got closer to go-time, the FBI team seemed calm, while the gravity of the operation weighed on Travis like an anchor. His job was simple, but critical. Contact the seller. Execute the transaction. Don't screw up.

No one said that to him in those terms, but Claudia came close. "I'll coordinate with the team. You don't press any keys until I tell you to. Are we clear on this point?" Her stance told him that the question wasn't rhetorical.

"Understood." His head bobbed in assent.

According to Maggie's elbow jabbing into his ribs, maybe his head bobbed a little too vigorously. Probably keeping time with his heartbeat.

Claudia leaned back on a hip. "Don't change the way you communicate with him. Don't use any language you wouldn't normally use." She rubbed her left temple. "I had an informant once who was supposed to text a simple message to his dealer. He turned it into a term paper."

He and Maggie couldn't keep the smiles suppressed. Neither could Claudia.

Travis had to admit the locker room pep talk bolstered his nerves. Claudia must've known he needed it.

"The seller will no doubt tell you how many cryptocurrency coins to transfer, but we want to confirm the current exchange rate before complying."

A female agent with short brown hair called from the table. "T-minus five minutes."

Claudia's attention returned to Travis.

"You just need to let him know you're ready for the transaction. He won't release the files until he confirms the crypto coins are in his wallet."

Travis knew this, but he didn't interrupt.

"I'll check every one of your messages, so wait for my approval before you hit enter on anything."

The theme was consistent. Travis didn't make a move without Claudia's approval. "I got it. Do nothing until you say so."

It was her turn to nod vigorously. She scanned him and Maggie. "We good?"

"Yes, ma'am." Travis clapped his hands together. "We're good."

She patted him on the shoulder as she walked away. "It's time to join us at the table."

Travis glanced at his sister. "Claudia's kind of a badass."

"I like her." Maggie gave Travis' hand a quick squeeze. "I know you told her you're good. But are you?"

He thought of the documents that indemnified him and Maggie from any consequences of this transaction. "We have a get-out-of-jail-free card." He hugged his sister. "We're both good."

Her eyes turned watery, her chin trembling. "Daddy and Trisha would be so proud of you." She wiped a cheek. "I know I am."

Ever since his parents died, Maggie felt some urge to play the replacement in Travis' life. The result was typically awkward.

Not this time. This time, it held meaning.

Any remaining tension fled him. Travis kissed his sister on the forehead and took a deep, satisfying breath as he walked toward the FBI team. It really was his turn to take a place at the table.

The next few minutes passed quickly, if not quietly. While Claudia focused on Travis, the redheaded agent named Gus led the cyber forensic team.

Gus wore a headset and looked a little like Damian Lewis, only tougher. "We are T-minus one minute. Is everyone in place?"

"Aye, sir," came from those round the tables.

"What about our guest?"

"Standing by."

"Comms?" Gus directed this comment to his headset.

Whatever answer he got, the team was apparently ready. Ignoring Travis, Gus's attention moved to Claudia. "It's go time."

Her seat was next to Travis's. She smiled. "Let's buy some stolen property."

"Yes, ma'am."

He opened the Tor browser on his dark web laptop while the FBI monitored and logged all the data packets from his computer. Before each click, he checked with his badass FBI handler. "Good to go?"

"Good to go," she said.

The background conversation around him continued. "Are we tracking?"

"Catching the hops."

As he concentrated on Claudia, their comments faded into ambiance.

The route he took to the dark web changed each time. With the FBI piggybacking off his keystrokes, they could see far more than if he were keeping this trip to the underworld a secret.

He opened his crypto wallet in another window for the transaction. Travis reached the website at the designated time and sent a Claudia-approved message:

On ur porch with coins

The phrase reminded him of the kid Travis chased the other night. Their young porch pirate. It was a shame Denesha couldn't find him. They all wanted to make sure the kid was safe.

"He replied." Claudia's voice snapped him back. "I need you to stay focused."

Travis wasn't sure how long he'd drifted elsewhere. When he looked up at Gus, the redhead glared. Travis checked the message on his screen:

Show me the coins

The seller quickly sent a second message with the address of his wallet and the expected payment. Travis waited while Claudia confirmed the amount.

"Transfer the funds," she said.

He entered the precise crypto coin sum listed by the seller and hit enter. Then, he sent the next approved message:

Wallet filling now

Blockchain technology enabled the trust factor in cryptocurrency exchanges. Blockchain was essentially a distributed accounting system that no one person controlled. Since the information was distributed, no one could change it to his advantage without alerting others in the chain.

When an exchange took place, the transaction was duplicated and recorded across the blockchain. Once enough blocks within the chain confirmed the transaction, the transaction was considered valid, and the funds were released.

Unfortunately, the blockchain confirmation process wasn't instantaneous, making everyone in the Fender house anxious. Baxter paced. The burly redhead in charge of the FBI team reviewed their monitoring as the sweat on his brow beaded.

After an excruciating 43 minutes, the seller replied:

Confirmed. Docs all yours.

Travis downloaded the R-Bot System's schematic files.

Claudia called Baxter over to validate their authenticity. Travis typed:

Verifying

As Baxter reviewed each file, his skin reddened. "These are legit." He backed away from the table.

Claudia kept her attention on Travis. "Let's finish this thing."

He typed a final message to the seller:

As advertised

The seller replied:

Great transaction. Have a nice day :)

Claudia touched Travis' shoulder. "We'll take it from here."

As Travis stood on shaky legs, he spied Maggie on the floor with their beagles. After all the excitement, the dogs slept on a shared pillow. She maneuvered around them and met Travis in the kitchen.

He held out an unsteady hand. "It was more tense than I expected."

"You were awesome, Trav." Her confidence encouraged him.

"Think so?"

"Look around." She gestured toward the hive of investigative activity. "This wasn't a normal Saturday."

He blew out stale air from his lungs. "No, it wasn't."

"Did they catch him?"

Travis scrubbed his hair with his hand. "I don't know. They're still working it, I presume."

Her expression turned serious.

"What's up, Magpie? Did you hear something?"

"No."

"What then?"

"It's probably nothing." She drew her hair away from her face. "There's a white car parked down the street. Seems to be watching the house."

"Who isn't? There's a lot to look at today. Carl Pinkerton probably sold tickets."

She didn't seem convinced. "But it was also here yesterday when Denesha arrived. I've never seen it park there before."

Travis wasn't up for more drama today. He was spent. "Probably lives in the area." He reached for the coffeepot.

She lifted an eyebrow. "Maybe."

From the other room, a hail of cheers thundered. Travis nearly dropped the pot.

Claudia leaned into the kitchen. "We got him."

47

From down the street, Marcus watched all the activity going down at the blonde's house with fresh wonder. There were multiple cars parked out front, but that van alone screamed surveillance. He just wasn't sure what kind. From the way the people acted, it looked like law enforcement, and if it was, Marcus didn't want to get in the middle of it. He already had enough trouble with the law.

But there were enough neighbors watching the goings-on that he could safely observe the action without becoming part of it. He'd cruised by the blonde's house earlier and saw the stream of equipment and people but didn't want to hang around. Too many eyes for his comfort. Instead, he drove by the yellow house on Custer where the blonde's black friend lived.

He believed her when she said she didn't recognize Toya, but if that were true, what was all the interest in this yellow house?

He drove by it again just as the petite sister disappeared into her place. It looked as if someone had gone in ahead of her, but Marcus only saw her. Was probably the roommate.

Marcus wanted to talk to the roommate, and see if she knew Toya, but it was too early for knocking on doors. He waited a moment to see if anyone came out again, but strangers in cars rarely sat well with neighbors. The last thing he needed was someone calling the cops to check on him.

Instead, he drove back to the blonde's house. With all the people and equipment now out of sight, Marcus parked down the road by a stand of trees and waited.

Marcus checked his GPS app for the Honda Civic. Since seeing it in front of the yellow house the evening before, it spent most of the time driving the streets.

The night before, he followed the tatted white dude in the Civic, taking care not to be seen. The car parked near the beach for a while, but Marcus didn't want to track the guy on foot. Again, the Civic drove by the yellow house on Custer, but the driver stayed in the car. Eventually, he found a liquor store, a burger joint, and returned to the motel. At the motel, Marcus saw two other people with the driver—a tall, blond man, and the stocky, black dude from the video at Toya's house. They were all in Half Moon Bay for a reason. But whatever they were looking for, they hadn't found it either.

Just then, the action heated up at the blonde's house, with people streaming out the front door. While Marcus was curious, none of them were Toya, and she was his primary target.

For the first time since tracking Toya, Marcus sensed that this was the end. He'd been close, but he never had this feeling of certainty. As if she'd finally stopped running. There was nothing in this place that he thought would ever hold her interest. Yet Marcus couldn't shake the feeling that Toya's long trail of deceit finally ended.

God, he hated that woman.

48

"A masked man in my house with a knife?" Denesha's eyes bulged at Sol like Mama's did when he was about to get smacked. "Are you sure about this?"

Denesha sounded like she didn't believe him.

Sol's stomach was flip-floppy again. He knew he shouldn't have said nothing. He leaned away from her.

"I haven't seen Sharla in over a day, Sol. When did you see her?" She sounded a little sweeter, but her voice didn't match her squinty face.

"Yesterday. When I plugged my phone into the outlet on your porch." He pulled his legs in toward him.

She reached out a hand to touch his foot. "You're not in trouble. Okay?"

Adults always said that, but it was never true. The banging in his head cranked up.

She stood now and leaned against the sofa. "Just tell me what happened."

"I was by the back door, and I thought I heard a dog crying." Each wheezy inhale brought another pang. "When I got close to the window—" He pointed at the bedroom door. "It was people sounds. So I looked inside." Saying that would surely get him a whooping.

"What did you see?"

"A big white man was in there with your friend. I saw you on the porch with her the other day."

"Sharla. Yes. She's my roommate. I was in her room this morning. Everything looked fine." Her arms crossed. "Tell me about the man with the knife."

"I don't know his name. I've seen him hanging around the beach."

She shut her eyes for a moment. "You said he had on a mask. How do you know what he looked like?"

Sol wasn't going to say anything about the man shooting Mama. She probably wouldn't believe that either. "I'm telling you what I saw."

"A big white man in a mask." She bit her lips. "What kind of knife?"

He tried to remember. "It was shiny."

Denesha said, "Show me which room."

He rolled onto his knees to get up.

"You stay here and rest. Just point. Which room?"

Sol struggled to his feet and walked to the bedroom door.

Denesha followed him and knocked. "Sharla. Are you in there?"

She leaned her ear against the door. She knocked again, only louder. "Sharla."

As Denesha opened the door, Sol entered. It was the room he remembered. Nice and clean like the rest of the house, but in here it was stinky.

"Everything looks fine." She covered her mouth and nose. "But something smells awful. Are you sure you saw her?"

"This is the room. The man with the knife was here, too. He was standing over her. She looked scared." Sol stepped closer to the bed.

"I haven't seen Sharla since the day before." Her head whipped from side to side around the room. Denesha opened the closet. "She's not here, Sol."

Sol held onto to a bedpost and checked under the bed. A woman looked back at him with empty eyes like a pigeon's. The woman he remembered on the porch with Denesha, her eyes smiled. "She's under here."

"Don't say that." Denesha's voice was sharp, not sounding so sweet now. "Get away from there!"

Sol moved toward the door. He knew she must be dead, but somehow, it didn't seem real.

Is that what Mama looked like now? Were her eyes blank like a pigeon's?

Mama never did like those birds.

Denesha squatted down, glancing at Sol another time before peering under the bed.

She scrambled backwards on the blue carpet. She pulled her knees into her chest. Her mouth opened wide like she wanted to scream, but she was quiet. Her head shook, and her eyes clamped closed. Both hands batted the air before she covered her face.

Denesha stayed there, rocking like she had a baby in her lap. When that scream of hers finally shook loose, it pierced his eardrums.

"Ahhhhgh!" She rocked harder, too hard for any baby. "Oh my, God! Sol!"

Sol dropped his chin to his chest. This was his fault. He should've said something.

"Sharla!"

That Sharla seemed like a nice lady. Now he was in big trouble for not telling someone about Angry Blue Eyes. No place was safe. Not San Francisco. Not his camp. Not even this nice, yellow house.

Denesha was saying stuff, maybe to him. He couldn't tell. Her words were all jumbled up with her crying. Sol leaned against the wall to get himself on his feet. He had to get out of here.

He was sorry for Denesha. Sorry about Sharla. But Sol didn't want to give the big white man a chance to kill him, too.

His coughing started up again, but he covered his mouth and kept walking down the hall. As he passed the clean brown sofa with big green leaves, Sol wished he could just lie down on it and sleep for a while. He didn't get much sleep last night with Black Hair chasing him, and all that shaking and sweating before wore him out.

How long had it been since he'd slept on a bed? Or even inside? He didn't know how many days, but it was a long time ago. Not since he was at home with Mama. That seemed like forever.

As Sol stepped outside, he tripped over the threshold, slamming his sore ribs against the hard tile. He gasped. Each short breath felt like a stab to the heart. Sol laid there a moment to rest.

He heard Denesha wailing for her friend. Denesha had been nice to him, but Sol only brought her trouble. Nothing was going right. Not since he picked up that stupid satchel. His thinking was getting all fuzzy. He pressed against the cool tiles to get himself upright and leaned against the wall.

Sol heard the door open, and Denesha burst onto the porch. "Sol. I'm so sorry." She tucked something behind her neck. She leaned over him, resting her hands on her knees. "Are you okay?"

"I'm fine. I'll be going now." He turned to leave, but she caught him by the hand.

"You can't leave." Her words came fast now, but her voice echoed in his ears. "You're sick. You need a doctor."

Doctors. They asked even more questions. Like everything was their business. Mama only took him to one when she had to for school shots. Even then, he wasn't allowed to answer anything. No matter the question, he didn't know the answer.

He pulled away from Denesha, but her grip tightened. He struggled to break free, but he was tired, and everything hurt. "Let me go."

She held him even tighter. "I called the police. You need to stay with me until—"

Her crying took over and got louder than her words. Sol couldn't understand the rest of her sentence.

But he was done with Denesha. Done with Angry Blue Eyes. Done with Half Moon Bay. He just wanted out.

The police were coming. He had to get away. He'd get the phone later.

Mama had a lot of rules. Some he didn't like at all. But one rule she made him swear to. She made him swear that he'd never hit a girl. Maybe she didn't want Sol hitting her back, or maybe she didn't like the way Tyrone and the others hit her.

But right now, Mama wasn't here to help him.

Sol reared back with his right leg and kicked Denesha square in the shin.

On impact, she sucked in air as if she were drowning. Her hand let go of his arm and felt for the wound on her leg.

He felt bad about kicking her, but she had no business keeping him there. Sol tried to run, but his body wouldn't let him go far today. He wheezed and dropped into the grass by the sidewalk.

"Sol. Wait!" Denesha hopped around on the porch. "I'm sorry."

He was sorry too. Sol checked behind him, and even with her hurt leg, Denesha limped up to him. He looked down the street. A car neared the house. By the time Sol saw Angry Blue Eyes in the front seat, it was too late.

49

The atmosphere at the Fender house turned jubilant. Conversation skittered among the agents, while Claudia hustled Maggie and Travis outside for a briefing.

They stood on the porch, as the dogs wandered the beach.

Claudia said, "I'm not at liberty to divulge all that we know about the seller, but it was the same person we'd been tracking. Until today, we didn't know his name."

Maggie had a thousand questions. No doubt Travis had more. "Where's he from?"

"We traced him to a location on the East Coast. Brighton Beach. We alerted the New York office, and they're assembling a team to arrest him."

Brighton Beach. Hearing the name stilled Maggie's heart. Probably a beautiful place with lovely people, but it was also the turf of the Russian mob. Her encounter with Vladimir Penniski left her acutely aware of their existence.

Travis voiced her concern, "Organized crime or a lone Russian gangster?"

"Too soon to tell, but given the product he was selling, he had to have associates. No one thinks the man at the keyboard was in charge."

While Travis asked more questions, Maggie dropped into a chair and stared at the crashing waves. Nothing ever changed. There was always someone desperate or evil enough to prey on others for financial gain.

It was just business.

R-Bot Systems—the mark was just another faceless corporation. A robotics company, no less, out to replace humans with machines. What was there to consider? No humanity required. The crushing impact on people held no weight.

But Yang had a face before it turned to vapor. Maggie remembered it. Maple colored, with intelligent, almond eyes, sensuous lips ever ready with a smile, as if they carried a secret.

Perhaps they did.

"Maggie." Travis's voice sounded stern. "Claudia wants to know about Vladimir."

Of course she did. Maggie shrugged. "There's not much to tell."

Claudia sat next to Maggie in their father's chair. "Indulge me."

Maggie gave her the verifiable version. The role her father played in the scandal was never made public. "Vladimir Penniski was one of Paddy O'Mara's jilted investors. My father was abducted by a man named Jack Scarson, but at one time, I thought Penniski might be the reason he was missing."

"You wouldn't be the first to accuse Penniski. They believe he killed Barney Reid, but they don't have enough evidence to arrest him. He's been especially careful since his release from prison. Hired a media team to rebrand his image."

"Maggie went to see him." Travis leaned against a pillar and grinned.

"Really." Claudia's shoulders squared toward Maggie. "Do tell."

Maggie discreetly stepped on Travis's foot to let him know his commentary wasn't appreciated. "We had a conversation about the matter. That's all. He said he wasn't involved with my father's abduction, and he was telling the truth."

While her father died anyway from the trauma, Vladimir helped him escape Scarson's noose. But only because killing her father didn't serve Vlad's purpose. Maggie wasn't sharing that story with anyone.

Travis was quick to change the subject. "So what next? Will you be able to reclaim the crypto payment?"

"We've got people working on that right now, but we want to secure the suspect first." Claudia rose and stretched. "Sorry. Long morning."

Travis called the dogs, and the beagles trotted over. Claudia held out a hand to each dog. They obliged her with wet noses. "I should get inside. The team will need to tear down and get our gear out of your house. Let you get back to your Saturday." She seemed to study Maggie. "We appreciate your cooperation. We'll tell you what we can as we develop the case."

She glanced at the eaves above Travis. "I notice you have some cameras out here. Smart idea."

Maggie hated the idea of having to live with surveillance, but the beach attracted many people and some unsavory characters. Given their family history, it served a purpose.

Travis shifted and pointed at the camera above Claudia. "We had a little trouble out here. Some stuff taken off the table."

"I'm sorry to hear that. Did you call the police?"

Travis blushed. "It wasn't a big crime. Just a kid swiping stuff."

"A kid. How old?" Claudia exhibited professional curiosity. "What was missing?"

"Maybe 8 or 9." His attention focused on their father's chair. "He took a jean jacket off that chair. Way too big for him."

"And some food." Maggie said, "Stuff left out from dinner." She could see Claudia processing the details. Even a petty crime held her interest. "The kid returned the food dishes. But the jacket is still missing. Hardly worth calling the cops over." Travis was far more upset over the incidents than was Maggie.

"I understand your reluctance." Claudia took a formal posture. "But crime is crime. A swift bit of justice by a loving parent at 8 or 9 could change the kid's future. Does he live around here?"

She had a point. "We don't know." Maggie tossed her hair behind a shoulder. "Travis followed him last night, but he ran away."

"I'm not sure he's got a home." Travis pushed off from the support pole. "We caught him on video late at night. Too late for a kid his age to be out alone."

"Can I see it? The video."

He scrubbed Bailey's head. "Well, sure, but it's not much." Belli came to get a turn. "In fact, the video doesn't show him taking anything. But Maggie's friend saw him on the beach wearing my dad's jacket."

Maggie thought it was much ado, but she led the way.

Inside their home, the FBI team was disconnecting their equipment. Baxter stood in the far corner and talked on the phone. His expression was the most relaxed she'd seen all day, but even with the success of this operation, this wasn't over for him.

Or Maggie. They still had a spy inside R-Bot Systems. Like taking out a drug dealer, finding the dark web seller didn't interrupt the supply or demand of stolen company secrets. It was just another skirmish in the war.

She wondered if this business she and Travis had started was worth it. Until Yang was killed, she never doubted. She'd only considered the adventure. After years as the family caretaker, her new role was exhilarating. But now, she and Travis were stalking a grade schooler. It brought her back to the low days, when she didn't know who she could trust.

If anyone.

As promised, Baxter brought all the new equipment to replace the components the FBI planned to keep for evidence. Travis' dark web laptop was now a link in the FBI evidence chain in the case against the man from Brighton Beach. Travis disappeared into his office.

Claudia went to Baxter's side when his call ended. Maggie enjoyed watching them interact, but it made her wistful. She hadn't seen Fyodor since the night at the shooting range, when he basically dumped her. Well, moved on if not dumped. They actually had to be a couple before she could get dumped.

She thought the success of this operation would cheer her, but so far, her mood was sliding downhill on a double-diamond run.

Travis returned with his video laptop. Maggie sat next to him and dropped her head on his shoulder. "You did good, little brother."

He smirked whenever she called him that. He patted the top of her head. "We make a fine team."

The video software fired up and Maggie watched again as the cute kid with short dreads tiptoed around their porch near the wall. What was he looking for? Their last viewing sent Travis out the door in a heated rush. This time, he just seemed sad.

Claudia broke off her conversation with Baxter and joined them on the couch. "Clint Masters wants to express his appreciation to you both for your participation in this operation. I'm sure Baxter will elaborate when he can."

Maggie read up on Masters. One of the better corporate types.

Travis restarted the video and hit the play button. Claudia watched intently as the boy came into view from the southwest corner of the house. He was probably coming from the beach. The time stamp listed 10:37 pm.

She said, "He is young."

The boy came onto the porch and looked around. When a dog barked from inside the house, the boy ran away.

Claudia tapped the table, "Would you start it over? And go to the shot when he first enters the property." Her expression turned grave. She searched for something on her phone. As the boy came into view, she said, "Stop. Now zoom in on his face."

In this view, he seemed older, even tired.

Claudia held up a photo of the same kid from the video. "His name is Solomon Price."

Travis pushed his hair back with both hands. "How do you know?"

She sighed. "Someone shot and killed his mother in San Francisco Monday morning. Happened on the street. We believe the boy was with her, but he fled the scene. On top of being traumatized, he's listed as a critical missing."

50

As the car approached the yellow house, Gilbert heard distant sirens start their familiar moans. Even if the cops weren't coming this way, the kid was all over the news. Gilbert didn't have time to question him here. Not with the dead girl in the house.

The kid and a woman sat on the grass by the sidewalk.

Gil had some tie wraps loosely zipped for such an opportunity. "Stop at the house. Those two are coming with us."

"You just need the kid," Rocco said.

"Witnesses, dumbass." Gilbert hated explaining himself. "Pop the trunk. We gotta be fast."

Rocco was loyal, but no one could accuse him of being smart. The tattoo on his neck proved that. Instead of the word "friend," the tattooist inked "fiend." Rocco didn't notice until someone pointed out the missing 'r'.

He jammed the brakes in front of the house.

When Gilbert jumped out, the woman looked up at him and screamed. He hit her on the jaw, jarring her long enough to lift her by the waist.

Gilbert clapped a hand over her mouth. With her whole body, she thrashed. But she didn't weigh enough to break his grip. He slammed her into the open trunk.

Yanking her arms behind her back, he pressed her face into the carpet. A smart girl like her probably knew there was a quick release inside the trunk. Couldn't risk her crawling out at a stoplight. After cinching the tie wrap around her wrists, he slammed the trunk shut.

Let her scream in there.

The kid was too frightened to move. Or too sick. Gil grabbed him under the armpits. The kid's body was warm, his clothes damp and smelling of

179

sweat. Gilbert didn't bother with the restraints and dropped him onto the back seat.

Gilbert slid in next to the kid. The operation took sixty seconds. The sirens grew louder. Gilbert slapped the headrest behind Rocco.

"Drive!"

51

While Marcus watched the action at the blonde's house, he also monitored the Civic on his tracker app after it left the hotel. It drove around the beach area and eventually returned to the yellow house on Custer. Marcus thought little of it, but then the car stayed out front longer than a drive-by. He fired up his Hyundai rental and drove over in time to catch the Civic on the move.

From what he could see, there were two people in the car. One in the front and one in the back, which was odd, but Marcus kept his distance.

He followed the car out the other side of the neighborhood, just as he heard sirens screeching in the distance. The Civic took the Cabrillo Highway south. He expected it to resume its normal pattern, essentially a grid search of the area, with occasional diversions to the beach or back to the motel. But it stayed on the highway.

This was a break from any of its previous activity. Maybe they gave up looking for Toya and were headed back to the city. But the car passed Highway 92, which would've been the fastest route over the range to the valley.

During his time in town, Marcus scouted the area by driving during the day and by checking satellite maps on his laptop at night. While there were a thousand smaller roads within the hills, there were few routes from the coast to the valley. Most roads that ascended toward Skyline Boulevard dead-ended near the top.

The Civic eventually turned east onto Tunitas Creek Road. While Marcus could tail it, it was a two-laner with no markings and no shoulder. Any half-observant driver would see him—even one with nothing to hide. He didn't want to risk it. Plus, with the tracker, he could find the car anytime.

Marcus stayed on Cabrillo after the Civic turned. He'd go back to the blonde's neighborhood and see what was happening. Something big was going down at her house, and he intended to find out what it was. Maybe he'd stop by the yellow house again. He wanted another chance to talk to the petite sister who lived there. Marcus had a growing feeling that she could lead him to Toya.

52

"You pick up any tails since we've been in town?" Gilbert watched the white car in the rearview mirror.

"No. I've been clean the whole time," Rocco said.

Gilbert saw the car earlier that day driving near the hotel and spotted it again when it followed them from the dead girl's house. The big, black dude was the same one they marked in Toya's house. Had to be.

His moves were pretty good, but Gilbert's were better. When Rocco turned off the main road, the other car turned too, before dropping completely out of sight. The road uphill was too small not to be seen. But how did he find them?

He wasn't a cop, but he was looking for something. Maybe the satchel. If the guy was following their car, he didn't have it yet.

Gil thought for sure it would be at the yellow house, but he searched everywhere. Most people aren't that good at hiding things. It takes a pro to make things disappear.

The cops might be at the yellow house now. Someone may have seen the kid and girl get snatched. But they hadn't found the dead girl's body. If they had, there'd be no end to the yellow tape and ruckus. Leaving her under the bed added the time he hoped to gain. But after twenty-four hours, a corpse can't hide if there's anyone around with a decent sense of smell.

Rocco glanced in the back seat. "Gil. Where are we going?"

"Just drive."

Gilbert warned Rocco not to say their names. He'd remind him later. Right now, they needed to get to their new base of operation and find out what the kid did with the leather case. After that, they were all expendable. Even Rocco, if he didn't keep his mouth shut.

The kid was facing the front of the car, but he didn't move. Gilbert had been tracking him for six days and still didn't have the satchel. Augie was out of patience. Gilbert had to end this today. A punk kid shouldn't be this much trouble.

Gilbert took a closer look at him. His face was streaked where sweat etched the grime. Maybe he'd been sleeping rough. The odor already made its way to Gilbert's nose, reminding him of a fast food dumpster. He cracked the window to let in some fresh air. He pictured the moment they made eye contact on the street. The kid was wearing the same shirt and jeans he had on Monday when it all went down on the street.

Sol. That was his name. What was he to the little black mama in the trunk? If she was taking care of him, she was doing a piss-poor job.

The road took a long upward slope for the first mile or so, winding through pastures and open space, while the Santa Cruz Mountains loomed ahead. Down the driveways they passed, houses might be worth millions or rotting in place. As they climbed, the road narrowed, the ravines deepened, and the trees grew thicker and closer together.

Gilbert never wasted expensive shoe leather when an internet search from his couch and access to a cold beer would suffice. After his arrival, he'd scoured satellite images of the local area to find well-concealed and unoccupied properties to take the kid to if needed. But Gilbert wasn't an outdoor guy. He needed some kind of building to use as their base. He searched property records and found those with structures and learned which were owned by out-of-towners or which were foreclosures now owned by the bank.

He'd narrowed his choices down to three remote locations for an on-site investigation. When a pack of dogs greeted him at the first place, he made a hasty U-turn. Whoever was there wanted the same privacy as Gilbert. Maybe growing dope or cooking meth. Either way, he left them to their work.

At the second location, he found an old cabin that met all of his requirements. The trees and growth obscured even the entrance. It had a rickety gate with a rusted lock and chain that hadn't opened in months. He busted the chain off the gate rail. His reconnaissance showed no sign of human life, and the cabin was big enough for his needs. Plus, it would take an explosion for any noise to reach the nearest neighbor.

As they traveled deeper into the forest, Gilbert couldn't see much past the trees, but he followed the directions back to the cabin. Deep in the forest, it was located off an old fire trail, where he could practice the brutal art of persuasion in private.

Beside him, the kid crashed like a frat boy during pledge week. At first, Gilbert thought he was just quiet until he heard the snoring. His breathing was wheezy, labored, unhealthy. Whatever he had, Gilbert didn't want to catch it. He needed to find the damn satchel and get back to his city. He missed the action and that willing redhead at the card room. Whatever her name was.

His mind drifted to the black dude in the white car. Gilbert mulled over the situation. What if there was a new player? The case sat in police lockup so long, he couldn't be sure of anything.

Or anyone.

He stared at Rocco in the front seat, but Rocco didn't know enough to be a threat.

How did the black guy from Toya's house find them here? Gilbert was already in Half Moon Bay before the video was recorded. The dude must've tailed Rocco.

Gil's gaze drifted downward along the dashboard. "Stop the car."

Rocco said, "What for?"

"Stop the damn car!"

Rocco pulled over on the edge of a ravine and stepped out the driver's side. "What the hell?"

Gilbert climbed over the kid and got out of the car. He looked under the dash of the Civic.

There it was.

"Dammit, Rocco!" He pulled an electronic device out of the OBD port of the car, normally used for engine diagnostics. "You've been driving around with a freaking GPS tracker! How long?"

Gil didn't wait for an answer. He dropped the unit on the road and ground it into the pavement with his heel. But now he understood. He felt for his gun strapped to his ankle. The black dude wasn't simply competition, he was a threat.

53

In his living room, Travis stared out a window that had a view of the surf. Hearing sirens in the neighborhood always gave him a fresh case of dread. The day they arrested him for hacking, he barely noticed them, until they pulled into his driveway. Maybe one day he wouldn't assume they were coming for him. But the chilling sound diverted a couple of streets away, and Travis could again breathe.

He knew it wasn't a rational thought. He just assisted a houseful of FBI agents in a successful sting. The Fender family made peace with law enforcement. Or vice versa. In time, the accusing memories would fade.

Maggie came to his side and looked out the adjacent window. "So the kid's really in trouble." She interlaced her fingers, touching them to her lips. "I feel terrible."

Her comments shifted his thoughts to Sol. With this episode, Travis felt the weight of new, accusing memories.

After watching his mother get shot on the streets, the Fender home should've been a safe haven for the kid. Instead, Travis' obsession with a jacket drove the kid deeper into hiding and further from rescue.

He kicked at the wooden floor. "You're not the one who made him run for his life."

Maggie's head tilted toward him. "Stop it." She glared. "I mean it. Stop it. We didn't know."

"I just hope we find him fast." He closed the curtain. "You know I don't love sirens."

She pointed toward the source of the noise. "Those can't be for the kid. For Solomon." Her stance softened. "Claudia's still on the phone arranging a search team."

"I'd join them, but I'm not sure he'd trust me."

"Or anyone after what he's been through." She frowned. "He's so young."

The sirens ended as abruptly as they started. Travis wondered where they landed in the neighborhood. Sirens never brought good news.

Maggie released her blonde hair from the ponytail and ran her fingers through it. "It's not even noon, and it's been a wild Saturday."

"I'm ready to grab a guitar and chill." He turned toward the FBI team, still disassembling and packing their gear. "Not happening too soon."

From across the room, Claudia motioned for them to join her near the kitchen table. Maggie led the way.

Claudia said, "We've alerted the local PD and the sheriff's department about the boy. They will take point on the search." She addressed Travis. "Since you had direct contact with him, they'll want to interview you. Do you know if anyone else spoke to him?"

"Yes." Maggie said, "My friend Denesha talked with him briefly. She was concerned about his welfare. We all were. She tried to find out more about him, but he ran away."

"They will definitely want to speak with her. Would you let her know to contact an Officer Standish at the Half Moon Bay PD? He's coordinating the search."

"Of course." Maggie glanced at Travis. Standish had questioned Travis in a previous encounter.

More glorious memories.

A knock came at the porch door, which wasn't common. The beagles woke from their nap and stuck their noses around the curtain to see who was outside. Wagging tails told him it was not foe, but friend. Travis padded over to the door. With the happenings this past week, his friend Javier was a welcome diversion. Travis met him on the porch, Bailey and Belli in tow.

"Dude." Travis fist-bumped his friend. "Busy doings around here."

"Can't stay long, and you look busy." Javie leaned against the house. "SWAT move in?"

"All but the sniper rifles." Travis said, "They're clearing out now."

"You catch your thief?"

"Which one?" His head lowered. "Remember the kid who was swiping stuff off the porch? He's been on the lam. His mom was killed in a shooting."

"No joke?" Javie tensed as if he was ready for a fight. As the eldest of his many siblings, he was also their staunchest protector. "That's stone cold."

Travis gave Javie a rundown on the video and his own search for the kid.

"You didn't know, man," he said. "Who's looking for him?"

Travis jacked a thumb toward the house. "Calling out the cavalry as we speak. Standish is in charge."

Javie grimaced. "Wow. Bad draw."

"I had the same thought."

Travis heard a ringtone, Boyz II Men's A Song for Mama, and Javier fished his phone out of his back pocket. He said, "Hang on, it's Mom."

Travis walked off the porch to find his pups. With all the commotion in his house, he didn't want them to roam. He whistled once, and both dogs bounded to his side.

Javier finished his call.

Travis didn't like the look on his face. "Is everything okay?"

Javie tucked the phone in his jeans. "The cops are at Denesha's."

The sirens from earlier, he knew they were nearby. "Denesha's. For what?"

He grabbed Travis' arm. "Be careful what you tell Maggie, but Mom heard there were cops all over the place."

The words made no sense. Why would the cops be at Denesha's? She didn't even drive fast.

"Carl Pinkerton told her that someone reported a murder."

Murder. Couldn't be murder. Not at Denesha's.

Travis broke free from his friend. "I gotta go."

"Sorry, man." Javie said. "Let me know what we can do."

The Modestos rode shotgun for every Fender family drama, scouting the rough terrain. "Thanks, bro." Travis clapped his friend's shoulder and went inside.

The FBI agents were taking down the tables and lugging equipment out to the van. The dogs went for refreshment at their water bowls, while Travis searched for Maggie.

He went upstairs and knocked on her door. "Magpie, you in there?"

"C'mon in." Her back was to him. As he entered, she turned. "I just needed a quiet mo—"

She scrambled to Travis' side. "What's happened? Is the boy okay? Did they find Solomon?"

He had to ease her into this. "Javie was here. Now don't freak out." His words had the opposite effect.

"Freak out! Over what?" Panic strained her voice. "Just tell me, dammit!"

"I don't know anything specific, but it's not about Solomon."

His sister seemed both relieved and perplexed. "Not about Solomon. Then what's wrong?"

He drew in a deep lungful of air. "Javie was here. He said the police are at Denesha's. Someone reported a murder."

Maggie hesitated only briefly, then bolted from the room. She was down the stairs and on the street, running to Denesha's, before he caught up to her.

"Slow down," he called. "I'm coming with you."

But she only ran faster. Down one street onto the next.

Before they turned the corner onto Denesha's road, police lights bounced off houses and trees confirming Javie's grim news. Travis' gut momentarily seized. Maggie surged ahead.

With so many vehicles and people blocking the road, he couldn't tell if Denesha's house was the center of the tragedy.

Patrol cars and ambulance surrounded the home, keeping all traffic diverted. Directly behind them, the short squawk of another siren announced the arrival of an unmarked police unit. Travis caught Maggie by the hand and pulled her to the sidewalk so the car could pass.

Across the street, spectators swarmed. The officers among them no doubt worked to gather witness accounts, gather evidence, and piece together events.

A murder.

Travis held his breath as he scanned for a body.

Maggie hesitated, then rushed toward an officer on the front lawn. He took a step forward as she approached. "Hold up, ma'am. This is a crime scene."

Behind him, officers cordoned off the area.

"My friend Denesha lives here. Where is she?"

He maintained his stance. "I'm Detective Montenegro from the San Mateo County Sheriff's Department." He had a pad with him. "What's your name, ma'am?"

"Maggie. Margaret Fender." She leaned into her brother. "This is my brother, Travis."

The detective took the information and offered no reaction, no recognition of Travis' name. Maybe his notoriety with law enforcement was yesterday's news.

"Where do you live?"

"A few blocks over." She gave them the address.

"What's Denesha's last name?"

"Roberts."

"Does she live alone?"

"No. Her roommate lives with her. Sharla. Sharla—" Maggie gripped Travis' shoulder. "I don't know her last name."

Travis said. "Denesha is a family friend. The two women recently rented this place." He rested a hand on Maggie's back. "We barely know Sharla, but we're very close to Denesha. What happened?"

The detective was about the same age as Baxter. He wore slacks and a golf shirt with the unit's logo. He addressed his comments to Maggie. "Please describe your friend and her roommate for me."

Maggie trembled beneath Travis' touch but complied with the request, describing Denesha in great detail, with a far shorter sketch of Sharla.

"I'm sorry, ma'am. This appears to be a homicide, and based on your information, we believe the victim is—"

Travis felt Maggie stiffen.

"—Sharla. Do you know the whereabouts of her roommate, Denesha?"

Before either of them could answer, an officer from across the street jogged over to the detective, who excused himself.

Maggie's eyes didn't seem to focus. "Sharla's dead." She covered her mouth. "My God."

Detective Montenegro rejoined them. "I'm sorry, ma'am, but an elderly neighbor witnessed the abduction of a young African-American woman and a boy. They were forced into a car in front of this house about thirty minutes ago." He hesitated. "The woman is likely your friend, Denesha, but you didn't mention a boy living at the home. Who is he?"

"Abduction." Maggie repeated the word without emotion. Travis knew she was numb.

"Was the boy her son?" The detective diverted his attention to Travis. "Was she in a custody battle?"

"No. The boy wasn't Denesha's."

It was the right answer, but not the complete answer. It had to be Solomon. Travis wasn't sure where to start with that story or what it had to do with their abduction.

The detective didn't give him time to respond. "I need to know if Denesha had any enemies."

54

Maggie squeezed Travis's hand. "Enemies. Denesha didn't make enemies." The only enemies around were Maggie's. "Everyone loves her."

"I'm sure they do, ma'am." The detective tapped his pad. "What can you tell me about the boy? If it's not her son, who is he?"

Images of the past week flooded Maggie's senses, drowning sights and sounds. Solomon scouting their back porch. Denesha's excitement about school. Yang's last smile.

Sharla. Maggie met Sharla once. Lovely woman. Now, all the memories Maggie conjured were grisly.

When the deluge receded, she heard Travis' voice.

"—critical missing. Officer Stanton is mounting a search of the bluffs, but it appears now that Solomon was kidnapped. Along with our friend." He said it calmly, without a detectable hint of fear.

Maggie let go of Travis' hand, wiggling her fingers to return some feeling. She needed a serious grip on her emotions. Losing it wouldn't help Denesha or Solomon. Poor Sharla was beyond help.

The officer searched on his pad. "Solomon Price, right?"

Even with her new resolve, words were slow to form on her tongue. Travis beat her to them. "That's his name. He's been missing since Monday when his mother was murdered." He gestured toward their house. "The FBI agents at our house might have more information."

Detective Montenegro stood a little taller. "And why do you have FBI agents at your home this morning?"

Maggie sustained herself with a sharp intake of air. "You're welcome to ask them, but we're not at liberty to say."

"I intend to." He called to an officer. "Take their statements. I need to have a chat with the FBI."

Over the next thirty minutes, Maggie and Travis answered questions independently

No, she didn't ever meet Solomon in person.

No, she wasn't aware of anyone stalking Denesha.

No, they didn't know Sharla's next of kin.

When Maggie and Travis could finally leave, they compared their conversations with the police as they walked home.

"They want a copy of the video, but I told them they'd have to ask the FBI." Travis stretched his neck to the sides. "Dude wasn't happy about that."

"They asked me a million times if I saw anything. Kept telling them I arrived after they did." Maggie picked up the pace. "Sol probably saw the person who killed his mom, but why would they take Denesha too?" She inhaled, her lungs filing with fear. "Should I call her mother?"

"No." Travis stopped his sister in mid-stride. "Let the police handle this." He hesitated. "Be the one who comforts them, not the one who brings them devastating news."

She knew he was right, but she hated the thought of Denesha's family hearing this news from the police. But her parents would want to know about the investigation, and Maggie couldn't answer those questions.

"Let's get home." She hit his arm with a backhand and broke into a run.

When they got to their house, Detective Montenegro was leaving. Claudia's car was still out front.

Maggie and Travis entered their home. All evidence of the morning cyber sting was gone, except for Claudia, who rubbed Bailey's tummy. She looked up. "I think they need to go out, but I wasn't sure what the rules were for them."

Travis called for Belli and let them out the back door. Maggie sat next to Claudia.

"Baxter had to leave, and I didn't want your house unattended. Given what transpired, I'm glad I was here." Her brow furrowed. "How are you holding up?"

Thread barely.

Instead of answering, Maggie said, "Do the police know anything about the abductor?"

"Not really. Two men. A blond and another Caucasian. They have a vague description of the car but no license plate. The only eyewitness is an elderly woman. They've asked us to assist, so we will."

Travis joined them. "Did you give them a copy of the video?"

"Yes. It may not give them much to go on, but it confirms that Solomon Price was in the area. The photo on his missing notice was fairly recent, and it matches the boy in the video. The police found a phone charging on your friend's back porch, which was confirmed to be his mother's. We believe Solomon Price was abducted with your friend Denesha."

"She went looking for him today." Travis said, "She walked with him the other day. We didn't know he was a missing child."

"His mother used a variety of false identities. It took the San Francisco police a while to tie her to an item picked up from Lost and Found."

"Lost and Found." Maggie hadn't heard this part. "What item?"

Claudia leaned forward to stretch. "Three months ago, the boy found a leather satchel in Blackburn Park that contained $8,500. An officer was in the area, and the boy turned it over to him. Ninety days later, since no one claimed it, the kid and his mother picked it up from SFPD. She was shot on the street just a few blocks away."

"Is the money tied to her murder?" Travis took a wide stance. "How did anyone know they were claiming it that day? And who lost it?"

Claudia offered a wan smile. "All good questions. We have a team assigned to the search for your friend and the boy."

More questions seemed to occupy Travis. For Maggie, this day had worn out its welcome. After their success in uncovering the dark web seller, it morphed into a nightmare.

Maggie recently lost her father. She didn't know what she'd do if she lost Denesha.

Claudia stood. "I'll keep you posted with whatever I can share. Anything you see or think of that might provide some answers, let me know. We aim to bring everyone home safely."

She said it with conviction, which tempered Maggie's urge to freak out. She had to keep it together for Denesha.

There was little left for Claudia to carry out of their house, just a shoulder bag and a small case. They walked with her to her car.

Travis said, "I've got some ideas on the spy at R-Bot, but nothing concrete. I'll let you know if I can confirm anything."

"You did good work today, Travis. My team was very impressed with you. Maybe when you're older, you'll consider applying to the FBI."

His face flushed. "Maybe I will. Thanks."

What started as a great day for him was now shaded by tragedy. Apparently, that was the family theme. Something to depict in the Fender coat of arms.

After Claudia drove off, Maggie lingered outside, wondering how long Denesha's house would be a crime scene. Maggie left before they brought out the body. No doubt Carl Pinkerton stayed for that show.

Down the street, a white sedan turned toward Denesha's. The car that parked down Maggie's street was white.

Yeah. That white car and the thousand others in her neighborhood. Maggie was officially seeing ghosts. Her nerves were frayed and threatening to unravel.

She went inside to where Travis was on his computer. He was in 'the zone,' a familiar state, and she left him to do his thing.

The agents put the kitchen back in reasonable order before they left, so Maggie took the dogs outside for a romp in the surf while she let her head clear.

But her thoughts were too thick to dissipate. The police didn't seem to have any concrete leads in the abduction. Did they expect a ransom note, or were the kidnappers after something else? If Denesha wasn't of value to them, how long would they keep her alive?

An icy stroke of fear chilled her spine. Denesha was too tiny to fend off anyone.

And the boy, Solomon. Regret steeped in her soul on his account. He'd been on his own for days with no help from them. They'd accused and condemned, but hadn't offered him any comfort. She wished she could have a do-over on that one.

Belli scampered back to her long enough to nuzzle Maggie's hand.

They tried to reach the boy, especially Denesha. But he was too afraid to trust anyone. After seeing his mother gunned down on the street, who could blame him?

The day was a chaotic mix, and Maggie couldn't solve anything by staring at the sand. She called the dogs and returned with them to the house.

Travis still exhibited an intensity to his work, so she left him alone and wondered where she could apply her restless energy.

If she did something to help find Denesha, the knot it her belly might loosen. But not today. Not unless someone found her safe.

Maggie decided to walk to Denesha's, to see if there was any news. She left by the front door.

That white car was parked down the street again. She saw it first when Denesha came over for dinner. It seemed to haunt her street ever since. But the police said someone in a silver car abducted Denesha, not a white one.

Someone was sitting in the front seat, and it was a public street. The car had a right to be there.

But no law said Maggie couldn't demand to know what the hell it was doing.

She ran upstairs and strapped the KelTec .380 holster around her ankle, covering it with her pant leg. Carrying it wasn't legal, but if the guy down the street was a danger, she wasn't going quietly.

55

Gilbert paced in the middle of the lonely country road, trying to figure out his next move. After finding the GPS tracker in the OBD port of their car, he wanted to shoot Rocco in the head for being that stupid. Dwayne, too.

The black guy driving the white car had to be the one seen at Toya's. He was in a taxi that day. Somehow, he got the tracker installed in Rocco's ride. Did that guy lie in wait at her house?

Probably hired the same crew in Toya's 'hood that Rocco and Dwayne paid to watch the house.

Enterprising bastards.

Can't trust anyone.

Gilbert kicked a pine cone into a ditch.

Which meant the guy in the white car had been tracking their Civic for days. The implications snapped together like magnets. The Civic had been to the motel, to the yellow house with the dead girl. Did the guy see Gilbert snatch the boy and the woman?

If so, he might still follow or call the police.

But he wouldn't call the cops if he was looking for the satchel.

With the GPS tracker, he could bide his time and attack when Gil didn't expect it.

The guy knew the Civic's license plate number, so Gil had to torch the car, but not until they were done. Smoke coming out of the forest attracted the wrong attention.

This black dude was nothing but trouble, and now he was Gilbert's prime target.

While the guy showed up at Toya's in a cab, he probably rented a car to come this distance—that white car. Even Rocco wasn't dumb enough to miss a yellow cab on his ass.

The tracker was off the Civic, but what about Gil's Chrysler?

He got on his phone and called Dwayne at the motel. "You see anyone on your tail? Here or in the city?"

"No, man. Would've reported that."

Dwayne was smarter than Rocco, but a toad could step over that bar.

"Think, man! A white car. Driven by a black guy."

"Maybe." Dwayne said, "There was a guy in the parking lot of the motel when we arrived. Saw him again the next day. But I figured he was staying there."

Gilbert's palms began to sweat. "Now listen carefully. You need to go out to my ride and check the OBD port. You know what that is?"

"Yeah. What am I looking for?"

"Anything plugged into it. Go now and call me back."

"On it."

Gilbert got back in the car. "Wait here," he snapped at Rocco.

The moments passed in silence.

Finally, Gilbert's phone rang. "Talk to me."

"Nothing plugged in. What next?"

Gilbert exhaled a long, anxious breath. "Good. That's good." He tightened his hand into a fist. "You clear our rooms and check out of the motel."

They'd used fake IDs and stolen credit cards, but the black dude was pretty smart. If he'd followed them this far, he was also dangerous.

"Pay the bill in cash. I'll send you a list of supplies to pick up. Then get your ass out here fast. You have the location locked on GPS?"

"Sure do."

"Good. It's tough to find otherwise. And make damn sure you're not followed. If you see that car again, I want to know about it." He didn't wait for a reply.

Gil considered his options, if he didn't get the information from the kid quickly. There was nothing up in the cabin but a few decrepit sticks of furniture and an old dog kennel. While no one was going to sleep until this was over, his crew might need some basic supplies. He texted a list to Dwayne:

Water, trash bags, shovel.

They had plenty of zip ties and a fresh roll of duct tape under the front seat.

Gilbert patted the headrest behind Rocco. "Drive."

Rocco kept the speed down as the Civic meandered deeper into the forest. The roads grew narrower, with deep ditches from runoff on either side.

"The turnoff is around the next bend." Gilbert motioned to the right.

Beside Gilbert, the kid's breathing labored. Heat and sickness radiated off him like a loser pony at the track. Gilbert kept to his side of the rear seat, where he hoped the air was safe. He'd dump the kid if he could, but Gilbert had to keep him alive long enough to find the leather case.

The girl in the trunk wasn't any trouble. The bumpy road alone probably bled off some of her attitude. But what they said about women was true. After an hour in the trunk, a dog was happy to see you, but never a woman. When they opened that trunk, Gilbert planned to be armed.

Augie didn't appreciate complications, but he couldn't leave the woman as a witness. Besides, she might know where the kid stashed the case. Women always knew more than they admitted.

He saw the slight break in the tree line that led to the cabin, matching the instructions on his GPS. "This is it."

The turnoff was barely a road. In the rainy season, it might be impassable without 4-wheel drive. Gullies on either side threatened those who strayed. Overgrowth long owned the property, but Gil's arrival earlier in the week beat down the foliage enough to ensure passage. Rocco dropped the speed to an idle.

When they rolled up to the gate, Rocco stopped and moved it out of the way. Once they cleared the fence line, he swung the gate back in place.

The kid stirred and coughed like he'd vaped a dozen vials. Even that didn't wake him. The car hit a rut, bouncing them closer together on the rear seat. Gilbert shoved him over with an elbow.

God, he hoped it wasn't contagious.

Gilbert wanted to be back in his city, but he was stuck in this foggy bottom until they found the satchel. It was probably in town somewhere or on the beach. He needed head room to think.

The old road was fairly straight, with towering trees blocking the direct sunlight. Gilbert knew the cabin was near, but the road ahead seemed to disappear into the forest. When they reached a gap in the trees, Rocco slowed the car and turned, following the tracks Gilbert had made earlier in the week.

A derelict cabin sat away from the road about a hundred feet amid a clearing. A few saplings dared to compete for light under the canopy while detritus and dark green ferns covered the rest of the clearing. Rocco pulled the car up to the front porch and parked.

It was a wooden, single-room structure roughly twenty feet square. The pitched roof, green with moss, extended about six feet to cover the front porch. A chimney rose from the back of the house, but Gilbert wasn't about to light a fire. The whole place looked like kindling. They were a match away from a forest fire.

Rocco found the nearest tree to relieve himself, while Gilbert went inside. It was as he remembered. The room held a table made of two-by-fours with a set of rail back chairs, now decorated with various colors of mold. A dog kennel occupied one corner, while a battered laundry basin sat in the other. A bookcase with collapsed shelves completed the sad ensemble. It lacked any amenities he would choose, but it sure was private.

First thing he had to do was wake up the kid. If Gilbert got the cooperation he wanted, he'd make it to a card club that night. Otherwise, for the girl and the kid, it was going to get nasty.

He went outside. Rocco leaned against the car.

Gilbert said, "Get the kid."

"What about the girl?"

"Unless we need her, she can stay in the trunk." She was bound to be trouble.

Rocco opened the back door of the Civic and dragged out the kid by his feet. When his shoes reached the ground, Rocco patted his face. "Yo. Wake up."

"Geez, he's hot." Rocco wiped his hand on his jeans. "And sweaty."

The kid sat upright, his eyes flickering open. His head lolled as if he couldn't bear its weight. "Where's Denesha?"

So the girl mattered to him. That was good news for Gilbert. Bad news for the girl. Another lever to pull.

Rocco grabbed the front of the kid's shirt and pulled him to a stand. His legs wobbled, but he stood.

Gilbert said, "Sol. His name is Sol."

The kid snapped his head toward Gilbert. "How do you know my name?"

"We've met before. I'm sure you remember where."

Sol nodded, but he didn't seem scared. "I remember." He wiped his brow with the inside of his elbow. "What'd you do to my mother? Where is she?"

Gilbert said, "Give me what I want, and I'll take you to her."

He rolled his lips between his teeth and nodded. "What do you want?"

"The same thing I wanted when we met. The satchel you picked up at the police station." He felt for the knife in his pocket. "If you'd given it to me when I asked the first time, we wouldn't be here now."

"It ain't worth all this." Sol rubbed his eyes. "You can have the money. I just want to go home with Mama."

Money. Gilbert wasn't looking for cash. He just needed the satchel.

The kid looked frantically around the property. "Where's Denesha?"

Gilbert pointed at the trunk. "She's in there."

"Let her out." The kid's voice cracked.

"Unless you want Denesha to get hurt, you better tell me where you hid the satchel."

He closed his eyes. "I buried it near the beach."

"Where near the beach?"

"Up above. In the bushes by the trail."

"Is that where you've been sleeping?"

He nodded. "I dug a hole for that."

Gilbert searched all over for him. Resourceful little punk.

"How close to the girl's house?"

"Not far."

"Kid, if you're lying to me, I will cause you and Denesha great pain. You feel me?"

He shook his head. "I'm not lying. That satchel's been nothing but trouble. I don't want it no more. I just want to go home."

"That's good." Gilbert patted his back. "You and I will go find it. Once we do, you and Denesha can go home."

The satchel was near the beach. Gilbert thought it might be. Even without the GPS tracker, the black guy wouldn't give up. Gil didn't know how soon Dwayne would get there, but driving the Civic put the job in jeopardy.

Gilbert motioned to Rocco. "Let's get her out of the trunk."

Rocco stood at a distance and popped open the trunk with the key fob. When nothing leapt out, he moved closer.

"Keep her in the kennel."

Sol trudged toward the trunk, but Gilbert stopped him from getting too close.

Sol glared at Gilbert. His furrowed scowl made him look like an old man. "Don't you hurt her. She don't know nothing about the satchel."

Gilbert poked Sol in the chest. "She'll be fine as long as I get what I want." He jacked a thumb toward Rocco. "If not, we'll shoot her like we shot your mother."

56

Travis worried about Denesha as much as Maggie, but he knew there was nothing he could do to find her that the police and FBI weren't doing. In the meantime, he poured his anxious energy into finding the spy.

The software update was due in three hours, but he had other things to review first. Even with their discovery of the dark web seller, the information had to come from inside R-Bot Systems. The FBI might get a name, but Travis doubted the seller knew it.

One question nagged him. If the DocuLocker software enabled the data breach, why weren't all their customer companies affected? Why only the startups? The company was reputable. DocuLocker sold this software in some form for over ten years. Management was stable, and financially, they were a steady pick on Wall Street.

Travis checked LinkedIn to see who else worked at the place. It wasn't a large company. Seventy-seven employees claimed them on LinkedIn. His screen-scraping script pulled their names and job titles into a separate file. He filtered the list for people involved in the technology. Travis doubted the accountants had the chops to infiltrate the systems. When he was done, his list numbered thirty-two.

He started at the top, entering each name into the search engine to see what he could find on the web and social media. With the first ten names, Travis found a couple of personal websites where the person blogged about technology and coding. Only one was still active. Another employee posted vids on his YouTube channel, while another held her wedding on the beach in Carmel, where the entire wedding party went barefoot.

From what Travis heard, his father married Maggie's mom on the beach. When she abandoned the family for a frozen food delivery dude, Maggie burned all the wedding pictures. Travis found a few other photos, but their father rarely talked about his first wife, and Maggie had nothing nice to say. Probably a good thing the woman moved out of the area.

Travis refocused on the beach bride. No reason to suspect she might be an industrial spy at DocuLocker, except a fancy wedding. Her title listed her as a frontend developer. Not someone who would have access to all the code, only the user screens she maintained.

Companies typically built software apps in three tiers. In the frontend tier, they developed the menus and screens seen by the users. The backend tier, the processing unseen by a user, the app accessed the database to save and retrieve information. In the middleware tier, developers applied the functional logic to data as it passed between the other two tiers. Middleware was the connective tissue of the application.

A coder skilled in all three tiers was a full-stack developer. But companies kept walls solidly in place between the code repositories. Access was on a need-to-use basis to prevent theft of their money makers. No one on Travis' list was senior enough to be a threat.

He started in on the next ten names and found similar results. Then he hit the name of Byron Suliani, whose title alone intrigued Travis: Cybersecurity Architect - IAM, Audit, and Compliance. IAM, or Identity Access Management. This dude designed the parts of the program that determined who got in and who stayed out. He was worthy of Travis' attention.

The smiling photo of Byron was a casual shot of him sitting on a porch step. He wore a San Francisco 49ers jersey and a pair of jeans. His elbows rested on his knees as he leaned forward. Dark hair and complexion, Travis figured his name was Italian.

Seemed harmless from the pic. He was no James Bondy super-spy. Carrying an extra sixty pounds and a second chin, he looked like someone's dad. Travis noticed a bulge in his shirt pocket, shaped like a pack of cigarettes. At least he hadn't rolled them up in his sleeve. Few people smoked real cigarettes anymore. Vaping was the current fashion for ingesting poison.

But the guy had serious tech chops. Byron Suliani began his career as a database admin, got certified in networking and moved into an admin role. Along the way, he taught himself to code, picking up multiple languages and framework knowledge, bolstering his technical arsenal. Then, he took over the cybersecurity team at DocuLocker, where he defined the architecture for the latest version of their software.

It was like the fireman who turns out to be the local arsonist. He had all the tools to do it and the knowledge to avoid getting caught.

But Travis was punished for a crime he didn't commit. Knowing how to infiltrate the software wasn't evidence against the man. Being able didn't make him guilty.

Travis searched for work-related hits and found guest blog posts at security websites written by Byron. Ransomware. PCI compliance. SQL injection. Not light topics. The man knew his trade.

But who was he?

Time for Travis to crawl Facebook.

Digital footprints were tough to erase. The European Union enacted the General Data Protection Regulation—GDPR—to give people a chance to reclaim their online reputations. Foolish indiscretions haunted people who'd changed, repented. No such laws existed in the U.S. If it was on the internet, good luck losing the bad press.

There were two people on Facebook listed with the name Byron Suliani. The kid from Parma, Italy, looked legit, but the smiling man wearing a Navy dress uniform had no history, no posts. Denesha said she got friend requests from those types all the time. Definitely spammy. Someone looking for money or sex. Or both.

Travis searched for anyone named Suliani living in California. The hits were plenty. Mostly girls taking bathroom mirror selfies. Didn't they know anyone who would take a decent picture for them?

Byron went to school in the Bay Area and wore a 49er's jersey. Sports team loyalties were die hard. No transplant from Milwaukee was giving up the Packers for the 49ers red and gold. The jersey was reasonable weight to anchor his initial search.

Combing social media was a simple affair, searching for a specific person through photo tags, family posts, and any references Travis could find to others in the person's circle. People posted about the big moments in life—vacations, weddings, reunion—events that returned the family strays to the fold long enough for a photo op. But wading through the minutiae of someone else's life was always strange.

Most of it was harmless, but why put it out there for mass consumption? Few people posted their worst moments in life, so the glimpses were staged and framed. After Travis' conviction, no airbrush could soften his media image. Only his troubles made headlines, not his exoneration. While his bitterness waned, his experience with the media was never particularly social.

Travis scanned the list of people named Suliani, eliminating a few accounts from a lack of activity. He needed someone who shared his junk. Travis chose one of the busier Sulianis to cyberstalk, Alfred from Daly City, just south of San Francisco. This Suliani made his living as an artist, creating origami sculptures out of glass.

Pretty cool stuff. Colorful and delicate pieces like the paper ones, but impossibly made of glass. Maggie would love his stuff, but she'd complain it was another thing to dust. The artist posted pictures of his artwork, but there wasn't a single personal image on his account.

Travis moved on to a Mimi Suliani, a woman who lived down the peninsula in San Mateo. Taken somewhere on the Pacific Coast, her profile picture was a smiling shot of her on the beach. Her interests included knitting and dog rescue. Posted activity centered on family, grandkids, and rescue dogs she fostered. Travis found a beagle on her page that looked a little like Belli. It found a home last month.

He scrolled through a few pics of items she knitted, and eventually landed on a post that stopped Travis cold.

Thank you to all my friends for your love and support. We lost my beloved grandson, Byron, far too early.

He was dead?

Travis checked the date. Posted about three months ago. He scanned the comments section. Nothing helpful there. Eventually, he found another post from earlier that same week.

Today, my beautiful grandson, Byron, died from a stroke. He was incoherent and someone called the police! By the time they realized it was a medical emergency, he was gone. Words cannot express the pain in my fractured heart—

Cherish your loved ones! Never let a day go by without letting them know you care! Please look at the symptoms below, so you can tell when someone—

Reading this left Travis a little depressed. Byron wasn't that old. The extra weight and smoking surely didn't help, but it still sucked.

The post offered a link to Byron's memorial website, where people who knew him lavished their condolences on the family. Travis checked the local news and found a report about Byron. He was found wandering in the neighborhood near Blackburn Park with no identification.

Travis navigated to a website that listed local police incidents. He filtered the information to the date of Byron's death and scrolled through the police actions for that day. The incidents ran the gamut of illegal activities and those where police offered help in non-criminal events. Travis found a non-criminal entry for Mental Health Detention for the Blackburn Park area.

If the dude was stroking out, his behavior probably scared the neighbors, assumed he was another drugged-up crazy. The police would've called the paramedics, but by then, it was bye-bye Byron.

Heck of a way to go.

A second entry within 30 minutes of the first one caught Travis' attention. Found Property also in Blackburn Park.

Sol's mother was killed after collecting found property at the police department when no one claimed it. Maybe the two incidents were related. Fortunately, Travis knew an FBI agent who could find out firsthand.

57

Maggie stormed out of the house with a head full of questions for the driver of the white car. Maybe the driver was waiting for someone. Or birdwatching. Or casing the neighborhood, choosing which house to burgle first.

The ideas clashed as she thought about Denesha. Where was she? Why would anyone kidnap her? And Sharla. My God! Maggie still couldn't believe she'd been murdered.

Before she'd made it past her driveway, she saw Ginger padding toward her in bare feet. Maggie stopped and waited for her friend.

"I heard what happened." Ginger called, running the last few yards to meet Maggie. "Is there any news?"

Maggie shook her head. "Nothing. But the police don't have me on speed dial."

"Denesha is smart, and she's tough." Ginger stretched an arm around Maggie. "We need to keep our spirits up for her."

"I can't imagine what she's going through." Maggie's voice cracked. "She was the one who found Sharla."

"And the police will find Denesha and the boy." Ginger glanced toward the house. "Are the FBI on the case?"

"Yes, but I keep thinking about when Dad went missing. I can't lose Denesha too."

"You're not losing anyone." The little Samoan woman laid her head on Maggie's shoulder. "When she gets back, we'll roast a pig."

Ginger's answers to life always included food. Buried underground with hot rocks, her roast pig was legendary. Maggie laid her head on Ginger's. "Yes, we will."

They stood together for a moment, and then Maggie caught movement at Fyodor's house. She stood upright. "He's been fanning an old flame."

Ginger put her fists against her hips. "Been wondering what's up with you and Frodo."

"He was engaged at one time. Katya." Maggie couldn't take her eyes off the front door. "Katya the Great. She's got to be beautiful."

"Your time will come."

His door opened, and a tall, but frail woman walked out on Fyodor's arm. His mother, no doubt. Maggie looked down at her clothes. Oh well. He'd seen her in worse condition.

Then she saw Katya, who fulfilled all of Maggie's worst imaginings.

Drop. Dead. Gorgeous.

Statuesque, regal, and with an air of ownership as she locked the front door behind her. Fyodor saw Maggie and acknowledged her with a lift of the chin. But he kept in step with his mother as he guided her to the car.

Katya scanned the surrounding area, but her eyes never landed on Maggie. Too insignificant for Katya to lower her gaze.

It didn't matter. Not today. Fyodor had his life, Maggie had hers. Today, one of her two dearest friends was missing. Everything else was just noise.

"You and Travis need anything?"

"No. The FBI sting went really well." She gave her all the information she could share about the operation.

"You still going to be undercover?"

Maggie had to stay close. Baxter would understand. "I don't know. All I can think about is Denesha."

Fyodor started his car and backed out onto the street. As he drove away, she saw the white car still parked under the tree. But after Ginger's intervention, Maggie wasn't sure if she'd approach him.

Ginger patted her hand. "I'm around. Call me if you need me."

"Thanks, Ginger."

While Ginger walked away toward her house, Maggie stayed outside, breathing in the fresh air. The onshore breeze brought scents of kelp and flecks of foam from the spray.

The effort fortified her, and she renewed her resolve to see what the driver of the white car was doing. But direct confrontation was always a bad idea.

She crossed the street and walked at a leisurely pace. If she saw anything suspicious, she'd worry about it then. Keeping her distance was safer. She could pass by, offer a friendly nod, observe, and keep moving. If nothing else, she planned to record the license plate number.

Her mind floated back to Denesha. She was the one who found Sharla's body. Even if Denesha wanted to be a nurse, finding her roommate dead under the bed must've been horrifying. She was abducted within minutes of reporting the crime. Those two events had to be linked.

By now, her kidnappers could be miles away. Over the hills, the highways led in all directions. Maggie prayed Denesha was safe. And Sol. After losing his mother in such a terrifying way, he careened into another nightmare.

Maggie was nearing the white car when the driver's door opened. A large black man stepped out and called to her. "Hi."

She stopped and checked her surroundings. If he planned her any harm, he wasn't worried that others saw his car. But after Denesha's abduction, Maggie wasn't taking any chances.

She stood her ground. "Can I help you?"

"Yes. Maybe. I'm looking for my sister, Toya. Maybe you know her?"

Is that what he was doing? Looking for a missing sister. Other than the woman famous for being a Jackson, Maggie didn't know anyone by that name. "No. I'm sorry. I can't help you."

But now he moved closer. "Could I please show you her picture? It's possible she's using a different name."

Something about his request seemed off. He sounded more like a private investigator on a job than a distraught brother. She and Travis had been in their business a short while, but she was apparently good at pretending she was someone else.

This guy? Not so much.

Carl Pinkerton chose that time to come outside and dig up a flower bed. For a change, his presence was welcome. At least if she were kidnapped, there'd be a witness.

"Sure." Maggie stayed on her side of the street and waved at Carl. If the man with the photo had evil plans, she wasn't going quietly.

The man was bigger than she realized, tall, solid, and nicely dressed in jeans and a long-sleeved polo. He had a calm air about him, even if Maggie thought he was a liar. He also waved at Carl Pinkerton, maybe to put Maggie at ease. She had to admit. It helped.

When he came near her, she noticed that the edge of his right earlobe was saw-toothed, as if torn or bitten. He stopped outside of her personal space and handed her a photo. "This is Toya."

She was a beautiful woman, with a slight resemblance to Viola Davis but zero resemblance to the handsome man with the ragged ear standing in front of Maggie. The woman's picture was probably a glam shot taken after a makeover.

"I'm sorry." Maggie returned the picture. "I've never seen her."

His shoulders sagged.

"What makes you think she lives around here?"

"Toya left home, and our mother hasn't seen her in a long time." His hand swept over the neighborhood. "I heard she was staying with friends in the area."

His story didn't seem real, but the disappointment did. Maggie was intrigued. More formal than the locals, his manner was polite, his voice carrying a slight Southern drawl. He wore the bearing of a military man.

She swept her hair behind an ear. "I don't know everyone around here, so I hope you have better luck."

He gave her a curt nod. "What can you tell me about the police action on the Custer?" He pointed toward Denesha's street.

The question reverberated in Maggie's head. She briefly shut her eyes to focus. "Why? What do you know about it?"

"Nothing. I spoke to a woman who lives down that street yesterday. This morning, looks like all hell broke loose."

All hell did break loose.

Maggie heard her own heartbeat. "Who? Who did you talk to?"

His eyes narrowed. "I didn't ask her name. Tiny, dark woman. Extra big smile."

Denesha.

"What did you say to her?" Maggie tried to keep the panic from tainting her voice.

"I take it you know her." He tucked the photo in his wallet. "I asked her about my sister. She said she didn't know Toya, but she'd check with her roommate when she returned. I wanted to follow up today, but the police had the road blocked, and I didn't want to interfere."

Denesha's roommate wasn't returning.

Maggie rubbed her left temple. The information was public knowledge at this point. A murder, and two missing. Carl Pinkerton would gladly provide those facts, plus his color commentary.

She struggled to put it in words. "The roommate, Sharla, was found dead this morning. I didn't know Sharla well, but the woman you talked to is very dear to me. After calling the police, she and a young boy were abducted." Maggie sought full eye contact with the stranger. "If you know anything. Saw anything. You must tell the police."

The man finally appeared animated. Something about Denesha's abduction sparked his concern. "Do they have a description of the car?"

"A silver car. That's it."

He wiped his brow. "Then I know who took them."

58

Rocco approached the trunk as if it held a rabid dog.

"Just get her out of there." But Gilbert understood Rocco's trepidation. Trapped animals were vicious. Women were far worse. His ear still throbbed where that dead bitch bit him.

Rocco lifted the trunk door. Inside, Denesha was motionless but breathing like a Greyhound after the last race. Gil recognized that look in her eye. She wouldn't play nice.

Rocco yanked her by the hair. "Scream all you want out here. No one will hear you. You bite me or kick me, it's going to get ugly. You got it, Denesha?"

At the mention of her name, she recoiled.

Gilbert put his hand on Sol's head and gave him a shove. "Yeah, the kid told us who you are. Now you better go easy, or little Sol here might get hurt."

Sol glowered at Gilbert—as if he could do some damage. The kid was feverish, struggling for every breath. Gil's biggest worry was keeping him alive long enough to find the satchel.

Denesha slackened under Rocco's grip. "Leave the boy be. I won't fight you."

Rocco grabbed her by the ankles and lowered her legs over the edge. From there, he pulled her by the arm until her feet hit the ground.

Denesha stumbled to a stand. "How're you doing, Sol?" She wiped her cheek on a shoulder.

"We ask the questions," Gilbert said. "Check to see if she's got a phone."

Rocco patted her down. "No phone."

"Where's your roommate?"

Her eyelids fluttered as if she might faint.

From that reaction, Gilbert guessed she found the body. He leaned in and whispered, "Unless you want the kid to get hurt, answer me. Did you call the police?"

Her shoulders straightened. "Her name was Sharla. We ran out of the house and you showed up."

When Rocco and he rolled up to the house, they were in a panic. Still, he had to be careful. "Get her inside."

"Wait," she said. "Sol's sick. He needs medical attention."

Gilbert laughed. "We'll get right on that. Just as soon as I get the leather case."

Rocco pushed Denesha toward the cabin. "Move it."

She complied, walking slowly, but kept an eye toward Sol while disappearing into the cabin.

The kid sat on the ground, hunched over his legs. His wheezing was louder.

Dammit. Where was Dwayne? Gilbert checked his phone coverage. Barely a bar.

Losing use of the Civic threw off their plans because they couldn't drive it back to Half Moon Bay—not with the black dude tailing them.

Who was he? Another buyer? Hired muscle? From the description of him, he was big enough. How did he find out about the satchel?

Gilbert didn't even know what the payload was in the thing. He just knew his life now depended on finding it first.

But they couldn't torch the Civic out here. Many of these old roads dead-ended in the hills, but they could get over the coastal range and onto a highway for home in about twenty minutes. When the job was done, Rocco could swipe some fresh plates, drive the Civic back, and light it up in the Mission. The alley fire might even warm a few winos.

Perpetual shade kept this location on the cool side. While it didn't bother Gilbert, the kid was shivering. He also snored like he'd been on a bender. Gilbert stepped over him and went inside to check on Rocco.

The girl was in the dog kennel with her hands tied behind her back. Rocco secured the cage door with more tie wraps. Gilbert approved.

"If she talks too much, tape her mouth. Unless she wants to tell us where the case is located."

He expected a flash of panic from her. She didn't even make eye contact. He had to give it to her. She wasn't hysterical like the last one he took for a ride. That one cried for two full hours until she gave up her loser boyfriend. After that, Gilbert disposed of them both.

Rocco leaned back in a chair with his arms crossed. "What do you want me to do?"

"Stay in here and watch her. As soon as Dwayne shows, we're taking the kid to get the leather case. I'll contact you as soon as we have it." Gilbert said, "How many bars on your phone?"

"None in here. I got one outside by the car. What'd you expect?"

He hated when Rocco tried to get smart. It didn't suit him.

Gilbert ignored the comment. "You got your piece?"

Rocco usually carried a Ruger Max-9, a small profile 9mm that concealed well. He patted his jacket pocket. "Always."

A rumbling sound lightened Gilbert's mood. Dwayne finally arrived. Gilbert motioned for Rocco to follow him.

Dwayne parked the Chrysler next to the Civic and unloaded supplies. He said, "I got everything on the list."

"Dwayne, you and I are leaving with the kid." Gilbert pointed at Rocco. "Check your phone for messages once in a while, in case we need your help. Once I have the satchel, get rid of the girl."

Dwayne dropped the trash bags on the ground and tossed a shovel to Rocco, who caught it midair.

Gilbert said, "Make sure the hole is deep. Don't want her dragged off by animals."

"What about the kid?" Dwayne jacked a thumb at the boy.

Gilbert backhanded Dwayne on the shoulder. "Get him in the Chrysler. We'll figure out what to do with him later."

As Dwayne picked the kid off the ground, his body draped like dead weight.

Dwayne pushed Sol across the back seat and got in with him. "Looks sick. What's he got?"

"Don't know. Don't care. Let him sleep until we get into town."

As Gilbert drove down the hill toward Half Moon Bay, he kept a constant watch over his six. No white cars following, but he wouldn't put it past the black dude to find a fresh ride. That's what Gilbert would do. But he didn't see any cars following him, so maybe they were safe.

As it was, having the kid in the car was dangerous. If he had more time, he'd dye the kid's hair and dress him in different clothes. While Denesha might not be considered missing yet, the kid damn sure was. Up and down the coast, authorities were looking for him.

Gil's phone rang. The call came from Augie's burner.

"Tell me some good news." His voice was shaky.

"I have the kid. Should be wrapped within a few hours."

A great sigh came from Augie. "It better be." He ended the call.

Gil was out of time, and so was the kid.

A few minutes later, the road flattened into the bottomland. When they neared the Cabrillo Highway, Gilbert said, "Wake up the kid."

Dwayne jostled Sol. "Hey. Get up."

Gil strained to see him. "Is he alive?"

"He's breathing." Dwayne applied more force. "Wake up."

Sol stirred. "I'm up." He pushed off the seat with both hands and slumped against the door.

They reached the stop sign at the end of the road. "Which way, kid?"

He didn't look out the window. "To the beach, near Denesha's."

Gilbert nodded and headed north.

Going back to that area was risky. He didn't know if the police knew about the roommate. The guy in the white car was another problem.

But Augie was the biggest risk. Disappointing him would be deadly.

Gil kept watch for anyone following him. No white cars. No black choppers, No drones.

No reason to get paranoid.

He wiped off the sweat from his palms.

The beach had various places to park along the bluff trail. Gilbert didn't want to park too close to the neighborhood, but he also wanted to get in and out as quickly as possible. He considered all the parking lots and remembered one with a secluded entrance. The access didn't offer a direct path to the beach, so fewer people used it.

Two grown men walking around with a sick kid might draw attention. They'd have to get in the brush quickly and stay away from the trail. Once they found the satchel, Gil would hustle back to the city. The kid's breathing was already bad. He'd be easy to smother, and they could leave his body in the brush.

59

Travis needed more information to interpret the events that occurred in Blackburn Park. Was the police blotter notice about Sol? If so, whatever he found and turned over to the police may have led to his mother's murder and his own abduction. Until Travis confirmed the connection, Byron Suliani's demise was merely a sad footnote in Travis' research.

Bailey and Belli trotted up to him for some attention. After the morning with a houseful of strangers, they reclaimed their turf, which included Travis. He wrestled with them on the floor until Belli left him for the water bowl. Bailey followed his sister. With the dogs satisfied, Travis turned his attention to his job for R-Bot Systems and logged into Baxter's laptop.

The DocuLocker software update was due to occur, and Travis wanted to monitor the process. The company used a popular update routine, ModifySoft, as a vehicle to update the DocuLocker software. Tens of thousands of companies used the ModifySoft routine, and it was highly vetted for security.

During a software update, the routine added the new files and deleted the old files. When all the changes were in place, the program restarted to ensure it found the correct new files and rebuilt the software to run the latest version.

To record these file changes, Travis set up a packet sniffer to record the DocuLocker update at R-Bot Systems. The packet sniffer looked at every single bit of information that passed between the two points. Not a keystroke nor a slippery bit of code could escape detection and capture for analysis. Most of the time, the data just flowed along a network, but at critical junctures, packet monitoring tools recorded the data and could even determine whether the action was allowed.

Parents relied on these types of tools to keep their kids safe from inappropriate websites, or to prevent an eight-year-old from betting on the fifth race at Pimlico. Travis heard about a kid who used his dad's laptop to bet on a cage fight. His parents were ticked until they found out the kid won two grand.

Packet sniffers were useful, but monitoring everything was impractical. The information captured in the log files was just clutter unless someone analyzed the data for meaning. It was also voluminous. The accumulated storage of these log files could quickly get expensive. The critical balance lay between need and obsession.

From what Baxter told Travis, the previous log files showed nothing unusual, nothing nefarious. But watching the packets get logged was the equivalent of waiting at a red light. Minimally interesting, and there was nothing to do until the process finished.

Travis usually confined his dark web activity to the computer that was now in an FBI evidence bag. His shiny replacement from Baxter was still in the box, and Travis wanted to check in with AreEff. While the dark web wasn't a place to blunder about, Travis knew what precautions to take and what to avoid.

He logged in to his main laptop using the Tor browser and went to the hacker forum. As expected, AreEff wasn't online. Travis left a message for him. Or her.

Solid as usual. o u

There were plenty of posers and imposters on the dark web, but AreEff was always 24 karat. While Travis relied on their relationship, it couldn't be one-way. He wouldn't break the law for AreEff, but Travis would do anything short of it. Sometimes the lines between were uncomfortably indistinct.

He checked on the progress of the updates, and it was nearly complete. He closed his main laptop and got back to work examining the data packets.

There were two critical parts to consider when software gave access to another program or a user: authentication and authorization. Authentication meant proving you are who you say you are, while authorization meant proving you were allowed to see what you asked to see.

Travis' father explained that, while Travis could authenticate that he was his father's son, it didn't give him authorization to eat a cookie without express permission.

Travis ran a script to compare the log data from today with the previous logs. He expected differences in the payloads, but the rest of it should be similar.

Travis' script scanned for known hacks, similar to an anti-virus routine. The results showed nothing alarming. The authentication and authorization processes looked like all the other updates, only with different dates and session IDs.

So far, so dull.

Until he saw the closing routine.

One particular command gave him pause. It was a delete command in the update software, ModifySoft. While it was only supposed to delete old files from DocuLocker, this command deleted a file that ModifySoft had just created. He dug a little deeper.

This created file showed up after all the main files were updated. While ModifySoft deleted the file it created, Travis recorded a copy of the code before it disappeared.

He stared at the code for a long while, trying to discern its purpose. Then he understood.

The file changed the permissions required to copy files from the system storage and gave itself authorization to copy documents from the DocuLocker system.

Travis gaped at the screen. The implications staggered his imagination.

This was R-Bot's thief. The ModifySoft update routine stole files from the DocuLocker system. Someone found a hole in the authentication routine and drove an Abrams tank battalion right through it.

Essentially, the routine was a Trojan horse, pretending to be both an authenticated and authorized user of the files. With full permissions, it copied the files to an external URL on the web. But the URL probably led to a hacked website that didn't know it was being used to transport the stolen files. The Trojan code then reset the permissions back to normal and deleted itself, leaving no trace it was ever there.

Unless the activity was logged. Even then, unless someone examined those logs, it looked like legitimate activity.

But Travis knew, code didn't write itself.

It was easy to blame the software, but a person was behind this. Either someone from DocuLocker, ModifySoft, or a cunning opportunist who discovered the vulnerability. Perhaps an employee at R-Bot Systems.

It made sense to run this scam on the startups. They had fewer resources to monitor and analyze these kinds of threats. Their systems were new and not as developed as companies with staff dedicated to protecting their intellectual assets. Startup employees spent days and nights solving problems. They didn't have time to look for obscure hacks in third-party software.

From what Travis could see, there was a delay in the closing session of the ModifySoft update routine, allowing an injection of the Trojan code at a critical moment. Like leaving a door ajar, it allowed in the burglars. As far as Travis knew, the software community was unaware of this vulnerability.

The code had a limited life span, but the ill-gotten gains would be phenomenal. Whoever owned it had to strike selectively and quickly.

Once the issue was known, ModifySoft would quickly fix it, but not before doing irreparable damage to other businesses. With the number of companies using ModifySoft, the targets were manifold.

Travis had to alert the authorities.

A concerted effort to attack industry leaders en masse could cause a technology transfer to nefarious buyers that gave them an illicit advantage.

For some, that was plenty worth killing for.

60

"I'm Maggie Fender." She grabbed the man's hand. "Come with me." Maggie broke into a run toward her house, and the man kept pace. When they reached her door, she said, "Who are you? And how do you know the people in the silver car?"

"Marcus Fisher." He seemed a little winded. "I told you. I'm looking for my sister."

Maggie burst through the front door and called out, "Travis!"

The beagles scampered up to Marcus and sniffed him before they entered the living room.

"Travis!"

"Maggie, are you okay?" Travis stumbled out of his office and looked the stranger up and down. "Who are you?"

Maggie pulled Marcus to the couch. "He saw the car that kidnapped Denesha."

Travis dropped into a chair. "No joke?" He pulled his phone from his shirt pocket. "We've got to call Claudia."

Bailey and Belli hovered around the stranger. He looked uncomfortable, so Maggie shooed them to their beds.

Marcus raised an eyebrow. "Claudia?"

"FBI agent." Maggie realized that sounded strange. No one had FBI agents on speed dial. "Long story, but everyone is looking for Denesha. Tell us what you know."

He rested his hands on his knees and drew in a deep breath. "I was told that my sister Toya was living at the yellow house, so I went by there yesterday." His eyes shifted between Maggie and Travis. "When I arrived, a silver car was parked in the street. I assumed someone would get out or come

216

out of the house, but neither happened." He held up his palms. "Then it drove off."

Marcus started to shake. "Excuse me." He reached in his pocket and pulled out a bag of almonds, before dropping a few in his mouth. "Low blood sugar."

He chewed a moment and swallowed. "I went up to the house, and Denesha and I spoke briefly." He dusted off his hands. "I don't know if it's the same car, but I have the license plate number."

Hope unknotted Maggie's stomach, allowing her the first deep breath since she heard the news. She wanted to hug this man. Find the car. Find Denesha and the boy.

Travis was on the phone with Claudia, relaying the bits of information from Marcus. Travis repeated the license plate number and waited for Marcus to nod approval.

"Yes, that's the correct plate number. It was a silver Honda Civic. Late model."

"Yeah. Of course." Travis handed the phone to Marcus. "She wants to talk to you."

Marcus took the phone. "Yes. Marcus Fisher, ma'am."

Maggie and Travis could only hear his side of the call.

"I did, ma'am. Three men traveled together. Tall, white guy with blond hair. White guy with tats on the neck, medium build. Stocky black guy."

Three grown men against Denesha. She didn't have a chance. Neither did Sharla. Bastards.

"No. I didn't see the driver today, but it was the same car."

Maggie wished she could hear both sides of the conversation.

"The car was also about halfway up Tunitas Creek Road. Maybe they have a place up there." Marcus bit his lips. "Yes. I'm happy to give a statement. But there's another car that you might find of interest. A black Chrysler 300. Just a moment, please." He checked his phone and recited another license plate number to Claudia.

He said to Maggie and Travis. "Agent Seagal is still in town and wants to interview me. Do you mind if we do that here?"

"Please do," Maggie said. With Claudia on the case and some fresh leads, things were bound to shake loose.

Dear God, she hoped so.

"The Chrysler was at the Manzanita Motel with the other car." He sighed. "Yes, ma'am. I'll be here." He ended the call and gave Travis his phone. "She's on her way."

While all this new information was good news, something didn't add up for Maggie. "Why didn't you talk to the police when they were at Denesha's house?"

"I didn't know what was going on. The road was blocked." He crossed his ankles.

Maggie thought he knew more than he admitted. How did he know those guys were at the Manzanita Motel or on Tunitas unless he followed them?

"Until you told me about the silver car, I had no reason to believe there was a problem."

Travis seemed to pick up on her concern. He stood, positioning himself near his sister. "Why were you watching our house?"

Marcus sat back in his seat. "There was a lot of commotion at your house this morning. Just waiting it out before I asked about my sister."

"But I saw you last night when I met Denesha outside." Heat gathered in her thoughts. "Were you following her?"

"No. I wasn't." He pressed his fingers into his eyes. "I'm just trying to find my sister."

The guy was in his early thirties. Maggie doubted his sister was a teenage runaway. Having an FBI agent on the way to her house emboldened her. She put her feet on the coffee table. "So why are you looking for your sister? She's an adult, right?"

His focus was intense, causing Maggie to lose some of her bluster.

Marcus said, "Is this young man your brother?"

"Yes. His name is Travis."

"Then you're fortunate. You both seem like well-adjusted members of society. My sister isn't."

Maggie felt a little bad for challenging him. He was the one link she had to Denesha. Why did Maggie always have to push until something tipped over? "I'm sorry to hear that."

"My sister's been gone for several years, and I want to make sure she's safe. Believe me, you'd do the same."

Maggie didn't know what to believe. He appeared genuine in his desire to find this woman. If his intent was evil, he wouldn't be so willing to meet with the FBI.

She said, "Let me see her picture again."

He got it out of his wallet and handed it to her. She studied it this time. Nothing about the woman looked familiar, except the Viola Davis thing.

The weight of the day didn't need more drag. She passed the photo to Travis. "This is his sister. Have you seen her around here?"

Travis was a more thoughtful person than Maggie. Not just kinder, though he was that too. But he put more thought into a thing before he reacted. When her crumbling family was adrift, all she could do was react, defending them against the salvo that battered their creaky hull. For all the ills Travis suffered, he didn't lose his humanity, just a choice part of his youth.

He studied the photo longer than Maggie thought necessary. "I've never met her. But she reminds me of someone. I don't know who."

Maggie rolled her eyes. "Viola Davis."

"Who's that?"

"An actress."

He shook his head. "Nah. That's not it."

Marcus leaned forward. "Who then?"

Travis raised his arms in surrender. "I don't know. If I think of a name, I'll tell you."

The doorbell sounded, sending the beagles out of their beds in a scramble for the front door. Belli was ahead of her brother as they hit the hallway.

Maggie quickly followed them and opened the door for Claudia.

"I stopped to get lunch before heading out of town, so I wasn't far."

They went into the next room, and Marcus rose from his seat.

Maggie introduced Marcus Fisher to Special Agent Claudia Seagal, and they all sat around the coffee table. Claudia pulled a laptop from her bag.

"The information you gave me about the vehicles might be very helpful. We're circulating it now to law enforcement. There's a BOLO on both vehicles, so hopefully we can locate them soon."

Her head cocked just a little as she looked at Marcus. "You certainly have my attention, sir. What else can you tell me about the car or the three men that you saw?"

"I was on Custer Street, prior to the abduction, and I saw the silver Civic stop near the yellow house. I thought it strange, so I took down the license plate."

"That's fortunate." She took notes and nodded. "So how was it you can give me a description of the three men?"

Marcus glanced at the ceiling. "I saw the same car later. At the Manzanita Motel. The men were standing near it."

"We'll send someone over there to check it out. If they were involved in the kidnapping, I doubt they're still guests."

Claudia typed for a bit and then addressed Marcus, "Tunitas Creek Road. Why do you think they were up there?"

"I couldn't say, ma'am. But if I wanted to hide out, there would seem to be plenty of places out that way."

Claudia apparently had the same questions Maggie did when hearing the story. Good information if any of it was true.

"This car got around the area. Wouldn't you say?"

Marcus adjusted his shirt cuff. "Yes, ma'am."

"Did you follow it up Tunitas Creek Road?"

"No, ma'am. I didn't."

"Then how do you know it was up there?"

Marcus pulled at his collar. "I'd rather not say, ma'am."

Claudia tapped the edge of her laptop. "Let's cut the crap, Marcus. Shall we? I had my team run a check on you. They say you own a trucking fleet in

Naples, Florida. What are you doing wandering the streets of Half Moon Bay?"

"A trucking fleet." Maggie said it louder that she planned. "I thought you were a private detective."

Marcus stayed quiet.

Travis said, "He's here looking for his sister, Toya."

Claudia cocked an eyebrow. "He has two brothers who run the business with him, and a set of parents, both living." She addressed her comments to Travis and Maggie. "There's no sign of a sister."

Claudia pushed up her sleeves and stood. "Now start telling me the truth before I arrest you."

61

Denesha's arms and back ached from her unholy imprisonment in the trunk. That creepy blond hit her so hard, it delayed her instinct to fight. By then, flight wasn't an option. Until she found a way out, she was trapped.

The view from the dog cage in the cabin brought Denesha's spirit to a new low, forcing her to look up at people who acted like animals. She never liked the use of kennels for dogs, but they had a purpose. Putting a human in one was unconscionable.

She barely had time to alert the police about poor Sharla. Poor, sweet Sharla. Extinguished before her chance to shine. Denesha choked on the memory of finding her body under the bed. None of it seemed real until she met the creepy blond who killed her.

Denesha wiped an eye on a shoulder.

She heard the car drive off. At least Sol wasn't stuck in the cage. In the city, someone might rescue him.

How long would they keep her alive? Or Sol.

And what was all the talk about a satchel? Sol said he hid it somewhere on the beach, but why was it important?

Denesha now knew he'd been living alone on the beach, hiding. But she didn't know for how long.

His life was in jeopardy and not just from their abductors. She barely started her nursing studies, but even she knew that boy was gravely ill. Feverish, fatigued, maybe suffering from exposure—he seemed ready to collapse.

The police might know Denesha was missing, since she was gone before they arrived. But she never mentioned Sol. Did anyone know he was with her?

These guys were armed and had no qualms about killing Sharla. The longer Denesha went without help, the shorter her life expectancy. Those thugs should be locked in a cage.

A vision of Sharla's empty eyes hovered like an apparition. What did they do to her? How long did she suffer before she was murdered? Horrific images ripped through Denesha's mind like a tempest.

She suddenly felt chilled. A shaking started in her shoulders that she couldn't control, spreading until her entire body quivered. She pressed herself into the mesh cage wall to stop the convulsion, to feel something solid, something real.

Denesha couldn't drown in fear. She had to stay sharp, focused. Right now, she only felt numb.

She stayed pressed against the mesh until it hurt her flesh, chasing away the fear with a new sensation. With the worst of it passed, she opened her eyes. She was alone in the cabin, giving her time to think.

The cabin was in the middle of the forest, but where? When she was in the trunk, she'd counted to nearly a thousand when the car stopped for a while, and she lost track. Someone was yelling. Probably the blonde. After the car started up again, she counted to six-hundred and eighty-six, when the car finally stopped at this location.

How long was that? Twenty minutes? There were a thousand places to go in the coastal foothills in that amount of time.

Her primary problem was getting out of the cage. Fortunately, it was designed for a big dog, and Denesha was small enough that she could sit cross legged. She examined it. While it was strong enough to contain a Rottweiler, Denesha was no Rottweiler. She spied several flaws in the old kennel that she could exploit, if her hands were loose. Right now, that was the trick.

The tie wrap around her wrists cut into her skin. Maybe she was bleeding. From the front, she couldn't tell. But tie wraps could be broken even when secured behind her back. Maggie showed her how.

After her father died, Maggie insisted that Ginger and Denesha come over for dinner and watch some videos of people breaking tie wraps bound around their wrists. They humored her because they love her. She was in shock from the loss. Plus, Travis roasted prime rib for the occasion.

The event was surreal. But since it was for Maggie, they played along. She wanted them to have a fighting chance in case they were ever restrained. They weren't sure if Travis was fully on board with the idea, but he stood by his sister. Ginger and Denesha figured it was some version of closure for Maggie.

After watching videos of several people snapping off the tie wraps around their wrists, Maggie insisted Ginger and Denesha try it themselves. Maggie taped their wrists, so the tie wraps didn't injure them during the attempts. Then she cinched their wrists with the tie wraps. Denesha and Ginger both repeated what they saw in the video until each could break free. Maggie popped some champagne for that moment.

While it was an awesome party trick, Denesha never expected to need it. She only did it for Maggie's sake. Her best friend, after all her suffering, Denesha thought Maggie lost a proper perspective on life.

Now, miles away, she was saving Denesha's.

She tried to break free while she was in the trunk but didn't have enough room. Now, the timing had to be right. Denesha couldn't let Rocco know her hands were free until she had a plan to escape the cage. Her phone was tucked inside her sports bra between her shoulder blades. It was a more comfortable place to keep it when she ran. Rocco didn't pat down that part of her body.

He also said the cell reception didn't work inside, so that meant she had to be outdoors before risking that critical call. Her life depended on the timing.

Just then, Rocco appeared at the cabin door. He carried a shovel but left it resting against the door jamb. He stepped inside and said, "We've got water if you need some."

Rocco looked like a guy following orders rather than someone who enjoyed inflicting pain. No doubt he would've fit in on the Southern plantations and the concentration camps. No moral true north—just following orders.

Denesha refused to curry his favor, and given her confinement, she didn't want to strain her bladder with liquids. "No, thank you."

He stared blankly at her a moment and said, "Suit yourself."

A gun hung now from his hip. It wasn't there earlier. Her heart thumped a strange beat. She heard them discussing a gun, knew it was around, but seeing the gun while she was imprisoned solidified the threat.

Rocco had been ordered to watch her, but he didn't sit in the chair, didn't settle himself indoors. Maybe he figured the kennel would contain her or just didn't want to deal with her. But he walked out the door, grabbing the shovel on his way.

Denesha winced.

Or he had to dig a hole to hide her corpse.

Bury the evidence, and let foothills keep their secrets. They tried to do that to Sharla.

Denesha thought about Maggie, some of the crazy stuff she said the night they watched the videos.

Don't you dare go gentle into that good night. Fight them! Fight them, dammit! You hear me? Or when it's over, I will kick your ass!

Both Ginger and Denesha laughed, thinking Maggie was joking. Or completely lost it. Now Denesha knew. Maggie already faced this danger. She suffered but prevailed. Maggie wanted to spare her loved ones the same scars.

Denesha understood intellectually. She knew about crime, but the concept was abstract. It happened to other people. She'd never had to contend for her life. Sharla did and lost. Denesha hoped Sharla put up a righteous fight.

Denesha needed to break the tie wraps before Rocco finished digging her grave. She raised herself up on her knees. The cage was too short for her to fully extend, so she leaned on the front panel, allowing her back to straighten. She stretched her arms up high, applying outward pressure against the tie wrap, then snapped them downward, striking her butt with force.

Nothing.

Denesha tried again and again. With each try, the nylon dug deeper into her skin, until she felt the slip of liquid on her fingers. She maneuvered the tie wraps higher up her wrists where it bit into fresh skin.

She took a deep sustaining breath and wondered what Rocco was doing with the shovel.

Just following orders.

Maggie's warning echoed in her head. Denesha wasn't going gentle anywhere with this lot. She raised her arms as high as she could, adding all the lateral pressure she could rally, and slammed them against her backside.

She felt a snap.

The instant release left her reeling onto the dirty floor of the dog cage with hands free and a new problem to solve.

Rocco was out there somewhere, planning her demise. Denesha had to break free before he broke her.

62

Lying to a hooker, a dealer, or even a cop didn't bother Marcus. Lying to the feds was an order of magnitude more stupid. Technically, lying to the cops was illegal, but it was a misdemeanor. He hunted Toya too long to sweat the small stuff. But lying to the FBI was a felony. He wasn't doing hard time for any reason, and the beautiful FBI agent with dark hair and olive skin demanded answers.

"Sir, either you're wasting my time, or you have material information that may help us find the perpetrators of an abduction and a murder."

Special Agent Claudia Seagal was tall for a woman. Marcus stayed seated while she loomed over him.

"Either way, you better tell me the truth."

She was no pushover. He couldn't evade her questions entirely. If he didn't cooperate, she could hand his sorry ass on a platter to the nearest judge and face a nickel in the federal pen.

Not. An. Option.

Marcus rode this trail for so many years. He was weary. Weary of the chasing, the running, the lying. It was a pattern he perfected. For the sake of the victims, he had to trust her with the truth.

"Everything I told you is true. But before I tell you anything else, I want immunity."

His comment raised eyebrows around the room.

The blonde, Maggie, was the first to voice her surprise. "Immunity. From what? What did you do?"

Claudia held an arm out toward Maggie, as if to keep her at bay. "Happy to discuss that, sir. Now why would you need immunity?" Claudia gently resumed her spot on the couch, touching the holster at her hip. No doubt her weapon was at the ready.

"I haven't told you everything." He glanced at Maggie and her brother with the black hair and green eyes. Even with the world rocking beneath them, their sky was still blue.

"That much is apparent, sir." She said, "But I don't give immunity for murder."

"I'm no murderer." Though in his heart, he'd committed that crime a thousand times. "You're right. I run a trucking business with my brothers in Pensacola."

"So, what are you doing here?" Maggie jumped into the conversation, but Claudia shot her a look to back off.

"I know you served your country in Afghanistan, so I'm inclined to give you some leeway if you tell me the truth." She said, "For starters, tell me how you know the silver car was on Tunitas Creek Road."

The breath he held for eight years stuttered on his exhale. "I am looking for Toya Price, but she's not my sister." Marcus told that lie to Maggie, not the fed. "She lives in San Francisco but wasn't home when I arrived last week." He leaned forward, resting his forearms on his thighs. "I hoped to talk to her when she returned."

Claudia's gaze was relentless. "What did you do?"

He tugged on his ragged ear lobe. "I put a camera in her home, and I paid a guy to put a GPS tracker on any car that stopped by her house."

"What else?"

"Nothing, ma'am. That's the extent of it."

"So where was the car on Tunitas?"

Marcus took his phone out of his back pocket and navigated to the tracker app. "Here." He pointed at the screen. "But I lost the signal after that. The device was in the OBD port, so the driver might've noticed and removed it."

She examined the map and then typed something into her laptop. When she'd finished, he could tell she was running triage on the million questions she wanted to ask. He offered a few quick answers.

"In San Francisco, that car drove a loop from Toya's house to the club where she worked several times a day, so I knew the driver was looking for her. I have video of the guys who were in her house. That's how I can give you a description."

"You're full of surprises." Claudia pulled a notepad from her bag and wrote an email address on it. "Send the file here. Now."

He shared the file to the address and then scanned their faces. He held everyone's full attention.

"When I saw the car travel south from the city, I followed it. There were three men staying at the Manzanita Motel. They drove the silver Civic and a black Chrysler 300." He rubbed his hands together. "I didn't know they were wanted until today when Maggie told me about the kidnapping."

"That Civic—" Marcus poked a finger into the air. "—drove a similar loop locally around the yellow house on Custer Street. Driving by. Parking down the street. Slowing down as it passed. So I expected to find Toya there."

"You have all the logs from the tracker?" Claudia said.

"I do." The information might not be admissible in court, but the files could help them find witnesses.

"I wanted to stop by on Friday to show Toya's picture around, but the Civic was stopped on the road in front of the house. I waited for it to leave before I approached the home. When I did, I met your friend—"

"Denesha." Maggie pulled her feet under her on the couch. "Her name is Denesha."

He nodded. "Denesha didn't recognize Toya."

"That's when you started watching our place."

How had he sunk this low? Breaking into houses—breaking the law. Scaring innocent strangers unfortunate enough to get sucked into his miserable orbit. He pressed on his left leg to stop his foot from bouncing.

"I drove by the yellow house a few times myself, along with watching the three men at the hotel. Friday night, I saw Denesha walk to your house. I knew then I wanted to talk to you."

When considering the events of this morning, his chest felt heavy. "I drove by Denesha's house again this morning, and I saw the Civic leaving." He motioned to Maggie. "I came by your house and saw the surveillance van out front, knowing it was a police action. So I observed from down the street. Eventually, I left to get a proper meal."

He saw the two beagles stir from their sleep. One of them scurried to his side, sending his heart rate into a canter. He gave it the evil eye, hoping it would go away.

Claudia glanced at the siblings and said, "Please remove the dogs."

Travis got up from his seat, hustled the beagles down a hallway, and returned.

Marcus' heart rate lowered to a trot.

"Thank you, Travis." Claudia said, "Please continue, sir."

"When I returned after eating, Denesha's street was congested with emergency vehicles. I didn't know her house was the center of attention, and I didn't want to interfere. So I parked under the tree down this street and waited. Eventually, Maggie came over to my car, and I asked her about Toya."

He sat back and rested his palms on his knees. "And here we are."

"Is that the entire story, sir?" Claudia continued to type without breaking eye contact.

"It is, ma'am."

"I've alerted the task team to the information you provided. It should help us locate the vehicles, so we appreciate you coming forward."

He hoped that was true. Denesha seemed like a sweet girl. Not the kind he usually encountered when looking for Toya. The crimes he committed might help them find her. At least that was a consolation. Perhaps the FBI would see things the same way and grant him immunity from the other crimes. While breaking and entering wasn't a specific crime in California, recording without consent was up to the prosecutor whether to be charged as a misdemeanor or a felony.

Claudia slid the laptop onto the coffee table. Leaning back onto the cushion, she said, "I might be persuaded to believe you, Mr. Fisher. Assuming we can confirm your story."

He was careful not to lie to this woman. His future was in the hands of this cool, dark FBI agent. "I've told you everything I know about the cars and the people driving them. I'm here to help."

She smiled in that way a cat looks when it pins the mouse's tail to the floor. Marcus rolled his shoulders to loosen the tension.

"You're not here to help."

His left foot bounced. "I came here with Maggie as soon as I found out I could be a witness."

"You flew from Naples, Florida, to San Francisco. Then drove here to Half Moon Bay to find this woman, Toya." Claudia's eyes narrowed, and she leaned in so closely, he caught a faint musky scent exuding from her body. "I want to know why."

63

Sol woke with a jolt from the sharp pain to his cheek. When his eyes cracked open, the black guy's face hovered over his. Dwayne. Sol heard one of them say his name. They called Angry Blue Eyes Gil.

"He's awake," Dwayne said.

"Get his ass out of the car." Gil's voice was screechy, like a rusty old gate.

The snatches Sol remembered came to him in fuzzy pictures and sounds of people talking that sometimes sounded like words. He heard them say Denesha was in the woods with the tattooed white guy, Rocco. Gil said he'd shoot her if Sol didn't give them the leather case. Like he shot Mama.

Dwayne grabbed Sol by an arm and a leg and dragged him across the back seat of the car until his feet hung off the edge.

"Stand up, kid." Dwayne's voice was low, like one of the tough guys in his neighborhood. The ones that grabbed you by the shirt collar or threw rocks at your head.

Sol kicked his feet out in search of some ground. When they touched, he pushed off the car door to stand, but his legs were shaky. He leaned against the door, coughing until he thought he'd puke. But nothing came up.

They were in a parking lot. Dwayne shoved Sol. "Let's move."

The ache in Sol's bones was big now, and the pounding in his head sounded like someone was chasing hard after him. Sol wanted some of those red pills Mama gave him when he got hurt. Ibuprofen. He remembered the word from the bottle. But he wasn't getting no medicine from Gil or Dwayne.

And Mama probably wasn't coming back. The day he got that satchel from the police, they hurt her bad.

Sol felt something ugly and sad in his chest. But thinking she might be alive kept him going. Now he didn't believe he'd ever see her again. And even if she was alive, they were going to kill him as soon as they got that case.

But he didn't want that for Denesha.

Sol tilted his head to see Gil. They weren't just angry eyes. They were mean. He liked it when others got hurt. When Gil started walking, Dwayne stayed behind and poked Sol in the back.

It was a day where the sun wasn't shining much, and the good ocean smells told him they were by the beach. He tried to breathe it all in, but his nose was plugged up. When he coughed, his chest stung. He lowered his head and followed Gil.

They parked right next to the trail but didn't follow it. Instead, Gil led them out into the brush. From what Sol remembered, they were down the beach from his camp. Maybe he could run away before they got there.

As they picked their way along, Dwayne kept poking Sol in the back. From somewhere, he heard people happy talking. Their voices were sing-songy like they were having fun. He thought about Denesha and her friends. They seemed happy and nice. They just didn't like Sol stealing their stuff.

Gil made Sol stop. He put his finger over his lips to shush everyone.

The happy talking people were on the trail and coming their way. If Sol yelled out, they might come and help him. Mama told him not to trust anyone, but they couldn't be meaner than Gil or Dwayne. Could they?

Sol didn't want Denesha to get hurt because of him, but no one could help Denesha if he didn't do something.

The pounding in his head made it hard to think.

The people on the trail were coming closer, and he decided to yell for help. But before he made much noise, Dwayne slapped his hands over Sol's mouth. These were powerful hands. Stronger than Tyrone's.

The people took their time walking by, and Dwayne held Sol tight. With his nose plugged up, he couldn't breathe. Sol felt a swelling inside, like his whole body might burst. He couldn't see clearly, his vision fading to black. His heart was fast-running now. His legs wobbled and gave out beneath him.

A picture of his Mama on the sidewalk flashed in his brain, and he bit hard into Dwayne's hand. Dwayne dropped him like he was on fire. Sol gasped in as much air as he could and fell to the ground.

Cool leaves met his cheek. He wouldn't yell for help now. He just wanted to breathe. Dwayne kept quiet during the biting, but Sol felt a solid kick to his leg. The cool ground felt almost as good as his bed.

He fell asleep or something. The next Sol knew, the voices from the trail were gone and someone lifted him by the back of his shirt.

"You bite me again, kid, and I will throw you over the cliff." Dwayne turned Sol around, glaring at him with buggy eyes. "You read me?"

Sol didn't answer. Talking made it harder to breathe.

"He broke my skin, Gil." Dwayne shook his hand like a cat with a wet paw. "If he has something contagious—" He slapped Sol upside the head.

"You covered his mouth." Gil rolled his eyes. "The kid couldn't breathe."

Dwayne said, "You take him for a while."

"Quit your whining." Gil put his hands on his hips. "Where is it, kid? We should be close."

He pointed toward his camp.

A breeze came off the ocean, and one of Sol's nostrils finally opened. He took in some of the air, but it was wet, like the fog. The mistiness made him cough, and the coughing made him so tired.

His Mama used to make him take naps. Especially when she had visitors at the house. Sol didn't like those naps, but right now, a nap sounded so good.

Gil came up and pushed Sol. "Get moving."

Eventually, they were going to take the satchel for real.

What would happen to Denesha then?

64

They built dog cages to keep an animal with paws contained, not a human. Unless it was locked, a toddler would find his way out once he saw the mechanism work a few times. Intellect coupled with thumbs offered substantial advantage.

In Denesha's case, Rocco upped the security ante with tie wraps. He tie-wrapped the latch mechanism like it was an Egyptian mummy. She couldn't snap those like the one on her wrists.

The cuts on her wrists were painful but superficial, scraping the skin until it was raw and bleeding. Bruising would follow.

A quick call on her hidden phone would bring help in full force, but it was useless inside the cabin.

No cell coverage bars. Just cage bars.

She couldn't let Rocco know her hands were free until it mattered. For now, she had to figure out how to get out of the cage.

A squeak came from outside. Denesha whipped her head toward the door and listened. It was rhythmic, with a cadence that sounded like a grocery cart with a bad wheel. She sat on the broken tie wrap and kept her hands behind her back in case Rocco returned.

Her breathing suspended as she monitored the open door. From her corner in the cabin, she only saw a sliver of the outdoors, and the two tiny windows were too dirty to see anything from a dog's eye view.

Whatever it was, the squeaking ended as abruptly as it started. Maybe it was a bird.

Fortunately, there was no sign of Rocco.

Denesha's chest filled with the damp air of the cabin, and she renewed her examination of the cage. The six-sided cage was constructed of painted metal wire that was three times the thickness of a sturdy coat hanger. Rust settled in the joints, but without tools, she wasn't bending the wire.

Designed to collapse for storage, she studied how the panels connected. Despite the tie wraps on the latch, the front panel held the most promise. Wire loops at the top edge bent onto the roof panel to keep it locked in place. Denesha would have to release the wire loops from the roof panel and pull the front panel inside the cage with her.

She didn't need to be Houdini to breakout. But where was Rocco?

He was the x-factor that played on her fears. He might hear the panel clatter and catch her before she crawled out of the cage. She might make it outside, only to have him gun her down before she could get help. If she did get outside, then what? All she knew was that she was in the middle of a forest. Her sense of direction sucked when she was downtown, but it was nonexistent in the woods.

Denesha had to find a spot where she could call the police. If Rocco caught her before then, she wouldn't get a second chance. She'd end up like sweet Sharla. Denesha channeled her rampant anxiety into making her escape.

Denesha pressed upward on the left wire loop that fastened the front panel to the roof. Yanking hard on the roof panel, the left side broke free.

Ten long seconds passed while she listened for Rocco. Nothing stirred.

She repeated the motions on the right side of the front panel, finally separating it from the roof.

With the front panel loose, it could only fold inside the cage toward her. Denesha cleared the panel past the other sides of the cage. But now, she was in the way. She scooted back as far as she could, with barely room for the panel to clear her. Now the panel lay on her lap.

It was an awkward exercise, but she held the side panels of the cage, her torso leaning over the front panel as it angled over her lap. With a firm grasp, she hoisted her butt off the floor, shimming her feet toward the rear of the cage.

Sweat dripped from her forehead, and her back ached from the strain. Denesha stopped again to listen for Rocco, but she heard only the thump-thump of blood coursing through her veins.

The panel now rested on her left shoe. She eased her foot away until the wire panel rested on the cage floor. Her fingers uncurled from their grip on the side panels, and she shook them to revive their motion.

Denesha stepped carefully onto the wire panel, making sure the pressure of her weight didn't create noise that would garner Rocco's attention. As she crept out of the cage, she tested each step before trusting it with her life.

Finally, she was clear of the cage door. She imagined a flock of birds let loose into a welcoming sky. But she still had to clear the cabin, which now just felt like a larger cage. Denesha moved to a wall near the cabin door and considered her next steps.

She didn't want to hang around, but a wrong decision was worse than none. She got her phone out from the back of her sports bra. No bars. She tucked it back between her shoulder blades.

From the front door, the porch overhang obstructed her view of the property. Was he standing around the corner or off in the trees digging her grave? Denesha glanced about the room for a weapon. The old fireplace had a lone stick leaning against it. Not much use against a gun, but Rocco wasn't the only animal in the woods.

With stick in hand, she peered obliquely out the front door from the right side. When Denesha decided it was clear, she backed away and went to the left. If he was around, he wasn't in the front yard. She said a quick prayer before stepping onto the porch.

Denesha worked the six feet of porch like a minefield. The ball of her foot touched first, bearing her weight on each creaky old board in fear. With each agonizing step, she scanned the area for Rocco.

As she stood at the edge of the porch, she craned to hear any clues to his location. The cool air offered only the smell of decaying leaves and cedar. Appearing to be alone, she scurried to a stand of trees near the vehicle.

She quickly checked her phone again. One bar, cutting in and out.

It would be difficult to make a call from this location. Rocco could return at any moment. There were tracks in the vegetation behind the car's wheels that had to lead to a road. The road was Denesha's best hope for help. She followed the tracks until she got a safe distance from the cabin.

While she sneaked from tree to tree, Denesha kept a keen lookout for Rocco. Sunlight came in flashes where the canopy allowed its passage. It would be dark within the hour, and she didn't want to know what else might live in the forest. She stuffed those thoughts and pressed on.

When she'd put some distance between herself and the cabin, she checked her phone. One bar.

She called 9-1-1 and hoped the single bar held out long enough to alert the police.

65

Marcus Fisher clearly heard Claudia's question. It seemed to make him uncomfortable. Or angry. Travis couldn't read him.

She leaned in closer. "Sir, I'm going to ask you again. Why are you stalking this woman, Toya Price?"

The question lit Marcus' face like a lightning bolt. "She stole my son."

Definitely anger.

Claudia's shoulders dropped. "Is she the mother?"

"Yes."

"What's your legal status with her and the child? Are you married? Who has legal custody?"

"Toya does. No. We never married." Marcus swatted his knee. "I deployed to Afghanistan. She never told me she was pregnant."

Claudia's posture softened, her gaze sweeping over Travis and Maggie. "I'm sorry, sir. I presume you consulted an attorney on this matter."

"Several. I have to find her before anyone can help me claim my son."

"Do you have evidence of paternity?"

It was a delicate way of asking who else might be the father. A fair concern, since the guy was overseas. The subtlety wasn't lost on Marcus.

"I don't. But I'm sure the boy is mine. He'd be over eight now." Water welled in his deep brown eyes. "I just want my son to have his father."

Whatever the truth of this situation, Travis admired the man's dedication. Every single day, Travis missed his own father.

It was a long day for everyone. Along with Travis, this conversation seemed to make Claudia weary. Her sigh was audible.

"I appreciate your situation, sir. Unfortunately, there's nothing we can do. Unless there's an outstanding warrant for parental abduction, we have no jurisdiction to assist."

"That's what they all tell me, ma'am." His voice was guttural, resigned. "Toya has outstanding arrest warrants for other offenses, but I have to find her before she can be extradited."

Something about his mannerism sparked Travis' memory. "Do you have a picture of the boy?"

For a half-beat, Claudia and Maggie froze.

Travis thought he saw a resemblance. It was between Sol and Toya. Now he saw Sol's resemblance to Marcus.

"No. We've actually never met."

Claudia reached over the table and held out her hand. "You have the mother's picture. Let's see that."

Marcus reached in his back pocket for his wallet and withdrew a rumpled photo. "This is Toya."

She studied the photo before handing it back. "Sir. I'm going to show you a photo of a woman that we know by another name, and I need you to tell me if this is Toya."

He drew in a sharp breath. "You know her? Where is she?"

"I'm sorry, sir. But the woman in the photo that I have is no longer living." She hesitated. "Do you think you'll be able to tell me if it's Toya?"

Marcus' focus seemed to wander as if he were afraid to let it settle. His head tremored in tiny declarations of dissent. When he replied, "Yeah. I can," his chin trembled.

Claudia's lips folded inward as she navigated on her laptop. When she was done, she turned the screen toward Marcus.

His brow dropped at the gravity of viewing a dead body, but Travis sensed no loss. Marcus blinked in rapid succession. "That's her." His jaw set, he refocused on Claudia. "Now where's my son?"

The conversation turned in a way none of them expected when Maggie first noticed Marcus down the street. Travis thought about Sol, this man's son, living on the beach.

As an FBI agent, Claudia was likely used to delivering devastating news. Her countenance bore only sympathy.

She gently spun the laptop around to her side. Her words were careful. "I'm sorry, sir. But the boy we believe is Toya's son was kidnapped along with Denesha Roberts. They were likely taken in the silver Civic you identified."

Marcus' steely façade didn't waver when he heard the news about Toya's death. He'd been searching for her for so many years. Whatever they once shared, there was no apparent surprise or grief over her demise.

After news of Sol's abduction, Marcus stared as if the words didn't permeate. When the truth finally cut through his fog, fingers covered his open mouth. Short, plaintive wails ruptured from lips. Marcus wrapped his arms around his torso and rocked.

"Oh, my God!" Maggie leapt up and ran into the kitchen, while Claudia stayed calmly in place.

Travis wasn't sure what to do. Maggie returned with a tumbler full of water and sat it on the table in front of Marcus. The big man continued to mourn while the rest of them could only pretend not to gape.

His motion slowed as two shaky hands reached out to seize the water glass, downing half of it in a continuous guzzle. He placed the glass on the table and glanced at everyone in the room. Marcus' knuckles touched his lips, and he closed his eyes. "Why was he taken? Why would those men want to take my boy?"

"We don't know, sir." Claudia said, "We're still investigating. But the information you gave us will help us find your son."

His sniffed loudly. "Where has he been staying?"

The question reignited Travis' guilt. He pursued the boy. Thought Sol was a budding local criminal, not an endangered child. But Travis owned this.

"We think he's been staying on the beach." He said, "I have video of him if you'd like to see it."

Marcus' eyes blinked open. "Yes, I would." He drew a handkerchief from his pocket and pressed it to his face, his body unfurling to its full stature. "You really have video of him?" Marcus' brittle voice was hopeful but cautious. "I've never actually seen him."

Maggie got up and sat next to Marcus on the couch, touching the back of his hand. "He's a beautiful boy."

He assented with a simple nod.

Travis had the video ready to play, but felt that it needed to come with a warning. "We noticed items missing from our back porch, so we set up cameras." He waited for a reaction, but none came. "He took essentials. Food. Warm clothing." Travis' conscience panged in guilt. While he obsessed over the loss of a jacket, a young boy needed its warmth to survive.

Maggie said, "He actually washed a dish and returned it with some seashells." Her face lowered behind a veil of blonde hair. "We didn't know he was living on the beach."

Travis hit the play button.

They'd watched this video many times. Now, as it played, they watched Marcus.

It was the brief clip of Sol coming onto the porch to scout for an outlet to charge a phone. After searching for his son all these years, it had to be disappointing for Marcus to see him this way.

But he grinned, laughter spilling along with tears. "That's my boy!" He moved to the edge of the couch. "That's my boy!" Marcus grabbed Maggie by the shoulders and kissed her forehead.

For most people, that would've been a dangerous move. A diner once tried to grab her when she was waitressing. Maggie accidentally stabbed his hand with a fork. With Marcus, she only smiled.

"He's extremely resourceful." Maggie added, "If we'd known—"

But the ugly truth remained. Sol was still missing.

"The investigation is ongoing." Claudia stood and said, "Mr. Fisher. I need to confer with my team. I'd like to get your contact information."

Marcus stood, sobered by the comment, and pulled a card from his wallet. "Here's my cell phone. Please let me know when you learn something. Anything."

"Of course." She studied the card for a moment. "We have a joint task force on this investigation, and the information you provided might be the break we need to locate your son."

Claudia packed her laptop in her case. "I'm leaving, but we will keep you apprised of any developments."

"I need to talk to you first." Travis gestured toward the backroom. He didn't have time to brief Maggie about his interest in Byron Suliani, but she stayed behind with Marcus.

Claudia followed him into his office. "You look like a man with concerns."

"Not about Marcus."

Travis told her about Byron Suliani's security work at DocuLocker, the document software company, and his stroke near the park where Sol found the leather satchel. "Maybe it was Byron's. The separate incidents on the police blotter were within the same hour."

"I'm listening." Claudia seemed to take his theory seriously.

"I think Suliani found a vulnerability in ModifySoft, the routine that updates other software, and he wrote some code to exploit it. The code creates an open window to steal files that are stored in DocuLocker." Travis paused, "Or other software."

Claudia low-whistled. "That code would be worth billions."

"I know, right? Suliani had the technical chops to pull it off. Maybe he was meeting a buyer in the park when he died."

She pinched the bridge of her nose. "Okay, send me any evidence you have, and my team will take it from here."

While it was thrilling to discover the connection, Travis felt his burden lift. "Thanks."

They walked back to the living room and Claudia said, "I'll let myself out."

Marcus and Maggie were still on the couch as the video of Sol replayed. Marcus said, "Do you know where he's been living? Can you show me?"

Travis expected the question and dreaded it. "After seeing the video last night, I ran after him. Found him out on the bluff." He couldn't think of a good way to say it. "When I tried to talk to him, that only scared him off. Now I know why."

Maggie was aware of his apprehension over that detail and added, "Denesha went to look for him early this morning. They must've connected."

In a near whisper, Marcus said, "Such a big thing for a small boy."

"Yeah." Travis rose. "I can show you the general area where he camped."

"Please do."

"We'll go out the back way."

Now that the excitement subsided, Maggie appeared pensive.

"You coming, Magpie?"

She strapped both arms across her chest. "No. I'll wait here."

Travis was worried for Denesha, too, but at least now they had some leads. "I'll be back soon."

He wanted to bring Bailey and Belli, but left them at the house. He led Marcus out the back door to the porch and said, "I guess you're not a dog person."

"Can't say I'm a fan." Marcus tugged his torn earlobe. "Rabid dog bit this off when I was in Afghanistan. The vaccine shots were worse than the bite. Not as bad as the old days when they hit you twenty times in the stomach, but I wouldn't wish it on anyone."

"That might do it for me, too." Travis pointed. "Sol stayed up on the bluff. There's more protection from the wind than on the beach, but it's fairly desolate. Lots of scrub trees and brush."

"Considering all the places I tracked his mother, it might be an improvement."

Travis could only imagine what Marcus meant, but it was clear he didn't hold the woman in high regard.

As they hiked up the hill to the bluff, Travis said, "There's probably nothing to see up here." He slowed to glance back at Marcus. "I'd hate to get your hopes up."

66

Denesha's heart drum-rolled as she waited for someone to answer her call. With each ring, she wondered. Where was Rocco?

Finally, an efficient male voice said, "9-1-1. What's your location?"

"In a forest in the foothills. I don't know where." The quiet of the forest now unnerved her. The sound of her voice seemed to boom. "They kidnapped me and a boy named Sol, but I escaped."

"What's your name?"

"Denesha Roberts."

"Stay on the phone with me, Denesha. Is your abductor near you?"

"I don't see him."

"Are you injured?"

"No. But they still have Sol."

"Who abducted—"

She clung to his last word, waiting for him to finish the sentence. But the call dropped. Her phone still showed a single bar.

Denesha pushed 9-1-1 again, but this time got dead air.

A branch snapped behind her. Her limbs tightened, and she pressed her body against the tree.

Several seconds passed.

The 9-1-1 operator would try to call her back. She found the volume control and lowered it to mute.

Denesha wasn't sure how long she waited, but after hearing nothing else, she had to move.

The dropped call with the 9-1-1 operator left her rattled, and she had to reorient herself to the road. With stick in hand, she picked her way from tree to bush, seeking cover and praying her tenuous steps were in the right direction.

She tried 9-1-1 again. No ringing. No connection. Only one fading bar and no way out.

Her thoughts traveled to Maggie, and Denesha hit speed dial.

Maggie answered on the first ring. "My God, Denesha! Where are you? Are you hurt?"

Hearing Maggie's voice, Denesha couldn't keep it together any longer, and she sobbed into the phone.

"Denesha, are you hurt?"

"No." The word came out as a wail. She sniffed hard. "I escaped from a cabin into the woods." The dark trees hovered like specters. "Now I'm lost."

"You listen to me." Instead of sympathetic, Maggie's voice was stern. "Focus! You're getting out of there. You hear me?"

Denesha's ordeal wasn't over. It was just mobile. Until Rocco was no longer a threat, she was still in the cage. She swept an arm across her face. "I hear you."

"Where are the kidnappers? How many are there?"

"Two went into town with Sol. Just one guy left to watch me. I don't know where he is."

"Did you call the police?"

Her body sank against the tree. "The call keeps dropping."

"I'll call them. Where's the cabin?"

"In the foothills. I don't know where."

"Can you get on the internet?"

"The internet? Why would I want—"

"If you have any access, get on the map software. Add my email address to the location sharing. I'll be able to track you on the map."

"Okay."

"Hang up and do it now."

Denesha didn't want to end the call, didn't want to be alone.

Maggie's voice was decisive and hopeful. "You need the bandwidth, Neesh. Trust me."

"I know. I do. Love you, girl."

"Love you, too. Now hang up!"

Denesha's finger trembled when it pressed the end call icon on her phone. Would she ever hear Maggie's voice again?

Denesha navigated to the map app, but it didn't bring up her location. She felt the phone vibrate. It was the same concerned male voice of the 9-1-1 operator.

"Denesha Roberts, are you still in danger?"

"Yes. I'm in the forest still. I called my friend."

"We need to keep you on the phone long enough to triangu—"

The call ended as abruptly as it came. She slapped the phone against the side of her leg.

If she could only find one more bar in the place, they'd be able to locate her. Rocco had to know she was gone by now. If so, he'd be on her trail.

Denesha gripped her stick and left her cover in search of that second bar. As she walked, she had no bars, no service of any kind. Eventually, she reached a spot where she found the scorched remains of a recent fire. Stripped of all foliage, only the blackened trunks remained of the trees, and she found her elusive second bar.

Navigating to the map app, she saw her location. She realized she'd traveled in the opposite direction of the road, deeper into the forest than even the cabin. Maggie's voice echoed in her ears. Focus!

Finding the location sharing feature, Denesha added Maggie's email address. Hopefully, she'd be able to get a blip now and again and feed the information to the police. But Denesha didn't plan to sit here in the woods waiting for Rocco to bury her. She called 9-1-1 again, and that's when she heard Rocco's gravelly voice.

"You're going to be sorry you ran away, Denesha."

67

Maggie was already in the car and driving toward the foothills when she received notification from the map app. Denesha's first location report! Maggie's hope soared as she called the police. They knew the general vicinity of her whereabouts from the cell tower information they'd gathered and dispatched some units from the task force. But this report was much more specific, offering actual coordinates of her location.

The location report placed her up Tunitas Creek Road, in a heavily forested area that matched Denesha's description of her surroundings. It also aligned with Marcus' report of the silver Civic. But the report was already nine minutes old, and Denesha wouldn't stay in one place. If the kidnapper noticed her missing, she was in danger. While she wasn't a rugged outdoor type, as a daily runner, she had speed and endurance as allies.

When Maggie spoke to the police, they were still trying to reconnect the call with Denesha. That mountain range was notorious for spotty access. In places, it was quite strong. In others, it was nonexistent. They wanted Maggie's help, since she had the link to Denesha's movements, but they wouldn't allow her up Tunitas Creek Road past the first checkpoint. Whatever, Maggie wasn't staying home.

She kept her GPS open while she traveled toward Denesha's location, hoping for another update. Even knowing she was in the same place would be a blessing. When the next blip arrived, it was clear Denesha was on the move. The police gave Maggie a direct number to contact Officer Standish when she got updates on Denesha. Maggie called him with the latest.

Officer Standish said, "Her revised position puts her closer to the main road, which is helpful. What we can't tell is if her captor is in pursuit. We plan

243

to infiltrate the area, but we need to make sure we don't create an incident by our presence. You're sure she's only being guarded by one man?"

Denesha was observant, careful. Yes, Maggie was sure.

"That's what Denesha told me. If she didn't know, she wouldn't have specified a number. She was quite clear. Two men took Sol back to town, and one man remained to guard her in the cabin. When that man left the cabin, she escaped."

"Excellent. That information will help both teams in pursuit." He said, "What's your ETA?"

"I'm about five minutes out."

"We appreciate your cooperation, Ms. Fender. We have a blockade closer in, near a cabin where we think Ms. Roberts was being held. When you get to the checkpoint, don't get out of your car for any reason."

"Of course," Maggie said. But the officer's voice gave her concern. "What's happened?"

"We don't want you to be alarmed, but we heard gunshots. Around here, it could just be a poacher."

A poacher or a killer.

Now it was Maggie's turn to keep her head on straight. Fear was a soul crusher. She couldn't let it control her. Maggie drove on.

The road narrowed at this elevation, and the first checkpoint was still a mile away. Out here, there weren't any homes or businesses near the road, only obscured lanes and acres and acres of woodlands. Glorious, majestic, and a terrifying place to be lost. On a good day, there were mountain lions, coyotes, and even bears. The thought of tiny Denesha fending for herself in that environment made Maggie sad and angry.

Just then, another location report came from her phone. Denesha's position was now about a hundred yards to the right of Maggie's car.

68

As Travis trudged up to the bluff, he felt the weight of the long day in his bones. The morning started with singular focus and sky-high energy, but now he was spent. He understood why Marcus wanted to see where his son had been living, and after hounding the kid, Travis owed them both.

It was nearing sunset, and the shadows cast exaggerated images of everything. He and Marcus appeared the size of giants, while the bushes loomed as monsters, clawing the earth with scraggy branches.

Marcus echoed the sentiments. "It's hard to imagine a boy out here by himself. My boy." His eyes squinted. "The place looks spooky now, and it's not even dark."

"Yeah. I've lived here a long time, and I don't come out here at night unless I have good reason."

Like chasing a scared kid.

They reached the top and continued along the trail. A young Asian couple coming toward them took the spur to the parking lot. Marcus checked his watch. "Not a lot of light left. How far from here?"

"Maybe five minutes." Travis remembered the spot where he'd found Sol the prior night. Even before he ran, Travis sensed the boy's fear. Travis planned to go back this morning and find him, but he'd relinquished that duty to Denesha. Now they were both in danger.

The trail wended along the bluff, offering glimpses of a technicolor sunset over a calm ocean. "Is it safe up here?" Marcus pointed toward the water without taking his focus off the trail. "I hear this town sees gigantic waves."

The stormy season was coming, which brought the legendary waves at Mavericks that extended up to sixty feet in height. While the conditions brought big-wave surfers from around the globe, Travis was purely a spectator.

"The monster waves occur in only one spot. Pillar Point. It's north of here and conditions have to be right. But, yeah, they are mighty."

They neared the area Travis saw Sol the night before. He slowed and tapped Marcus' arm. "Let's head into the brush."

Marcus scanned the area as they moved off the trail. "How long has he been out here?"

"We noticed something missing from our porch on Tuesday morning. So maybe since Monday."

Sol's fatigued silhouette in the moonlight had etched Travis' memory in vivid detail. If the kid had taken anything but that jacket, maybe Travis wouldn't have so thoroughly lost his mind.

They entered a clearing among several copses, and Travis said, "I'm not certain where Sol camped." One section of the brush looked much like the next. "But it's probably around here."

Marcus stood still, hands on hips, and seemed to breathe in the environs.

Scrubby yellow flowers claimed their turf among the tough coastal greenery that clung to the earth. With the ocean at their doorstep, wind was constant, and the terrain yielded under its perpetual sway. Now, the wind scented the air with pine and brine.

Travis left Marcus to his thoughts until he heard someone or something moving through the brush. Travis held up a hand so the intrusion wouldn't take Marcus by surprise. The beach attracted all sorts—wild animals and wild people. His father taught him to always be prepared.

Two men pushed their way through a small stand of trees, one black and stocky, the other big and white, and with them, the young boy Solomon.

Marcus gasped.

The white guy had his hand around Sol's wrist. Sol coughed and wobbled to a stand, his eyelids at half-mast. The men matched the description of the kidnappers.

Travis noticed the pistol pointing his way.

Whatever these two wanted out here on the bluff, they didn't expect company. While Travis and Marcus wanted to help Sol, neither of them were prepared for a gunfight.

69

Maggie hadn't made it to the police checkpoint when she stopped the car. Denesha was close.

She left the engine running and called the police again.

"Officer Standish here."

"I got another report on Denesha. It shows her in the woods near me." Maggie referred to her map. "I'm still a mile south of the checkpoint."

"We're sending a car to your location, and we'll keep you on the phone until it arrives."

"Okay."

"You need to leave the area immediately, ma'am. The perpetrator may be in pursuit."

"In pursuit?" Maggie imagined someone chasing Denesha. "I hope not." While her normal speed would be tough to match, she may have been hurt since they last talked. "How long before the police get here?"

"It's rolling now, ma'am. Just drive down the hill. Let us handle this."

Denesha was a soccer field's distance from the road. On the flat, she could cover that ground in under twenty seconds. The police car had to drive a mile on bad roads. At sixty miles an hour, that was sixty seconds before it arrived.

Denesha might not have forty seconds to spare.

Craaack! A shot sounded nearby in the woods.

Maggie ducked, dropping her phone on the floorboard. She felt for the KelTec pistol still strapped to her ankle. The magazine was full. She cycled a round into the chamber and laid it on her lap.

Where were the police? Had it been a minute? Two?

She scanned the car floor for her phone, finding it under the brake pedal. The call was still live. "Are you there?"

"Yes, ma'am." Officer Standish's voice was calm. "Have you left the area?"

"I heard a gunshot in the woods," Maggie panted the words.

"You need to get out of the area immediately."

"I know." She should. It was stupid to stay. But Maggie couldn't leave until the police arrived.

No doubt the officer had more sage advice, but she dropped the phone in the cup holder. It made sense to at least turn the car around, so it pointed downhill. She swung the vehicle in a wide arc for a U-turn, but the road was too narrow for a single maneuver.

Then Denesha burst onto the road.

She sprinted to the passenger's door and scrambled to get inside. Maggie quick-reversed onto the road, rocks spraying behind them. As she threw the gearshift into drive, a man bolted onto the road.

When he saw the women, he glared.

"That's him!" Denesha shrank in her seat.

Maggie spotted his gun. He leveled it at the car and fired.

The blast rocked the car, punching a jagged hole in the windshield. Thunderous reverberations muddled her thoughts. Images flashed of Yang at the moment he met death.

She felt for the gun in her lap.

The man strode toward her car with no apparent fear. He saw two weak women. When he smiled at them, Maggie's anger boiled into rage.

She released the pistol, gripped the steering wheel with both hands, and floored it.

He leveled his weapon a second time, looking perplexed when Maggie's car didn't stop.

The front bumper slammed into his body with a sickening thud. His body flew into the air, but she didn't slow down. When her heart rate dropped to a stampede, she resumed her call with Officer Standish.

The police were welcome to take their time now.

70

Sol coughed into his elbow until his chest hurt. When he looked again, there were two other men standing near him. At first, he couldn't tell who they were. Sol's eyes were achy, and sweat from his forehead rolled in, making them sting. He tried to catch a breath, but even with the breeze, he couldn't pull in enough air to stop the wheezing.

Seeing the raggedy-eared man with Black Hair from the nice house didn't seem real, more like a bad dream. How did they know each other?

With four of them now, the money Sol had left would give them about $2,000 each. Gil pointed a gun at the new people. He probably didn't want to share.

"So you followed us here." Gil stood wide like a TV gunfighter. "Big mistake." He waved the gun at the raggedy-eared man. "What's your name, big man?"

"Mar—Marcus Fisher."

Mama said to watch out for this one, but she never said his name was Marcus. The way she talked about him, Sol expected him to be giant-sized and maybe breathing fire. Right now, he seemed more scared than scary.

Marcus watched Sol the way the lady from the services did after Mama was arrested.

"And who the hell are you?" Gil sounded angrier at Black Hair than Marcus.

"Travis Fender," he said, "I live nearby."

Marcus stepped toward Sol. "The boy's sick. He needs a doctor."

Dwayne said, "You stay right there." He now had a gun, too.

"If they move, shoot them both." Gil squeezed Sol's shoulder, digging his fingers in until it hurt. "This is all on you, kid. Where is it?"

Sol knew what Gil wanted, but his head was fuzzy from the throbbing. Couldn't he just sleep for a while?

Gil dug in his fingers again.

Sol shrunk under the sharp grip, but it woke him up a bit more. He tried to focus. Maybe they'd let Denesha go once they got the money. Maybe they'd let him sleep.

He pulled away from Gil. The elbow tree was around here somewhere. Sol was pretty good at figuring out directions. The ocean was on his left. He backed up to check the trees and knew this wasn't the right spot.

"It's this way, Gil." He pointed.

"It better be, kid." Gil was like the mean kids on the street. Couldn't say nothing without adding a threat.

Sol didn't bother talking back. Never helped. Just bought more trouble.

He knew it was the right way because there was a worn-down spot between the two groups of trees. After staying here for a while—How long had it been?—He knew the area pretty well. Mama taught him that.

Whenever he and Mama moved, scouting the area was the first thing they did. Had to find a grocery store, drug store for makeup, a gas station if they had a car, and a hair place for Mama. They didn't always look for a school right away. Mama wanted to make sure they were going to stay.

Sol's legs weren't happy about having to walk. They acted all rubbery like Tyrone's did when he brought Mama home from work. Sol held on to the branches to keep himself upright.

It was weird having all the grownups follow him. They usually didn't pay him much attention. When Sol set out, that Marcus jumped in right behind Sol, patting the same shoulder Gil squeezed. Mama should've warned Sol about Gil. So far, Marcus with the raggedy ear didn't seem so bad.

On the other side of the worn-down path was another patch of brush. Sol's lungs felt heavy like that time he had bronky-itis, only worse. Sol grabbed onto the branches, pulling himself through to the other side.

And there it was. The elbow tree.

Sol leaned against a different tree to rest and faced the group. "The case is in a hole at the bottom of that tree." He tried to breathe, but he wasn't getting much air in him. "The one with the elbow."

Gil walked ahead of them all and stood in front of the elbow tree. He was finally smiling. "It's about damn time. Let's get it, Dwayne."

Travis leaned in to look and got his face real close to Marcus' ear. Dwayne stepped up and poked Travis with his gun. "Dig it up."

Travis didn't seem too happy about being asked to do that, but he got on the ground and started feeling around for the right spot. Dwayne stood to the side and pointed his gun at Marcus.

Sol did a good job hiding the case, covering it with the dirt after making the hole and adding dead tree stuff, so it looked like the rest of the ground. No reason to look at that tree and think there was hidden treasure.

Travis found the right spot, taking off all the dead leaves and branches piled on until he was down to the dirt.

He reached for a stick, but Gil said, "Use your hands."

When Travis stared at Gil, Travis' olive green eyes reminded Sol of that old cat that came around their place in Detroit. He looked ready to hiss and spit, too.

Once Gil got the case, maybe Sol could get some sleep. He hoped Gil would just let him stay out here by the elbow tree when this was done, but he wasn't sure what would happen to Denesha. And now, to Travis and Marcus. Sol thought of Sharla with pigeon eyes under the bed. Gil would probably leave all of them the same way.

Sol's body shook from a rush of cold. He had to get out of here before they dug up that satchel. He didn't want to end up with pigeon eyes under no bed.

Travis scratched at the dirt with his fingernails. When he got enough loose stuff together, he scooped it with both hands and tossed it outside the hole. Dwayne kept the gun aimed at Marcus' side, while Travis dug.

The light wasn't so bright now. Sol couldn't tell, but the sun might've already slipped under the ocean. He felt moisture gathering in the air.

Travis squatted over the hole, digging deeper, when he said, "I found something." Gil and Dwayne both inched closer to the hole.

When Gil leaned in to look inside, Travis threw dirt in Gil's face.

His hand covered his eyes. "Dammit!"

Marcus elbowed Dwayne so hard in the nose, Sol heard something crack. Dwayne dropped his gun. Marcus kicked it into a bush and then punched Dwayne in the jaw. He didn't get up again.

Gil blinked to clear the dirt. Those old blue eyes were angrier than ever. But he still had his gun, and he aimed at Sol.

Was it the same gun that shot Mama? Sol was so tired. At least maybe Mama was resting now.

Travis spread out his arms. "You've got what you want. Leave him alone."

Gil waved the gun. "Back off!"

Marcus stepped in front of Sol. Sol looked up the full length of his back. He was such a big man.

Sol's head pounded. Being so tired, his eyelids wouldn't stay open any longer. Darkness crept through his brain, blocking the light. He couldn't stay awake anymore. Sleep was coming even with the grownups talking loud, arguing. Sounds got muffled and echoed, and he couldn't make out any of their words. Black patches took over his vision, pushing out all the other colors, right before he heard the gunshot.

71

The bullet ripped through Marcus' arm. He fell to the ground, taking Sol down with him. Blood spurted from Marcus' bicep like a geyser. His covered the wound with his other hand.

Gil momentarily froze. The satchel he so desperately desired still lay at the bottom of a dirty hole.

Something in Travis snapped. He lunged at Gil, ramming his head into Gil's chest. They were equal in height, but Gil was heavier. He didn't expect the hit and landed hard on his side. Travis crouched over Gil, flailing at his head and chest with both fists. Gil shrank beneath the assault, arms blocking, trying to thwart the blows.

He scanned for the gun. Gil didn't have it, but Travis wouldn't move. He yelled, "Call the police and get an ambulance. A man's been shot!"

Travis didn't know if anyone could hear him, but Marcus' arm needed immediate attention, or he might bleed out in front of his son.

Dwayne stirred. He pushed himself to an unsteady stand.

With Travis's attention on Dwayne, Gil knocked Travis to the side. He tumbled into the brush. Something under the elbow tree glinted in the waning light.

Dwayne noticed it too and stumbled toward the spot. But Travis was closer. He crawled on his belly, stretching out his arm to seize the weapon.

He rolled onto his back and pointed the gun at Dwayne's crooked bloody nose.

Gil lay groaning, holding onto his side.

Travis sat upright, locking glares with Dwayne. "Face down. On the ground now!"

Dwayne complied, giving Travis a chance to get on his feet. He kept the gun on a constant sweep of the two men.

He wanted to help Marcus and Sol, but Travis couldn't risk letting the two men loose. Maybe someone heard the gunshot and called for help. Without medical care, Marcus didn't have long to survive, and Sol wasn't moving. Travis didn't know if he'd been shot, but the kid sure was sick.

And then, sirens penetrated the clamor inside Travis' head.

Sirens.

Instead of judgment, these sounded like mercy.

The police arrived first on the scene with weapons drawn. One of them had a bead on Travis. "Put down the weapon, sir."

Travis' body sagged. He laid the gun on the grass and raised his hands over his head. "These men kidnapped Sol. "

The officers took control of Dwayne and Gil. Another officer restrained Travis while they verified his story.

With the immediate threat contained, police gestured, and EMTs converged on Marcus and Sol to assess their injuries. The medical team quickly loaded Marcus onto a stretcher and hustled him out of the clearing. Sol's stretcher followed close behind.

The police didn't handcuff Gil. Instead, the EMTs loaded him onto another gurney.

The officer said, "Broken ribs."

Broken ribs caused severe pain.

That worked for Travis.

His mind tripped over the events leading to this moment, when Claudia appeared with an entourage of people wearing FBI jackets. She spied Travis and came toward him.

"It's good to see you in one piece. You hurt at all?"

He wiped his chin with the back of his hand. "No. No damage." He motioned toward the hole in the ground. "Byron Suliani's leather case is buried under that tree. They forced Sol to show them where he hid it."

Claudia motioned to her team and said, "Ace in the hole. Dig it up."

A group of three converged on the spot. They retrieved a tan-colored case and a large jean jacket.

Travis winced at the memory. "How's Marcus? Sol?" The boy was so sick.

"Both are in critical condition. Airlifting them to San Mateo Medical right now."

Travis hadn't noticed the helicopter land or takeoff.

Claudia said, "I'm sorry, but you'll need to give the police your statement."

Travis remembered his sister. "I need to let Maggie know. She must be worried sick. Is there any news about Denesha?"

Claudia laid a hand on his shoulder. "Denesha is fine." Her smile went wide. "Let's talk about your sister."

72

Travis had the wine ready when Maggie arrived home with Denesha that night. Denesha quickly showered and returned wearing Maggie's pajamas. They huddled on the couch to share their stories.

Denesha recounted her harrowing capture and escape first, right down to that moment of relief when she saw Maggie on the road. Maggie still reeled from running over Rocco. He was taken to the hospital with multiple fractures and internal bleeding.

After the women gave their statements to the police, they were allowed to go home. Fortunately Denesha's physical wounds were superficial. The mental wounds might take a bit more time.

Travis regaled them with his story last. Denesha particularly enjoyed the part where Travis broke Gil's ribs before his arrest. They called the hospital, but thanks to HIPAA regulations, no one would tell them anything about Marcus or Sol.

Adrenaline kept them awake long enough to hear the details of each one's ordeal, but eventually sleep became the collective priority.

The next morning, Travis made coffee and carried two steaming mugs up to Maggie's room. He listened at the door for their voices before setting the mugs on the floor.

He gently rapped on the door. "Coffee outside the door, ladies. Breakfast in about thirty."

"Thank you," both voices called from the room.

Travis returned to the kitchen to let the dogs in from their run. His phone rang before he reached the back door. It was Claudia.

"How're you and Maggie holding up?" She sounded groggy. The marathon day before took its toll on them all.

"We're good here." He let the beagles inside and went to the kitchen for their food. "What do you know about Marcus or Sol? The hospital won't tell us anything."

"They operated on Marcus last night, and he was in the ICU this morning. He'd be dead if he hadn't stemmed the bleeding before the EMTs arrived. The next hurdle is saving his arm. With the bone and nerve damage, he could lose the use of it." Claudia sighed. "Gunshot wounds are rarely a quick recovery."

"He took that bullet for Sol. Saved the kid's life." Travis scooped out some dog food for the pups and put it in their bowls. "What about Sol? He was in bad shape."

"That's one sick little boy. He contracted fungal pneumonia. Most likely from his exposure to bird droppings on the beach or from his sleeping in a dirt hole for a week. Obviously, we want to interview him, but his health is still in jeopardy. He was dehydrated and physically exhausted. They have him on an anti-fungal treatment and are monitoring him in ICU. The boy needs lots of rest, but they're hopeful."

"Glad to hear that." He scrubbed his hair with a hand. "Do you think they're really related?" From what Travis heard about Sol's mother, it was a reasonable question.

"Marcus is convinced, but he'll need a positive paternity test if he intends to make a legal claim. For both their sakes, I hope so." Claudia paused. "Will you be around in about an hour?"

"Yeah. What's up?"

"I need to talk to you about what we found in Suliani's satchel."

Maggie and Denesha roused from bed and ate breakfast with Travis before Denesha's parents arrived. They drove over from the valley to take her home and coddle her for a few days. After all that had transpired, she didn't object. They also planned to visit Sharla's family to pay their respects.

When Claudia arrived, Maggie ushered her into the living room, while Travis hovered like he was playing one-on-one defense. "What did you find in the case?"

Maggie shot him a quick glare, and he took the hint.

"Would you like some coffee?" He offered Claudia.

"Black, please."

He returned quickly, and they settled in around the coffee table.

Maggie had much to be thankful for, but with the wreckage of the past week, she was fighting a righteous funk. "All the arrests, and we still don't know who killed Yang. He deserves better."

"His murder was egregious." Claudia softened her expression. "Witnessing it as you did was equally appalling. But it's still an open case," she said. "We may not have instant results, but we will follow the evidence."

"I know." Maggie pulled her bare feet onto the cushion.

Claudia sat back with her cup. "To be clear, I can't tell you all that I found in that case. Young Sol turned it in to police because it contained a sizable amount of money. $8,500 when he collected it. But it also held something much more valuable. A micro SD card." She blew away the steam and took a sip.

Maggie just bought a 1TB micro SD card for her phone. Tiny enough to hide anywhere.

"It was tucked inside the satchel where the leather overlapped. Had a string taped to it to retrieve it from the recess." Claudia massaged a temple. "The code you found in the ModifySoft update routine came from the executable code we found on the SD card."

"How did the code gain access?" Travis leaned forward, elbows resting on knees. "Was it through ModifySoft's identity routine?"

"Yes," she said. "The code exploited a vulnerability that bypassed ModifySoft's multi-factor authentication, leaving the system completely unprotected. A user with no legitimate rights could access the system." Claudia sipped her coffee. "Once in, the person could download the schematic files from DocuLocker."

"So it broke the Zero Trust protocols." Maggie wasn't the computer whiz of the family, but she understood the concepts. "But why wasn't the illegal download recorded by R-Bot Systems?"

"Good question." Claudia said, "Since DocuLocker was being upgraded, the exploit code deleted the files that enable monitoring just before the theft. After the theft, the monitoring files were returned and enabled."

"And no one was the wiser." Maggie beamed at Travis. "Except my brainy little brother."

"He captured the information during the disrupting routine. After the routine runs, it erases the registers, so it never appears to be the problem."

"The problem was never with the DocuLocker software." Travis said, "With Byron Suliani's code, someone could steal files from any company using ModifySoft."

Claudia cradled her mug. "I can neither confirm nor deny that assertion."

It was clear from her expression that Travis was right.

"Hypothetically," she continued, "if that were true, the exploit presents an international security risk, which I would not be at liberty to discuss. Companies all over the world use ModifySoft to update critical software. Even if ModifySoft's development team patched the exploit today, many companies won't implement it immediately."

Maggie said, "Travis was right. Byron Suliani was going to sell the code."

Claudia smiled. "Hypothetically, Byron Suliani could've been at the park to meet a buyer. The code on that SD he carried is worth a fortune."

"Any idea who was buying?" Maggie wondered if Gil and his cohorts were talking to the FBI.

"I'm not at liberty to say. The men we arrested immediately lawyered up, and they probably don't even know who the buyer was. Too far down the food chain." Claudia addressed Maggie directly. "But they have ties to the Russian mob."

Vladimir Penniski.

Maggie wondered if it might be him. He lived in the heart of high-tech and had a penchant for easy money and other people's.

She went to his penthouse when her father was missing. Not a social call. It was a perilous climb up the leopard's tree.

The memory of that encounter made her anxious. Maggie didn't want Vladimir Penniski in her widest circle.

73

Monday morning rolled in as if the weekend events resembled normal. Before the sun cracked an eye over the mountains, Maggie hustled out of the house for her fake job.

Travis tried to sleep in, but his mind kept replaying the scenes from the FBI sting and finding Sol on the bluff. Too many images to process.

He plodded into the guitar room and cradled the 1965 Strat. Starting slowly with a riff from Red Hot Chili Pepper's Under the Bridge, he segued into a blues riff inspired by Stevie Ray Vaughn, which paled by any comparison. Travis didn't care. Making music delivered a rare, unbridled escape.

Eventually, the beagles wandered in and parked at his door. Travis shut down the amp and rested the guitar on the wall rack. With his thoughts untangled, he let the dogs outside and returned to his computer for more research.

The death of Yang Tunan had to be related to the document theft. His murder was a targeted hit. Travis spent a few hours reviewing Yang's social media outlets. He didn't dabble on the various platforms, other than his profile on LinkedIn. A search of his connections revealed nothing Travis thought might be a clue.

He directed his effort back to Byron Suliani's history, a brilliant tech, who kicked over that first domino by discovering the vulnerability in the update software. Did he intentionally look for a way to steal company secrets, or did he find the security hole and decide to charge admission?

He went back to Byron's LinkedIn account. Travis already reviewed his list of coworkers, but Byron had 478 direct connections with people at other companies. His secondary and tertiary connections numbered in the thousands.

Automation was Travis' friend. He ran a script to pull the names of Byron's direct connections from the website and write them to a file. While the process was easy, it wasn't fast. After launching the script, he went to find his dogs. By the time Travis and The Firm returned from the beach, the process was finished.

Now that he had the list, he wasn't sure what to do with it. He searched for anyone also named Suliani. No hits.

Travis scanned the names of Byron's associates. Nothing rose in interest, but everything at LinkedIn was sanitized for corporate consumption. No drunken political rants at two in the morning. No inappropriate pics from the boat party. No flaming accusations leveled at strangers. He returned to Facebook, where the real and unreal shared a single dimension.

He started with Byron's grandmother. She was an active poster, picture taker, and had a gazillion people she called friends. Travis dove headfirst into the rabbit hole, scrolling through her list of contacts. Lots of people named Suliani here, plus other names, none of which looked—

Then he noticed one he'd seen before. Lyons. He checked the list from LinkedIn. There it was again. Imelda Lyons. Byron Suliani's older sister.

Imelda worked as a wedding planner in Redwood City. He clicked through her images, most of which were of brides and grooms. But a few seemed personal. He checked carefully the names tagged in each photo.

He found images of Imelda and Byron from when he was younger, thinner. On bikes in the driveway. Digging sand at the beach. In a smiling group photo at Imelda's wedding reception. There were few tags on the reception picture. Travis scanned the faces.

And then he found a person to link the late Byron Suliani and R-Bot Systems. Were those two related?

Travis ran a records search at the county to confirm his theory.

How many degrees of separation was that? Two? Three? Still a long way from Kevin Bacon.

Just then, Travis got a call from Claudia. "We have a lead on the spy at R-Bot Systems. Can you meet us there at eleven?"

Maggie and Baxter met up with Travis and Claudia in the R-Bot Systems lobby. Maggie knew there were developments, but she hadn't been told what they were. She'd missed an earlier call from Travis when she was in a faux meeting with the engineering team, pretending to care about changes in a design.

Baxter ushered them into a conference room off the lobby. "Do you have enough evidence to make an arrest?" He seemed apprehensive.

Claudia nodded with such conviction, Maggie was glad she wasn't the suspect. "Travis provided corroborating evidence this morning. We still need to build a case for trial, but our evidence is solid."

Baxter ran a hand through his hair. "Then let's do it." He made a quick phone call, and a few minutes later, Gail Everly strode into the conference room.

She wore tan sandals that laced up her ankles and disappeared under a flowing flowered dress. Oversized hoops dangled from her ears. A jasmine scent wafted in with her. She looked ready for a garden party, not an interrogation.

"Hi, all." She didn't seem surprised to see the group assembled. "What can I do for you, Baxter?"

He closed the door and leaned against it, while Claudia took control of the conversation. "Ms. Everly. Please have a seat."

A flicker of concern crossed the accountant's face. Everyone at the company understood that Claudia was FBI.

"What's this about?" Gail sat closest to the door.

Claudia rested against the chair back. "I have agents searching your house right now. You worked with Byron Suliani to steal engineering documents from R-Bot Systems and other companies so you could resell them on the dark web."

Gail's eyes cut from person to person. "You can't be serious."

"Oh, but I am." Claudia gestured toward Travis. "Our colleague discovered the code used to steal the documents. You were a consultant at various companies prior to joining R-Bot Systems. Several of them were hacked as well."

Claudia paused for a reaction and then continued.

"He also confirmed that Byron Suliani's older sister is married to your brother. So you've known Byron for what? At least ten years."

Travis raised an eyebrow at Maggie. So that was the reason Travis called that morning.

Claudia said, "Did Byron approach you on the deal? Once he wrote the executable code to breach company defenses, he had to verify that it worked. You were in the perfect position to help him and yourself."

Gail always seemed so cheery, not the iceberg sitting across the table with a scowl. "I want an attorney."

"You're a CPA, Gail. You know how it works. We follow the money. You made several deposits totaling $50,000."

Baxter contained his outward anger to a grimace. Hearing this news must've been a blow. He hand-selected all the members of this team. Gail came highly recommended by several people who knew Clint Masters.

Claudia tapped the table with a fingernail. "But we couldn't understand what happened to Yang Tunan. Who would shoot him? Then we found the emails on his personal computer sent to your private account."

"I didn't kill Yang."

"He threatened to expose you, Gail. He figured out you were the one stealing the design documents. Only he didn't want to stop you, he just wanted his cut of the money."

The news jolted Maggie, recalling images of Yang's death. She tried to reconcile the revelation with what she remembered. While she hadn't known him long, she liked him. He seemed too well-mannered to be a blackmailer.

Gail put her hands on the table and rose. "I didn't kill him."

"Sit down." Claudia's voice was sharp. "Then who did?"

Gail returned to her seat. She was shaking now, her lips flattening into a thin line. "I'm not talking to anyone except my attorney."

Claudia gestured to Baxter, and he opened the door for two men wearing FBI jackets. "Ms. Everly has invoked her right to counsel." She stood. "Gentlemen, please take her into custody."

74

On the 42nd floor, Yuri and Anton played cribbage at the coffee table, while Vladimir Penniski watched a sailboat tack across the San Francisco Bay. This was Vlad's favorite view, as the city cloaked herself in nighttime.

The sailboat headed toward the Golden Gate Bridge, where the Pacific lay beyond. While the waters inside the bay were white-capped and choppy, the treacherous waters beneath that bridge ebbed and flowed, churning with a force that surpassed the Mississippi River at flood stage. Like the rest of the city, from this height, the boat was tiny, insignificant.

The doorbell sounded a few minutes early. Vlad adjusted the button line on his white silk shirt and stayed by the window.

Yuri stowed the cards and cribbage board, while Anton returned from the door with Augie Barrett. Augie walked toward Vlad, but when the brothers flanked him, he stopped in the middle of the room, shifting his weight between his feet.

Vlad surveyed the underling. "You're late."

Augie's eyebrows rose as he checked his phone. "You wanted me here by six. It's three till."

"Months." Vlad tapped the oyster on his wrist. "Not minutes."

Augie flinched at the comment.

"I had multiple buyers for that code. I had to go back on my word with long-term and dangerous associates." Vlad stepped slowly toward Augie until they were face to face. "You cost me far more than you're worth. That doesn't happen twice."

Sweat beads erupted on Augie's forehead. "It was a good plan until Byron stroked out."

"So I've heard. But you left loose ends." Vlad gestured to the chairs, sitting in his favorite. Augie's hand shook as he unbuttoned his jacket and sat on the edge of his seat.

"Gil and Dwayne. You know their reputations. They won't talk. And, well, with Rocco dead, there are no loose ends."

Rocco died during surgery after Maggie Fender ran him over with the car. While Vlad admired her spunk, this time, she was too close to Vlad's business.

"I'm not talking about them. The Everly woman. She's now in FBI custody."

"Gail?" Augie's voice cracked. "Since when?"

"This morning, *mudak*. They know it was her selling the engineering documents on the website. They found the code." Vlad beat his chest. "Code I was supposed to sell three months ago!"

Augie scanned the room as if there were an exit. "Gail won't talk. She knows what happened to Yang Tunan after he threatened her."

Yuri was the quiet brother, and he was also one hell of a shot. Vlad thought about eliminating the Fender woman the same night. Two birds, two rounds from the modified Mosin.

"My boys cleaned up that mess." Vlad reached over and poked Augie in the chest hard enough to make him recoil. "This is yours to clean up. Get rid of the accountant."

"Yes, Vlad."

"Now get out until it's done."

Augie scurried toward the door with the brothers on his heels.

Vlad expected to see the headline of the accountant's death within a week, or the news would carry Augie's name. Either way, Vlad wasn't leaving any of them alive to reveal his part in this debacle. The accountant. Augie. Dwayne. That idiot Rocco, if he lived. While Augie was the only one with a direct link to Vlad, this was no time to be careless.

Only the young beauty Maggie Fender gave him pause. He instructed Yuri to shoot Yang Tunan in her presence to force her back to her simple world. But few men Vlad worked with had her mettle.

This was the second time their lives intersected. Vlad would not give her a third opportunity.

While shooting her would be easy enough, Vlad had his image renewal to consider. Plus, she had contacts in the FBI.

He wandered to the bar.

The city was embracing him as a reformed benefactor. A man of substance and style.

Lousy hypocrites. It was only when his wallet opened that polite society doors followed.

No, he wouldn't kill Maggie yet. There were other ways to control someone like her. Subtle ways. First, he had to find the best angle. Her friend Denesha was clearly a lever. And her brother. Finding the proper pressure point for someone like Maggie might even be fun. The notion intrigued Vlad.

Like the computer systems the code could exploit, where was Maggie most vulnerable? How could he best breach her formidable defenses?

She might even be a worthy challenge, but if not, he still planned to neutralize her.

He poured a snifter of cognac, swirling the liquid against the sides of the glass before downing the contents in a single shot.

Some things shouldn't be rushed.

Vladimir Penniski would eventually find Maggie Fender's weakness.

75

A few days later, Maggie and Travis arrived at San Mateo Medical Center with a bag full of toys and books for Sol. He was still weak from the effects of pneumonia, but alert and out of danger. Marcus' operation was successful, saving his life and his arm, but the nerve damage was significant. Time and physical therapy would determine how much functionality he could regain.

Marcus was in Sol's room when they arrived, with one arm in a sling and the other holding on to his IV pole. Both their faces lit up when Maggie and Travis entered the room.

"Man, it's good to see you two!" Travis grinned at Marcus and swung the bag onto the bed, landing it next to Sol. "Magpie and I picked out some goodies for you, little buddy."

Sol's voice was scratchy. "That's a big bag."

Travis emptied the contents on the blanket. Sol reached for a book titled Tippy Lemmey by Patricia McKissack.

"Maggie used to read that one to me." Travis said, "It's one of my favorites."

Sol glided his hand across the smooth cover. "Will you read it to me?"

Travis pulled a chair in close and started. "In 1951 there was a war going on in—"

Maggie sidled up to Marcus. He let go of his IV pole long enough to give her a hug. "Glad you came."

"How are you?" She said, "Does he know yet?"

He shook his head. "The paternity test was positive, and I've been planning the legal arrangements to take him to Florida with me for years." His smile beamed with pride. "And now, there he is."

"He's a beautiful kid."

"Toya never told me she was pregnant when I left for Afghanistan." His body heaved out a long breath. "When I got back, she was gone. It was Toya's mother who told me I was a father." Marcus glared at the ceiling. "Toya didn't want me knowing."

"That's cold."

"That sums up Toya. She was sub-zero."

He let go of his IV pole and adjusted his sling. "Not only did Sol grow up thinking he didn't have a father, Toya's been telling him I was a threat. Right up there with Candyman from the horror flicks." His head dropped. "I can't lay all that on him at once."

Toya rivaled Maggie's own mother for being selfish. "What are you going to do?"

"I'm working with a child counselor. Together, we'll ease him into the notion." Marcus bit his lips. "And for the boy's sake, we need to give his mama a proper burial."

Maggie had no words for Marcus. He and the boy were in for a season of change—not unlike the one Travis and she still endured. Especially for young Sol. Grief was a solitary place. She once hoped Fyodor might brighten her darkness, but he had his own sorrows.

At least for now.

She watched as her half-brother read the book to Sol. Travis was so good with kids.

"Pensacola, huh?" Maggie said, "That will be a fun place for Sol."

"One thing I have going for me," Marcus said, "That boy loves the ocean."

FROM THE AUTHOR

Thank you for reading ZERO TRUST. If you enjoyed it, please tell your friends and leave a review. Your good opinion matters to me and encourages other readers to try my novels. I'd consider it a favor.

When you read books in my other series, characters from ZERO TRUST often make an appearance. Mine is a single story world, where storylines and people cross into other lives—Travis Fender plies his trade to assist Mycroft Merlin in THE MASTERS' KEY. Kurt Meyers and FBI agent Claudia Seagal chase murderers and missing artifacts in ECHOES FROM DEATH. Vonda Creevy helps Beth Sutton cope after they are abducted in 3 LIES.

You're invited to sign up for my Thrillers Behind the Firewall readers group, and you'll receive a FREE Thriller, plus a story about one of my nefarious characters. Your information will remain confidential (the NSA excepted), and I promise to send only items that won't bore you . . . . like the time I solved hit-and-run

HelenHanson.com/free-thriller

A personal note about ZERO TRUST:

ZERO TRUST covers a personal patch of turf for me. Having several beloved siblings, I considered the relationships we forge in our youth. Seemingly simple for some families, yet deeply complicated in others, certain events drive us inextricably together, while other situations create that impassable schism. People without a familial base must blaze another trail, finding those worthy of their trust among the throng of passing strangers. We're creatures who need a pack. May we all enjoy a place of welcome and refreshment in this realm.

As for me, I'm not a corporation. I'm a writer with a couple of goofy dogs and an active keyboard who relies on satisfied readers, and I hope to hear from you. If you've got a comment about this story or a great book recommendation, let me know. I read too.

Thanks. It means a lot to me.

All the best,

Helen

When you're out and about, please visit with me at the following pixels:

www.HelenHanson.com

http://www.amazon.com/Helen-Hanson/e/B004FD2MR2/
https://twitter.com/helenhanson
https://www.facebook.com/Helen.Hanson.Author
https://plus.google.com/111614494099474096937/posts
http://www.goodreads.com/author/show/608798.Helen_Hanson

WriteMe@HelenHanson.com

HELEN HANSON

NOVELS

BY

HELEN HANSON

~ THE MASTERS CIA THRILLER SERIES ~

3 LIES
THE MASTERS' KEY
DEAD STORM

~ THE CRUISE FBI THRILLER SERIES ~

OCEAN OF FEAR
SPIDER GAMES
ECHOES FROM DEATH

~

DARK POOL
ZERO TRUST

3 LIES

A MASTERS CIA THRILLER – BOOK 1

CHAPTER ONE

The water bead on her chest slalomed south to join the others on the black-diamond run to her groin. Beth Sutton wrapped the thick, white towel around her dripping hair. Both hung to her hip. As she stepped onto the bath mat, the arterial catheter bounced off her inner thigh muscle. She wiped down the rest of her body and draped the towel on the rack.

Clint left her house at eleven the night before with a promise to return for breakfast prior to their fishing trip. Another evening absorbed in unguarded conversation. Their two months together passed with an easy contentment.

She should have dialyzed last night, but she'd fallen asleep too soon, cocooned in fading dreams, down, and enchantment. The evening proved too satisfying to interrupt for blood filtering. He'd offered to help. Again.

Maybe he could really handle it. Maybe not. Maybe she wasn't ready to test him.

A knock came from her door as she dressed.

Six-fifteen. He was early.

Once over in the mirror—baggy pink jeans and a pink thermal shirt sufficed for cooking breakfast.

Omelets. Everybody liked omelets.

She hustled to the door. The deadbolt resisted. "Just a second." The lock popped. She threw the door open with a flourishing smile. "Good morn–"

Her chest inflated with fear. A stocky man wearing a blue ski mask shoved her inside. He covered her mouth before a scream loosened. A piece of paper dropped from his hand. Footsteps fell behind her. She struggled, but she couldn't escape his grip. A sharp jab pierced her bottom.

Her pulse staggered. A needle. Oh dear, God.

Dreaminess surged. Her focus failed.

CHAPTER TWO

According to Paige Masters, Clint's almost ex-wife, he never noticed anything. But the white Chevy van pulling out of Beth's road caught his attention. At least the sound of the V-8 engine rumbling under the hood did. Between a full-size and a mini, that van never left the factory boasting anything larger than a V-6. Dull and gutless by reputation, the piece of junk couldn't get jacked during a riot.

A throaty roar from the vehicle broke his expectation, like a Swedish accent from the lips of a black man. While the kiddies tried to give the illusion of raw power under the hood without the trouble of an actual engine swap, this van camouflaged its strength with exhaust silencers. Sporting rear-wheel drive and a torquey V-8, that homely white box could spank a Mustang in a quarter mile.

Don't say he didn't notice anything. Hell yes, he noticed.

Clint parked his black pickup on the main street of Clement, Massachusetts but stayed in the cab to finish his coffee while the seaside burg enjoyed the remaining minutes of slumber. He preferred walking down to Beth's house so his black lab, Louie, could sniff the flora on the way. Beth's road was nearly half a mile long and ran mostly downhill on a headland. It led to four houses and a winery. Each home occupied five wooded acres; and the winery, fifty. If Clint drove down to her house without letting Louie romp, then for the duration of their visit the young dog would whimper, paw the floor, and sulk.

Clint had heard the van coming before it emerged from the patchy fog a car length away. Two swarthy men stayed behind blue-mirrored sunglasses and Red Sox ball caps as they crested the hill. Probably a delivery to the winery. In spite of not knowing these men, Clint waved, as a gesture.

The men either didn't see him or weren't up for friendly this early. Neither waved back. The van's rear tires spun, searching for a hold in the loose gravel. It lurched onto the roadway staying long enough for Clint to see a dirty patch of bumper sticker glue in the shape of Australia that adorned the back door. Virginia plates. It roared off toward the highway through the dissipating mist.

A beautiful day barely underway. What's the rush? Smell the flowers. Will ya?

He emptied the last of the coffee from his paper cup and tossed it onto the floorboard before getting out of the truck. A glance to his watch showed the time as six twenty-two. He was early, but extra hungry. Somehow, that made up for the early.

The ocean-side chill receded under the constant gaze of the new sun. He pushed the sleeves of his sweatshirt back to the elbows. "C'mon, Louie."

The glossy black dog bounded from the back seat of the cab. A wag started at the tail and rippled through to the other end of his sleek body. A drooling red tongue flapped amid the pearly-whites of his mouth.

"Good boy." Clint clipped a leash on the leather collar and patted Louie's firm flank. "Let's go, Lou."

Louie led Clint on a tour of every white oak, sugar maple, and pitch pine before scampering up the porch to Beth Sutton's door. A nineteenth century bungalow with the Atlantic Ocean slapping its back, the whole place boasted only 820 square feet. Clint lowered the anchor-shaped knocker onto the strike plate. She would hear the clatter from any room. Echoes settled into silence. He knocked again.

No shower noises. Even if she were in there, she'd at least call out and tell him to wait. A growl undulated from Clint's empty stomach. Beth specifically invited him to breakfast. He was early, but she ought to be up by now. He knocked again. Louder.

Another full minute passed. Clint walked around to the back of the house and rapped on the kitchen door. He peered through a sliver of uncovered windowpane. The hemodialysis machine she named Dracula stood sentry at the bedroom wall. The doors to both her bedroom and bath were open. Her vacant computer table occupied the near corner in the still, Beth-less room.

The next round of belly noises came with spikes. He turned around and leaned back against the gray clapboard house. He dropped the leash and closed his arms across his chest.

Louie ran straight to a cricket hopping near the garage behind the house. He pounced but missed. It jumped out of his reach through a gap in the carriage door.

Clint forgot to check for her car. Maybe she went out. The garage door lock dangled from the latch. He pushed the solid door in as much as the latch would allow. Even in the low light the small utility vehicle was easy to see.

Beth probably stayed up late reading again or writing. She owed her editor some chapters but not until early next month. Maybe she had her treatment. She was due for one yesterday, but he'd stayed late. She said she felt washed out after dialysis. He should have gone home sooner so she was free to dialyze. She wouldn't start a session with him around. It was selfish of him to linger, but time with her dissolved like sugar.

Still, leaving a guy outside, a hungry guy–

"This violates some rule of social etiquette. Right, Louie?"

Louie pawed the ground. Being right didn't fill his belly, and Clint still had to rouse her lovely butt.

Damn. Moments like this rubbed. He couldn't call her. He'd ditched his cell phone along with the rest of his electronic tethers, and he needed to find one. At this hour.

He was the only one he knew without a cell phone: dockworkers, old ladies walking their ankle-biters, certainly all the drivers in all the cars in all the merging lanes of I-93 had one. Hell, even school kids. He could afford one. He just didn't want one. Like so many people, most of that crap was unreliable.

Beth's neighbor Janet Raffety—she'd let him use the phone. He walked across the street and looked for any sign of activity. If she was working in the kiln, he didn't want to disturb her. The house was quiet, but a glow came from her shop.

The next pang hit him harder as the extra-bold French roast etched a hole in his stomach lining. Louie probed a Mayflower cluster when Clint caught the leash and went back to the truck. Louie scrambled into the back seat, and Clint drove off.

Thirty-five miles from Boston, the tourist town of Clement had few businesses operating this time of year. Even fewer opened at this hour. Clint decided his best shot was near the freeway. The congregation of trucks outside Maggie Mae's Blue Bird Diner lit his hope.

Maggie Mae was a large, hairy man in his sixties with a round, fleshy face. Clad in a red-striped apron and matching cap, his picture could only be completed with the addition of a burning cigarette dangling from the side of his mouth. Armed with twin decanters of fresh coffee, he made his way round the tables of regulars chatting up each in turn. A quiet man by diner standards, he gave instructions to the kitchen staff by means of hand gestures, facial expressions, and head movements—a performance Marcel Marceau would have admired.

Clint found the pay phone by the restrooms—naturally. He dropped in some coins and called Beth.

After four rings Beth's voice answered, "Hi. I can't take your call right now. Please leave a message, and I'll return it when I can."

"Hey, it's me. Pick up the phone." He waited for the click of her receiver, for the happy lilt to her voice when she said his name, for a swift end to his growing sense of loss.

"Beth, are you there? We had plans today, remember?" No reply. "I'll try your other phone."

He smacked down the receiver. Damn it. They'd made a date. Breakfast was her idea, and she promised breakfast would be ready at six-thirty sharp. They planned to go fishing for striper and meet up with Abe later. It was nearly seven. Where the hell was she?

After digging around his pocket, he came up with more change and placed a call to her cell phone. Voice mail kicked in after three rings. "It's me, Clint. I've tried all the numbers I know. I'm going to grab something for us to eat and come back. Hope you're up by then."

The clank of dishes rising from the dining room joggled Clint's attention to his hunger. He ordered four breakfast burritos and coffee at the counter. He took the to-go bag and drove back to her house.

He banged on her front door until his hand hurt. She would have heard that. Fear tiptoed through his veins. If she could.

He ran to the kitchen window. From here, he could see her bed and Beth wasn't in it. He moved to another window to check the bath. The shower curtain was pulled back, and unless she was in the tub, she wasn't there either. Calm down. She's in good health, considering. She's not going to keel over from a day's delay in her dialysis. At least that's what she told him.

"Enough of this. Let's eat."

Clint turned on the water spigot long enough to make a puddle for the dog and plopped down on Beth's porch rocker. His long legs draped over a milk can painted with rose buds, cherry blossoms, and blue hydrangeas that Beth said were the same hue as Clint's eyes.

Yeah. Sure.

He poured salsa from a plastic ramekin onto one burrito and tossed another to Louie. The dog intercepted the package like an NFL cornerback. He hoisted the food around with his teeth, biting it and choking large chunks down his throat.

Clint finished his meal and wadded all the trash back in the original bag. He took his boot knife out of the sheath and threw it into a tree. Louie retrieved it. With each toss, the knife stuck where he aimed. The activity helped pass the time and freed his brain for thinking. Interest in the game waned before he'd done any lasting damage to the bark.

He stared at Beth's door, but decided against trying again. "It's her turn. Huh, Lou?"

When he hit the road in front of Beth's, he saw Janet pulling a large box from an old Subaru wagon. He called to her and ran over to her side. "Allow me?"

"Why thanks." She hauled out another box. "These go in the shop." She led the way.

"I was looking for Beth. Have you seen her this morning?"

"No, I've been loading my kiln. What's up?"

He stepped into the shop and set the box down. "I was due at her place for breakfast, but she's not around."

They returned to the wagon for more boxes.

Clint knew Beth hadn't told Janet about the dialysis. Beth preferred to keep some details of her life private. After the continuing saga of Paige, he found such discretion refreshing.

They landed the last load into Janet's shop.

"Thanks for your help."

"If you see Beth, let her know I came by."

"Will do."

Louie led him back to the truck by the main road for the all-important tree survey. For a dog that lived on a boat, wooded lots represented the ultimate in luxury. Clint loaded Louie in the truck. He threw the bag with Beth's burrito on the floorboard and drove off for home, spinning his rear wheels in the effort.

Along the coast road, the surf vibrated with a crystalline sheen. They should have been out there by now, together. He and Beth.

He'd never seen a more beautiful woman. Not perfect, but simply enchanting. Ah hell, admit it, she was perfect. Her bamboo-shoot green eyes sparkled amid her heart-shaped face. Golden tresses cascaded in loose ringlets all the way to her gorgeous butt.

Botticelli painted her only in his dreams.

But beauty never kept Clint engaged. Not like his buddy, Todd. Todd swapped women like designer ties. For Clint the packaging intrigued but any genuine gift remained hidden inside.

While Beth's illness didn't seem to worry her, it left him unnerved. She loomed fragile, ethereal, a morning mist that might seep through his hand. Like catching a butterfly, then opening your cupped hands slowly to see if it was there. When they were together, he caught himself checking to see if she was still in the room with him.

He tousled Louie's furry neck. "I've only known her two months. Who needs this?"

Stood up by a damn butterfly.

Clint pulled into Clement Marina and parked. Louie stood on alert while Clint cleaned out the last two days mail from his box.

Merlin, one of the Clement Marina staff, walked up to them and sidled in close. "Guess what landed in your slip?"

"What do you mean?"

"A lass. An angelfish. She came looking for you, so I let her in. You let me know if you want to throw her back, mate. I'll get my net."

Jungle rhythms pummeled Clint's chest. He wiped sweaty palms down the front of his pants. "Where is she?"

"At your boat." Merlin rubbed on his scraggly chin. "A real swimmer, that one."

Clint threw his backpack over a shoulder and headed to the security gate, down the gangway to his slip at the end of the dock. This time, Louie followed.

He looked back at the dog. "Why'd she come here?" Louie's expression didn't change.

Half the damn morning—gone. She knew they were meeting at her house. But he couldn't stay mad because Beth was here, now.

He hated this feeling. Neediness. It didn't suit him. He didn't want it to suit him. But his relief trumped any anger.

She was here now. That's all that mattered.

She didn't stand him up.

She just changed the plans.

She—

She wasn't Beth.

Paige Masters sat on the port gunwale of Clint's 45-foot sailboat. Even with the expansive view of the harbor, the glorious Atlantic beyond, there she sat filing her acrylic fingernails.

"I've been trying to reach you. Your cell phone isn't working." She finally looked up at Clint. "What's the matter? Can't afford the payments anymore?" Her third-grade smile glowed with the intensity of a lighthouse as seen from the battered ship.

For a moment, Clint stopped breathing.

In less than five months, their divorce would be final.

Technology and future ex-wives. Both highly unreliable.

OCEAN OF FEAR

A CRUISE FBI THRILLER – BOOK 1

CHAPTER ONE

By six-thirty a.m., Baxter Cruise lounged at the corner table of Whitney's Coffee Bar, wiping away a frothy milk moustache with his sleeve. He swirled the dregs of a Cappuccino in the ceramic mug while a gangly freshman tried to make time with the surfer-girl barista. She was clearly uninterested. The young man's frustration passed for entertainment while Baxter waited for Professor Sydney Mantis. Syd usually sent their client's pitch-list via email, but today, he'd sent a text from a new phone demanding face-time.

Instead of wasting a precious morning, Baxter should've blasted another 225,000 emails or let his ratware scrape more addresses from the geezer forums. Either action would have netted him enough cash to cover the cost of the java and maybe some additional credits at UC Santa Cruz. Unlike the rest of the losers, he didn't plan to get stuck with any student loans to repay.

His fingertips hit the tabletop in rhythmic succession. He should have brought his laptop. Where the hell was Sydney? Didn't he know? Time was money, man. Time was money.

A smiling coed in a UC-logo sweatshirt opened the front door for an elderly couple shuffling at the pace of the old woman's walker. When Sydney Mantis jockeyed around all three of them to enter first, the young woman's mouth dropped to a scowl.

Sydney hadn't even thanked her for holding the door. His usual easy charm seemed under pressure. Wearing a Baja hoodie and aviator sunglasses, he looked like the Unabomber.

"Bax, thank God you're still here." Syd withdrew a shaking hand from the pouch pocket and tossed a flash drive onto Baxter's lap. "I need you to take this to Dr. Bisch. She'll be in the office by the time you get there. But don't leave it on her desk." His gaze ricocheted around the room, his voice lowering to a near whisper. "Make sure you hand it to her personally. I need to leave town for a few days."

Baxter retrieved the flash drive from the folds around his crotch. "What about our new client?"

But Sydney's attention fixed outside.

A man in harmony with the '60s, he dialed to mellow even if it required herbal assistance. Baxter figured he was one toke over his usual line.

"I can't stay here." For the first time since arriving, Sydney pulled off his sunglasses to make eye contact. "Will you take care of Gertrude for me?" A thick vein throbbed at his neck, muscles twitched across his face, and his pupils dilated to ripe-olive proportions.

Sydney didn't look stoned. Simply terrified.

"Trudy?" Baxter always liked Sydney's Border collie. "Sure, I'll watch her for you." Baxter didn't know what else to say.

"Thanks, man." Sydney wiped an eye. "I've got to go." He put on his sunglasses and returned to the dull gray of the morning fog.

Baxter stared at the front door as if it might open to a parallel universe. The good professor taught computer engineering, not theater arts. And while he tilted dramatic, this performance was worthy of a nomination. Ever since Baxter joined his gig nearly five years ago, Sydney's feet routinely got frostbite, especially lately. But he always found something to return him to calm—usually a bong, a warm hippie chick, or both.

But something had Syd rattled. Perhaps the pitches for the new email campaign contained sensitive stuff. Sure, they were spammers, but they didn't run just any email pitch. Baxter maintained strict standards: Viagra. Yes. Online casinos. Yes. Girls from Russia. No. His girlfriend, Natalie, wouldn't let him keep one anyway. Their robot butler offered enough contention. Baxter squeezed the flash drive in his fist.

The weird encounter faded as his thoughts focused on his schedule for the day. Hitting Science Hill on campus would waste another thirty minutes just to run an errand, but he could claim the hours for his work-study position with Sydney. Then he could crank on their email campaigns until Natalie came home in the early evening. No time to catch a wave, though. Maybe tomorrow. Pocketing the flash drive, he stood and left the coffee bar.

Outside, fog patched the skyline while cars moved with caution along the streets. Baxter chirped the car alarm and trailed the sound to reach his ride.

He fired up his 370Z, wended his way to High Street, and putted up the Empire Grade until he reached the western entrance to UC Santa Cruz.

As life stirred along Heller Drive, bikes and backpacks bumped uphill toward their destinations and then disappeared behind an evergreen veil. Baxter tucked his car into the second level of the Core West parking garage and headed across McLaughlin Drive to the third floor of the Jack Baskin Engineering Building.

The first classes were over an hour from commencing, but the early nerds were busy catching their worms. Baxter barely remembered when he was that eager to impress. As a graduate student within the department, he needed eighteen units for his master's, and then he planned to pursue his doctorate. Given his lucrative arrangement with Sydney, he wasn't in any hurry. He swiped his card key in the exterior door and headed for the stairs to the third floor.

Professor Alessandra Bisch held degrees in mathematics and electrical engineering from Oxford, a Master of Science in naval architecture and marine engineering from M.I.T., and a Ph.D in robotics from Carnegie Mellon University, and Baxter still didn't like her. She came to UCSC because of the degree program in robotics. And the funding. Academic researchers stalked funding like the paparazzi stalked celebrities. Most of the faculty were accessible and friendly, but Alessandra—or 'The Bisch' as she was known by students—reeked of condescension.

A student passed him on the stairs, but when Baxter entered the hall on the third floor, he was alone. The Bisch's office was on the exterior wall with the window-endowed members of the engineering department, but the fog choked off any sunlight this morning. He'd taken two classes from her. He only knew the location of her door because it was perpetually closed.

The Bisch was severe for the sake of it: Close-cropped hair. Flinty smile. Constant reminders of her education. Strictly enunciated diction. Brilliant or not, she possessed the warmth of the UC Santa Cruz mascot—a banana slug.

Baxter knocked on her door. He waited a polite few moments and tried again. Sydney said she'd be here by now. Another knock, only louder. She might be on the phone in which case the knocking could seriously piss her off.

Eh, what the hell? He knocked some more.

If she were in there, he would have roused her by now. He could leave the drive on her desk. Syd would never know, anyway. Baxter gripped the door handle and moved it downward.

With a slight push, the door swung freely to a crack. Since his intrusion didn't elicit any yelling, he posted an eye at the opening to survey the interior. The Bisch wasn't here.

Sweet. In. Out. No fuss. No muss.

The light was on as he pushed the door open and slipped inside. With open files and a lamp lit on the desk, the room looked like she should be working. Then he noticed the papers on the floor. Cabinets and drawers splayed open. As he neared her desk, he saw a reddish-brown pattern in the carpet unlike that in any of the other offices. It glistened.

Nausea swelled in his belly.

Baxter stumbled to avoid stepping in it. He peered around the cherry wood desk and saw her. Dr. Alessandra Bisch lay face down on the floor with a hole at the nape of her neck.

ABOUT THE AUTHOR

Bestselling author Helen Hanson writes thrillers about desperate people with a high-tech bent. Hackers. The CIA. Industry titans. Guys on sailboats. Mobsters. Their personal maelstroms pit them against unrelenting forces willing to kill. Throughout the journey, they try to find some truth, a little humor, and their humanity — from either end of the trigger.

While Helen writes about the power hungry, she genuinely mistrusts anyone who wants to rule the world.

Helen directed operations for high-tech manufacturers of semiconductors, video games, software, and computers. Her reluctant education behind the Redwood Curtain culminated in a B.S. in Business Administration with concentrated studies in Computer Science. She also learned to play a mean game of hacky sack.

She is a licensed private pilot with a ticket for single-engine aircraft. Helen and her husband spent their first anniversary with their flight instructor studying for the FAA practical. If you were a passenger on a 737 trying to land at SJC, she sends her most sincere apologies. Really.

Born in fly-over country, Helen has lived on both coasts, near both borders, and at several locations in between. She lettered in tennis, worked as a machinist, and saw the Clash at the San Francisco Civic Auditorium sometime in the eighties. She currently lives amid the bricks of Texas with her husband, son, a dog that composes music with squeaky toys, and another dog that's too lazy to bother.

ACKNOWLEDGMENTS

This was a hard book to finish because of the gap in time from when I started it. Who did I leave dangling on the cliff? Which gun was hidden in the closet? But I had some amazing help. Always my husband and son, providing wit, inspiration, and the occasional cup of coffee.

Many thanks to my wonderful writing tribe, Jayme, Carolyn, Jan, and Skip, who help curb my excesses and provide wise counsel.

A grateful shoutout to my generous and learned early readers who keep me honest and offer their valued expertise. John Spillman, who finally approved of my choice in wines. Paul McDonnell, who did not find an alliterative pattern in this work. Scott Nichols, a veritable bloodhound when it comes to timelines. Dave Savage, a computer security expert who kept me technically legit. Chet Richards, who offered both valuable critique and hearty encouragement. As they say here in Texas, all y'all are amazing! I'm grateful for your contribution. Thank you!

Maybe I should leave out my Lord, Jesus Christ, because His example loses vibrancy in me. I struggle, flounder, and stumble. Through Him, somehow, it all still works.

In the end, any errors, omissions, or epic fails are fully mine. Thank you for reading!